S,S.Brigden

THE CLAWS OF MERCY

JOHN HARRIS

THE CLAWS
OF MERCY

178-202 GREAT PORTLAND STREET
LONDON, W.C.1

First published 1955

Made and printed in Great Britain by
TAYLOR GARNETT EVANS & CO., LTD.
BUSHEY MILL LANE
WATFORD, HERTS.

"... People who do not like spending any time alone or who are dependent on amusements not of their own making are unsuited to a country like Sierra Leone."

From a paper prepared by the Information Bureau, Royal Empire Society, and duplicated by Her Majesty's Stationery Office for the Colonial Office.

CONTENTS

	Page
Part I	9
Part II	127
Part III	241

Part I

One

IT was already hot, with the breath-catching closeness of an oven, as the rays of the sun—still far from its summit in the brassy sky—rebounded off the surrounding mountains with a violence that was almost physical. In spite of the early hour, Freetown wore a jaded mid-day look, dusty and drained of energy, and as the sun flared higher over the hills, the heat began to radiate even from the old grey walls near the river and the port seemed to huddle under the slopes like a shabby old beggar.

It rose, white and brown and gaudy green, up from the Portuguese Steps to Tower Hill; from Clyne Town to Kongo Town; from the Mohammedan quarter beyond Kissy and past the stained green statue of William Wilberforce; past the Law Courts and the Cathedral; through the flat, unshaded façades of seedy bars and cloth shops, that mass of cast-iron balconies and tin roofs from a dead era; and up the slopes of the hill where the bungalows of the Creoles and Whites stood among the trees. Farther to the east and west among the palms were the unpainted box-wood houses that abutted, dry and sun-drenched, on the town centre; and beyond them the mud and beaten-tin dwellings of the poor with their rusting roofs and their air of old junk.

Jimmy Agnew, approaching the wharf between the glaring whitewashed buildings, led by a small boy in a pair of torn shorts through which his shining black bottom showed, felt as though he were being slowly fried. There was no air and no shade and the streets appeared to sizzle in the sun.

11

He mopped his face, half stifled, and told himself cheerfully he'd soon get used to it. *"Those who enjoy a sunny hot summer in England will probably enjoy the tropics,"* the Colonial Office pamphlet had informed him enthusiastically when he had taken the job, but there was nothing in England he could ever remember like this breathless West African heat which had caused him to toss on his bed throughout the night feeling like a herring on a griddle. Even now, he could feel the sweat trickling down his spine and legs and the dampness of his shirt. He was already beginning to wish he had taken a car to the wharf as he had been advised instead of deciding to walk as a means of seeing the place.

Only a trickle of brightly-hued, chattering people was moving about the streets yet, and the song of the town, that swelling, high-pitched sound of an African crowd, was still only a murmur. A black clerk went past, stiff in a smart starched suit of dazzling drill, and wearing a white topee with a conscious superiority over the lesser men around him—the Hausa trader in a dust-sweeping robe of striped pyjama cloth and a tawdry gold-embroidered smoking cap who was crouched over his calabashes of wares; the labourers with their banjo-voices striding for the waterfront with slapping feet and flying shirt-tails ; the farmer with the trussed live pig on his head; the mammies, in chemise-like frocks and bearing baskets of fruit, or paper-stoppered ginger-beer bottles, their heads knotted in gaudy Madras handkerchiefs.

Absorbing the noise and the riot of breathtakingly crude colour, Jimmy stared about him, bemused by the impact of this teeming new land upon his senses, which were still used to the less dramatic environments of England. Its smells, its colours, its vast life, were all of them too rich, too full, to have anything but a hammer-blow effect on a newcomer.

And, at that moment also, he felt a little dazed. The enthralling first glimpse of flying fish which was the indication that he was approaching the Equator wasn't far behind him;

12

and the roar of the anchor cable as it crashed into the water—the sound of a portcullis clanking down in front of all his former life—still echoed in his ears.

He stared as a bus load of Africans chugged by, the bus inevitably overloaded, noisy, old fashioned and creaking, its passengers chirruping like a lot of excited monkeys. A pair of vultures in the centre of the shimmering road skipped clumsily to one side as the vehicle passed; ugly, bald old ladies in rusty black, their scaly feet stirring the dust in little puffs as they moved.

An African girl, her face bluish with the powder she wore, her dark lips faintly purple under her lipstick, ran past him up the worn steps to a set of offices, and Jimmy was instantly aware of something about her that he had sensed in the whole of Freetown immediately he had passed through the Customs Sheds the previous day—something strong and vital but not yet completely civilized, something that showed in the fatal application of white powder on a coal-black skin, something gaudy and over-coloured—something that was in the too-green lushness of the vegetation and the too-rich redness of the earth. . . .

It was while he was in this absorbed trance that Earnshaw found him.

"Oy! You there! You Agnew?"

Jimmy found himself facing a lean withered man with a face wrinkled like a walnut. He wore oil-stained shorts faded with too much washing and held up by a length of electric light cord, and a battered bush hat with a brim like a switchback which, when he lifted it to scratch his head, disclosed a dusty-looking thatch of iron-grey hair that seemed to have been thrust on end by an electric shock. Grubby stockings wilted over unpolished shoes and he had the hard-bitten look of a stable-lad—a burnt, brown man who belonged not so much to Africa as, with nets and ferrets, to the broad autumn fields of Shropshire.

13

"That's right," Jimmy said, turning towards him. "You Mr. Twigg?"

The other's wily grin showed broken stained teeth. "Not me, old lad," he said slowly. "Earnshaw's my name."

He lit a cigarette with the deliberate air of one who had never done anything impulsive in his life, and stood smoking, obviously in no hurry to depart; and Jimmy, casting round out of the corner of his eye for an escape from the sweltering sun, took advantage of the pause in his progress to slip unobtrusively into a patch of shade under the awning of a shop doorway.

"What did you say your first name was?" Earnshaw was asking.

"I didn't." Jimmy's reply was accompanied by a sheepish grin. "I never do if I can help it. It's Francis Theodore St. John Agnew."

"Jesus!" Earnshaw looked sharply at him. "Honest?"

"Most people call me Jimmy."

"I should think so." Earnshaw regarded him with the bright-eyed interest of a sparrow. "It's a proper jaw-breaker, isn't it? I know how you must feel. My name's Archibald."

He thrust out a grimy fist to a fellow-sufferer and Jimmy took it, mopping the perspiration from his face with his other hand.

"Twiggy sent me down for you." Earnshaw held out his packet of cigarettes. "Couldn't get away from the mine. One of his nigs creating a bit of trouble. He sent his regards and hope you don't mind. Fag, old lad?"

While Jimmy was lighting the cigarette, Earnshaw turned to the carriers with Jimmy's baggage. "Okay, mate," he said out of the corner of his mouth to the nearest of them. "Shove it down here. My blokes'll take it now."

Edging farther into his patch of shade from the glare of the sun—Earnshaw seemed able to stand in the full awful blast of it and enjoy it—Jimmy paid off the carriers, and

14

Earnshaw set off again in a flat stride that was almost a strut, like his neighbours wasting no time on anyone else, far ahead of the more polite and less experienced Jimmy who was pausing to apologize to the mammies he jostled.

Earnshaw moved with such dexterity through the growing crowd that Jimmy, his eyeballs already itching with the sweat that ran off his forehead, was finding it difficult to keep up with him. They were walking in the centre of the road now with the rest—the narrow sidewalks, cluttered up with salesmen and tailors and fruit vendors, seemed too full already for comfort—and for a minute, as he did a hop, skip and jump to avoid a small black boy on a bicycle, Jimmy almost lost Earnshaw among the noisy African throng with its satellite hordes of dogs and children.

"Hot, isn't it?" he said, manfully cheerful as he gained ground a little.

"Gets 'otter."

"Much hotter?"

"Like the 'Obs of 'Ell."

"Oh!"

Earnshaw's hurry slackened a little out of sympathy. "We thunk you like to go up by river," he said as Jimmy caught up with him again. "Give you a treat. Roads is so bloody dusty this time of the year. I seen 'em. And them ferries! Gawd! Gev me the pip years since." He spoke with a magnificent disregard of past and present tenses, in quick, dancing phrases which were like a poacher's footfalls. His voice was a low boozy shadow that matched them. "You feel better when you get to Ma-Imi," he said. "It's cooler there."

"I'm not for Ma-Imi," Jimmy shouted over the heads of the passers-by. "I'm going beyond there to a new mine at Amama. At least according to the letter I got from Twigg—with a chap called Otto or Gotto or something."

Earnshaw stopped dead, so suddenly that an African

15

labourer following close behind cannoned into him, apologized and passed on without his batting an eyelid in his concentrated stare. He looked at Jimmy for so long without speaking that Jimmy began to feel there was something wrong with his clothes and glanced quickly down at himself.

"Gotto?" Earnshaw said at last. "Gotto? You going to to be stuck up in Amama on your own with *him*? Oh, you poor bastard! You got it cut off the crusty part, old lad. You have, proper."

Earnshaw's grubby clothes gave him a raffish appearance startlingly contrary to everything Jimmy had expected of a white man in Africa, but they also gave him the air of knowing what he was talking about, so that he seemed horribly prophetic. Suddenly the heat striking out from the whitewashed wall of a cloth shop alongside that was candy-striped with the shadows of a palm-tree's fronds seemed twice as choking.

"What's wrong with Gotto?" Jimmy asked.

Earnshaw gave a low cackle of mirthless laughter that sounded like the rattle of dry palm leaves. "What's wrong with a nail in your shoe?" he asked.

"Sounds a nice chap."

"Ever broke your leg? Ever rupture yourself?"

"Go on," Jimmy said. "I'll buy it. What *is* wrong with him?"

Earnshaw glanced at him again with a shrewd, shining glance under his eyebrow that made him look like a scruffy old fox. "You not heard about Gotto?" he asked in that shifty drawl of his that was sly and yet oddly boisterous. "No, of course you not. Oh, well, you soon will. He got ever such a jolly nature. You'll curl up laughing."

He looked again at Jimmy with a bright black eye that gleamed like a polished raisin under a bushy eyebrow as shocked into stiffness as his hair, and tried to reassure him.

16

"Nemmind, old lad," he said. "I hang out at Amama meself. I see you right if you in trouble."

"Trouble?" Jimmy was beginning to feel unexpected tremors of apprehension. This job he had come out to do had seemed straightforward enough in the advertisement he had read in the *Daily Telegraph* and through the ordeal of the interview in the London office, but now it seemed to have hidden complications he hadn't bargained for and he felt vaguely as though he had been lured by a set of false pretences to a climate that was enough in itself to wither all his ambitions without any other difficulties arising from some unknown individual with a flair for confusion.

He looked sideways at Earnshaw. "What sort of trouble?" he asked again, warily this time.

"With Gotto, I mean." Earnshaw sounded almost casual —as though trouble and Gotto were synonymous.

"I see. And why trouble?"

"It's usual."

"Oh, is it?"

"Yah. He's like that."

Earnshaw shrugged, as much as to suggest that if Gotto hadn't driven Jimmy post-haste back to England within a fortnight, there was something wrong with his calculations. Then he blew the cigarette end from his mouth with a popping noise and set off once more at a speed which made Jimmy gasp as they threaded through the growing crowds, paying no heed to the climbing sun which made the roadway a pattern of violent blacks and dazzling whites.

At the wharf, quivering and alive in the swift water of a falling tide, an ugly boat wallowed in the sunshine which drew waves of heat up from her iron decks. Beyond her, the river stretched, flat and glittering, to Tasso Island and the opposite shore.

As Earnshaw hailed her, Jimmy was conscious of several

17

black faces turning in his direction, all of them curious, and suddenly his neat khaki seemed indecently new and unmarked.

Earnshaw bent to the starters of the engines as Jimmy's luggage was lifted aboard. "O.K. Suri," he called into the cabin. "Let's 'ave some music!"

A black face bearing a martyred expression popped up abruptly through the hatchway. "Music, boss? *Again*, boss?" The words were a plea for mercy.

Earnshaw stared back aggressively. "Yes, again. And why not?"

"Boss," the African protested in a whine. "Already plenty times today. Plenty plenty times."

"What about it? Let's have it plenty plenty more times. I like a bit of good music."

Suri sighed visibly and disappeared, and a second later the howl of an ancient gramophone roared out.

"I yi yi yi yi I like you vairy much,
      I yi yi yi yi I theenk you're grand."

An unrecognizable voice screeched out the almost un-recognizable words as the tune roared across the shining water, as incongruous as a drunk at a funeral in the glowing African forenoon.

"Pretty, isn't it?" Earnshaw said.

"Enchanting."

"Carmen Mirandy." Earnshaw, a touch of awe and reverence in his voice, failed to notice the expression on Jimmy's face. "Only record I got left. Had it years. She musta sang that song hundreds of times up and down these 'ere creeks."

"She sounds a bit hoarse."

The sarcasm was lost on Earnshaw. "Oh, that's where it's worn," he pointed out. "Down to the laceholes, it is. But all the rest got bust so this one got used a bit more than normal. Had 'em sent out special, too. Costs money, that does. Knew

18

a barmaid in Swansea useta sing like that. Like a linnet. Honest. Tattoed down both arms and a voice like Vera Lynn. Finished up taking in washing. Gin," he ended. "Voice went."

He squinted at the brassy ball climbing over the palm-tufted green of the hills and wiped the sweat off his wrinkled face with the back of his hand. "Jesus," he commented. "And they call it the Dark Continent!" He glared round at his crew. "O.K., you keggy-handed set of bastards, let go them ropes and let's be off. Jump about a bit."

The black boys grinned bright betel-mouthed grins and let go the ropes and the boat began to move forward, dodging a heavy sprit-sailed Susu canoe loaded to the gunwales with fruit as it glided into a mooring.

For a while, Earnshaw's attention was engaged as his boat swung out into the river and turned up-stream away from the port. He threw his weight on to the wheel to swing the vessel round another fruit boat, swore at its helmsman in a stream of oaths whose eloquence matched their picturesqueness, dodged a bumboatman's canoe, revved the engines fiercely to avoid being swung by the tide on to the anchor cable of a merchant ship, and eventually came back on to his original course, all without turning a hair, while Jimmy watched open-mouthed throughout the manœuvring. Africa's rivers seemed as shockingly overcrowded as its streets, he decided.

Earnshaw accepted the compliment of his astonishment with the bland boredom of one who had seen everything—most of it twice—and Jimmy, gagging in the heat that swept up to him in waves from the engines, studied him for a while, trying to make out his official capacity at the Ma-Imi mine.

"You work for the mine, too?" he asked eventually.

"Nah! Not me." Earnshaw's contempt was withering. "I work for meself and happy as a parrot on a kitchen table doing it, I am." He appeared to be impervious to the heat, and indeed his withered frame looked as though all the

19

moisture had long since been dried out of it and he had been left with the dehydrated look of a prune.

"Admiral of the Sierra Leone Navy I am," he said. "Do all the fetching and carrying up-river. Supplies for Amama. There isn't no deep-water anchorage, see? Spare parts for Ma-Ima. Petrol and goods for the United Africa Company farther up at Moyamba. I got a fleet o' wog boats converted to barges and scows and a few of these here powered jobs to tow 'em. Archibald Earnshaw Incorporated. Large as life and twice as nasty. Mayor of Amama. That's me. Anything you want, just mention my name."

They moved across the bright, blinding surface of the water, through the steamers and tugs and the crowding canoes carrying fruit down-river to the market at Kru Bay, through the clusters of bumboats still hovering round the ship which had brought Jimmy to Africa the day before, their occupants offering all manner of cheap merchandise as souvenirs, or shouting their willingness to dive for shillings while wearing top-hats, frock-coats or even water-wings.

Earnshaw's eyes were narrow as he studied Jimmy, whose round pink face, just a little dazed still, wore a look of intense curiosity that made him seem even younger.

"You met Twigg, your boss, yet?" he asked.

"No." Jimmy grinned. "What's he like?"

Earnshaw replied with another question. "You play cricket?" he asked.

"No. Why?"

"You soon see."

Henry Twigg, the manager of the Ma-Imi mine, a handsome man, lean and stringy like a faded athlete, met them with a jeep as the boat drew into the landing-stage there.

The sun had reached its summit in the sky by this time and the heat-saturated earth was flinging back the glare. Sirocco waves were coming from the engines in blasts that scorched the face and the cabin roofs were too hot to sit on. The early blueness of the heavens had changed to a shrill metallic glow that was reflected dazzlingly in the unruffled water.

The landing-stage was a bare stretch of broken concrete slabs where small green lizards basked in the sun, disappearing in sudden zigzag flashes like coloured darts of flame as the boat nosed alongside. A grimy, rust-covered coaster with awnings rigged and sagging in the stillness was loading in a hanging cloud of dust below a conveyor that was bleached to the colour of old bones.

Twigg drove them through the dense vegetation to the mine area, talking all the way through the fumes from a faulty exhaust that wafted back in cloying folds, dulling Jimmy's mind and taking away all thought beyond the desire to get out of the jeep and breathe what would be comparatively fresh air.

"Laid on a party for you tonight," he was saying. "Might as well enjoy yourself, old boy, before you pass on. Quieter up at Amama where you're going. No club or welfare up there. Bit of tennis, that's all.

"Me, I prefer cricket," he went on almost casually and Earnshaw muttered under his breath from the rear seat.

"Oh, Gawd," he said. "Hold your hat on. Here it come."

"You play cricket at all?" Twigg turned to Jimmy with disarming unconcern.

"A little," Jimmy lied, deciding to be diplomatic in view of Twigg's obvious enthusiasm and Earnshaw's shifty muttering.

"Good show. You can organize a team up at Amama and we'll arrange matches. Earnshaw can transport the teams."

"Ho, can 'e?" Earnshaw growled almost inaudibly just behind Jimmy's ear. "Catch 'im doing it."

"We've got a matting wicket here," Twigg continued gaily through the clouds of dust that came into the jeep at

21

one side and out at the other. "On concrete. Only trouble, there's a crack at one end and it leaves a bad patch. Damned annoying. Cost me a lot of money, that pitch, and it'll have to come up in the end, I suppose."

Jimmy was staring about him, wide-eyed, enjoying the experience of being in Africa. "What sort of top soil is it here?" he inquired.

"Oh, the usual," Twigg replied casually. "Damn' dusty. Crumbles too quickly for cricket. Jolly keen on cricket here. Pity you've got to go up to Amama tomorrow. Might have found you a game."

He blew a blast on the jeep's horn that sent a couple of mammies scuttling for their lives and roared into the residential area of the Ma-Imi mine.

The concrete bungalows, like a neat army camp, fronted on to a dusty square, where a group of black boys lazed with the dogs under a cotton tree whose buttressed trunk seemed as antique and immovable as Africa itself. Overhead, the inevitable vultures hung, like jagged rents in the shining sky, and beyond, the forest crept down from the hill where they dug the ironstone. Over the tops of the trees, Jimmy could see the roofs of uglier, more utilitarian buildings which he assumed were the crushing plants, the offices and laboratories, and the head of the railway that ran through the bush to the water's edge.

He was itching to see more of the mine but it was only after a meal and a sleep and a great many hints that Twigg condescended to conduct him round. He had been showing him photographs of his cricket team, a lot of bored Africans, with, in the centre, Twigg himself holding a bat and wearing a striped blazer, and he looked up, faintly irritated by the interruption.

"The mine?" he said. "Well, yes, I suppose I *can* show you round. Come on. Might as well go now. Mustn't be long. Got

22

to be back for the party tonight. Welcome to Africa sort of thing. Help you to get to know everybody."

He drove furiously away from the bungalow, wiping his moist face with a purple handkerchief as he negotiated the blind bends between the trees, while Jimmy hung on with both hands and began to wish he'd kept his mouth shut.

"You'll be on your own up at Amama." Twigg said through the dust, which Jimmy had by now added to the heat and the crowds as the major discomforts of Africa. "Except for Gotto. He's all right," he went on in a non-committal manner which was hardly a recommendation. "Not exactly a thing of beauty and a joy for ever. Doesn't play cricket," he ended, as though this failing placed the absent Gotto beyond the pale. "Doesn't play any damned game, in fact," he said with a burst of irritation. "Can't understand a chap who doesn't play anything."

He waved a hand vaguely in the direction of the river "He went up today. He'll show you around. He's been up before on relief and he knows his way about. It's dead easy, of course. No overburden. You can nearly scrape up the iron-stone with a teaspoon. Opencast, of course, like this. Rich. Damn' rich. Always had a sneaking regard for the place myself. Nice and quiet.

"Only thing against it is the distance. No telephone, y'see. If there was, you'd always get the wrong number anyway. You always do out here. Between you and me, we're not making much profit out of Amama. It's too small and we need a heavier and faster railway, but I want to prove its potentialities. God, this heat!"

His concluding sentence was tacked to the others, almost as though it were more information about the mine.

He halted the jeep to mop his face with the purple handkerchief and, having finished, showed no inclination to start it again. "Of course," he said, sitting back. "You've no crushing plant or anything like that. All you've got to do is see that

23

the stuff's loaded on the old railway and sent down here. We'll do the rest. Just look after Gotto, that's all. That's enough for anybody. I'll be up in a couple of months to see how you're getting on."

He stopped flapping the flies away with his handkerchief to light a pipe, blowing out clouds of blue smoke which hung motionless on the still, dry air. "You've no engineer," he continued between puffs. "Earnshaw sees to anything like that if you need it. If it's too much for him, we send up from Ma-Imi. And you've got Alf Momo. He's shift boss. African. Very clever. Fine type of chap. Pity he don't get on with Snotty Gotty."

Jimmy's growing apprehension burst out of him at last. "What's Gotto like, sir?" he asked.

"He's all right," Twigg said again, but, Jimmy noticed, once more without any marked enthusiasm. "Pity Jarvis got malaria and had to be sent home. Still—" he flashed his brilliant smile at Jimmy "—chance to get rid of Gotto, eh, till he goes home. Only a few months now, thank God. I shall miss Jarvis, though. Jolly good cricketer. All these blasted people they send out to me these days are tennis players and it's a hard job getting the Africans interested. The bastards prefer football."

"About the mine, sir," Jimmy prompted feebly as he saw Twigg's attention wandering again. The red scar on the hillside was not much nearer to them than when they had set off.

"Oh, yes, Amama." It seemed to require an effort of concentration for Twigg to return to the subject. "A sort of experiment. Any setback would shut the place down immediately. We're not as big as the Development Company people at Marampa. We can't afford snags. They only want results in London. Easy money, that's all. Big returns for no outlay. Still, they have agreed to a new concrete jetty so the lorries can get closer to the conveyor. That'll be part of your job. There's a gang of Africans handling it. I know it's not strictly

24

our line of country but we have to do these things out here. Especially in a place like Amama. It ought to be ready before the rains come."

He sighed. "That's the trouble with this coast. The rains. A hundred and fifty inches of it and all in a few weeks. It ruins everything. Farming. Soil. Sport. You get sick of it. Sort of 'Oh, what the hell!' It gets under the concrete, y'know."

"The concrete, sir? Which concrete?"

"The cricket pitch." Twigg's eyebrows lifted in surprise— as though Jimmy had not been paying attention. "Have to re-lay the damn' thing after every rainy season. Always cock-eyed or something. And the damned rats eat the string off the bat handles. Awful hard to keep going."

Jimmy was beginning to see himself arriving at Amama with no more foreknowledge of the place than that cricket there was difficult.

"What equipment have you got up there?" he asked.

"Cricket equipment?"

"No. The mine."

"Oh, the mine. Not much. All the usual. Diggers. Scrapers. A dumper. A few lorries. Euclids, most of them. All old stuff. All we could spare from here. Plenty of labour, though. Wonderful material for a cricket team."

"You seem keen on cricket, sir."

"Oh, rather." To Jimmy's anxious eyes it seemed that their tour of inspection was over. Twigg had switched off the jeep's idling engine. "Rather. Cricket breeds gentlemen. Wouldn't have half the trouble we do out here if they only played more cricket."

He mopped his face again. "Look, old boy," he said abruptly. "Let's head the other way. No need to mess about round the workings. It's hot and dusty at this time of the year and there's no sense in sweating more than necessary. I don't suppose you're all that keen on seeing them, are you?"

"Well, no, sir." Jimmy had felt it was his duty to find out

25

something about his work but Twigg didn't seem concerned. "I just thought I'd like to get to know a bit. That's all."

"Plenty of time tomorrow, old boy."

"Aren't I going up to Amama tomorrow?"

"Oh, hell, yes! And while you're at it, you're taking one Samuel Assissay with you. Bloody agitator——"

"Agitator?"

"Yes. One of these mission-educated Africans who thinks he's Christ's brother-in-law. Spouts the Bible and wants the Whites out of Africa." Twigg waved a hand airily. "Shipping him back to his home village. Comes from up-country somewhere beyond Amama. Earnshaw will take him up with you and drop him there out of my territory. Let someone else worry about him."

"Is he dangerous?"

"God, no, old man! Just a nuisance, that's all. Stirs my boys up. More ju-ju than agitator. Too much mission talk in his head. Keep him away from Gotto, for heaven's sake."

In spite of Twigg's words, Jimmy's first sight of Gotto at Amama the following day was disappointing.

As they turned into the creek out of the main stream—with Carmen Mirandy going full blast once more like a fair-ground steam organ in the cabin—the spit of land with its amphitheatre of trees looked shining and golden in the deep tranquillity of the afternoon and, to Jimmy, sweating on the foredeck as far away from the engines as he could get, disturbingly hot.

A rusting conveyor overhung the glittering brown water—obviously a home-made contraption rigged by the departed Jarvis. It looked as though it needed as many men to keep it standing as were required to see that the ironstone was loaded on to it and into the string of barges below. The landing jetty, a ramshackle affair of grey weathered wood on stilts, as impermanent-looking as the conveyor, with a hut

26

at its shoreward end, looked incapable of holding a dozen people let alone the throng which was gathered on it. There appeared to be no space anywhere for another human being. From one end to the other it was packed with black figures, most of them children. In the middle at the front were two solitary white people, a man and a woman.

Earnshaw peered over the edge of the steering well as they rounded the bend. "Oh, Lor'," he said. "Swannack's waiting to give you an 'ero's welcome. He always does this for strangers."

"Who's Swannack? More trouble?"

Earnshaw shifted his fag-end from one side of his mouth to the other with his tongue. "Nah. Missionary. Bible-basher. Praise the Lord and pass the ammunition. Yankee, but he's all right. Don't get in your hair much. His daughter's here on a visit. From the look of her photo on her ma's dresser, she's no Carmen Mirandy but she got it in all the right places and in the right amount." He smirked at Jimmy, sly, wily and suggestive. "Company for you, old lad. Company's a good thing to have here. I got Zaidee."

"Zaidee?"

"Zaidee Soloman. She's my girl. She's a widder. Don't use her married name, though. Her old man runs the store at Amama. There isn't no United Africa Company here, see. Indian Joe's his name—Joseph Soloman. Yusef Suleiman, if you want his real monicker. He's a Syrian and he'll be out to do you."

"Thanks for the tip."

"That's all right, old lad. Watch him. When it comes to fiddling, he could blind you with science. He's a right boy. If he wasn't, there'd be no Zaidee. The Syrians don't mix much normally. They stick to their own kind."

"And Zaidee?"

"Her ma had a bit of nig in her somewhere and Zaidee's butter-colour. One of coffee, two of milk. Heat don't affect

27

her. Nig blood keeps her cool." He glanced at Jimmy and went on in his flat whine as the boat approached the jetty. "We been going steady for a bit, y'know. She likes a white bloke. Fancies she's white herself. Makes her a bit crusty sometimes when she finds she's not. Mind, I'm not one of these blokes what have a different darkey girl hanging round the place every other night. They're dead common, they are. All you get outa that lark is a bad reputation and kinks in your spine."

Earnshaw grinned and scratched his dusty hair. "But you need company, old lad. You get sick of being alone. You got to keep it on the run, you know."

"I'll be all right," Jimmy said defiantly. "I've got Gotto."

Earnshaw gave a bark of laughter and Jimmy frowned. "What's wrong with this Gotto?" he demanded.

"You see soon enough."

"Listen," Jimmy said angrily. "Everybody seems to know this blasted Gotto. What *is* wrong with him? Has he got two heads or something?"

Earnshaw grinned shiftily. "If it was me coming to work with him," he said portentously, "I'd call out the perishing Navy." He glanced shorewards where they could hear a voice counting slowly—"One—two—three—" and he turned towards the cabin.

"O.K., Suri," he called. "Switch off the gramophone. 'Ere it comes."

Even as Carmen Mirandy was cut explosively short in mid-sentence, fifty young trebles, led by an aggressively high-pitched contralto, came across the water in a wavering hymn, slightly too slow and a little off-key.

"Onward, Christian Soldiers," came the brassy contralto.

"Marchy nasty war," came the fifty young trebles.

"Wither Crossy Jesus,
    Goin' Gone befar."

The hymn followed them as Earnshaw edged in and out of the mud banks, back-tracking on itself as they turned in a

28

big sweep under the towering mangroves that edged the river and finally blaring off in a triumphant serenade as the engines were switched off and Earnshaw signed to his crew to make fast.

"Them Swannacks do it better every time," he commented heavily. "Nice timing, Rev.," he shouted to the jetty. "Finish just as we arrive. Proper smashing it was. Solid bar gold."

"The new guy like it?" The white man on the jetty grinned proudly.

Nudged by Earnshaw, Jimmy nodded hastily. "Jolly good," he said enthusiastically and Swannack grinned again.

"It's the one we know best, brother," he said. "We all like that one. It makes a nice welcome."

While his wife fussed among the black children, marshalling them into order—"Bryma. Malaki. Into threes. Hurry up there, you, Lamina. Back to the schoolroom"—Swannack climbed down on to the boat. He was a hefty man with black hair growing in tufts all over his face—from his eyebrows and on his cheeks—so that he looked a little like a worn-out old broom.

"Pleased to meet you, son," he boomed as he shook hands with Jimmy. "Glad to have you join our little flock."

Mrs. Swannack was climbing aboard the boat now, a middle-aged, bony woman with a straight back and a thin mouth, obviously bursting with energy despite the heat that dewed her upper lip and made her hair lank with moisture.

"This him?" she said, staring with bold eyes at Jimmy who felt a little like an exhibit in a sideshow. "Pleased to meet you, son. You play tennis?"

Swannack flapped a hand in protest. "Give the boy a chance, Mother."

"Let him answer for himself, Father." Mrs. Swannack's tones were brisk and authoritative. "He'll be glad to play tennis before he's been here very long. Soon get sick of sitting. You play tennis, son? My daughter's arrived," she pointed

29

out, as though this were an event of considerable importance—not only to her but to Africa generally. "Father fetched her from the airfield yesterday. Graduated at Morrisonville Academy, Idaho. She'll want a partner and that Gotto sure is a wet hen. You play tennis, son?"

Her manner was as aggressive as her voice, demanding not only attention, but an immediate answer. Her bright piercing eyes, glowing in the shadow of the bush hat she wore top-dead-centre, were fixed intimidatingly on Jimmy and he said that he did, instantly aware of the aggrieved look that would have appeared on Twigg's face had he been there.

"That's good," Mrs. Swannack was saying briskly, obviously having little time for the Christian virtues of patience and resignation. "All I wanted to know. Come to the party tomorrow. After afternoon service. Cup of tea. Home-made wine. A prayer. Meet my daughter."

Jimmy had begun to think that if Mrs. Swannack's daughter were anything like Mrs. Swannack, meeting her might prove a doubtful pleasure. He began to foresee a hard-bitten devil-dodger like her mother with a mouth full of thundering Bible texts and a mind convinced of the sanctity of her mission in life.

Swannack was mildly rebuking his wife.

"Give the boy a chance, Mother," he was saying again. "Let him land first."

"While my daughter's here, I don't want her to say Africa's no place for company," Mrs. Swannack retaliated loudly. "We shall need her. Working for the Lord doesn't bar us from friends. Come on, Father, back to the schoolroom."

She bustled from the boat, cocking a leg over the rails and climbing from the catamaran to the jetty as easily as if she'd been mounting a staircase in her own home.

Swannack offered Jimmy a cigarette. "You attend church, son?" he asked placidly. "Always pleased to see newcomers at our services. How about tomorrow?"

30

Jimmy was on the point of finding out Swannack's religion and, as an excuse, claiming allegiance to a different one, but the ground was cut from under his feet as Swannack went on. "Doesn't matter whether you're Baptist, C. of E., Methodist, Total Immersionist, Holy Roller or what, son. I cater for 'em all. I cover all denominations, so's not to miss anybody. Come tomorrow."

"Father," Mrs. Swannack bawled peremptorily from the end of the jetty. "Back to the schoolroom. Routine, Father, routine."

Swannack made a moue of disgust which seemed girlish in one of so much bulk. "Women!" he said angrily, and climbed off the boat after his wife.

"Christ!" Earnshaw sighed with relief, and, lifting his hat with its switchback brim, mopped his forehead. "Them Swannacks fair exhaust me. O.K. tie 'er up, Suri, you black sinner," he said. "And don't go making a muck of it, or I nobble you. By God, I will."

As they stepped on to the catamaran, a white man came towards them down the jetty and Earnshaw turned quickly back to the boat.

"Oh, Gawd," he said to Jimmy. "Here it comes. You-too-can-be-the-life-of-the-party hisself. You nip off and have a good laugh with him and I'll get the boys to bring your luggage up."

The newcomer was very tall and yellow with mepacrine, and with a large, bony nose like a beak below pale hair and eyes. As he peered forward, he reminded Jimmy for all the world of the herons and cranes they had seen among the mangroves on their trip up the river. His long awkward legs, their skin tinted by the climate, heightened the impression.

"Hallo," he said in a sharp, high voice without offering his hand. "You'll be Agnew, I suppose. My name's Gotto."

31

TWO

His head buzzing as much from the implied warnings about Gotto as from Twigg's last-minute instructions, Jimmy felt vaguely let down.

For two days, from the scraps of conversation he had heard, the odd impressions and opinions he had gleaned from other people, he had been building up a mental picture of him quite out of proportion to the real thing. This weedy yellow young man with his pale hair and eyes and his bony nose, and the ill-fitting bush jacket that hung on his skinny body, was far removed from the swart-browed, ugly-tempered individual he had expected.

In point of fact, Gotto seemed tediously dull and boringly ordinary. He was long-windedly talkative about trivialities and awkwardly laconic about everything else.

He drove Jimmy up the dusty road to the bungalow they were to share close to the Amama mine, his eyes fixed on the red ribbon cut out of the mangroves, his attitude one of nervous affability.

"You any good at cricket?" he asked, as they reached the top of the hill where the bush started abruptly with the firm soil, and Jimmy cast him a trapped look over his shoulder.

'Oh, God,' he thought. 'Another one!' He decided to be honest this time, even if it ruined his career. Honesty, even in disfavour, seemed better than the nightly bouts of cricket Twigg was reputed to inflict on the juniors at Ma-Imi.

"Not very," he admitted with an apologetic smile.

"Well, that's all right," Gotto said with obvious relief.

"I got sick of hearing cricket down at Ma-Imi." He leaned back in his seat, apparently satisfied to have settled a long-standing worry, and stared ahead again where the dying sun drew long straight shadows across the ground from the base of the palms and the eucalyptus trees. Without waiting for him to continue, Jimmy took it upon himself to ask the obvious first questions that would break the ice.

"Been out here long?" he began.

"Nearly finished my time. I was mostly at Ma-Imi." Gotto gave him a sidelong smile and, remembering Twigg's obvious pleasure at getting rid of him, Jimmy found himself wondering what was wrong with him. He seemed depressingly unexciting and so excruciatingly ordinary that Jimmy was quite certain he'd seen him somewhere before. He wore provincial England on him like a stiff Sunday suit.

"I've fixed it with the houseboy for you to have the room on the river side of the bungalow," he was saying. "That's the best side. It gets less sun and it's cooler—or rather, it's not so hot. He'll have moved my stuff out by the time we get back."

"Don't let me take your room," Jimmy protested.

"That's all right," Gotto said quickly. "I don't mind. Trying to make you comfortable, that's all. You can keep my drawers. They stick a bit but they're bigger than the others. It's a nice room," he went on eagerly, obviously more than anxious to be friendly. "As nice as you can get in this hole, anyway. The bush doesn't come so close on that side so you don't hear the frogs and crickets and you don't get so much wild life—bugs and things."

"It's jolly decent of you to move out," Jimmy said, as willing as Gotto to be co-operative—especially in view of the assorted warnings he'd received during the past two days.

"I've got bags of khaki you can borrow if you're short," Gotto went on. "And I've got a camera you can have if you've not got one. I've taken a lot of pictures myself—to show the people back home. Girls, you know. They'll never believe how little they wear and the village girls will always pose for you—without clothes if you give 'em a couple of bob. I've got quite a collection. I'll show 'em to you some time if you like."

Jimmy smiled feebly and decided to change the subject. "Do this job back home?" he asked.

"Yes. Lincolnshire. At least, that's where I worked before I came to this dump."

"My old man's in this line in Lincolnshire. He helped me get this job. Experience, you know, before I go into the family outfit. I suppose you decided to have a look round the world, too?"

"Not really. Got fed up hanging about."

"Hanging about?"

Gotto gave him a sad sidelong smile, and stroked his large nose in an involuntary effort to hide it that drew Jimmy's attention to it immediately. "Got the push," he said. "The manager had his knife into me. Like the chap where I worked opencast coal. Staff alterations, they called it, but it was the sack all the same."

"Oh." There was an awkward pause. "Didn't you fancy coming out here, then?"

"Nowhere else."

"What about Northamptonshire?"

"I went from Northamptonshire to Lincolnshire."

Jimmy was on the point of asking why when it occurred to him that Gotto had probably got the push from there, too, and that Africa was the last chapter in a long history of sudden changes, and the conversation halted once more as he sought a change of subject. "You married?" he asked at last.

Gotto's bony face brightened for the first time and his expression softened almost to wistfulness. It was a sudden warm shyness that fleetingly transformed his features, and he seemed to get his teeth into the conversation at last, as though the trivialities of home towns were desperately important to

34

him. He seemed to be grasping for something familiar in a strange land.

"Not yet," he said with a smile. "But I'm engaged—or nearly." His eyes still on the road, he fished one-handed in the breast pocket of his bush jacket and produced a photograph case containing the conventional snapshot of a girl against a garden wall.

"That's my girl. Doris is her name."

Jimmy affected to be interested and Gotto went on enthusiastically.

"*You* married?" he asked, tucking the case back again.

"No." Jimmy grinned. "But all my old girl friends promised to write. They all swore they'd try and miss me."

"All? How many have you got?"

"There must be at least six of 'em jockeying for position."

"Six!" The expression on Gotto's face was suddenly one of resentment. "You ought to have been born with a nose like mine. They don't jockey round *me* much."

Jimmy smiled. "What's this Swannack girl like?" he asked.

"I've got an invite round there tomorrow. I expect it includes you too." Gotto spoke as if it were a triumph of diplomacy on his part, though having met Mrs. Swannack, Jimmy was quite certain it wasn't.

Gotto looked over his shoulder, beginning to show something like warmth again. "Stella's her name. She's nineteen."

"Bit young."

"They're best young. When they get older, they start talking to you as though you don't know the score. Nineteen's a nice age. I'm looking forward to meeting her. Doris is nineteen." Gotto mopped his moist face with the handkerchief that lay on his lap as he drove. "Pity there's nowhere to take a girl round here," he concluded, the resentful tone returning to his voice.

"There's shooting, I'm told——"

"Catch me carrying a rifle round all day in this heat!"

"Well, fishing then——"

"From a wog canoe?"

"Well, there's a beach not far away, isn't there?"

"Get jigger worms in your toes if you run round without shoes on out here. You'll soon find out. I've had a bit."

"Well——" Jimmy was still wondering what it was about Gotto that so upset everyone and had privately arrived at the conclusion that the only effect he could possibly have on anyone would be a slow death from boredom. "Well—" he said again—"Earnshaw's offered to take me in one of his boats up the creeks after crocodiles."

"Earnshaw!" Gotto laughed sarcastically. The sky was beginning to turn jade green now as the sun began to sink but his eyes were as blank as marbles and his face showed no sign of interest.

"What's wrong with him?" Jimmy asked the question cautiously. In spite of Earnshaw's obvious immorality and the fact that he was none too clean and probably not very honest, he had taken rather a liking to his spicy conversation and his sly, croaking voice.

"Well——" Gotto made his reply slowly. "That gramophone of his for a start. And 'Old lad' this and 'Old lad' that. And he obviously doesn't wash very often. He's got a woman in tow—that Zaidee——"

"One of coffee, two of milk."

"That's her. And he's friendly with the Syrians. He gambles with his crews. He—well, he sets a pretty low sort of example, that's all, and you can't get on out here when you're familiar with the Africans."

"Oh, can't you?" It had seemed to Jimmy that Earnshaw's relations with his crews were very good, despite his insults and familiarity.

"Funny thing—" Gotto looked puzzled—"he seems to get on with the Swannacks. He often goes up there. They asked me once when I was up with Jarvis. They didn't rush to ask me again. Not till now and they couldn't very well avoid it this time. Everybody'll be there."

Gotto stopped the car at the little bungalow and when Earnshaw arrived in a lorry shortly afterwards, he began to direct the off-loading of supplies, shouting orders in a harsh high voice that seemed like a whiplash to the black boys who were scurrying in and out of the bungalow with boxes and cases.

Earnshaw watched him for a while, his hands in the pockets of his dirty shorts, his eyes heavy and disinterested. Then he glanced at Jimmy and saw the startled expression on his face.

" 'Ot, ain't it?" he asked.

"Gets hotter," Jimmy replied and Earnshaw grinned.

"Makes you wonder if you hadn't best stayed at home," he observed. "Me, I coulda taken over the old man's business but I couldn't see meself behind a counter. He was a herbalist. Sarsaparilla and hot drinks. 'Ead and neuralgia 'erbs. Backache and kidney stuff. All the nonsense. The war finished him."

"A bomb?" Jimmy asked, squinting into the glare of the sun.

"No, old lad." Earnshaw gave his slow tired smile. "Tobacco shortage. He find they was coming for his herbs to fill their pipes with."

As he finished speaking, he halted one of the Africans hurrying from the bungalow towards the lorry for the last of Jimmy's baggage.

"This here is Amadu Komorra, your boy," he said over his shoulder. "Biggest liar, biggest thief in Amama. Aintcha, Amadu, old cock?"

The black man's face split in a wide grin as he stared back at Earnshaw's bored blank face.

"No, sah. Not Amadu, sah."

"Go on, you bloody old rogue. Who pinches the sugar

37

and tea to give to the mammies? Who bribes the girls with flour?"

"Not Amadu, sah."

"I've *seed* you with me own eyes. Keep 'alf the blackies in Amama with what you swipe, dontcha? Who used to tell Boss Jarvis his clothes was all wore out and then took 'em up town and flogged 'em to his pals?"

"Not me, sah. Not Amadu."

The black man was wriggling with delighted embarrassment.

"You want to watch him, old lad," Earnshaw said to Jimmy, cocking a thumb in the direction of the African. "He pinch the smell of a goat if he could."

"No boss." Amadu crowed with mirth. "Not me, boss."

"Why, you're the biggest rogue, mammy-chaser and wangler in the whole of Amama. You know you are. What are you?"

"Boss"—Amadu almost collapsed with merriment—"I de biggest rogue, mammy-chaser and wangler in de whole Amama."

"That's right," Earnshaw agreed. "Glad you know it. Watch him, old lad, or you've had it. He's pretty smart for a darkey."

Amadu's grin faded as Gotto reappeared.

"O.K.," he was told brusquely. "Get moving! What about a meal?"

"Yessah, boss! I get!" Amadu hurried nervously away and Gotto stared after him, his eyes narrow and suspicious.

"Brassy-faced little swine, that," he commented. "Too much cheek for an African."

As he disappeared inside the bungalow again, Earnshaw turned towards Jimmy and shook hands solemnly.

"Goodbye, old lad," he said heavily. "Enjoy yourself. I'll see you get a decent burial."

"I heard the mortality was high out here." Jimmy was peering into the bungalow, his eyes puzzled.

38

"It got 'igher since His Lordship arrived," Earnshaw commented.

Jimmy closed the last of his suitcases and, kicking it out of his way, turned towards a damp-warped chest of drawers in the corner of his bedroom. Gotto was lounging on the bed and as Jimmy turned, a pile of clothes in his hand, he sat up. The conversation had found its way round to work and Gotto was suddenly animated in an aggressive, eager way.

"Listen," he was saying as he explained his plans. "I don't know about you, but this job here means a lot to me. A damned lot. I've sent a message to Amama Town where the shift boss lives. I've told him to meet us at the office first thing on Monday morning. We'll talk this lot over with him, tell him we expect him to pull with us, let him know straight away just where he stands. What say?"

"Good!" Jimmy slapped the clothes into a drawer and pushed it to with a squeak of tortured woodwork.

"After all, he's only an African. He's got to be told. They're loyal enough if you let 'em see you're not standing any damn' nonsense." Gotto paused to let his opinion sink in before continuing. "I've got to make a good show of this place," he said. "I've a mother to keep. She can't do much for herself and she's dependent on me absolutely. Got a bad heart. Makes her a bit difficult at times. You see," he went on with a trace of spite in his voice. "*My* old man didn't own some firm I could take over when I left school."

Jimmy hurried past the complaint before it developed further. "I'll back you up," he said, thankful that at least Gotto wasn't going to demand that he play cricket and prepared to overlook the threadbareness of his personality because of it.

"Well, it's nice to know you're not just the Ma-Imi type," Gotto went on. "They called me Snotty Gotty down there. Did you know?"

Jimmy gave him an embarrassed smile and said he didn't.

"Oh, yes. They thought I didn't know but I did. They never got on with me. Never even tried. They sent me up here to get me out of the way." Gotto seemed to take a queer delight in his isolation.

"Anyway, I'm with you, whatever you do. Listen——" Jimmy closed the last twisted drawer on his clothes with an effort that brought beads of sweat to his face—"let's go and sit on the verandah and talk, shall we? It'll be cooler there than in here."

Gotto sat bolt upright against the bare concrete wall. "Outside?" he said. "It'll soon be dark."

"I know. I like sunsets, don't you?"

Gotto's look seemed to suggest he was mad and then it changed abruptly to a smile.

"Yes," he said quickly. "I do. That is, I suppose I do. Never particularly noticed them, to tell you the truth. Always too busy trying to find something to do."

They moved out on to the verandah, through the stifling little bungalow with its characterless company-issue furniture and its native cloth curtains, its carved canoe-paddle wall decoration, its African leather pouf and the drum that was used as an occasional table. The palms in the distance were blue and velvety by this time and the sun, just disappearing behind the hills, was a bright golden orange in a sky of pale green and salmon pink. They could hear the honk of a hornbill in the distance and, pulling up a chair, Jimmy caught the first cricket's cheep.

As they sat down, a figure in white rose from the side of the verandah and appeared in front of them, suddenly and unexpectedly, and Jimmy noticed that Gotto jumped nervously.

"What do you want, you fool, coming up like that?" he demanded sharply.

40

"Sah!" The African grinned, his face slit across with a water-melon slice of white teeth, and Jimmy caught a glint of spectacles. "Jus' me. Clerical Officer Smith."

"Clerical Officer, my Aunt Fanny," Gotto said in a high thin voice that sounded like jangled nerves. "You're just a bloody pen pusher."

"Thass right, boss, sah." The African beamed at Jimmy. "Chief bloody pen pusher. Clerical Officer Joseph Windsor Buckingham Smith, sah. I read. I write. I type better dan de Queen England. I come greet de new boss, sah. Fo' de African people I greet you, boss. Fo' dese po' black folk, dese uneducated black trash with no reading, no writing, no civilization."

"Thank you very much, Mr. Smith."

"I work hard fo' you, boss," Smith continued, the slash of his white teeth dividing his black face into two halves. "I de best clerical officer in all de worl'. Any black boy give you cheek I kick him backside one-time, all-same de police."

Gotto interrupted the flow of self-esteem with an irritated wave of his hand. "O.K. You've said your piece. Now shove off. And don't come here again at night, savvy?"

"I savvy, boss." Smith gave him a nervous flickering glance and turned again to Jimmy. "I come greet fo' de African people. Dass all. Boss, you like dis Africa country?"

"Tell you better in a week or two."

Gotto gestured again, more angrily. "Go on, hop it," he said.

"O.K., sah, I go now." Smith looked once more at Jimmy. "I see you in de mornings, sah. I yo' clerk. I polish yo' desk. I spit on yo' chair and polish wit' de handkerchief. Make smoot' for yo' backside. I read, sah. I write. I type better dan de Queen England. Goo' night, boss."

As he disappeared, merging abruptly into the swiftly growing dusk, Gotto stared after him. "Too smooth, that Smith," he said. "Clerical officer my eye. Just reads enough

41

and writes enough to be useful. Recruited round here. Twigg picked him. The educated Africans won't have this joint. Too quiet. And I can't say I blame 'em."

It was now almost dark and there was a chorus round them of sounds. To the bark of the frogs and the cheep of the crickets, an all-enveloping chorus that seemed to have surrounded them suddenly, without any beginning, was added the sharp whine of a mosquito, and Gotto flapped angrily.

"Blasted things. Malarial. Pick it up from the natives." He slapped at his wrist and stared at the smeared insect with an expression that was a mixture of disgust and indignation.

"Look," Jimmy said hastily. "How about a shower and a trip in the car up to the town?"

Gotto turned abruptly, his eyes startled. "A trip up to the town? That's not a town. It's a collection of scruffy huts. There are no bright lights," he said pityingly. "This is Africa. Not the West End."

He was obviously reluctant and Jimmy put it down to a desire to remain at home and work at nights.

"I'm not proposing to make a habit of it," he pointed out quickly. "It's just that I'd like to see it before I start work. That's all."

"I wasn't thinking of that. It's just that it's dark. Nothing to see."

"If you've got something else to do, I'll go on my own. But I'd like to know what it's like and where I am."

Gotto stared at him, then again his face broke into a hesitant smile.

"Oh, well," he said. "I suppose you might. All right," he added. "I'll drive you up. Let's go and visit the illuminations. I'm not staying here on my own again."

Dark masses of giant cotton trees hung over the highway that ran through Amama Town, shutting out the tremendous African moon and making the road a chequerboard of blacks and silver-whites. Beyond the cotton trees, the great dry leaves of the palms rustled in the hot wind and beyond them the sky, slashed by the curving boles of trees, was pricked by starlight.

The mud and wattle huts huddled among the banana plants were thrown out here and there in silhouette by the yellow light of an oil lamp or the glare of a fire, and what few stone buildings there were picked up the moonlight on their white-washed fronts and tossed it back nakedly. The aromatic air was heavy with the smell of wood smoke and vegetation, that exciting smell of Africa that Jimmy had noticed as soon as they had turned into Amama Creek.

In front of a hut near the roadway, a couple of women sat, still prepared to sell mangoes or bananas to all comers from the calabashes on the ground before them and, in the open doorway of a wood and tin dwelling, a tailor crouched over an ancient treadle sewing machine by the light of a kerosene lamp held by his wife. From among the shadows at the rear came the murmur of African voices and the monotonous plink-plonk of a single-octave tune on an instrument made from a tin box—in splinters of broken sound as though the melody had been dropped and shattered to fragments. And like a bass accompaniment, across the still hot air the thump of a Bundu drum beat through the crowded trees that flattened the sound to the steady throb of a pulse.

"Those blasted tomtoms," Gotto said as he drove. "Always at it. They get to be a part of the landscape."

He halted the car as they entered Amama Town—given the title out of courtesy because of the half-dozen two-storeyed buildings in its centre and the few stone dwellings along the roadside.

"Well, here you are," he said with a snigger. "Gay, isn't it? Full of night life. What say?"

Beyond the small group of stone buildings, Jimmy could see more clusters of native huts in the darkness but it was

43

really the flickering lights inside them and the number of people about the road that indicated a community, for even here the cotton trees clustered thickly along the edge of the bush and the place was jetty with shadow.

Gotto indicated a couple of naphtha flares that set the foliage glowing greenly outside a brick and wood building just ahead of them, next door to the home of an artisan that showed its Edwardian bric-a-brac and black-skinned portraits in a glow of pride under the light of an oil lamp.

"Amama's Café Continental," he said. "Indian Joe's Bar."

The whitewashed store alongside had its shutters in place and looked more like a lock-up garage than a shop. The three or four Africans who sat on the steps at the front with bottles in their hands were delightedly watching an argument that was going on over the counter inside the drab little den, a mere hole in the wall peopled by drinkers with black faces which somehow with the arrival of darkness looked vaguely sinister.

"How about a drink?" Jimmy asked, greedy for the lights.

"They're all Africans," Gotto said.

"Well, does it matter? There's no colour bar."

"Ought not to drink with Africans. Damned important. Colour bar or no colour bar. Besides, I don't want foot and mouth disease. They drink out of the same glasses." Gotto seemed to fidget with uneasiness. "Look, we ought not to be up here at night at all. I never trust these devils after dark."

He tossed a hand in front of him nervously. "Momo lives down there somewhere. The shift boss."

"Yes, I heard about Momo. They said he was pretty hot stuff."

Gotto turned in his seat and in the weak glow of the dashboard light, Jimmy could see he was smiling. "So they got you, did they?" he said. "They tried to give *me* that yarn. 'Nothing you know that he doesn't know,' they said. 'Get him to help you.' Help me! My God! *I* went to mining school back in England, which is something Mr. Momo didn't do. What did they tell you about the rest of 'em up here?—the native labour, I mean."

"Much the same," Jimmy said doubtfully.

"They smell." Gotto's comment was vehement. "Like all Africans. I suppose they did their song and dance act about Amama, too?"

"Song and dance act?"

"You know—how marvellous it is and all that. They're always preaching it, Twigg and that crew. They told me it was a clean, pretty place. It's pretty scruffy if you ask me." Gotto sniggered again in a curiously high-pitched way and wiped the sweat from his face and neck. "Like all the rest. Empty tin cans. Dirt. Half-starved dogs and pigs that look like greyhounds. Scrawny chickens. And always a kid asking you if you want jig-jig with his sister." The list of dislikes was in danger of becoming a jeremiad.

"Look," Gotto said in conclusion. "I can't say I like this damn' place very much at night. Never did. Let's shove off. What say?"

"Shove off?" Jimmy felt flattened, his excitement at all the new sights and sounds and scents withered. It was hard for enthusiasm to flower in the face of such bitter opposition.

Gotto was already fiddling with the starter. "Let's get back to the bungalow," he said, his manner growing suddenly warmer, as though he had suddenly become aware of his boorishness and were trying to make amends for it. "We can have a drink there. More cosy than in that bar. What say? We can talk about the mine better, too. Look," he went on in a flooding affability that screamed out loud of loneliness, "when I heard you were coming up, I got a bottle of scotch in. Let's go and make a hole in it. We ought to celebrate. I've got a feeling we're going to get on well together."

45

Three

IT was after lunch next day when Gotto first appeared, dressed in clean drill and shining with energy. Jimmy was outside in the sizzling heat, sweating cheerfully with a broken hand fork over the neglected garden in front of the bungalow. As he dug in the dusty earth, a naked urchin watched him, his hands behind his back, his round black belly stuck out like a pudding basin. Amadu, the house-boy, sat blinking in the shade of the verandah, wondering whether he were mad or worth assisting.

Jimmy looked round as he saw an angular shadow fall across the scorched flower bed where he crouched, and his eyes rose to meet Gotto's.

"Ready to meet Stella Swannack?" Gotto asked cheerfully. "There'll be a crowd, y'know."

"I'm ready." Jimmy tossed down the hand fork. "Just putting things to rights a bit. I didn't know we'd got a garden."

"We haven't. At least, not what I call a garden. This is just a burnt-out dust heap. Nothing grows here. Nothing decent, that is. Just native stuff."

"I'll bet *I* make something grow."

Gotto hesitated. "You want to leave that kind of work to the boys, you know," he pointed out. "White men don't do sweated labour out here."

"I don't mind." Jimmy grinned. "I like gardening. In fact, I thought I might plant a few geraniums in petrol tins and shove 'em on the stoep there. Make the place look homely."

"Homely!" Gotto laughed. "This hole?"

"Well, we can try. Listen, I was rooting round the bungalow

46

last night and I found a butterfly net in a cupboard. Amadu tells me it was Jarvis's. I'm going to see what I can catch. I used to collect butterflies at school. If Jarvis found it interesting, *I* might."

"I thought that was a kid's game."

"It is, but it'll do to keep me busy."

"It gets a lot hotter than this."

"I'll chance it."

"Can't see the point." Gotto stroked his long nose and strolled off towards the car.

"Always something to do," Jimmy pointed out as he caught up with him.

"Probably get sweat rash as a result. I've had a bit."

"I might not." Engrossed with being alive, Jimmy weighed up the sweat rash against the possible excitement and decided it was worth risking. "Like to have a go with me?"

"Me?" Gotto stopped with his hand on the door handle. "I've got something better to do than indulge in nursery pastimes." He paused and went on with an encouraging, understanding smile. "Everybody starts off like that, you know—dashing all over the countryside like mad, looking at things and chasing butterflies. Tourist stuff. But you gradually settle down. Keep that pace up and they'll take you home on a stretcher. When I arrived out here, it didn't take me long to make up my mind about that. That's why I've kept fit. Nothing wrong with me."

Nothing beyond a little mental stagnation, Jimmy thought spitefully.

"Sorry," he apologized. "I thought perhaps you found time hung a little heavy."

"It does. By God, it does," Gotto said vigorously. "But to hell with sweating your guts out after butterflies. That's the sort of thing Earnshaw does."

It was only a short run to the church, but the sun on the

47

roof of the car made it seem like an oven long before they arrived. The district of Amama, which took its name from the largest inhabited place, was almost an island, jutting out into a bend of the river and joined to the mainland by a narrow isthmus which carried the only road out of the area, a fact which left it isolated and lost to officialdom, for its contentment caused it to be overlooked. The promontory contained, in addition to Amama Town, half a dozen other places with names which to Jimmy, as a newcomer, all sounded extraordinarily alike—Rotumba, Marama, Miambi, Kamara—and the fishing village of King Tim tucked away in a rocky bay on the south side. The mine was driven into a small hill at the river end, a red bite out of the earth, levelled by zigzag roads that descended to the mine office and a small petrol railway, and eventually to the rickety jetty where the conveyor loaded the ironstone into Earnshaw's dumb barges.

In spite of the heat, the place looked fresh in the morning sunshine, with its bright green foliage and gaudy earth and the iridescent butterflies that abounded on the fringe of the trees growing like a cliff at the side of the road. They could hear the clipped simian cries of monkeys and the shriek of parrakeets, and could see glossy purple starlings and lemon-coloured weavers darting among the leaves. Inevitably, they passed the eternal solitary traveller, a symbol of Africa almost, a woman wrapped in a gaudy lappa decorated with great scarlet handprints and carrying on her head an umbrella held down by a large Bible—obviously a member of Swannack's flock on the way to prayer.

At the little rose-red church set in a vault of rustling palm trees, there was a record crowd, obviously all turned up to see the new white missis. The bell, begged from the burned-out wreckage of a Liberty ship torpedoed and run ashore in the Bunce during the war, hung on a wooden framework by the gateway and was tolled by an enthusiastic and tireless small boy in a loin-cloth. It had been clanging for an hour when Jimmy and Gotto arrived.

The overflow from inside the church had gathered in a mass of colour in the dense, dappled shadow, chattering in that peculiar high-pitched note of an African assembly, the men at the front and the mammies, some of them with children at the breast, twittering like a lot of excited monkeys at the back, seeing what they could between the brawny frames of their lordly menfolk. The girls stood to one side in a giggling group and the children, mother-naked except for a ju-ju of cowrie shells or chicken feathers, stared solemnly from any point of vantage.

Mrs. Swannack met them at the gate with the shriek that did duty for her laugh. The powder on her face was crusted by the perspiration but she seemed otherwise unmoved by the heat.

"Big day today," she shouted in a voice like the bray of a trumpet. "Father's in back with the choir. Usually I'm with him—routine, I guess, just routine—but today I thought I'd meet everybody here and give a welcome in the name of the Saviour."

The church was already crammed tight and as they appeared in the entrance, more than a hundred pairs of eyes, white in black faces, swung in their direction. For a church, it seemed remarkably noisy to Jimmy. There were suits and stiff collars on the few who could afford them, Clerk Smith prominent among this opulence in a starched white outfit he had worked on personally all morning until it had the consistency of a plank. The rest wore shorts, pyjama cloth robes, or the gaudy loin-cloths of the village.

At the chattering which broke out at their appearance, half a dozen babies, asleep in their mothers' arms, awakened with a series of yells and cotton dresses and lappas were opened for them to be breast-fed and quietened.

Mrs. Swannack indicated a seat at the front of the church

where, to Jimmy's surprise, Earnshaw already sat, dressed for the occasion in a striped shirt and an ugly satin tie. Underneath his chair was a grey American fedora.

"Didn't expect to find you here," Jimmy whispered as he pushed past.

"Anything's exciting, old lad, when there's nothing to do," Earnshaw pointed out simply. "Me and Old Doc never miss nothing new. Helps to keep it on the run."

He indicated the man sitting in the next chair who turned and held out his hand.

He was plump and elderly and his face was damp with perspiration. Down the back of his shirt was a dark moist patch.

A pair of shrewd blue eyes stared appraisingly at Jimmy through thick, old-fashioned spectacles. "Seems we'll be neighbours," he said. "Name's Romney." He shook hands hurriedly, as though it were a hardship, using Jimmy's arm like a pump handle.

"*Doctor* Romney," Earnshaw corrected him. "You get your first dose of malaria," he informed Jimmy with weighty foreboding, "Old Doc'll pull you through it. Twenty-five years and more on the Coast and him nearly seventy. He's the reason this place ain't known as the White Man's Grave any more."

"Not enough malaria to worry your head about," Romney assured Jimmy gruffly. "Healthy a place as you'll find in Sierra Leone. Took long enough but it's working." The old man's eyes, shining under his bushy eyebrows, had a sudden absorbed look, as though they stared out on his life's work.

"Ain't the diseases, old lad," Earnshaw said gloomily to Jimmy in a stage whisper. "It's the food. This wog cooking. It's awful. I got stomach ulcers out of it big as house bricks."

"God, those ulcers," Romney interjected wearily without turning round.

"I suffer terrible," Earnshaw continued. "Everything outa tins. I can't hardly eat a thing afore I start getting pains in

50

my guts." He screwed up his wrinkled face into an agonized grimace for Jimmy's enlightenment. "That and foot rot. I always got that. Foot rot, gut rot, and nut rot. That's Sierra Leone all over."

"Nut rot?"

"Melancholia, old lad. Going off yer chump. Like I said, you got to keep it on the run else you go barmy."

"So we buy a gramophone," Romney said, "and drive everyone else barmy instead." He glanced at Jimmy. "You'll already be acquainted with the apotheosis of Carmen Miranda."

"She's a good singer," Earnshaw pointed out.

"Doubtless. It's just that you have her sing so often."

Earnshaw looked at him pityingly. "You got to have something to do of a night, aintcha?" He turned to Jimmy and the Africans nearby leaned forward to listen. "Me, I got everything to keep you busy, old lad. Canasta. Monopoly. Dominoes. Cards. Beer. Gin. Everything that opens and shuts. I shown the boys how to play——"

"In fact," Romney interrupted again over his shoulder, "we've brought mental atrophy to a fine art, and now we're instructing the natives in it."

Earnshaw's voice became high with indignation. "It's either that else boozing," he said. "Twiggy goes for the booze. The way he drinks sometimes, you think he got holler legs. I go in for Carmen Mirandy and tiddly-winks with Suri and the boys. Cheaper and better for me ulcers. You sure they're ulcers, Doc? I think they might even be gallstones. Thought I could hear 'em, in fact, rattling round like a lot of marbles."

"Teeth. That's what it is. You should have your teeth out. I've been telling you so for years."

"What, all of 'em? I'd look like the entrance to the Severn Tunnel."

"There's such a thing as false teeth."

"I'd look dandy going to see Zaidee with a set of machinery

51

in me mouth." Earnshaw flicked a hand across the church. "That's Zaidee," he said to Jimmy. "There, with her dad. Pays for the dressing up, don't she?"

At first, Jimmy thought the girl alongside the elderly Syrian was white. Her hair was black and straight, like an Italian's, and her skin was olive—one of coffee, two of milk, as Earnshaw had said—but her clothes stamped without question the coloured blood in her. She was wearing a tight yellow blouse and a purple scarf in a way no white woman would have dared and a pair of bright green trousers which, leaving nothing to the imagination, were studied with awe and envy by the mammies who stood nearby.

'Three-D and colour by Technicolor,' thought Jimmy, who had never seen anything in his life like them before. Obviously they had been made by an over-enthusiastic African tailor with a keen eye to fit and Jimmy couldn't take his eyes off them. She looked wanton and as lusty as a young animal.

"Walks like Marilyn Monroe," Earnshaw pointed out proudly. "She don't come 'ere much but ole Swannack's a sport. Always a welcome for 'er——"

He fell silent in mid-sentence and, looking for the cause, Jimmy saw the intimidating figure of Mrs. Swannack heading down the church again.

"Big day today." She flashed her false teeth at them like a badge of office and shouted out the words so that the whole congregation could hear her. "There's my daughter, Stella, at the organ."

Jimmy, who had expected something like Mrs. Swannack with a mouth as hard as an old hack's and a bush hat flat on top of mousy hair, was startled to see a tall girl cool in a white frock and straw hat sitting at a small harmonium. Her features were certainly her mother's, however, and he realized that in later years, unless she had something of her father's gentler nature, she would probably look exactly like that intimidating gospeller.

She waved at them with her fingers, and smiled, and Jimmy smiled back, blushing with embarrassment at the sudden wide grins that appeared on the interested black faces round him at the gesture.

"We won't be long now," Mrs. Swannack boomed. "Never late here. Routine's the thing. My, I've never seen such a congregation before. It's all you young folk, I guess. The Lord loves young folk."

Apparently at a signal from her father, Stella Swannack started to pedal the harmonium and a bronchitic wheeze came from it as she started to play, plucking up the keys with her finger nails when they stuck.

"Stand up, stand up, for Jesus!" Mrs. Swannack suddenly faced front like a drill sergeant and began to bellow in a deafening contralto alongside that made Jimmy jump. "Ye Soldiers of the Cross."

"Lift high His royil banner," came an answering shout that was half drowned in the scuffling as the congregation scrambled to its feet from chairs, benches and the hard earth floor. "It mus' not suffer loss." The sudden noise started the babies howling once more and for a moment there was a considerable amount of agitation as black breasts were uncovered again.

From the back door of the church Swannack appeared, the tufts of black hair sticking straight out from his face in his fervour so that he seemed to be staring through a quick-set hedge. He was followed by a choir of small black boys whose high-pitched treble voices, none too much in tune, flung the echoes crashing to the apex of the iron roof where the cheap coloured-glass window finished. A woman in the row behind, whose over-youthful yellow frock and picture hat looked oddly out of place against her black face, passed over a dog-eared card without halting her singing, but, too occupied with staring, Jimmy merely mouthed the chorus of the hymn. On one side of him, he could hear Earnshaw and Romney

53

clearly enjoying themselves at the top of their voices and on the other, Gotto, like himself, only murmuring the words.

As the choir passed, Mrs. Swannack swung into line with the precision of a guardsman and joined on the end, eventually taking her place on the bench that acted as the choir stalls where she could keep a sharp eye on the small boys.

"Praise the Lord," Swannack intoned loudly. "Praise the Lord Who has brought us once again to this glorious Sabbath Day."

There was a chorus of *Hallelujahs* and Stella Swannack ceased pedalling the harmonium which wheezed to silence as she sat back and mopped her face.

"Brothers and sisters in God," Swannack said. "Let us praise the Good Lord."

"Amen," shouted Mrs. Swannack intimidatingly.

"Hallelujah," responded the congregation.

"I say," Jimmy whispered to Earnshaw. "What denomination is this?"

"Gawd knows," Earnshaw whispered back. "Between you and me and the gatepost, I think it's one old Swannack made up hisself."

The service consisted almost entirely of hymns, all popular tunes which the congregation apparently knew and enjoyed, and they bellowed them with all the gusto of a Saturday night Salvation Army meeting. The sermon was one which offered blood and fire and eternal damnation as the alternative to a good life with salvation hereafter, but the black flock lapped it up, though at one point when Swannack paused for a breath before a final assault on their consciences, Jimmy distinctly heard Earnshaw saying in a loud whisper to Romney next door, "Yes, but you should of led clubs, Doc, then I could of got out my ace."

Apart from the heat—and that crowded church in the windless humidity of Sierra Leone seemed to swell with it so that it came up from inside his shirt in waves and almost

54

suffocated him—Jimmy found himself thoroughly enjoying the experience. There was a strong smell of charcoal, cheap perfume and perspiration from the black lady behind which mingled none too successfully with the scent of flowers, dust-dry wood and the baked corrugated iron of the roof.

Jimmy was watching Zaidee Soloman staring at Stella Swannack from her position by her father, the old Syrian. She sat bolt upright, untroubled by the temperature, her eyes constantly in the direction of the harmonium instead of on Swannack, bold and brightly-hued as a parakeet and conscious of her own beauty.

For a moment, Jimmy wondered what had brought these two to the welcome service for Swannack's daughter, particularly as Indian Joe would inevitably be a Muslim. Then it occurred to him that for them as well as for himself and all the other people in the town, Stella Swannack's arrival was an event, something which lifted that particular day out of the long succession of dazzling days that stretched through the year. It would have been the same, he realized, if there had been an accident or a mad dog.

The Swannacks' house was next door to the church, beyond the little graveyard where the red headstones of dead missionaries crumbled among the ant heaps. It was full of people when they arrived after the service, and their entrance was made through an avenue of grinning Africans assembled outside to see the fun so that once again it was brought home to Jimmy that anything that happened in Amama was exciting, however trivial it might be.

As they pushed through the crowd, a storm of shouting broke out at the back among the banana plants and Jimmy heard a deep voice chanting with the timbre of a big drum.

"An' I see a new Heaven an' a new eart'. For de fuss Heaven an' de fuss eart' are passed away; and de sea is no mo'. An' I see de Holy City, Jerusalem——"

55

"Samuel Assissay," Earnshaw commented, placidly unmoved. "Playing it big and using both hands. It ain't taken him long to wind hisself up. 'Im and Jesus is buddies," he explained.

Assissay, an incredibly tall man, gaunt in his tattered clothes, was standing on the fringe of the crowd, waving long arms like antennae. Jimmy had seen him before on the boat on the way up-river from Ma-Imi but then he had huddled on the stern, a disconsolate bundle of arms and legs. This wildly gesturing sermonizer was a different person and it was obvious that Mrs. Swannack recognized him as a threat to her influence.

"This is the Lord's house," she shrieked from the doorway. "If you're blaspheming His name, Samuel Assissay, take yourself off His Holy Acre."

"Have no fear," Romney commented to Jimmy. "Assissay will lose this round. The opposition's more than strong enough to hold its own."

He studied the uproar for a while. "I'm glad you've seen him in action," he said. "He's a sort of black John the Baptist and it's a help to know all about him if you have to meet him socially."

The crowd were laughing and jeering at Assissay now, tormenting him and shoving him from one to another as he continued to chant his plaint at the top of his voice.

"All black men downtrodden," he was yelling. "By-n'-by, black man savvy white master de oppressor of de poor and lowly. He rise up——" he staggered across the road from a shove in the back and collapsed on his knees in a puff of dust—"De Lord of Hosts hab sworn it. It shall come to pass."

The crowd was shrieking with laughter now and trying to drown his noise with a chant of its own.

"Arfar Chart Nevn. Harold be thy name. Thy Kindon come. Thy Willie Dunn. . . ."

Two or three men advanced on Assissay whose mouth was

still opening and shutting ineffectually against the din as he waved his dusty pink palms, and picking him up they tossed him into the undergrowth to the huge delight of the onlookers.

"O.K., Missis Swannack," they grinned, turning towards the house. "We fix 'um."

"The forces of the Lord have prevailed once more," Romney pronounced solemnly as he mounted the steps to the bungalow. "We can now enter into the Kingdom of Heaven."

The party consisted mostly of black people—with the addition of a couple of white ministers who had driven out especially from Freetown and were obviously keenly interested in Stella. There was also a black minister from up-river, three or four black school-teachers, and one or two foremen from the mine, among them Alf Momo, a lanky man with a lean sensitive face and the sad spaniel eyes of his race.

Mrs. Swannack, unmoved by the stifling heat that glowed through doorways and windows in spite of awnings and slatted blinds, was in her element, noisy and happy and energetic as she helped the black servant to pass round the cakes and tea and the discreet glasses of home-made wine.

Like the church the old-fashioned little parlour was packed to its limits. All the white men and one or two of the black men huddled in a group round Stella Swannack, vying with each other in their attempts to claim her attention. Even Gotto managed to put in a stiff, humourless remark from time to time but no one appeared to take any notice of what he said and his conventional chit-chat was soon swamped in the noisy comments of the others so that whenever Jimmy looked at him he appeared to have been elbowed out of the conversation.

Later, when Swannack had handed round nips of gin to the men—Earnshaw downed his at a single gulp before the rest were served—Jimmy found himself alone with Stella in the garden.

Earnshaw watched them through the window, disinterested, weary and bored. "Think he going to shape up?" he asked Romney.

"Why shouldn't he?"

"Gotto, o' course."

"What can Gotto do?"

"What can a boil on your neck do? Twiggy oughta kep' him down at Ma-Imi for a bit and sent someone else up— or kep' Gotto down there. Blimey, he's only a few months to go before he's finished. Why they have to send him up here? If I was young Agnew, I'd be feeling like Joe Rotten."

"I shouldn't worry," Romney said, glancing through the window at Jimmy. "That young man has a lively look. He's the sort who survives."

Meanwhile, outside in the tumultuous garden where gaudy flowers hid beneath gigantic banana leaves, Jimmy was finding Stella Swannack as bewildered as he was himself by the confused impressions of Africa.

"I guess it takes some getting used to," she was saying. "I was born out here, but I'd forgotten what it was like and it comes at you a bit unexpected when you come back."

"Miss the bright lights?" Jimmy was thinking of skyscrapers and sleek cars and neon patterns and ballyhoo.

"You don't know Morrisonville," she smiled. "The only difference between Morrisonville and Amama is that back home we've got a drug store and a pool room."

"And how long are you staying?"

"Oh, just a little while."

"And when you go back?"

"Teach, I suppose." She didn't seem too sure and didn't appear to relish the prospect. "I've got truckloads of notebooks and pencils. I'm going to fill 'em all and give a few lectures to the kids back home. I've got three cameras and films by the crate."

"What do you want with three cameras?"

"Take pictures, of course. Why?"

"Yes, I know. But wouldn't one do?"

"Three will make a better job of it. Some pictures will be this shape"—she gestured vaguely with her hands—"some will be that shape and some will be another shape." She laughed. "That'll make for variety even if the pictures are lousy."

She hoisted herself on to the verandah rail and sat swinging her legs, her eyes on the ground. "The United Evangelists will always be interested in lectures about the work out here," she said. "The only trouble is, I'm not sure that I am. At least, not interested enough to make it my life."

"What shall you do then?" Jimmy hitched himself up at the other end of the verandah rail and sat facing her.

"Oh, look around. Visit Europe on my way back to the States. I stopped at London on the way here—that's some city! Guess I might try Paris if the funds run to it. I might get a job in England for a bit on an exchange system. I'd like that. Then I suppose I'll eventually get married."

"Oh! Who to?"

"Oh, just somebody I know, I suppose."

"Engaged?"

"Gosh, no!" She sounded indignant. "I've only just started looking 'em over. I mean I'll get to know someone and decide to settle down with him. That's all. It's quite usual around my age."

"Why not marry me?" Jimmy grinned. "I'm free just now and it'll save you the journey home."

She laughed heartily for the first time. "Sure is nice of you," she said. "But I hardly know you."

"You will before long."

"You the persistent kind?"

"Not particularly." Jimmy stubbed out his cigarette in a pot of geraniums and blinked in the sunlight that pierced the leaves in needling shafts of light. "But I've been in Amama long enough already to know you'll see a lot of everybody before you've finished. Even Gotto."

"That's a queer guy." She wrinkled her brows in bewilderment.

"Sure is a queer guy," Jimmy agreed. "Anyway, to come back to this proposal of mine——"

"Take it easy. I'm used to proposals. I once had three in one night at a college party—only one of 'em for marriage, too!"

Jimmy laughed. "Since you don't know me very well, I'll tell you all about myself. Name, Francis Theodore St. John Agnew——"

"Gosh!"

"Earnshaw was blunter. I think *he* said 'Jesus'. Personally, I've never believed it but my mother insists it's true and you can't argue with a birth certificate."

Stella held out her hand. "Shake. If the truth were known and my grandfather had his way, mine would be Swanakaczicki."

"Pretty name," Jimmy said politely. "To return: I'm domesticated. I help with the washing up. I'm good at fixing things. I do card tricks. I can whistle between my teeth——"

"You sound just the type I'm looking for."

"You bet I am. I like good music. I save my money and I'm all for Anglo-American relationships—especially in Amama—I'm fond of kids——"

She stared at him, her large grey eyes faintly mocking. "Kids, too? This is too much. Honest?"

"Honest. I've got dozens I write to regularly. I don't drink—at least, not much, and then only when I'm thirsty."

"You'd better put your application in writing and I'll consider it with the others."

Jimmy grinned. "Well, anyway," he said. "There's no need to be lonely out here. I'm told there's always someone willing to look after you."

60

Stella laughed again and she seemed suddenly much more at home than she had been when he had found her. "The house-boy's made me my own private privy already. Mother says it's quite an honour, only he *will* insist on asking me if it fits."

"No, but seriously," Jimmy persisted, "I'd like to show you around—when someone's shown *me* around."

"Seems we ought to look around together. Be much easier. Be much smarter. Then what we don't know we can guess at."

"There's some good swimming not far away, I believe," Jimmy went on gaily. "There's fishing and shooting. Plenty to do if you don't weaken and the sun doesn't get you. I believe we've even got a gas-lamp in the middle of Amama which some old chief bought from the London County Council after he'd visited Queen Victoria's Jubilee, and erected here on a stone plinth. He lost quite a bit of face when it didn't light up."

Stella laughed.

"At least, it's something for a photograph," Jimmy said. "You're going to need something with three cameras. I'll help you take it. How about it?" he concluded with a sweeping enthusiasm. "Tomorrow?"

She held up her hand in protest.

"You mustn't rush me like this. You've got to give me time. My folks will want me around here for a while."

"Nothing wrong with meeting an eligible young man for a bit of swimming between times though, is there?"

"Maybe not. But give me a day or two. Just a day or two. Say a week. I'm here for the dry season."

It was late when Jimmy left the Swannacks, and Gotto and the car had long since disappeared. He got a lift with Romney and Earnshaw and stayed talking with them for some time, before walking slowly back to the bungalow through the scented night, occupied with thoughts of Stella Swannack.

The mine bungalow appeared to be deserted when he arrived and he assumed Gotto had gone to bed, though the light was burning and the moths were banging and buzzing round it like a dust storm and the air was full of the smell of singed wings.

The house-boy, who was sitting in the shadows on the verandah playing with a chameleon on a piece of string, greeted him sleepily.

"You wait for me, Amadu?"

"Yassah, boss. See you safe home. I go now."

Jimmy pulled off his shirt and threw it, wet with sweat, with a plop to the floor. He lit a cigarette and, indifferent to the whine of mosquitoes, went outside to let the cooler night air play on his body.

"That you, Agnew?"

He turned as Gotto's voice came sharply from his bedroom. He was lying on his back, staring at the ceiling, his yellow face shining with perspiration. There was a half-written letter on the bed and an ash-tray full of crushed cigarette ends on the chair alongside.

"Hallo," Jimmy said from the door. "Thought you were asleep. What have you been doing?"

"Lying here."

"Staring at the ceiling?"

"Yes."

"That's a poor way to pass the time."

"Is it?" Gotto turned his head slowly and stared at Jimmy. "Enjoy yourself?" he asked.

"Not half," Jimmy said enthusiastically. "Nice kid, Stella, don't you think? More than made up for the home-made wine." He grinned at Gotto. "I'd have passed out if Earnshaw hadn't told me about the case of beer he had round the back. Did you get one?"

"Nobody tells me things like that."

62

Jimmy laughed. "Hard luck. How about you? Did you enjoy yourself?"

Gotto shrugged. "Might have, if you hadn't hogged the girl all day. Nobody else got a chance."

Jimmy grinned. "Modern girls like speed," he said. "This is the jet age, you know."

"We're not all lady-killers," Gotto replied. "All of us haven't had your chances. Some of us have had to look after their families. Like I have with my old mother. I wasn't always able to get out and run around like you."

"Hm." Jimmy began to suspect that Gotto wasn't joking and he was a little flattened by the realization. "Rotten hard luck," he commented heavily.

"I had to stay back and fetch and carry. And I didn't always get much thanks for it when I'd done, either."

The resentful tone creeping into Gotto's voice depressed Jimmy.

"Well," he said in a weightily cheerful tone. "Now's your chance. You're your own master now. You can go in for riotous living as much as you like."

"I need all *my* money," Gotto said pointedly. "I haven't got a father who owns a business. Besides, I wasn't born as lucky as you. Being able to get people falling on my neck—just talking like that, shooting a line."

"I'll give you lessons if you like," Jimmy said, unable to keep the sarcasm out of his voice. "It's quite easy."

"Not for me. They just turn their backs on me when *I* talk and find there's something they've forgotten to do." Gotto paused for a moment and lit a cigarette before continuing, casually—almost too casually. "What did she say about me?"

"Say about you? Nothing as far as I know. What should she say?"

"What they all say. That's a queer-looking clod, with a snout like a prize sow."

63

"Don't be silly, man." Jimmy was beginning to feel irritated by the acid self-sympathy, all the more so as Gotto's guess was so nearly right. "As far as I know," he lied, "she never even mentioned your name."

"She didn't like me all the same. I can always tell by their looks."

Jimmy was on the point of losing his temper when he pulled himself up short. He had to live with Gotto for a considerable time yet, he remembered, and arguing wasn't going to help either of them.

"Listen, Gotty," he said as calmly as he could. "I think you're quite wrong. Stella's not that kind of girl. I'm sure she's not, in fact. I've arranged to see her again——"

Gotto smiled, like an advocate who has caught out a witness in a lie. "Hogging the women," he commented. "See what I mean?"

Jimmy ignored him. "I've arranged to see her again," he repeated. "But if you feel you want to know her better there's nothing to stop *you* seeing her, too."

"Only a great ugly snout!" Gotto laughed harshly. "Besides, I can imagine your face if you arrived at the Mission and found she was out with me." The eager chumminess of the morning was swamped by obvious jealousy, and as it suddenly occurred to Jimmy that Gotto lived in a cheerless little world of his own to which he clung unwillingly as a defence against the rebuffs his humourlessness brought him, he began at last to understand Twigg's warnings.

"Look, Gotty," he said. "Don't let's quarrel about it."

"I'm not quarrelling." Gotto spoke with a patient, too-reasonable smile that made Jimmy grit his teeth. "You're the one who's getting upset."

"Am I?" Jimmy forced a grin. "Well, it isn't worth it, anyway, is it? Nothing to stop us sharing the lady. Why not come with us when I see her again? We're only going swimming or something."

64

"I'd look fine playing gooseberry. No, thank you."

Jimmy stood by the bed, lost for words, anxious to break off a difficult conversation that led him into greater confusion with every reply, and eventually Gotto waved his hand, and he seemed a little more cheerful.

"Don't forget we're meeting Momo at the office tomorrow," he said. "Talk things over."

"Yes. I'd better get some sleep."

Jimmy left the room thankfully. He had a sudden uncomfortable feeling that perhaps Earnshaw's first estimate of life with Gotto had been more right than he had thought. Whether his stay in Amama was to be one of weeks or months, he decided, it was going to seem an awfully long time.

Four

THE bright blinding sun roused Jimmy early the next morning. As it rose behind the hills, a shaft of flame touched the misty blueness of the early daylight, then the sun itself appeared, a yellow eye staring clear across the curve of the earth, its orb curtained by the dark palm fronds that intervened.

The empty sky was lit by its glow and the tips of the hills were tinted gold. As it rose higher, Amama blazed with its daylight brassiness and the new cycle began to burn its way to its zenith.

Jimmy woke slowly, after a drugged sleep in the airless night that was broken only by the whirr of a faulty fan and the croak of the gaudy little toads that hid under the doorstep. His mouth was dry and his body was already moist with perspiration.

He sat up and, reaching for a towel, mopped his face, then hurried naked for the shower. Recovering his wits under the splashing water, he began to sing loudly until he remembered his conversation with Gotto the previous night, and his song stopped abruptly as he became obsessed with a feeling of depression. Then he began to sing again, louder and faster that ever, combating the thoughts that had turned off his happiness as though with a tap.

'There must be no depression in *this* house,' he decided as he set off for the office, whistling defiantly. 'There must be no thought of defeat.' With Amama as small as it was and with Gotto constantly treading on his heels, there could be no room for cheerlessness.

66

He thrust his foot down on the accelerator of the rattling old station wagon that had been assigned to him and skidded it in the dust round a corner just for the fun of the thing.

The chatter of the diggers and the grinding roar of lorries in low gear penetrated through the bush as he approached the workings. The bright foliage on either side of the road was dulled with the dust that the Euclids' wheels had churned up, and the bite out of the hillside seemed to glow like blood in the hot morning sunshine, a rich semi-circle in the flat quarry-face, like a slice out of the red flesh of a paw-paw. The whole complicated operation of getting iron out cf the earth to feed the furnaces of the world was in progress. Fringing the workings and along the top of the great arc were the giant trees—baobab, cotton, palm—in a solid mass as though huddling together in fear of the steel machines that carved into their midst. Even as Jimmy watched, he saw a towering eucalyptus topple to make way for a new road and heard the muffled thump of an explosion as rock was blasted on one of the lower levels.

The mine office was in a wooden hut that looked as though it had had its origin in an army dump. It was a plain concrete-floored room filled with sparse furniture, the only decoration being a calendar on which Jimmy noticed someone—he presumed Gotto—had started to tick off the days. From next door, the sound of a typewriter beat unsteadily as Smith, the black clerk, started work.

Jimmy sat down and, for lack of anything better to do until Gotto arrived, loudly shuffled the papers and plans on the desk which were gritty with the dust that had settled everywhere. Then he studied the rock samples which were used as paper-weights when the Harmattan, the cold wind off the Sahara, blew across from the north, and examined the surveyor's tripod in a corner of the office with a paper of compass bearings and distances attached to it by an elastic band. For ten minutes, he glanced through the geological survey memoirs of the area, and studied a drawing of a Mather and Platt pump, while all the time the office shook to the rhythmic thump of a digger's bucket on the earth not far away.

After a while, as no one appeared, he lifted a drilling bit from a chair to the table and sat down. "Smith," he shouted through to the other office. "Clerk Smith. What's the time? This clock doesn't seem to work."

"No, Boss." Smith's grape-dark countenance appeared round the door and beamed. "No work. All rusted up. De rains fix 'um."

"Oh!" Jimmy stared at the damp-spotted face of the clock. "Can't it be mended?"

"No, Boss. Plenty too much damn' rust."

"I see. Anything else that doesn't work?"

"Yassah, Boss." Smith nodded enthusiastically. "De drawers all stick. De typewriter no good. De keys of de safe done get lost. And, Boss, de telephone to de workings——"

"What happened to that?"

"De rains, Boss. Or de ants get in de works. Eat de wire. I t'ink de rains."

"How do you get in touch, then?"

"Go down, Boss. Send boy on bicycle. Boss Earnshaw fix 'um mebbe. Boss——" Smith's cheerful countenance became gloomy and confiding. "Boss Earnshaw—you see de gramophone? He play 'um for you some time?"

"Not half." Jimmy was disinterestedly trying to make head or tail of the tangle of dusty papers left unsorted on the desk by the departed Jarvis before his dose of malaria. "On the boat coming up. About five million times. Why?"

"Boss—" Smith smiled sadly—"gramophone good for black man. Plenty dance. No cost money for drums when he give party."

"I suppose you're right." Jimmy looked up, beginning to wonder what the other was getting at.

68

"Plenty times I ask Boss Earnshaw give me gramophone. He got wireless. Why he want both?" The African's black face was suddenly indignant, as though he'd been cheated.

"I suppose he likes to hear his record," Jimmy said. "He's only got one——"

"Yassah. Carmen Mirandy."

"Well, I think he likes Carmen Miranda a bit. So he probably wants to hang on to her." Jimmy dismissed the subject and prepared to return to the papers in front of him.

"Boss——" Jimmy looked up this time with an expression as near irritable as his face could get—"I go buy gramophone from Boss Earnshaw. Only I not get paid enough money. He want ten pounds." Smith's face was outraged. "Ten pounds, Boss!"

"Well, work hard, old son, and study in your spare time," Jimmy said hastily, repeating a well-worn formula which had been flung at him times without number. "And then you'll earn more money and you'll be able to buy a gramophone and a Carmen Miranda of your own."

"Boss——"

"Oh, God," Jimmy said under his breath.

"Black man like me, plenty write, plenty read, type better dan de Queen England, why I no earn more money?"

Jimmy was sitting with his head on one hand now, staring sightlessly at the papers in front of him, trying to battle with the baking heat and Smith's droning voice.

"Clerk Smith very important black man in Amama. All mammies like Clerk Smith. Boss, I get gramophone, plenty girls come to my party, mebbe. Make dance. Boss, why Boss Earnshaw no give me gramophone?"

"Listen——" The sweat was beginning to run into Jimmy's eyes now and make him blink—"Be a good chap and go and boil your head, will you?"

Smith drooped sadly back to the other room where he

69

began to pound an ancient typewriter that seemed to shake the hut as he thumped laboriously on its keys.

Alf Momo, the shift boss, and Gotto arrived almost together, Gotto more like a crane or a heron than ever with his bony knees and a yellow face that was moist with the heat. He went straight to the water container and, filling a tin mug, swallowed it quickly. "Chloride!" he snorted, pulling a face. "Chloride of lime."

He sat down at the table, mopping his face and ignoring Momo. Jimmy, at the other side, watching him, was a picture of brisk energy and efficiency.

"Right!" Gotto smacked the table with encouraging enthusiasm. "Let's get on. I've got the gen on everything from Twigg. It's a piece of cake."

Momo was still standing by the door and Jimmy indicated a chair. "Sit down," he suggested and Gotto looked up quickly. Momo caught the glance, hesitated, then pulled up a chair and sat uncomfortably on the edge of it.

"Right," Gotto said again, even more heartily than before. He moved the papers in front of him briskly and a cloud of dust rose and the expression of distaste that appeared as he waved it aside chased away his look of bright alertness as though a blind had been drawn across his features.

"That's one thing," he said sharply, staring at the dust motes in the sunshine that streamed into the room. "Too much damn' dirt around here for comfort." He looked aggressively at Momo, almost as though it were his fault. "Down at Ma-Imi we had sprinklers to lay the dust. Can't we do something like that here?"

"We have not got sprinklers, Boss," Momo pointed out.

"No," Gotto said, and his brisk voice had given way to a fretful snap. "And we haven't got a lot of other thing either, as far as I can see. Is it always like this?"

"Not when the rains come, Boss." Momo flashed him a
70

broad grin. "All mud then. Too much mud. All-same glue in the office."

"Don't you use a pump?" Gotto's eyes were sharp and needling and Jimmy was reminded of the angry glance of a ferret.

"Yassah. As much we can. But the rains come faster than the pump work. Sometimes, it stop loading. The lorries cannot move in the mud."

"We'll have to use shovel boys, then."

Momo grinned again and spread his hands with a shrug. "Boss, the shovel boys cannot move also."

As he laughed heartily with an African's belly-laugh, Jimmy joined in but Gotto's expression didn't change.

"Because of mud?" he said. "Is that all? Mud doesn't stop *me* working. I'll chase 'em up."

Momo began to sense the hostility in the questions and he flashed a nervous glance at Jimmy who was immediately reminded of his own reactions the previous night when he had discovered that Gotto was not given to appreciating jokes.

When Momo continued, his voice had acquired the cautious note that had already become part of Jimmy's.

"Boss—" he said, his dark eyes sad. "Black man on Amama Island best in Africa. But black man funny man. Plenty queer in head. Boss Jarvis leave 'em to me. I'm black man, too. I understand black men. He put me in charge the black boys."

"Oh, he did, did he?" Gotto said. "Well, listen. Boss Jarvis isn't here any longer. He's gone home. My name's Gotto. Ivor Gotto. I'm in charge now. Savvy?"

Momo's face was calm and dignified as he replied. "I understand, sah," he said.

Gotto stared at him, hot and uncomfortable in the stifling room, his shirt sticking to his back, the dust creeping down his collar and into his eyes and nose.

71

"Right," he said. "Let's have no more about Boss Jarvis then, eh?" He shuffled the papers again, nervously, his manner belying the briskness of his words, then his pale eyes lifted and rested on Jimmy's face.

"Agnew, how about you keeping an eye on that gang who're supposed to be building the jetty? I'll look after the workings and you look after the jetty."

"Haven't we got a foreman on that job?" Jimmy sat up, puzzled.

"I'm not trusting any damned African."

Gotto used the word as an insult and Jimmy's eyes flew to Momo's face, but the shift boss sat impassively, his features expressionless. Gotto looked up, saw Jimmy's glance, and waved a hand.

"Not you, Momo. Not you," he said. "Don't start getting touchy, for God's sake. I wasn't thinking of you. But you have to admit some of these chaps of yours have to be watched, don't they?"

Momo licked his lips. "African good worker, Boss," he said deliberately. "Give him trust, he work well."

Gotto laughed flatly, softly. "Oh, that's all boloney, Momo, you know. Some African workers, maybe. But ninety-nine out of a hundred you can't trust as far as you can throw a grand piano. You can't kid me. I've been around a bit. You have to get up early to put one across me. What say, Agnew?"

Jimmy flushed and wriggled uncomfortably in his seat. For lack of anything to say, he lit a cigarette and offered the packet to Momo, defiantly, conscious of Gotto's disapproving eyes.

"All right, Agnew," Gotto went on. "I'll look after this end and you look after that." He sat back and smacked the table again, his enthusiasm returning. "That's all, I think. Everybody satisfied? All weighed, all paid?"

Jimmy pushed his chair away, conscious that the conference

had produced nothing but uncomfortable silences and embarrassing *faux pas*. He glanced instinctively at Momo who had also risen.

"Boss," the shift boss said. "One thing. Rice."

"Rice?" Gotto, who had half risen, sank back into his chair. "Rice? What's that got to do with an iron mine? We're not growing rice, are we? They're doing that down at Bonthe, not here. Or is this a rice quarry, eh?" He laughed loudly at his own joke.

"Boss—" Momo's black face was serious—"boys tell me rice short in Amama Island."

"Oh?" Gotto's glance was hostile. "And why should they tell *you* particularly?"

"Boss, always they ask me speak for them."

"Trouble-maker, eh?"

"No, Boss." Momo remained unmoved. "I am educated black man. Other black men trust me."

"Oh, do they? Well, they'd better not trust you *too* much or *I* shan't." Gotto sat back. "O.K. Spit it out. What are you belly-aching about?"

"Boss, good rice harvest this year. Indian Joe collar it. Syrian trick. Joe Soloman not good Syrian. He hang on to the rice and charge high price for it. Black boy can't buy."

"Well, what about it? That's not my affair. That's between the boys and Indian Joe. It's nothing to do with me."

"Plenty trouble, Boss," Momo said earnestly. "No rice, black boy go hungry. Plenty trouble then."

"Well let black boy sort that out." Gotto sniggered and rose quickly. "I'm damned if I'm going to worry my head about black boys' grub. Let black boy look after that. I've plenty of other things to occupy my mind."

"Boss," Momo put in earnestly. "I get rice. I am son of chief——"

"Chief of what? A scruffy little village? That doesn't mean a thing to me."

73

Momo's expression remained unaltered, though his eyes flickered towards Jimmy. "Boss, I take lorry. I bring back rice. I know where there is plenty rice."

"Yes," Gotto said. "I know you lot. You'll take the lorry and have a damn' good holiday. Plenty mammies and plenty booze. Then you'll come back and say, 'Boss, no rice. No got. Rice done get lost en route.' It's just a damn' good excuse for a holiday. You're paid to work here, not go jazzing round the bush looking for mammies."

Momo looked angry for the first time. "Boss, I have got wife. I am a Christian."

Gotto laughed. "Go on. Tell me another. Listen, I'll write to Twigg and the appropriate Government department. That's what I'll do and that's all I'll do. But you're not going off up-country. Savvy? O.K., Momo, off you go and let's see you get those boys *moving*. And I mean *moving*. And no dodging it yourself in the foreman's hut."

Momo paused, as though to say something further, then changed his mind and went out without a word. Gotto stared after him, his hands on his bony hips.

"Mr. Momo's going to cause trouble, Jimmy," he said sharply. "He's trying to tell me my job already. Trying to get me mixed up with the local politics. He doesn't like me and he's looking for a chance to do me down. A proper barrack-room lawyer by the sound of him——"

He spun round, studying the office, then he turned to Jimmy again. "Right, let's have Smith in now," he said. "He might as well know what's expected of *him*, too."

He sat down at the desk again as Smith stood before him, rolling his eyes.

"Well, Smith," Gotto said cheerfully. "What do you think of this office? You think it's a nice office? A good office? A well-run office?"

"Boss——" Smith's eyes seemed to be spinning in their sockets. "Dis fine office. Plenty fine-fine. All same de Bucking-

74

ham Palace. All same de Houses of Palleyment. All same—"
he searched for a rapturous description worthy of the occasion
—"Boss, all same paradise wit' de angels."

"Well, it isn't, see?" Gotto shouted and Smith's feet
seemed to leave the floor as he jumped. Gotto slammed his
hand to the table and the cloud of dust rose again. "Look!
Dust! Muck! Filth! The place's grimy. Get a brush and sweep
it out—not now, you fool!" Smith, who was already half way
into his own office, thankful to be free of Gotto, shuffled
unwillingly back in front of him. "When I've gone. And every
morning. Throw water down. Lay the dust. And get that damn'
clock repaired. And that telephone. It was like that when Jarvis
was here. Broken. Useless. See it's done. Get the place tidy.
All these papers——"

"Boss Jarvis tell me no move de papers. He say I lose 'um."

"I'm not Boss Jarvis. I'm sick of Boss Jarvis. Everybody
throws Boss Jarvis down my throat. I say get the place tidy."

"Yassah. I get."

"And see we have fresh drinking water every day."

"Sah, labourer boy do dat. I tell him."

Gotto sat back and studied Smith, his lean face twisted
into a crooked smile. "Who's in charge of the office, Smith?"
he demanded.

Smith beamed proudly. "Clerk Smith, sah. He in charge,
sah."

Gotto leaned forward abruptly, his long nose out-thrust.
"Well, Clerk Smith can damn' well do it himself. O.K.?
When Jarvis was here, it was always left to a labourer and it
was *never* done. From now on, you can do it. Savvy?"

Smith bobbed his head nervously. "I savvy, sah."

"Right. Now about furniture." Jimmy saw Clerk Smith's
eyes widen. "Get some different furniture."

"Furniture, sah?"

"Yes, furniture. Are you deaf or something? Furniture.
Tables. Chairs. This chair's falling to pieces."

75

"Boss, sah, where I get?"

"Oh, God, look around." Gotto was on his feet now and walking up and down the office, using his hands to gesture as he talked. "If your chair's better than this, bring it in here."

"Boss, what *I* sit on?"

"Get a box. Or stand up. I don't care. But I'm not sitting on a chair that's on its last legs."

"Yassah, Boss, I get."

"And get a different table."

"Sah, where I get?"

"Oh, God!" Gotto flung his hands heavenwards. " 'Where I get?' Is that the only tune you know. There's a carpenter, isn't there, building huts in the workings? Get him to make one."

"Yassah. But, sah, de carpenter he busy making de huts."

"Well, tell him to stop being busy making huts and start being busy making a table."

"Yassah. I tell him."

"And get some of these cobwebs shifted. And let's have the place sprayed for insects. I detest insects. They give me the creeps and there are too many in this place. If I see so much as a fruit fly in here I'll flay you alive."

Smith's face was growing longer and longer, and his eyes were widening more with each sharp word. Just as he seemed about to wilt to the floor, Gotto turned on his heel and made for the door. As he passed Jimmy, he grinned encouragingly. "Got to let 'em know who's boss, Agnew," he said. "Idle hands, you know. Keep 'em busy and they haven't time for complaining then. They're like children. They only understand this sort of treatment."

Puzzled, Jimmy watched him stride away across the clearing in front of the office towards his car, then he turned round and almost bumped into Clerk Smith standing behind him, staring at Gotto through the door.

76

As Jimmy moved away, the African raised mournful eyes to his face.

"Boss," he said, wagging his head dolefully. "Boss Gotto, he plenty hard man. He plenty difficult. He make plenty trouble."

Jimmy grinned and patted the black man's thin shoulder. "Smith, old boy," he said. "You don't realize it but I think you've really said a mouthful."

Five

JIMMY drove the station wagon slowly between the trees down the curving road towards the river, wondering what his application for a job in Sierra Leone had let him in for. He was annoyed to discover the depression he had fought off earlier had returned.

Earnshaw, who appeared, smothered in copper oxide paint, from underneath a boat dragged from the water on its cradle, listened to the story of the conference in silence, then he lit an old fag-end and flipped the match into the water.

"What he want," he grinned, "is a little nig to take his mind off hisself. I could find him a darkey girl easy, nice and clean and willing. Better men than him have done it and at least it'd prove he got red blood in his veins 'stead of dandelion and burdock."

He laughed softly in a dry cackle, sly and vulgar and scruffy in his sweat-stained shirt and with one sock hanging over his shoe. But to Jimmy he suddenly seemed twice as wholesome as Gotto.

"He gives me the pip," Earnshaw went on. "Allus did. Every time I offer a bit of advice about the jetty, off he go, full of the old acid. Di-da. Di-da. Di-da. Just like that. Three bags full. And him looking at me like I've come to the front door of Gotto 'All selling bloomer elastic and cards of buttons."

He was still talking when Clerk Smith came rattling down the rutted road on an ancient bicycle, trailing a little cloud of dust from the wheels.

He almost fell off at Jimmy's feet and began to wipe the sweat from his face with the sleeve of his starched white suit.

"Boss Jimmy," he panted. "Boss Gotto say come quickly! Plenty trouble."

"Take yer time, kid," Earnshaw shouted as the station wagon drew away. "It won't be nothing. Somewhere a voice is calling. That's all."

When Jimmy arrived at the workings, choking with the dust his furious drive had thrown up, Gotto was standing beside one of the diggers whose huge boom towered over their heads. The digger handler was waiting in front of him in the shadow of the machine, his eyes rolling, watched at a distance by a group of labourers and lorry drivers who were trying hard but unsuccessfully to pretend they were working.

"Ah, here you are," Gotto said gaily. "Taken you long enough."

"I came as fast as I could."

"Make it faster next time." Gotto smiled and indicated the digger handler. " A point here: This lunatic almost scooped me and the car up just now. We've got to post a chap near these people, Agnew, with a red flag or something as a warning. They don't understand machines. Never will. I've seen it before."

"You mean, you want a look-out of some sort?"

"Yes. See to it, will you?"

"It's not usual, is it?"

"Perhaps not. But it's going to be. I'm not going to be held responsible for accidents. Besides, I don't want half a ton of ironstone dumping on me. Tell Momo. He fancies himself at handling things like this. Let him have a go."

"It seems a bit of a waste of a man, don't you think?" Jimmy ventured to protest. "If we all keep a sharp look out that ought to be sufficient."

"Surely," Gotto said with a touch of asperity in his voice,

79

"we're not going to start off together by having a disagreement."

"No—but—one man out of every gang——"

"Let's have it fixed, shall we?" Gotto turned his weary smile on Jimmy. "And worry about that when the output falls, eh? What say?"

"So," Jimmy said to Earnshaw the following day as they stood by the fringe of the river listening to the clatter of the concrete mixer, "a boy from each team does nothing all day except sit in the sun and swipe flies. That is, until His Lordship appears, then he really goes to town. He shouts, dances, waves, sings, turns somersaults, fires rockets, and generally puts on a gala performance to let him know he's on the job. He does everything except turn inside out."

Earnshaw squinted into the glare of the sun that cracked the surface of the mud into a crazy mosaic peopled by land-crabs and mud-hoppers.

"Son," he said slowly, "he suffers from a funny idea that he knows how to handle wogs."

As the sun rose higher above the river, even the shade grew stifling in the pitiless overhead glow and the earth looked gorged with sunshine. Africa seemed suddenly unfriendly with its fierce colours and the deep silences in which, like a child's cry in the wilderness, was lost the stomachic chug of the steam engine. This ancient contraption that drove the concrete mixer and the pile-driver and kept the dozens of chattering barrow boys running from its side to where the first foundations of the new jetty were being laid, was so dilapidated that it blew its safety valve regularly or leaked steam through the confectionery of patches on the boiler, and work had to stop for hours at a time until it cooled down sufficiently for repairs to be made to it.

Every time this happened, those labourers not involved in the noisy display or histrionics round Earnshaw and the pile-driver stretched themselves luxuriously in the sunshine, avoiding Jimmy's eye whenever there was anything to be done. But, bearing in mind Gotto's stated desire to see things achieved and the example of his drive up in the workings, Jimmy forced the foreman to chivvy them to other duties and he was delighted at the end of a fortnight to see some progress.

"Couldn't have done it no better meself," Earnshaw shouted, a shrivelled figure on the old wooden jetty. "Not if you give me the time and place. How's it go, Jimmy, old lad? I just seen Sonny-Boy outside the office carrying on alarming to Alf Momo. Proper got his knife into Alf, hasn't he? I bet he's a bright 'erb to live with. Jolly as a handful of worms. You want any funny stories to make him laugh?"

At the thought of Gotto laughing, Jimmy laughed himself.

He drove cheerfully towards the bungalow when he had finished work, trembling with fatigue and with the dust chafing his neck along the collar of his shirt. He was feeling well content and was looking forward to seeing Stella Swannack later in the evening.

Already, for some time, he had been arriving regularly every day at the Mission bungalow to make some dubious inquiry as an excuse to see her, to produce battered magazines she might like to read; to drive her to the hills for air, or to Mansumana beach for a swim; to practice photography with one of her three cameras, or more simply to discuss the ever-absorbing subject of Gotto, whom Stella now knew by repute as well as Jimmy knew him by fact.

He stopped the car outside the mine bungalow and went inside, looking for Gotto, proud of his achievements at the river's edge and quite prepared to boast about it. But his triumph fell flat as an old love affair. Gotto had already lapsed into the bored vacuum which seemed to come over him the minute he left work. He made no comment on the news but, talking nervously all the time, followed Jimmy from his

81

bedroom to the shower and back again as he changed from his dirty shorts to his clean evening drill.

At first, Jimmy had thought smugly that this habit of his was because Gotto found pleasure in his company, but it suddenly dawned on him with a shock of amazement that the real reason was that Gotto found no pleasure in his own company, and couldn't stand being alone. The knowledge came to him while he was in the bathroom and he stopped in the middle of shaving. As he realized how right he was, he nodded to himself in the mirror, with a new feeling of confidence.

The realization helped him through the evening which, like all the others since his arrival, ended with Gotto stalking round the bungalow, unable to read, unable apparently to interest himself in anything, constantly treading on Jimmy's heels as he busied himself with the exciting newness of the place.

Finally, when Jimmy started to write letters, he crouched awkwardly in a chair alongside the table, fidgeting heavily, his long legs twisted round each other until they seemed deformed, making noisy comments on the month-old newspapers he rustled, obviously itching to get away from his own unbearable self.

After an hour or so, Jimmy found himself repeating a phrase from the Colonial Office pamphlet he had studied back home in England, a phrase which, since meeting Gotto, had taken on a very real meaning—'People who do not like spending any time alone or who are dependent on amusements not of their own making are unsuited to a country like Sierra Leone.'

"With which I entirely concur," he said aloud.

Gotto looked up. "What's that?" he said.

Jimmy lit a cigarette to hide his confusion. "Nothing," he said. "Just thinking aloud. That's all."

Gotto grunted. "What beats me," he said in blank bewilderment, "is what you are supposed to do in the evenings here?"

He looked hard at Jimmy, his eyes begging him to respond, but Jimmy only bent his head closer to the paper and wrote faster until the sweat dripped from the end of his nose. His letters home had suddenly become a burden to him, for his time had become too occupied with Stella Swannack for anything more than an occasional cursory attempt at correspondence.

Gotto watched him for a while, then he fetched pen and paper himself and, placing a blotter under his wrist to soak up the sweat, also began to write.

"I'm writing to Doris," he pointed out loudly.

"Good show," Jimmy commented, his head still bent.

"I don't get many letters back," Gotto said, after a long silence during which he chewed his pen end to splinters.

"It's not the number. It's what they say in them," Jimmy encouraged.

To his surprise, Gotto promptly pushed across a letter, a cheerless, badly-written epistle scrawled in a round schoolgirl script. Jimmy looked up at him, holding the letter in his hand.

"It's from my girl," Gotto said. "It's from Doris. What do you think of it?"

"You want me to read it?"

"Yes. Go on. Tell me what you think."

Jimmy glanced at the letter, which was devoid of affection or a great deal of interest. There was no reference in it to being married.

"Not a very demonstrative type," he commented cautiously.

"Well, no," Gotto said, taking the letter back and searching through the ill-formed lines for something to reassure him. Like a dog looking for someone to pat him, Jimmy thought. " 'Hoping to see you soon,' she says here. Think she's wanting me to get home?"

83

"I should say myself," Jimmy said with the assurance of half a dozen light-hearted love affairs, "that she means exactly what she says: that she's hoping to see you soon. Though, I must admit," he continued, "she doesn't seem very enthusiastic about that even." He glanced across at Gotto and saw unexpectedly a look of earnest anxiety, a desire to learn the art of making friends that made him seem unutterably lonely.

"You're sure you're not attaching too much to these letters, are you?" he asked more sympathetically.

"Well—" Gotto rubbed his nose—"we were always very friendly."

"I thought you were almost engaged."

"Well, we are—almost."

"Ever kissed the damned woman?"

Gotto sniggered and Jimmy began to doubt even this. "You know, Gotty, old boy," he said, "women like a bloke to be pushing these days."

"Think it's a good idea?"

"It always was with me."

It was only when he looked round and saw Gotto's resentful eyes that he realized that he had said the wrong thing again and he bent hurriedly to continue his letter.

For a long time the room was silent. Outside, the evening chorus from the frogs and the crickets was going full blast.

"My God, that row," Gotto said savagely, jerking a cigarette end through the window.

"What row?"

"The bloody livestock outside. When a chap wants to concentrate, that racket doesn't help. It's bad enough in the workings all day with the boys shrieking at you. Believe me, I had a bellyful this morning. I caught a nice old packet of trouble."

"Trouble?" The word had occurred so often in Jimmy's

84

early hours in Sierra Leone that it brought him upright in his chair immediately. "What trouble?"

"I had to sling out half a dozen shovel boys."

"Half a dozen? What for?"

"One of 'em was talking about bellyache and wanted to go up to Romney's for treatment. Sheer laziness, that's all. Momo stuck up for him, of course. Just as I expected. I told you he was a knife-in-the-back merchant. The bloke just wanted an hour's slacking."

"What about the others? Were they sick, too?"

"No. They just joined in. Brothers or something. I told the lot of 'em to get the hell out of it and I told Momo he'd be the next. That was the sort of thing that always got me the push back home. Chaps who wouldn't do as they were told and went whining to the union when I tried to insist. It used to happen at Ma-Imi and for some reason Twigg always let 'em get away with it. Never supported me. That's why I'm here, I expect. I think it was an insult sending *me* to Amama when I'm nearly due to go home. It was a job for a new man, not an old hand. I think it was a deliberate attempt by Twigg to spoil my record. Chap I never liked."

He looked round the bungalow with its shabby furniture and its unpainted doors, weathered by sun and rain to a flat silver grey, at the dusty concrete floor and the whitewashed walls marked by dirty fingers.

"It's a bit of a hole when you think of it, isn't it?" he said, fanning himself with his writing pad.

Jimmy was beginning to feel depressed under Gotto's resentment when Romney appeared in the doorway, fat and heavy and hot. He seemed angry.

"Hello," he said, dropping into one of the chairs and fanning himself with his hat. "I've come to make a complaint. One of your people has been forbidding the boys to come up to my surgery."

Jimmy looked quickly at Gotto, who went white and said nothing.

"Afraid they came, anyway," Romney said, wheezing in the silent room. "But perhaps you'll tell whoever it was that they're always allowed to come up to my place when they're sick. Jarvis encouraged it as a sort of welfare scheme. If they think they're going to lose their wages by coming, they'll not come and then the whole point of the surgery will be lost."

Again Jimmy looked at Gotto, who eventually offered a reply.

"As a matter of fact," he said. "It was me."

Romney looked surprised. "You?"

"Yes." Gotto's expression was defiant. "We'll never get anything done if they can just walk out when they like. It's a good excuse to disappear and there isn't a wog born who likes work."

Romney stared at him for a while without speaking, then he very deliberately took out his pipe, filled it and lit it. "Don't be too certain, son," he said quietly when he had finished brushing the tobacco from his trousers. "And don't be too harsh."

"We pay them to work," Gotto said stiffly, dogmatically. "There's nothing they can hold against me. It's all within the rules. There's nothing under any agreement that says they can go up to your place in working time."

"They always have."

"Well, they'd better stop. It's a good excuse for slacking."

"Son"—Romney smiled gently—"when they come to my place they're sick. They're not concerned with getting wages without work. If they were really after hard cash, they'd be down in Freetown or Ma-Imi where they could earn more."

Gotto was pale and strained-looking. "I've got instructions to run this place," he said. "Twigg put me in charge."

86

"Twigg wouldn't have insisted on this," Romney said, more sharply. "He encouraged it, in fact. It makes the boys content and gives them a feeling of security."

"He put *me* in charge," Gotto repeated with stubborn desperation.

Romney took a deep breath. "There's one other point," he said. "All the men you sacked are Mende."

"Who?"

"Mende. The whole of Amama—the whole of Sierra Leone, come to that—is made up of Mende and Temne tribes, with a few other odds and ends like Kru and Kissy and Mandingo to make weight."

"I know. I'm aware of that."

"You've already got more Temne working here than Mende, I think you'll find. Now you've got rid of half a dozen more Mende."

"What about it?" Jimmy, watching the discussion with interest, saw that Gotto's face was blank.

"It's very important to the Mende if you appear to show favour towards the Temne. You must know that."

Gotto's face was sullen and unfriendly.

"It isn't serious in itself," Romney continued. "As you know, they get on, but a quarrel between one or two of them can spread like wildfire." The old man puffed sparks from his pipe and watched Gotto under his eyebrows.

"I know they make a hell of a noise," Gotto said.

"It's more than a noise. They each fetch their brothers and cousins and uncles and great-uncles, until it becomes a tribal affair. Then they start bringing in the septs of the tribe until it becomes quite big. I'm not trying to tell you your job, but I've lived here quite a long time. Why not leave it to Alf Momo? He's very reliable and he knows the people."

"I'll manage without consulting any African shift boss," Gotto said, staring at the floor. "There's nothing he knows that I don't know. I went to mining school. *He* didn't."

"Maybe he didn't, son." Romney rose and moved to the door. "But he's an African. And *you're* not."

The room was silent as the door shut. Jimmy sat waiting for Gotto to speak, agreeing with everything Romney had said but knowing that, since he had to live with Gotto, it might not be diplomatic to say so.

"Silly old ass," Gotto observed to himself after a while and Jimmy felt he was unhappy and unsure of himself. "Nosy old devil. What's it got to do with him?"

"There might be something in what he says," Jimmy pointed out in the vague hope that Gotto might be persuaded.

"*Doctor* Romney!" Gotto's voice was a sneer. "Him and his hospital. Where does he get his money from anyway? Fiddle it?"

"Earnshaw says he performed an operation on one of the chiefs out here who thought he was for the high jump and the old boy responded with a little hospital. It's pretty rough and ready, of course, but Mrs. Swannack and the mission help."

"A likely story. I don't believe it. He and Earnshaw are as thick as thieves anyway. He comes from Birmingham and I lived there for a long time so I can soon get to know. There were a lot of Romneys round there. A big family of 'em. All doctors. I'll bet he was one of 'em."

Gotto's eyes had a blank bleak look in them. "Come to that, I'll bet he's not a proper doctor at all. I'll bet there's something fishy about him. Or why would he be out here in a God-forsaken joint like this when he could be earning thousands back home?"

"Perhaps he likes it."

"More likely he was mixed up in some scandal and had to come out here to lie low. I seem to remember something about a Doctor Romney when I was a kid, now I come to think of it. I'll write to Doris. She'll know."

Jimmy was staring at Gotto now with a mixture of amazement and dislike.

"That's doing it a bit brown, isn't it?" he ventured.

Engrossed with his own thoughts, Gotto didn't hear him. "I'll get Doris to find out," he continued, suddenly more cheerful. "There are plenty of Romneys still in Birmingham. I'll bet people will remember. I'll soon stop him coming here and telling me what to do. I'll fix the old fool."

Six

GOTTO's threats and the growing certainty that he was living with a trouble-maker stayed in Jimmy's mind for some time and, hard as he tried to avoid thinking of them, he could not thrust them aside. And, with each day that ended in its flare of gold among the palm trees, he found life being complicated further by a series of trivial incidents concerning Gotto and the African labourers. To be true, these were more wordy than important for the most part but, in the end, while Gotto was disinterestedly rattling the out-of-date newspapers after dinner, he found an excuse for leaving and made his way up to Earnshaw's.

Earnshaw's house was like Earnshaw himself. Even outside, it looked untidy and none too clean. The path to the front door was edged by buried and up-ended beer bottles and at the side the bush encroached too closely for health. But, oddly, at the front, mixed up with old shoes and a dirty shirt and giving it a homely, lived-in look, were half a dozen white-painted petrol tins containing geraniums whose blood-red blooms looked purple in the moonlight. Suri, Earnshaw's coxswain, and another African were sitting on the verandah, playing a native game similar to five-stones, noisy and excited and laughing.

Unwashed and unshaven and still in his oil-stained shorts, his damp shirt on the chair back despite the darkness and the pinging of the mosquitoes round his bare flesh, Earnshaw sprawled under a lamp at the table, playing patience, in front of him a glass of water and a jar of stomach powder. His iron-grey hair stood straight up, uncombed and unbrushed, like the stubble in a newly-cut wheatfield. Behind him, balanced precariously on the old sewing machine Suri used to patch his shorts, his gramophone screeched barbarically across the room.

He looked up as Jimmy entered and gave him a crafty grin.

"Just keeping it on the run, old lad," he said. He shoved the gin bottle across the untidy table and signed to Jimmy to find a seat.

Jimmy removed a plate, a tin mug and a rifle and cleaning rags from a sagging basket chair and sat down.

"I'd like—" he began but the music roaring across the room drowned the rest of his words.

Earnshaw saw the glance he gave the gramophone and, becoming conscious of the noise for the first time, snatched the needle off with an indigestive 'brrrrp'. "Gawd, what a bloody row," he commented.

"Thanks," Jimmy said heavily.

"What's up, old lad?" Earnshaw pushed his chair back and swung round. "You look proper in the dripping. Old How-To-Win-Friends-And-Influence-People been upsetting you?"

Jimmy nodded. "I'd like a bit of advice," he said.

"Let it rip, kid. You got the deck."

Brushing occasionally at a too-venturesome mosquito, Earnshaw listened to Jimmy in silence, then suggested calling on Romney.

"Old Doc'll know," he said. "There's a bloke what wasn't born yesterday. *He* don't know what to do after thirty years out here, well, it's time I ett my granny's hat. He seen it all. He's on the second time round now."

They found Romney sitting in the shabby little closet he used as a surgery, beneath an oil lamp that crowded the room with shadows. He was facing the doorway so that his view in

91

daylight had contained the expanse of the hills in all their varying tints.

The place was empty except for a bright native rug on the floor and a case full of books which were pock marked with mildew. It was as bare as a prison cell—as bare as Romney could get it of trivialities—and it smelled of the hospital odour of antiseptics.

Romney slowly dabbed at the perspiration on his forehead with a handkerchief and waited patiently, a little resentful at the intrusion into his leisure, as Jimmy laid out his facts. He looked comfortable and elderly with his book on his knees and his spectacles on the end of his nose. An insecticide spray gun was on the floor alongside with a glass in which a beetle was quietly drowning in the last drop of gin. He had had his evening swim in the pool behind his house that had been dammed from the clear mountain stream which ran into the river—the usual three times up and three times down—and he had a feeling of languor in his limbs. The evenings were the time of the day that Romney liked best. It was in the evenings when the night scents rose from the crowding undergrowth and the darkness turned the harshness of the day to the velvet of the night, and Romney didn't welcome any interference with his enjoyment of them.

He looked up over his spectacles as Jimmy spoke in an explosive indignation, odds and ends of law and order and the rights of man rattling round in his head like an armoured cavalcade.

"Good heavens, son," he said when he had finished. "What people say about me doesn't worry me any more. You stop worrying about those things long before you reach seventy. In any case, he's quite right. There *was* a little trouble with the Medical Council."

Jimmy's jaw dropped and Romney waved a fat hand.

"I stopped worrying about that years ago though, too. Don't trouble yourself about me. Think about the Africans.

92

They're the ones who're going to need your help, I suspect."

"He seems to have a thing about black men," Jimmy agreed, still a little surprised by Romney's revelation. "And, hell, they're not half-wits. They've got feelings like he has. There are good ones as well as bad ones."

"In fact," Romney commented slyly, "you've unearthed a basic truth that never ceases to surprise people when they discover it for the first time—that there's nothing to choose between the white and black races."

Jimmy blushed. "No, there isn't," he said, "and there's no need to chivvy 'em as he does. I wouldn't mind," he added with a shrug, "but they're beginning to associate not only him with the bullying but *me* too."

"One of the burdens of the righteous is to be misjudged."

"You know what's wrong with Gotto?" Earnshaw offered from the doorway where he sat with his back to the lintel. "He's nuts. That's what."

"On the contrary," Romney said, "he's being very normal. Insecure people are often bullies. It's a sop to their ego, a consolation prize, if you like."

"Well, he's quicker off the mark than anyone I've ever come across," Jimmy said. "He's got the Temne and the Mende at each other's throats already. There was a fight the other night in the town—just as you said there'd be—a party or something, and too much palm wine and native beer. There were casualties——"

"I know," Romney said. "I got one here. He'd had his ear half torn off in the scuffle."

"It was quite a party, I believe."

"An African crowd enjoys emotions to the full. Even other people's."

"I only hope he hasn't got one of these circuses going when Twigg arrives. That's all. He's due to look us over any time now."

93

"Don't worry, kid," Earnshaw said. "Twiggy'll dodge Gotto like the plague."

Jimmy looked puzzled and unhappy. "There's no warmth in the man anywhere. Ever since I came here, I've been trying to find some spark, and apart from a half-hearted effort from him at the start, I can't."

"Not surprised," Earnshaw commented. "He's as cold as an old fried egg. Perhaps 'e's congealed. Perhaps 'e's dead even. They pretty good at embalming these days."

He turned his head sideways to apply a match to the scorched cigarette end between his lips. "You seen the mammies frightening the kids to bed with his name?" he asked as he blew out a cloud of smoke. " 'Gotto's coming'," he squeaked in imitation of a black woman chasing her piccaninny indoors. " 'Gotto's coming. He eat you up.' I've heard 'em. Honest. They run like there was a crocodile after 'em. Cripes—" he sighed heavily and tossed the burnt match through the door— "if only he'd laugh sometimes."

"For Gotty," Jimmy said with a grin, "life is real, life is earnest. Much realer and earnester than for the rest of us."

Romney didn't join in the mirth. "I think it is and that's the whole trouble," he said quietly so that Jimmy felt vaguely ashamed of his levity.

Romney began to wipe the mistiness of perspiration from his spectacles. Behind him, the yellow light threw his face into darkness as he sat motionless, only his hands moving. Against the dusty wire mesh of the window, a moth beat itself to death with soft flutterings like the hammering of tiny fists.

"I suppose," he said at last, "it wouldn't matter half so much it it weren't that he could be such an asset to Indian Joe."

"Indian Joe?" Jimmy looked up in alarm. "Where's he come into it?"

Romney sat back, holding his spectacles on his knees.

94

"Indian Joe didn't know sufficient to start a mine here," he said, "but he's clever enough to listen to what's said in his bar and he'd like to buy it—the cheaper the better."

"How do you know?"

"I'm a doctor—the only one in Amama. Everybody comes to me. And people talk to doctors." He paused before he went on. "He'd sell it again, of course. He's no engineer. But he'd make a big profit. Perhaps all this is the reason for the rice shortage. They can still manufacture them. He's probably trying to make the output drop by stirring up trouble."

"Trouble!" Jimmy said. "God, that word!"

Romney put his glasses on, hitching them round his ears with care, and placed his finger-tips together to make a pyramid of his hands. Then he looked up, his old eyes distorted by the strong lenses. "I notice Samuel Assissay's still in Amama," he pointed out. "That wasn't what Twigg intended when he sent him up from Ma-Imi. He came to see me this morning with what would be a black eye if he were white. Somebody hit him."

"What for?"

"The usual." Romney shrugged his fat stooping shoulders. "Haranguing a crowd. They're not keen on him in Amama."

"Well, he doesn't seem to be doing any harm."

"He isn't at the moment, but it hasn't taken him long to realize our friend Gotto isn't popular."

"Oh, Lord! Now I see what you're getting at."

"He's three parts ju-ju, but he *could* get a crowd moving, and violence spreads like the green bay tree, especially among primitive people. You see, in an isolated place like Amama, an organization like the mine grows a little out of proportion and tends to become a power it was never intended to be. And so, hence, does the man who runs it—in this case, Gotto."

Jimmy studied the floor, watching the slow trudge of a centipede along the wainscoting. He was a little overwhelmed by what Romney had said.

95

"Gotto sacked half a dozen Mende the other day because one of them came to my surgery," the old man went on, laying facts before them like cards in a game of patience. "He was stupid enough to set on five Temne and only one Mende in their place. He wasn't to know. They all look alike to a white man—a newcomer, anyway. But he didn't bother to find out. So Samuel Assissay finds half a dozen followers with a grievance immediately. He'll find others before long, I suspect."

Jimmy was staring through the open door now at the clumps of yellow cannas that threw their massive blooms up from among large flat leaves, like gushing fountains. Behind them were brilliant hibiscus bushes, their solitary flowers closed for the night, and on either side of the path that led to the front door, bougainvillaea, white spider lilies and red irises crowded beneath a frangipani tree with orange blossoms. Even in the moonlight, he could see the colour and guess at the splendour of it all.

"Go on, Doc," he said slowly. He was beginning to suspect that he had become involved in something more complicated than he had imagined.

Romney made himself more comfortable and went on with the air of a lecturer delivering a talk. "Indian Joe's watching events, Jimmy," he said. "He has been for some time. He was even when Jarvis was here though he could do nothing then. Now it's different. He's given Assissay a job in his store. He doubtless feels he can use his peculiar talents to good effect. Assissay knows how to talk to crowds, even if he can't sort out ju-ju from white man's politics, or politics from religion."

Earnshaw leaned forward. "You want to report that Gotto," he said to Jimmy. "Let Henry Twigg know. It's his pigeon. He send him up here to get rid of him. That's all. But you have him out, kid, before you get yourself some trouble. Slap him down—sharp! They don't want him down at Ma-Imi, they want to send him home."

96

Jimmy had sat up abruptly, a look of unhappiness on his face as a disconcerting thought occurred to him.

"Oh, Lord, no," he said involuntarily. "You see, this seems to be his last chance. I gather he's been pushed from one job to another and he was hoping to make a go of this one."

"Upsetting Alf Momo and all the other blokes won't 'elp him. Have him out, Jimmy. Tell Twigg when he arrive."

"Hell, I can't. He's got a mother dependent on him. Besides, he's due to go home soon and surely Twiggy won't put anything in his way if he knows him. He's nearly finished his tour."

" 'E ain't learned much."

"He probably wouldn't if he stayed all his life but, God knows, I think he's tried hard to be friendly with *me* at least. It won't be long before he's gone."

"It'll be *too* long, however long it is." Earnshaw had a stubborn look on his face. "Leave him to me," he offered. "I sort him out quicker than that. I'll set my boys on him and give him a bit o' clog. I done it afore with blokes I've found hanging round Zaidee." He made the statement with the bland pride of a Borgia announcing the removal of a rival.

Jimmy looked hard at him. "Surely we can put up with him for a month or two. He might never come back. What do you say, Doc?"

"I agree. The man could be a damn' nuisance but in view of the fact that he's due home soon, I think we might cover up for him a bit."

Earnshaw tossed away his cigarette. "I suppose that might make it a bit different," he said thoughtfully. "Like the parrot what laid square eggs. All the same, I don't like it. Something might go wrong. It might be longer than you think. Months, in fact. You know 'ow these tickets 'ome get lost."

"We can chance it," Jimmy said. "We can stand him a bit longer if necessary."

"I think we ought to do more than that," Romney pointed

out. "*Standing* him isn't enough. We ought to try and bring him round. Nobody else has ever bothered. That's probably the trouble. We might even show him there's more to this place than the heat and the dust."

"Pull the plug on it and let it run out by itself," Earnshaw said. "That's what I say. Blow having tea-parties."

"He should be taken up-river and shown the sights."

"In my boats, I suppose?"

Romney nodded and Jimmy sat up delightedly, his uneasy conscience salved.

"Let him stew in his own juice," Earnshaw said heavily.

"It's only for a while," Jimmy said. "Otherwise, I'd go to Twigg. You don't think I'd put up with a clot like him indefinitely, do you?"

"I'll *put up* with him, but to hell with kiss-and-be-friends."

"Oh, come on, man," Jimmy said eagerly. "It's all in a good cause."

"O.K., O.K.," Earnshaw said wearily. "If that's what you want. So long as he's not staying, I'll kill the bastard with kindness. I'm going up-river tomorrer. Bring him along. You want to see a bloke be nice to him, you just watch me. I'm dead 'ot on friendship."

When Jimmy returned to the mine bungalow, Gotto was sprawled on his bed, still in the dusty khaki he had used in the workings. Outside, the sound of the bull-frogs, the crickets and the mosquitoes made music with the cheep of a bat or the screech of an owl. From time to time he heard the rats making love under the bungalow and the noise of a beetle roaring round the room like a flying bomb. The thermometer on the wall registered eighty-nine and the heat stood in the room with the menace of an assassin.

He was suffering from a sweat rash and he felt the discomfort was a personal imposition not inflicted on Romney or Earnshaw or Jimmy.

He was just pondering a miracle, the miracle of the boat crews' affection for Earnshaw—Earnshaw, the dishonest, the immoral, the uneducated, the crafty, the vulgar and the sly— an affection which was obvious and always had been obvious in the wide delighted grins that split their black faces at his crusty shouts, an affection which, to Gotto, seemed to draw sustenance only from kicks, insults and bad language, but an affection which to his amazement existed nevertheless. He had that morning watched Earnshaw's coxswain, Suri, wriggling with shyness, hand over as a birthday gift on behalf of the other boat crews a handkerchief full of limes for Earnshaw's gins. There had been no word of thanks, not a word, but the explosive "Why, you old black bastard, I'll bet you pinched 'em," brought only broad smiles to the faces of the Africans. Gotto was still trying to work it out.

His own arrival in the workings or down at the jetty was heralded only with silence, a brooding silence and eyes that followed him disapprovingly wherever he moved, while behind his back the jesters among the shovel boys, with their African gift for mimicry, mocked his slow walk for their comrades, prancing and caracoling with a fist before their faces as a symbol of his bony nose.

Even Jimmy, in his short stay in Amama, had found no difficulty in recruiting friends among the workmen who shook with laughter as he tormented them about their lady friends or their nagging wives, and among the small black boys who had taken to hanging round the bungalow. The children he organized into football teams and gave them a green West African orange for a ball, joining in their laughter when someone finally trod on it and it burst and they all rolled, naked and dusty, on the ground convulsed with mirth. From among them he could always get an assistant for his butterfly hunting forays and, in spite of his careless indifference to whether he was liked or not, could hardly move away from the mine without being surrounded by a dozen screaming black children

99

all eager to carry his net or his jam jar or begging a ride in the station wagon.

To Gotto, crucified by his loneliness, that Jimmy could be just Jimmy and still, without effort, be of as much interest to the illiterate labourers and the small black boys who thronged round him as he was to Stella Swannack, was also in the nature of a miracle.

He had never found it easy being Ivor Gotto—never, from the first stricken silences when his mother had taken him out visiting, or the pathetic embarrassment of children's parties; from the first awkwardness at school where his thin limbs and bony nose made him the perfect butt for the bullies; from the first hopeless attempts to get to know the opposite sex. Gotto's secret mind—that elusive, shut-off, shuttered place behind his anger that hid like a deformity the pain of frustration and unhappiness, the nagging misery of being Ivor Gotto and the crawling worms of faint-heartedness—it had never contained much that Gotto could bring himself to like but he had never realized just how much until now when he had nothing else to do but study it.

He stared at the ceiling in silence until he heard Jimmy outside talking to Amadu, the house-boy.

"Boss, mammy get piccaninny," Amadu was saying. "Boy piccin. Amadu Komorra got son."

"Nice work, Amadu," came Jimmy's voice. "What are you going to call him? Amadu, after you?"

"No, Boss Jimmy." Gotto could hear the black man laughing delightedly. "Boss, I call 'um Jimmy after you. Jimmy Komorra. You like?"

"Well, that's jolly nice of you, Amadu." Jimmy sounded surprised and touched.

Gotto sat up abruptly and went outside, brushing aside the bunch of bananas that had been hung in the doorway out of the way of the ants only to become instead the haunt of a million tiny fruit flies. Amadu stopped in mid-sentence as

100

he appeared, his grin fading, then he melted away into the darkness beyond the verandah.

"This bloody place," Gotto said heavily, flicking his cigarette away so that it curved, a vermilion arc, and landed in a shower of sparks. He stared into the darkness for a while at the distant sparkle of a village fire, and listened to the slow thump of a drum. "Don't you ever get fed up here?" he ended.

Jimmy's eyebrows rose. "No, of course not," he said. It came as a surprise to him to find that he liked the unhurried life of Amama and every lazy sound of the place—the thump of the grain pestles and the sharp chatter of the women wielding them, the flat barking of a village dog or the honk of a hornbill, to say nothing of the rich, unquenchable laughter of the African labourers.

Gotto watched him, clearly puzzled by the fact that Jimmy *could* find pleasure in the absence of civilization. "I mean"— he endeavoured to explain—"nothing ever happens."

"What *could* happen here in Amama?"

Gotto looked desperate as he tried to explain. "Well, I mean—same old mountains. Same old sun. Same old palm trees." The familiar petulant irritation was creeping back into his voice. "Same bloody wogs. Christ," he said feelingly, as he thought of the half-naked black girls he watched with a thin, bitter lust as they went about their business on the dusty road that ran past the mine. "What I'd give to talk to a girl."

For a while, Jimmy listened to him working himself up to the same old rigmarole of resentment, then he hastily outlined Romney's plan for a trip up-river, with the obvious reservations about the reason for it.

"It's not much," he explained. "Just up beyond the mud banks. That's all. We might see some wild life."

To his surprise his offer was accepted, and the alacrity with which Gotto snatched at the opportunity to get away from Amama indicated how bored with himself he was.

Immediately the weak appeal for friendship, the wretchedness of loneliness and the awful inability to do anything about it began to show again through the façade of harshness.

"What about Earnshaw, though?" Gotto asked doubtfully "I always thought he didn't like me."

"Hell, man, it was Earnshaw's idea," Jimmy lied vigorously. "He thought you'd be interested."

"Did he?" Gotto was pathetically pleased by what he took to be evidence of comradeship. "Did he honestly?"

The ghost of a smile crossed his features and for the first time Jimmy heard him whistling—in a tuneless monotone as he prepared for bed.

After several weeks in Amama, Jimmy was still entranced by what he saw every time they moved into the quieter creeks up-stream where the dainty terns splashed like dive-bombers into the river after fish, and pelicans took off and landed like clumsy grey flying-boats. From the bank, crocodiles slithered without a ripple into the water, watched from the mangroves above by cranes and herons, beautiful and incredibly frail-looking, and by the bright kingfishers hunting among the clouds of flies in the shallows. Between the trees as the boat moved up-river the air was alive with the screech of monkeys and birds, and the occasional eruptions on the surface of the muddy water indicated the teeming life below where a shoal of small fish fought to avoid the jaws of a barracuda. To the enchanted Jimmy, Africa was breathtaking in its over-crowded life, and since the trip made no demands on his energy, even Gotto's frown disappeared and Earnshaw, grey and dusty-looking, his smile the essence of immorality and slyness, began to be weightily friendly.

"I won't half show you a good time when we get settled down a bit," he said with a wink. "Have a day out in Free-town, me and you, we will. I can introduce you to a girl or two. Nice bit of milk chocolate. Pale-'ands-I-loved-beside-the-

102

Shalimar. Nice and clean. Plenty of scent. Most of 'em pong like billy-o—talk about the sweet breath of murder—but not the ones I know."

The river, the old route of the slavers and the breeding ground for the fevers that stretched through the Coast's grim history, was a winding brown flood that twisted its way between the trees from where the turbulent mountain streams rushed into it over rocky falls, down to the port which clustered, ramshackle and beautiful, along the water's edge; down to the beaches where the blue Portuguese-men-o'-war trailed their vicious stings along the surface of the waves, and where the wide mouth broke into a maze of tufted islands on which ancient cannon, erected against the French, rusted in decaying fortresses. And in every yard of its glittering surface there was some new point of interest that Earnshaw pointed out to them—the tumultuous wild life, the fishing villages where women sat outside their daubed huts weaving baskets, and men, balancing incredibly upright in their pencil-slim canoes, flung circular nets touched into meshes of gold by the sun; the scenes of old disasters and older pagan ceremonies, and of Earnshaw's own raffish adventures.

For Gotto's benefit he took the boat close in under the trees that overhung the water and showed him the grey parrots that shrieked among the branches, and once, a long green mamba that coiled whip-like among the leaves.

"Them's the boys what make no noise," he observed cheerfully. "They get their fangs in you, kid, you drop down dead immediate. I seen it. You 'ave to be careful out 'ere, with spiders and scorpions and one thing nor another.

"There's lizards and spiders and snakes green and black," he sang, "and bloody great scorpions that fall down yer back."

As the sun rose higher, Gotto, infected by Jimmy's enthusiasm and Earnshaw's hilarity, began to lose his suspicious expression and to show an interest in the things he saw about him—the big basking iguanas under the tortured arcs

103

of the mangrove roots; the oysters that clung to the bottom-most branches as they dipped the water at high tide; and the two-legged mud-hoppers that flipped and jumped with the land-crabs on the mud strips of the shallows.

"Oysters on trees and fishes that walk," Earnshaw pointed out in the manner of a Thames boatman indicating the places of interest. "That's what Livingstone said about this joint, ain't it? Spent years round here, I'm told."

"God, why?" Gotto said. "No wonder he snuffed it. Probably died of boredom."

Earnshaw laughed—a little forcedly—and they leaned towards each other like a couple of old cronies.

"Once saw a sea serpent in this 'ere river, I did," Earnshaw continued. "Twice, in fact. Then it disappeared."

"Perhaps that died of boredom, too," Gotto sniggered.

"Perhaps it did." Earnshaw winked conspiratorially at Jimmy.

"Perhaps that's why there are so many kids about," Gotto went on, developing his theme with more enthusiasm than judgment. "Nothing else to do of a night. A way to dodge the boredom."

"A way to dodge the boredom!" Earnshaw slapped him on the back. "I never heard it called that before. You aren't half a card."

He turned to the steering wheel with a look towards Jimmy that indicated he was suffering nobly in a good cause.

"No wonder they're allowed to have more than one wife," Gotto sniggered. "It gets dark early and the nights are long."

Earnshaw's grin was dying now and, unseen to Gotto, he glanced at Jimmy and tapped his temple.

But Jimmy laughed. If Gotto's jokes were not good, at least his temper was, and his humour was an indication of a barrier broken down. Jimmy had been on edge all day for some acid remark he would have to gloss over, some narrow

104

opinion that might offend. But sharp words had been remarkably few and even they had dwindled and disappeared as the day wore on.

Gotto even seemed to enjoy the manœuvring round the mud banks as Earnshaw found his way with boat-hook and lead-line, even taking his turn at the wheel, passing over the bottles of beer he had brought with him and joking over the cold chicken Amadu had packed for them.

By the late afternoon, when the red heat of midday had vanished and the golden glow was rising from the sinking sun, Jimmy was beginning to congratulate himself on the success of their scheme. Gotto, relaxed and almost smiling in the stern, was watching the passing of a great Susu canoe as it roared down-stream under its bellying sail, bound for the market at Freetown the following day.

"Hegg, Boss?" roared the helmsman, holding up a wicker basket of eggs as he leaned on the great steering oar on the poop. "You want hegg? You want chicken for cook? You want fiss?"

From among the mangoes and paw-paws and bananas and oranges that weighed the boat down until the water lapped over the scuppers, he brought out a bundle of the dried mullet with which fishermen tempted to a stop the drivers of the narrow-gauge railway train that ran from Freetown to Pendembu as it passed their riverside halts.

"Urtcher, you pudden-headed ole git," Earnshaw shouted back. "I can smell 'em from 'ere. If you're selling anything, I'd rather have the dark lady in the middle."

The ribald reply brought a shout of delighted laughter from the black crew and grins split the faces of the piccaninnies and the gaudily-dressed mammies who crouched in the well of the vessel.

They watched as the boat swooped past, the sun touching the sail with gold as it passed the panorama of the shore where the banner-like leaves of the palms drooped in the heat.

Gotto's eyes were alive with interest and he seemed to be won over at last.

It was while Jimmy was planning the next move towards his reclamation that they ran aground on one of the mud banks that the swiftly-flowing waters threw up in unexpected angles of the creeks, and as the boat began to shudder they came to a dead stop.

Gotto sat up abruptly. "What's happened?" he asked quickly, the smiles gone from his face.

Earnshaw listened to the labouring engine and studied the muddy foam that the screw was churning up. Then he rose and poked all round the vessel with the boat-hook, staring silently at the brown swirls he stirred to the surface. He tried the engine again without effect, then finally switched off and sat down.

The others had been watching him in silence.

"That's it," he said, scratching his head with a rasping sound. "We stuck. Tide's falling, too."

"Stuck!" Gotto's face was suddenly thunderous, the calm wiped off like a shadow when the sun fades. "Does that mean we're going to be here all night? The place'll be alive with mosquitoes."

"That's O.K.," Earnshaw reassured him, still in a cheerful mood. "Malaria ain't one of the diseases in season just now."

"Can't we push her off?"

"We can try."

Leaning on the boat-hook, they swore and thrust at the unresisting mud until their arms ached, and jumped up and down on the stern while Earnshaw raced the engine until they were wet with sweat. Finally, gasping in the still hot sun that beat low across the water into their aching eyes, they collapsed again into their seats, exhausted, limp and dispirited.

"This is a fine thing," Gotto said between his teeth. "Marooned."

106

"Just like Robinson Crusoe," Earnshaw said with maddening cheerfulness. "What a lark!"

"I can't see anything to laugh at."

"Neither can I, come to think of it. Still, hold your water a minute. There's some canoes over there. They fetch us off."

Putting two fingers in the corners of his mouth, Earnshaw gave a piercing whistle which echoed flatly across the water to the mangroves, and the fishermen turned and waved.

As the canoes drew alongside, Earnshaw tossed the anchor overboard. "That'll hold her for the night," he said. "O.K., old lad," he went on with a grin at Gotto. "This is where you 'ave your first trip in a wog canoe. Ain't you seeing the sights today? Tourists would pay thousands for this. Give your fare to the driver. Ten bob fine for spitting. And, for Gawd's sake, sit still, else you'll both be in the dripping."

Gotto's face was livid under its saffron colour as he climbed gingerly into the frail boat and sat amidships, his bony knees under his chin.

From the foredeck of the dinghy, Earnshaw watched Jimmy climbing into the next canoe, and indicated Gotto already moving away across the water to the village on a spit of sun-baked land. "Son," he commented. "I think summat's gone wrong. He looks as happy as a load of mad dogs."

Gotto, who was on the sandbank waiting for them when they stepped ashore, refused to eat any of the scrawny roast chicken Earnshaw conjured up from the headman. His manner was suddenly unfriendly again.

"No, thanks," he said coldly. "I'd rather die of starvation than food poisoning."

Earnshaw looked hard at him for a long time, while Jimmy racked his brains for some means of retrieving what appeared to be a deteriorating situation. The tautness had returned to Gotto's figure as he stared disapprovingly at the gaunt chickens that scratched the dirt, the lean dogs and the dark, mosquito-haunted huts among the trees where the food had come from. The interest he had shown in Africans during the afternoon was choked with dislike again as they jostled round him, grinning and interested, smelling of perspiration and charcoal, the bare black breasts of the mammies rubbing against his arm as they crowded closer to hear Earnshaw chivvying the headman with sly smutty jests to produce the paw-paws and bananas that grew about them.

And, as a small boy, eager both to please and to make money for himself, edged up to him and whispered, "You want lady, boss. My sister very clean," he seemed to draw back with the revolted horror of a maidenly spinster accosted by a drunk.

"Get away," he said in a high strangled voice as he tried, blushing furiously, to push his way through the naked women around him who had taken up the small boy's chant and were tossing it in delighted shrieks from one to another.

"But, Boss—" the small boy's voice rose to a thin wail— "she school-teacher."

Unable to get away, Gotto gave the boy a push and, as he fell in the dust, a murmur of protest ran through the crowd, silencing the laughter. Earnshaw quickly yanked the boy to his feet, gave him a coin and pushed him aside.

" 'Op it, Joe," he said.

"Boss——"

" 'Op it, I said, or I'll give you one acrost the ear'ole."

Earnshaw turned to Gotto, his tired eyes angry. "That was a bright bloody thing to do," he snorted, "when I'm trying to get 'em to 'elp."

"You heard what he was saying, didn't you?"

"Sure I did. But you're a big boy now. You oughta know about them things. And you oughta know 'ow to behave when you're out visiting."

"I didn't ask to be dragged up here into this hole."

"Well, of all the nerve!" Earnshaw slammed the banana

108

he was eating to the dusty earth. "Gawd, *I* didn't ast to bring you."

Hours later, after a seemingly endless argument conducted entirely in shouts between Earnshaw and the headman and the passing over of money, they were paddled down-stream beneath the gaudy stars, sitting among the dirty water and fish guts and rotten oranges in the bottom of a fruit canoe.

The mangroves that brushed against them had lost their daytime silence and had come alive with sound. Even above the chatter of water under the boat, they could hear the grunts of strange creatures in the shadows, the splashes of jumping fish, the peculiar whirr of crabs and the queer creaking and groaning sounds from the trees themselves. Now and again the strong musty smell that meant a crocodile close by came to them through the acid scent of the water and the mud, and as Earnshaw flashed his torch round they saw the gleam of bulging eyes and then the swift slither of a heavy body and the faint splash as it hit the water.

In spite of his anxiety, Jimmy felt awed by the vastness of the swamp forests but Earnshaw in front was a little drunk on native wine and was boasting loudly of his prowess at organizing things.

"Ten bob it cost and cheap at half the price," he was saying. "You want something fixing, leave it to yours truly. Just mention my name and it's all yours. I'll send Suri up for the dinghy tomorrow. Better than staying there half the night waiting for the tide."

He was cut short as Gotto interrupted in an angry voice from which all traces of friendliness had disappeared. "You might have thought of that before," he snapped. "Saved us coming home like a lot of wogs. Like a lot of wogs," he repeated bitterly. "Just like a lot of wogs."

Earnshaw turned round in his seat and tossed his fag-end overboard. "I didn't know there was a mud bank there," he retorted, suddenly incensed. "They come up in different positions every rainy season and nobody charts 'em."

"Then why take us up there?" Gotto said with the icy, infuriating reasonableness of a Torquemada.

Earnshaw glared, his humanity forgotten, his friendliness withered. "Always the chance you'll fall overboard," he snorted.

He sat in silence for a while and Jimmy could hear his heavy muttering in the darkness, then he leaned over, breathing his bad breath and old fag-ends over him.

"That's it, old lad," he said. "That finish it. I've tried just to oblige you and Old Doc. I've tried heavens hard to be matey with him and against me own better nature. That's it, though. I've had a gutser of him."

"Oh, Lord, man," Jimmy pleaded. "Give him another chance. It was rotten luck the boat running aground like that. We might have pulled it off otherwise."

"Yes, you might. And tomorrow he'd 'a' got up all smiles and brisk as a kipper—and probably slipped on a banana skin and broke his bloody neck. And then 'e'd 'a' been in a rare ole temper, wun't 'e? What's the good of trying with a bloke like him? No, mate, he's had it. He was drowning, I wun't give him deck space. Not if he went down on his knees and begged of me, I wouldn't. It's bad for me ulcers to get meself worked up like this 'ere. He's finished now as far as Archibald Earnshaw's concerned."

110

Seven

EARNSHAW'S defection from the scheme to amuse Gotto might not have resulted in its complete and utter collapse, but another blow towards it occurred the following week which completely destroyed all their hopes of making friends.

The arrival of the mail at the week-end was probably the beginning of the failure. It was another bright brassy day like all the hundreds of others but this one was marked by an atmosphere of excitement. Both Jimmy and Gotto had heard by the intangible but very real bush telegraph that existed from village to village that mail had arrived in the port down-river, and they both went about their work hardly able to restrain their excitement until it arrived in Ma-Imi and finally in Amama.

Earnshaw had gone down overnight to fetch the letters up and tossed the packet—a disappointingly small one after the rumours—into the mine bungalow as they were sitting down for the midday meal.

"There y'are, me old china," he croaked, very pointedly only to Jimmy. "If I was a postman and that's all I had to fetch, I'd be out on me uppers in a week. Right honest I would."

Gotto snatched the package from the floor and took it to the old-fashioned settee where he began to sort the letters. His manner was bright and eager and he was obviously as yet as unaware of any scheme to help him habilitate himself in Amama as he was of Earnshaw's growing opposition to it.

Jimmy pushed his chair back and stood impatiently along-

111

side him as he unfastened the string with shaking fingers.

"One for you," Gotto said brightly, throwing down the first letter. "Another for you. And another——"

His voice died away and he began to flip through the packets in silence.

"One for me," he said at last, showing Jimmy the envelope. "From my mother." His voice seemed to droop with disappointment as he tossed it down.

"Some people have all the luck," he commented with a thin acid bitterness.

"I write a lot of letters," Jimmy pointed out in an attempt at light-heartedness which only made him feel guilty in front of Gotto's unhappiness.

Gotto glanced at the bundle of letters in Jimmy's hand and turned over the last few in his own hand cautiously, as though afraid to read the addresses.

"Here's one from Doris," he said quickly, an obvious delight in his voice. Then the joy went out of his tones again immediately. "It's a thin one," he added sharply.

Jimmy had taken his letters to the table and was reading them as he crammed paw-paw into his mouth.

"All my old girl friends missing me. Just as they promised," he announced. "Anything in yours, Gotty?"

"The usual." Gotto's voice was dull and disinterested. "One page from my mother in pencil. She's got rheumatism again and the Vicar's not been to see her. Complaints as usual."

Jimmy studied his wry face as he stared at the scrawled piece of notepaper.

"What about Doris?" he asked.

Gotto was opening the other letter gingerly, as though afraid of the contents, then he took out a single sheet of paper and turned it over slowly, staring at both sides. His eyes showed the disappointment he felt.

Jimmy watched him as he read it. His features showed no
112

pleasure and when he came to the end of it, he lowered it slowly.

"Still love you?" Jimmy asked gaily, though his bright expression had faded.

"She says she's going out with another bloke." Gotto spoke in an uneven voice. "She say's there's nothing to it—not yet, anyway. And she says she'll be glad to see me any time I go home on leave."

"Is that all?" Jimmy felt almost as disappointed as Gotto.

"That's all." Gotto threw the letter aside savagely. He had the manner of one who is always disappointed and yet has never learned to expect anything but gratification. "God," he exploded. "She might have taken the trouble to write a bit more. She knows I'm stuck in this blasted hole!"

Jimmy watched him stamp out of sight into the bedroom then he shrugged and followed. After a shower he changed and began to toss swimming trunks and towels into the station wagon. He was whistling as he stuffed cigarettes and matches into his pockets, and he was on the point of climbing into the driver's seat when an angular shadow in front of him that could belong to no one but Gotto stopped the tune on his lips and set him stuffing the swimming costume behind the seat and bringing the butterfly net into greater prominence.

"Going somewhere?" Gotto asked.

"Er—yes," Jimmy said. "Up to Amama Town."

"Out with Stella Swannack?"

In Gotto's voice was a plea to be included and for a moment, Jimmy was on the point of inviting him, too, then he panicked at the last instant, appalled at the thought of the awkward silences that would take the place of the laughter that was normally a part of his outings with Stella, and he decided to put off the invitation to another day.

"No," he lied, hating himself for his selfishness. "Just

113

going up to see old Swannack about some butterflies he's caught. Thought I might just look in. That's all."

That lonely glance of Gotto's showed he didn't believe him and Jimmy drove off between the palms, conscious of a pair of eyes burning a hole in his back. . . .

The narrow arc of burnished sand at Mansumana was picked out by the sun into a dazzling crescent against which the metallic sheet of the sea nibbled in wavelets too small even to cause a splash as they broke. Behind it and about it, the tall grey boles of the palms curved gently out of the shadows cast by their own crests and into the sunshine where the great green leaves trembled in the breeze like tattered fans.

Beneath them in the shade the native children tumbled about, playing shrilly round the canoes upturned on trestles to dry. The chatter of women as they pounded the dirt out of their clothes on the smooth round stones of the stream, and the flat screech of a scrawny cockerel as it ruffled its feathers in the dust seemed to make the day lazier.

"This is when I begin to like Sierra Leone," Jimmy commented, blinking at the palm-crested spit of land that curved out into the bright sea. "You'd almost imagine it was Hawaii——"

"Or Palm Beach," Stella put in.

"Apart from the smell of the mangroves." Jimmy indicated the unhealthy green of the foliage where the swamp area in the distance encroached almost to the sand.

"And the absence of juke boxes and hot-dog stalls and soda fountains and convertibles. I could just do a coke now."

Jimmy rolled over on to his stomach and was about to kiss her when she drew back sharply.

"Jimmy! There's someone watching us."

"An African, I expect," Jimmy said easily. "Nothing to worry about."

They turned to each other again, engrossed in themselves, then Stella turned round once more.

"Jimmy!" Her voice rose. "It's a white man!"

"By God, it is, too!" Jimmy had started to his feet. "It's Gotto, I think," he said. "What's *he* want? Perhaps he came for a swim, too," he added with a feeling of shame at his own lack of charity. "I'll fetch him over, poor old bloke. He'll be glad of company."

"Jimmy," Stella whispered to him, laying her hand on his arm. "I think he's spying on us."

"Spying on us?"

"I thought I saw him once before but I didn't say anything in case I was wrong."

Jimmy looked at her, his face suddenly grim, then he stared towards the bush again. "He's gone now, anyway. Must have seen us looking."

"Jimmy, he gives me the creeps. Why should he follow us about?"

"Lord knows. Lonely probably. People like Gotto always follow the bright lights back home. They get a sort of cosy feeling from seeing other people enjoying themselves. A sort of reflected glow, I suppose you'd call it. Haven't you ever seen 'em, walking round the shops looking lost and hoping someone will be matey to them?"

Jimmy dismissed the subject with a wave of his hand. "He's quite cracked, you know. He imagines he's in love with some half-baked kid in Birmingham or somewhere who writes chatty notes to him and never mentions the word. Then, when he gets one of her dreary little letters, he sits brooding over it for a week or so, trying to read affection into it when there isn't any."

"He frightens me, Jimmy. He stares at me as though he'd like to get his hands on me."

"He probably would," Jimmy grinned.

115

"Suppose he's thinking of attacking us?"

"Not Gotty. He hasn't the spirit."

"All the same, I don't like him."

"Can't say I like him a lot myself, Stella."

"Listen—" Stella sat up angrily—"if he's following us about, he's dangerous. He's probably nuts."

Jimmy laughed out loud, rolling back on the sand and crowing. "Not he, my love. It probably excites him when he sees me kissing you. That's all. Probably that's the only warmth he ever gets out of life. Listen, Stella," he said as he sat up, "there's craziness and craziness. Gotto's the second kind of crazy. He does queer things. He broods. He's as broody as an old hen on a pot egg. He imagines things. Take this non-existent love affair with a kid just out of school for instance —God knows how he's managed to persuade himself it exists but he has." He paused, his eyes thoughtful. "To be fair to the poor old duffer," he went on, "he was blessed with none of the advantages of life and quite a lot of the disadvantages. I mean, that nose of his. If somebody wore it on the stage, it would be enough to make a cat laugh. But it's not funny for Gotty.

"He ought never to have come here. He can't stand himself alone. I reckon he must have had quite a surfeit of himself in his lifetime."

Stella looked up quickly. "You think we ought to bring him along with us some afternoon?"

"What!"

"Well, *sometimes*."

Jimmy snorted. "No, thanks."

"Jimmy, I know how he feels. I've been lonely, too. Many a time back in the States when I was at school and my folks were out here. Can't we do *anything* for him?"

Jimmy looked up soberly. "As a matter of fact," he said, "I tried. I asked him once. After the party. For our first date, in fact."

Stella looked indignant and Jimmy shrugged. "Well, you haven't got a monopoly on soft hearts."

"What did he say?"

"That he wasn't going to play gooseberry."

Stella considered for a moment. "You think I ought to get him up for tea or something? I will if it will help."

"You can try," Jimmy said slowly. "But I don't think it would do a scrap of good. He's got a suspicious nature and he'd probably think you were trying to take the mickey out of him. I suspect he's suffered quite a bit at the hands of bright young things who thought it was funny to jolly him along and then toss him over just when he was completely gaga. I imagine it doesn't take long to get him to that state."

"I only want to be friendly," Stella said indignantly.

Jimmy grinned and kissed her. "If you'd shown the slightest interest in him, you'd have had him hanging round your neck like a feather boa. You'd never have shaken him off. He'd have followed you around looking like a sick spaniel, all eyes and sighs."

"And mumbled compliments?"

Jimmy nodded.

"Oh dear. And flowers?"

"Probably. He'd inevitably have fallen over something as he gave them to you and then you'd have spent the rest of the evening trying to make him feel at home again. Friendship with a girl's a deadly serious thing for Gotty. In fact, I suspect that's what always frightens 'em away, poor old bloke. Gotty just hasn't got the technique and unfortunately there aren't a lot of useful books in the library you can read up on the subject."

When Jimmy returned to the bungalow, he was tired and the sight of Gotto's pathetic letter from Doris lying on the table reminded him of the spying incident that afternoon and he made up his mind to tax him with it there and then. As

117

he opened the door of Gotto's room, he was certain he heard a movement but Gotto's eyes were closed and he was motionless under the mosquito netting. Jimmy stared hard at him for a while, waiting impatiently for the flicker of an eyelid, certain he was feigning sleep and irritated because he couldn't work off his sudden temper on him. But Gotto didn't move and Jimmy went out, frustrated and angry.

The following morning, he rose late, still annoyed with Gotto but, as soon as he arrived at the river edge and the jetty, he became happily involved in one of Earnshaw's operations and clean forgot about it.

Earnshaw had collected a team of shovel boys and had dug out a square basin in the mud alongside the jetty where the fishermen from King Tim dried their nets and kept their canoes during the day. In this, he had erected parts of a dismantled cradle on to which he proposed to float his pinnace at spring tide to paint its hull.

"Now we'll get a drum of cement," he said, as he wiped mud off his hands, "and drop it in here. Spread it around a bit and let it harden off overnight, then when the spring tide comes up, Bob's your uncle and Kate's your aunt."

He climbed out of the basin and disappeared to steal one of the drums of cement from under the nose of the foreman in charge of the pile-driver.

Leaning on the cradle, gulping at a cigarette and wiping his streaming face, Jimmy looked up as he heard Gotto above him on the edge of the basin.

"Fraternizing with Earnshaw, I see," he commented.

Jimmy tossed his cigarette aside abruptly, ready to join battle with a few of the things he had had to leave unsaid the night before, but Earnshaw's return, rolling the drum of cement, interrupted the angry reply that rose to his lips.

Earnshaw poised the drum on the edge of the basin and proceeded to hack off the end with a spade.

118

"O.K., that's it," he said after a while. "Here it come. Keep your 'eads down unless you want a mud barf."

Jimmy dodged behind one of the cradles.

"Here," Gotto shouted. "That's *our* cement. Where did you get it?"

"Borrowed it, old lad. Tuck your head in."

"You've no damn' right to borrow our cement."

"No, I haven't. And you've no damn' right to come shoving your nose in what don't concern you. Keep your 'ead down."

Earnshaw thrust at the drum with his foot and as it dropped into the thin slime at the bottom of the basin with the wet slap of a whipped dishcloth, Gotto, still protesting on the edge, got the wave of mud and water full in his face.

For a complete minute, Earnshaw and Jimmy stared in horror at the black, glistening figure struck motionless with shock on the bank, then one of the shovel boys behind them choked and sniggered explosively. Immediately, another one laughed out loud in a deep rich chuckle and within seconds three or four dozen black men were rolling on the ground weeping and shaking with noisy laughter while others came running along the concrete to see the cause of all the merriment.

Gotto stood still for a moment longer, gouging two clear white spots round his eyes as he dug out the mud.

"You did that on purpose," he choked.

Earnshaw was laughing too, now. "Oh, my aching back," he said. "Sorry, old lad. I never meant—but, honest, you should of kept your 'ead down like I said."

Gotto blew black bubbles of rage, then he turned on his heel and stalked away, dripping slime, followed by the shouts and shrieks of laughter from the helpless shovel boys.

Earnshaw suddenly became sober as he stared after him. "It was the nigs laughing what done it," he said. "Somebody going to catch it now."

119

That afternoon, Gotto announced the removal of all canoes from the mud near the concrete wharf and the rickety wooden jetty. The announcement took the form of a typed slip of paper, well marked by Clerk Smith's grubby thumb, which was pinned to the side of the foreman's hut.

"*All fissermen*"—Clerk Smith's adventures in the art of spelling were hesitant and none too sure—"*from King Tim*," it read, "*will remove their canoes from mine property by tomorrow morning or they will be*"—here Clerk Smith had had three attempts to spell '*confiscated*' before he had persuaded Gotto to substitute the final words—"*taken over*."

"Well, I'm a monkey's uncle," Earnshaw said loudly. "They been using that bit of mud since before this jetty was thought of. Jarvis never bothered 'em. Why *he* got to?"

Jimmy's first reaction was also one of anger but the more he studied the notice the less important it seemed.

"I shouldn't waste your breath on it," he said. "Nobody will worry. They can't read anyway."

But if the fishermen from King Tim couldn't read, it was inevitable that the edict would be seen by someone who could, and as the news spread during the afternoon, there was a noticeably noisy agitation round the jetty.

Even so, Jimmy regarded it lightly enough to forget all about it when he returned to the bungalow for the evening meal and even, remembering Gotto's humiliation that morning, to manage to be friendly with him—a labouring effort, however, which brought little response from the other side of the table.

The following day, though, when he arrived at the jetty, he was startled to find a dozen brawny labourers from the workings already engaged in a noisy tug-of-war with the fishermen over the nets that had been strung up to dry. There was a milling crowd swirling round the canoes, and the first loud argument as the order was put into force had become a shoving match and the shoving match had become a brawl so

120

that now half the labourers employed round the pile-driver seemed to be as much involved as the fishermen, all shouting and waving their arms and quarrelling with anyone within reach, no matter which side they belonged to. Even as Jimmy drew near, hurrying across the concrete apron, he saw fists start flying where one corner of the uproar exploded into a fight and the whole crowd began to surge backwards and forwards along the water's edge, breaking up and re-forming in a vast concertina-like movement.

"My God," he said, "This is getting serious."

Storming into the foreman's hut, he found Gotto watching with interest, but white-faced and agitated at the resistance, while Earnshaw raved at him from the doorway.

"You're nuts. You're balmy. You're off your rocker," he was saying in his harsh, rasping voice. "You must be proper sawny if you think they'll stand for this."

Jimmy pushed him out of the way and stood in front of Gotto. "Have you gone off your chump?" he demanded. "What the hell's the idea?"

"You know what the idea is," Gotto said tautly.

"It's a crazy one, whatever it is."

"It's made 'em think, though." Gotto's lips stretched in a cheerless smile that died again immediately. "They're not supposed to be on mine property."

"They been there ever since the mine come," Earnshaw growled.

"I'm clearing away dead wood. They're not necessary here, so I'm getting rid of them."

"They're doing no harm," Jimmy's voice reached a high pitch of indignation. "You're not serious, are you?"

"Yes, I am. They're in the way. I'm going to use that stretch of mud."

"What for?"

"He going to scrape it up and use it for a beauty treatment," Earnshaw said cruelly. "He need it."

121

Gotto went white, but Jimmy went on without sympathy. "Go on," he insisted. "What for? Let's have it?"

Obviously Gotto had no idea but before he could reply, the crowd, sorting out its grievances and making up its mind about the identity of the enemy, split up and streamed across the mud to re-form outside the foreman's hut, creating a high-pitched hubbub so that the doorway was filled with black faces and the hut rocked violently as it seemed for a while that they would push it over.

Jimmy turned spitefully to Gotto.

"What are you going to do when you want to go up for a meal, Gotty?" he asked. "You'll never make your way through that lot."

"They wouldn't dare lay hands on me."

"Wouldn't they? What do you think they're waiting for? —for you to sign autographs?"

Just when the situation was looking awkward, the crowd parted for Alf Momo who had been fetched, as he always was in times of crisis. As he entered the hut, the noise subsided a little until it murmured with the uneasy fits and starts of a damp firework.

"Boss," Momo said earnestly, very conscious of the responsibility he bore and the esteem with which his wisdom was held. "Always these men leave their boats there. All white bosses let them."

"Well, this white boss has stopped them," Gotto said.

"He's going to stop something else, too, one of these nights," Earnshaw hinted darkly. "These blokes won't take it lying down."

"They'd better not try anything with me," Gotto said. "I'd have 'em down to the calaboose one-time."

"Boss—" Momo made another effort—"for many years these men leave their boats here. Many years," he stressed.

"Well, now they'd better find somewhere else."

"Boss, there is nowhere else. Farther up the creek, there is
122

no mud. Only mangroves. They bring boats here to sell fish to the shovel boys. Plenty trade. If they leave their canoes at King Tim, they muss walk through Amama Town. No good, Boss. Too far."

"Do 'em good." Gotto turned his back on Momo and stared through the window. "Anyway, they shouldn't be selling their damned fish here. They should sell it in the market in Amama."

"Boss, always they sell it here."

"Well, now they've stopped."

"Boss, black men buy fish because rice is short."

"Listen—" Goaded to fury by Momo's persistence, Gotto whirled round on him, pointing a skinny forefinger—"don't bring that nonsense up again. It's nothing to do with me. If they want to complain, they can complain away. There's nothing they can do about those damn' boats. This is mine property and I'm in charge of it and what I say goes. Savvy? If they're not off it in an hour, I'll have the police down from Amama Town to shift 'em."

"Boss," Momo said. "I tell them. But I do not like it. It is wrong. It is dangerous."

"O.K., Momo." Gotto thrust his hands into the pockets of his shorts with an air of finality. "You seem to know so much you'd better go and get yourself a better job—perhaps as a manager somewhere. They're employing black men nowadays, I hear. Perhaps you'd like to start your own mine. I'll find another shift boss. You can consider yourself out as from now."

Momo's expression didn't alter, and his eyes were steady on Gotto's face.

"Boss, you sack me, you change my job, I want to see Boss Twigg."

Gotto glowered at the black man, his fingers twitching. "Trying to pull the big-time stuff, eh? Trying to kid me you're important enough for Twigg to go over my head, eh?"

123

"Boss, I want to see Mister Twigg."

Gotto glared a moment longer, then he threw up his hands and turned away. "O.K., O.K.," he said. "I'll forget it this time. I don't want to cause Twigg any trouble. He's got enough to do without you going belly-aching round him. Forget it. I'll overlook it—but it's only to save Twigg the effort of having to come up here." He whirled and pointed. "That's all though. Get that straight. Only to save dragging Twigg up here."

Momo watched him with placid confidence. "Boss, I go down there," he said. "I don't mind. I see Boss Twigg at Ma-Imi."

"Oh, God, man," Gotto said irritably. "Forget it, can't you? I withdraw it if you're going to make a song and dance act out of it. Now get on with your own job. Go and tell those fishermen to clear off and let's have no more of it."

As Momo left the hut, Jimmy turned on Gotto, his temper bringing the colour to his face. Outside he could hear Momo's low voice describing the interview, then there was a sudden burst of shouting and a stone landed on the tin roof.

"I suppose he's told 'em some cock-and-bull story," Gotto commented coldly.

"More likely he's told them the truth," Earnshaw said.

"Listen, Gotty," Jimmy said angrily. "Are you going on with this nonsense?"

"You can't go back on your word. Saying what you mean represents a lot to these people. They can't trust you otherwise."

"Are you going on with it?"

"Yes, I am."

"Then, count me out. I'm having nothing to do with it."

As Jimmy stamped from the hut, suddenly unable to be within a yard of Gotto and keep a civil tongue in his head, he had to fight his way through a forest of waving black arms. Behind him, lumps of ironstone were starting a clamorous tattoo on the roof and the wooden sides of the hut. Then the

124

crowd spotted Gotto's labourers taking advantage of the diversion to drag the canoes off the mud once more, and the shoving match started all over again. For a while neither side showed any willingness to set about the other seriously but in the end the fighting began again, spreading in fits and starts as friends and relations of the combatants joined in. Stakes appeared from nowhere and boundary posts were wrenched out for weapons. Several people fell into the water and one or two of the small boys shrieking excitedly on the fringes of the uproar were trodden on. The jetty began to look like a battle-field with pieces of ironstone and stakes scattered everywhere and the few casualties limping painfully to safety.

While the attention of the crowd was engaged in forming sides for a final free-for-all, Gotto managed to escape from the hut to his car, and, as the shouting and the shoving started again, he hurried off up the road towards the trees.

Ten minutes later, Sergeant Asimani and three court messengers—the Protectorate police—very upright and very correct in their blue uniforms and sandals, climbed out of his car and marched down towards the jetty and advanced on the fishermen.

For a moment, the shrieking crowd became silent, mostly with surprise, then the shouting welled up again. There was another noisy argument and black arms gesticulated more violently and one of Gotto's unwilling labourers was stretched flat on the mud with a swing from a two-by-four stake. As one of the fishermen started a struggle with a policeman, Sergeant Asimani felled him with a scything blow from his fist and the stones and brickbats began to fly again. Asimani and his men were well disciplined, however, and they advanced in a straight line on the stone-throwers who backed away and eventually began to jump into the water and swim for safety. As the noise died down, the canoes were dragged sullenly off the stone-littered mud into the river and paddled towards King Tim by their owners.

There was an ugly silence round the jetty as they moved slowly downstream and out of sight round the bulging mangroves.

Jimmy watched them go from the rising ground beyond the mud, his eyes squinting against the sun that glittered on the water. Behind him, Earnshaw flicked his fag-end away. His face was set and angry.

"Son," he said. "Remember what I said when I first seen you?"

"You said a lot of things." Jimmy was still staring at the canoes, only half his attention on what Earnshaw was saying. "Which one was it?"

"I said you'd got it cut off the crusty part. That's what I said." Earnshaw drew a deep breath and reached for another cigarette. "And seeing 'ow things is working out, old lad, I reckon I wasn't far wrong."

Part II

One

THE dry season advanced and as the new grass became parched and brown, Jimmy's pink face changed to a healthy sunburn and eventually to the sallow yellow of West Africa.

The dusty mine office grew dustier as the heavy hanging cloud over the workings covered everything with a fine flat film, and always they could shake the red powder out of the folds of the plans, or write their name in it on the seats of the chairs.

Clerk Smith, entering the office with his sweeping brush in his hand for his daily diffusion of the dirt on the floor, stopped dead as he found Gotto sitting in his chair staring in front of him with that blank fretful manner which characterized him. Smith turned slowly round, one eye all the time on him, and tried to edge past him towards the verandah, holding his breath as his large feet in their white shoes shuffled on the gritty concrete floor.

Gotto was aware of him but for some time he didn't speak. He was hot, his hair plastered to his forehead, his face coated with the dust that caked on the perspiration oozing from his skin. His mind was withered with the awareness that he was now as disliked in Amama as he had been in Ma-Imi.

He sat up abruptly as Clerk Smith reached the verandah. "What the hell are you creeping about like that for, you fool?" he demanded loudly.

Dropping the brush with a clatter, Smith leapt a good two feet in the air and came down facing Gotto, his eyes rolling in his black face, his mouth open and flabby. He spread his pink palms in an agonized gesture of explanation.

"Boss, I see you t'ink," he babbled, the words tumbling off his tongue in his haste to appease. "Plenty important t'ings. 'Okay, Clerk Smith,' I say. 'You go for be quiet'."

He stared at Gotto, jigging from one foot to the other and itching to gain the safety of the verandah.

"What's the matter, you stupid idiot?" Gotto growled, his stiff upright posture subsiding slowly. "You afraid of me or something?"

Smith laughed, a nervous high-pitched cackle that convinced neither of them. "Afraid, Boss? Clerk Smith no afraid anyt'ing. Clerk Smith fight de lion. He wrestle de bush-cow. He go chase de leopard."

"You're a liar. You hate my guts, don't you?"

Smith's face split in a nervous smile and he spread his hands again, trying to impress the angular angry man at the desk. "Boss, you good man. You braver dan de lion. You de cleverest, bravest, wisest man in all de world."

He paused to watch the reaction.

"You're a liar," Gotto said again, but this time there was no hostility in his voice.

Smith's eyes stopped rolling immediately with the certain knowledge that he had touched on Gotto's soft spot with his flattery. He leaned forward anxiously. "Boss, you sick? You got belly humbug?"

"No." Gotto's reply was a fretful bark.

"Dat ole Earnshaw? Dat ole Boss Jimmy? Dat Doctor Romney? Dey make you angry, Boss?"

"They always make me angry."

"Boss, dey plenty bad men." Smith's concern was touching, and Gotto's posture relaxed still more. "Boss, dat Romney villain man. He steal black man's sister, black man's wife."

Gotto's eyes brightened as he stared through the doorway where the sunshine, by its sheer strength, was forcing itself

130

into the shaded room. "You mean that self-righteous old fool has black girls?" he asked.

"Boss," Smith went on, "dat doctor no doctor at all. I t'ink he t'ief man. He pinch t'ings. Sergy Asimani promise bring his police boys and take him calaboose, but Sargy Asimani plenty afraid. Boss, I t'ink he kill people in dat ole hospital."

Gotto's eyes widened, then he scowled as he realized it was only Smith's imagination that was running away with him.

"You're a liar," he snarled again, his relaxed expression disappearing immediately.

"No, Boss. I no lie to you. I 'gree for you too much." Smith's black face was distorted with earnestness as, never one to miss the histrionic possibilities of a scene, he beat his breast to prove his words. "Other black boys no like hard boss. Hard boss make black boy work. Black boy no like dat," he ended eagerly, quivering like a spaniel in his efforts to please.

"You're damn' right there, Smith," Gotto said dreamily. "But it's all they understand. It's a pity a few other people don't see it my way. The output's started to go down and a bit of the old-fashioned spur's what's wanted to push it up again."

"Boss," Smith said eagerly, anxious to consolidate his success as he found Gotto's temper improving. "Other white bosses too soft."

"Think so, Smith?" Gotto glanced sideways at the black man without moving his head.

"Boss, I suttinly t'ink so. But, *you* good boss. Why dey no make you bigger boss? Why dey no pay you more money?"

"That's something *I'd* like to know."

"Boss, we two both alike. You clever man. I clever man." Smith pursued his theme enthusiastically. "I read. I write. I type better dan de Queen England. Don't I, Boss? Boss," he concluded as his enthusiasm ran away with him. "Dey no pay me 'nough also."

Gotto lifted his head from his hands and stared hard at the black man, who backed away quickly.

"You're not a bad little bloke," he said, to Smith's surprise, suddenly friendly. "We'll have to see what we can do for you."

Smith's eyes widened until they seemed to be all whites and he did a little fandango of glee. "Boss, you give me big job?" His voice rose to an excited squeak. "You make me important black man so I go buy gramophone by-'n-by? Boss, I 'gree for you. I 'gree for you too much." Then he stopped dead, a dismayed expression spreading across his face. "Boss, what dat ole Boss Jimmy say when he find out?"

"He can go and jump in the creek," Gotto growled. "He can go off with his precious Stella and do what he likes with her."

"Boss——" Clerk Smith's eyes opened wider at the suggestion of scandal—"what he do? He get her with piccaninny? Missis Swannack she plenty mad den, dat old Jesus lady."

Gotto said nothing and Smith went on, his eyes dreamy as he contemplated his own future. "Boss Jimmy get plenty trouble. He get sent home to England. You give Clerk Smith his job. Black boy call me Boss Smith. I get black trash for clerk. I get plenty money, buy gramophone and Carmen Mirandy, all same Boss Earnshaw." His face split in a shining anticipatory grin which faded slowly into an expression of bewilderment. "Boss, where you get de wages for Clerk Smith's new job?"

Gotto had moved to the door now and he prodded at the dust between the cracks on the verandah with his stick. His eyes still had a far-away look in them. "We can always find we're overstaffed with labourers," he said. "We can always get rid of one of them!"

Smith's expression became crafty and a little malicious. "Dat ole Melikuri Tom no-good black man," he commented thoughtfully. "He say you bad boss. He say you drive black boy too hard. He say too much work in Amama mine. He kick Clerk Smith udder day. Say Clerk Smith lazy good-for-nothing black trash. He too big-for-boots."

"Well, we'll have *him* out for a start, eh? We don't want *his* kind."

Clerk Smith grinned again, his happiness gurgling in his throat. "Boss, you de finest boss all de world. Any black boy say you bad boss, I kick him backside."

Gotto spoke over his shoulder in reply. "Much better you tell me his name," he said distantly. "Then *I* kick his backside—or I sack him. Savvy? We don't want people who make trouble. Boss Twigg is coming from Ma-Imi soon and we want a good mine when he arrives. See what I mean?"

"Boss——" Smith was prepared to accuse half of Amama for the privilege of being important, willing to sell his soul to the devil if it meant getting his hands on a gramophone like Earnshaw's. "I tell you plenty. I listen all time to de black boys."

"And the white boys, too."

Smith halted, his eyes swinging again in panic. "White bosses, too?"

"Why not? The whole bloody shower of 'em are working against me, aren't they?" Gotto's bitterness burst out once more. "The whole damn' lot are trying to edge me out of here. Just because I'm not soft with the boys. No, if you want to be the Gestapo, Smith, you've got to be the Gestapo *all* the time."

"Gestapo, Boss?"

Gotto grinned. "Personal assistant," he said.

Smith nodded gleefully. "Yes, Boss. Gestapo, Boss. Dat good job."

He watched Gotto, an angular silhouette in the harsh light, overcome to the point of faintness by the desire to please, to provide him with news about everybody, real news or imaginary news. Where there was no real news, imagination

133

could easily supply it. "Boss," he said. "Dat Momo bad man also. He tell black boys no work hard so Boss Gotto get de sack."

"I thought something like that was going on."

"Boss, he tell 'em knock you on de head. Dat Momo man black savage, Boss. He in de pay dat Doctor Romney. Dat Ole Doc he want you for his hospital. He want for chop you up——"

Gotto sprang to life, and snatching up a book from the table threw it at Smith's head. "You bloody black liar," he stormed. "You're telling your damned lies again!"

Returning the following morning to the office from the creek where he had persuaded the ancient pile-driver to drive the first upright into the mud for Earnshaw's jetty, Jimmy found Clerk Smith sitting at his desk with his feet up on the plans, just as he had often seen Gotto doing.

Hot and dusty and shrivelled by the sun, the sweat in his shirt smearing a blue blotch from the indelible pencil in his pocket, Jimmy stood in the doorway wiping the inside of his hat and grinning at Smith.

"What's all this, Smith, old son?" he asked cheerfully, not surprised by anything he found in Africa, least of all in the volatile Smith. "You been promoted? Only the big shots can put their feet on the desk, you know."

"You go 'way, Boss Jimmy." Smith waved a hand pompously. "I pussonal clerk. I tell pussonal t'ings. Clerk Smith got new job."

Jimmy's brows came down in a frown as he immediately suspected Gotto of some new foolishness. "What's that?" he snapped, slamming his hat on his head. "New job? What new job?"

"I Gestapo," the black man pointed out haughtily. "Boss Gotto make me. I sit in de chair. I tell all people what to do."

"Do you, by God?"

134

Jimmy was advancing round the desk now and Smith's eyes began to roll as he made a desperate attempt to regain control of the situation. "Boss Jimmy, I pussonal clerk."

"Get your shoes off that desk and get back to your own damned office," Jimmy shouted in an explosion of anger that was directed chiefly at Gotto, and Smith dropped his feet and backed away, knocking over the chair. "I don't know what all this damned gibberish is that you're talking but you can get the hell out of here. If you want to be a personal clerk, go and be a personal clerk next door where you belong."

When Gotto appeared, Jimmy faced him angrily.

"What's all this nonsense about you setting Smith on as a personal clerk or something? What do you want with a personal clerk?"

"I can trust him."

"Does he get more money?"

"Yes."

"Ha!" Jimmy snorted. "I'll bet that wasn't what Twiggy intended."

"Twigg put me in charge. He trusts me."

"Like hell he does. Where are you getting the extra wages?"

"I've sacked one of the shovel boys."

"Have you, by God?" Jimmy was beginning to shout now. "Listen, man. Twiggy expects us to provide him with ironstone not personal clerks. Who did you fire?"

"Melikuri Tom."

"Another Mende!"

"What about it?"

"God, man," Jimmy said disgustedly, "you've been warned half a dozen times. By Alf Momo. By Romney. One of the boys got half his ear bitten off last time. These black boys take it seriously."

Gotto had backed away to the door, suddenly white-faced and desperate. "Leave me alone," he burst out. "You're

135

worse than my mother. She was always at me like this. 'Why don't you do this?' 'Why don't you do that?' 'You wouldn't have neglected me like this if your father had been alive!' That was her special moan and, God, I was always doing things for her. I never went out. I stuck in with her to keep her company until I wanted to scream, listening to the same old wireless programmes. Moan, moan, moan. All the time. And you're the same. I don't believe half of what Romney says, anyway. He's a bloody old rogue. I hear he sleeps with the African nurses he employs at the hospital."

Jimmy laughed. "Who's been telling you that rubbish? Personal Clerk Smith?"

Gotto flushed and Jimmy went on mercilessly. "I suppose he's told you Alf Momo's fomenting strikes. And Earnshaw ate his grandmother. And I'm Jack the Ripper. He wants kicking out, not promoting."

The irritation Gotto had caused was still evident when Jimmy saw Stella that evening. But, after the passage of a day and a great deal of searching of his conscience, it was tempered by a genuine worry that they weren't doing sufficient to help, and a feeling that, since the episode concerning the fishermen, events were moving too fast to be decently controlled.

"But what can I do?" he asked Stella. "He won't take any damn' notice of me. All I can do is bite my nails and hope to God another little episode like the row with the King Tim fishermen won't arise."

He sat for a while, smoking his cigarette slowly, deep in thought, while Stella watched him, waiting for him to speak again.

"He possesses the pernicious gift," he went on eventually, "of infuriating you to the point of exasperation and beyond and then, just when you've given him up as a bad job, of looking so blasted lonely and unhappy that you start getting agitated about his welfare. He gets me so I'm mad with myself

136

for upsetting him and then I get madder still because I know damn' well it's not my fault."

"Of course it's not your fault, Jimmy darling. You've tried hard enough."

Jimmy sat up angrily. "I'm sick of suggesting things to amuse him," he said. "I had another awful row with him this morning over Clerk Smith. When I told him he was no damn' good, Gotto pointed out that at least he didn't clear out of the room every time *he* came in."

"Oh, Jimmy! Do *you*?"

"You know jolly well I do. He makes me depressed."

Stella looked thoughtful. "Poor man," she said. "Jimmy, if we were back home, we'd get a psycho-analyst to look him over. You any good at psycho-analysis?"

Jimmy grinned and shook his head.

"Pity. Couldn't you try?"

Jimmy shrugged and grinned again at Stella. "Of course not, child," he said, suddenly more cheerful. "Only Gotto can be ringmaster to his own soul. You and me—because we're tougher, or stupider, if you like—we've got subconsciouses like performing fleas. They do as they're told. But not Gotto. Inside him, there's another little Gotto screeching to get out, like a claustrophobia case locked in a clothes closet. And *that* Gotto's afraid and insecure and lonely. You can see people like Gotto every five minutes back home. This place just brings it out more. I'll wager there are more in America than anywhere else in the world."

"Why America?"

"Because it's bigger and faster and slicker, and in big, fast slick places—London's one—there's no room for lost people like Gotty." He paused and looked at her, suddenly serious. Then he studied his feet for a while before he spoke. "You know, Stella, I can see a great danger to you back in the States. You ought to live in England and get away from it."

"I liked England," Stella admitted.

137

Jimmy took her hand. "Listen, Stella darling, I shall be going home when my tour's over out here. I shall be settling down to growing old and comfortable. Why not grow old and comfortable with me? It's a nice cosy thought."

Stella smiled and patted his hand.

"Marry me, Stella."

"Jimmy, you're a clown."

"I'm not clowning now, Stella."

Stella's eyes widened as she became aware of his expression. "Jimmy darling, are you getting serious?"

"Yes." Jimmy looked her squarely in the eye. "I am. I have been for some time."

Stella stared back at him for a moment, then her eyes fell. "Well, that's my big moment over," she said ruefully.

"Big moment? What big moment?"

"Every girl dreams of the day someone'll ask her to marry him. I was looking forward to orchids and moonlight and all the other things. What I get is a casual 'Marry me, Stella,' straight out of the blue, without any warning, without any soft lights or sweet music. Just like that. No romance. No poetry. No 'I love you'. Nothing."

Jimmy fiddled with his cigarette awkwardly for a while. "I'm sorry, Stella," he said. "It slipped out that way. It seemed the natural way to do it. Surely that's the best way."

"Couldn't you have put on a bit more of a show? Got down on your knees or something?"

"I'll do it again if you like." Jimmy shifted uneasily in his seat.

"No, Jimmy dear." Stella smiled and touched his cheek. "I'm only tormenting you. It's just that it came a little unexpectedly. I never realized you felt like that."

"Perhaps I never made it very clear. Gotto got in the way rather."

They sat together in silence for a while. Suddenly the easiness that had always been a mark of their companionship
138

had gone and there was some new emotion in its place—
something more serious and adult and tender. Jimmy watched
her for a moment or two before he spoke, hesitantly: "You
haven't answered yet."

Stella fingered his hand—shy and a little touched. "I guess
I'll have to think this one over," she said. "It's taken my breath
away a little."

"Why? We've been seeing each other very nearly every day
since we met. It's like night following day. It's a perfectly
normal step to take."

"It seems such a big one all the same."

"Think so? There are plenty of arguments for it. You kiss
me as though you mean it. I know *I* do. And, after all"—
Jimmy laughed a little nervously—"it's nearer to England
from here than it is to America. If you ever want to run home
to Mother, you won't have so far to go."

Stella began to play with the leaves of a geranium on the
edge of the verandah alongside her. "Honest, Jimmy dear, do
you really and truly mean it?"

"I've never been so serious in my life."

"It's these warm evenings, Jimmy, and the moon. These
African moons are pretty big."

"I'm too old to get moonstruck, Stella."

"Then it must be Gotto and all this fuss."

Jimmy stared at her suspiciously. "You're putting me off,"
he said. "You're trying to avoid answering me."

"No, I'm not."

"Well, what do you say?"

"Jimmy, I can't."

"Why not?" Jimmy looked startled and a little hurt, as
though her answer was unexpected.

"Now you're rushing me and I don't know."

"You must know."

Stella turned towards him. "I guess I like you an awful
lot, Jimmy dear, but we've not known each other very long."

139

"Long enough for me to be certain."

"Oh, Jimmy——"

"You don't love me." Jimmy's voice was suddenly flat.

"Yes—I mean, no. Jimmy, I don't know what I mean. I can't say 'yes' just like that. Give me time."

"Time!" Jimmy sounded a little indignant. "I thought you wouldn't need to debate it with yourself. The way you kissed me, the way we—well, the way we get on together, I thought you'd know. Do you want me to rescue you from a burning building or something before you make up your mind?"

"Jimmy, don't tease me. Just give me a little time. Just carry on as we were before——"

"You're asking something, Stella."

"I mean, just let it lie for a while. That's all."

"Let it hatch? Like an egg? That what you mean?"

"Jimmy, don't be unkind."

"I'm not being unkind. I feel pretty grim about it. I've said I want to marry you. You won't. That's why I feel grim. It's simple enough." He shrugged. "Strikes me," he commented glumly, "I've been paying too much blasted attention to Gotto and not enough to you. Here I've been for weeks gaily telling him how to run his love affairs and it seems I've been neglecting my own. From now on, he can sink or swim. I'm going to concentrate."

140

Two

JIMMY's mind was still in a state of turmoil when Twigg arrived—early the following morning when no one was expecting him. Relations between Jimmy and Gotto had remained strained and Twigg's appearance threw Jimmy, who was the first to meet him, into a state of panic. He must have set off before daylight for it was not long after breakfast that he bowled down to the bungalow in a cloud of red dust that swept on and past him in diminishing swirls as he halted his jeep.

"Hallo, Agnew," he said gaily, mopping his face with his purple handkerchief. "How's it going? Settled down yet? Everybody happy?"

"Oh, yes, we're fine, sir," Jimmy said with a sweeping enthusiasm he didn't feel. He regarded his superior nervously, dreading his reaction to what to him seemed an obviously dissatisfied mine. Gotto's behaviour had been growing more and more unpredictable for some time.

"Oh, yes," he repeated automatically, his mind chasing furiously through the events of the last few days. "We're fine."

"Good." Twigg gave him a sidelong inquisitive glance. "How are you getting on with friend Gotto?"

He seemed to be inviting confidences and it was on the tip of Jimmy's tongue to tell the truth, but a guilty feeling of plotting treachery behind Gotto's back led him to put the idea aside. After all, he decided weakly, there was no sense in causing trouble for a man with quite enough on his hands

141

already. He managed, therefore, to conceal the unrest from Twigg, and when he was asked about the fall in output, blamed it on faulty machinery.

Twigg seemed more than relieved not to be informed of friction but his eyebrows rose in surprise and he looked hard and unbelievingly at Jimmy. "H'm," he said. "Well—how's the cricket team going?"

Jimmy searched for an excuse. "Well, you see, sir," he pointed out, "we've been so busy getting things going, putting up the huts and all that, we never had the chance. But I think I've found a good spot for a pitch. A jolly good spot. We'll start as soon as we can."

"Good show." Twigg was looking round him as he talked. "Look slippy. I'm anxious to arrange a match with you up here. I've got a new fast bowler. Bee's knees, old boy. Laid out one of the foremen yesterday."

He flicked the dust from his clothes with an elegant finger. "Look, I'll just slip down to the workings and have a look round. Don't let me stop you doing whatever it was you *were* doing. See you at lunch."

Jimmy watched him with a sense of dread as he drove off but at lunch time when he sat at the table with Jimmy and Gotto, his amiability had not diminished. His questions showed that he had not missed much, however.

"Not got very far with the new level," he commented. "And that explosive store wants hurrying along a spot. Watch that. By the way, Momo tells me Joe Soloman's trying to corner all the rice in the place." He bent his head and tucked heartily into his curried chicken. "Can't have that, old boy," he said in mild rebuke to Gotto. "Better go along and see him. Use a bit of a threat if you like."

Jimmy looked up quickly, anxious to recruit Twigg's help. "How about you coming along yourself, sir?" he suggested hopefully. "Indian Joe might take more notice of you than us."

142

Twigg glanced out of the corner of his eye. Then he waved a hand without raising his head. "Oh, no," he said casually. "Leave it to you, old boy. Got to get back. You have a go at him. You'll be all right. Experience for you."

"Samuel Assissay's working for him now," Jimmy pointed out, tossing the ball back again.

Twigg's horse face lifted curiously at last. "Is he, by God?" He seemed on the point of a decision then he shelved it abruptly. "I thought he was going up-bush to his village. That's a bad thing."

"Think you'd better look into it while you're here, sir?" Jimmy hinted, remembering all that Romney had said.

Twigg flashed him a glance and ducked his head again. "Oh, I don't know, old boy. Just leave it alone. Just wait and see. I can't force him out. Mustn't be accused of harrying the natives. They're so touchy these days. So long as he's not on the mine premises and causing any trouble, let someone else worry about him. He's harmless. Just caught a dose of Sinner's Misery from Mrs. Swannack. That's all."

Jimmy subsided with a feeling of disappointment and Twigg turned to Gotto.

"Momo tells me you had a bit of trouble with a few shovel boys," he said. "And what's all this about fishermen?"

"The fishermen were trespassing," Gotto said quickly, his eyes on his plate.

"Can't do much harm, can they?"

"There are explosives about."

"They wouldn't know how to use them, old boy." Twigg shrugged amiably. "Have it your own way, of course. So long as there's no trouble. That's the important thing. And this shovel-boy business? What was that?"

"Only a fight between Temne and Mende," Gotto said. "They couldn't agree."

"I know." Twigg was busy with his food again. "Got to watch the devils. They're always squabbling. Mustn't have

143

too many of one or too many of the other up here. Jarvis always kept a nice balance. Ma-Imi doesn't matter so much. Nearer Freetown. More sophisticated. Don't worry about it so much there. But you're a bit isolated up here and they get jealous so damn' quickly. Pays to watch that."

Jimmy saw Gotto flash a quick glance at him, then he lowered his head and stared at his plate again.

"See Momo," Twigg advised cheerfully. "He'll fix it. Momo's a good man. See what he says."

"He's not very helpful," Gotto mumbled. "He doesn't like me, I'm afraid."

"Really? Why ever not?" Twigg's eyebrows shot up as though he couldn't believe it possible for anyone to dislike anyone, least of all Gotto, and Jimmy realized with a wretched feeling of frustration that his chief aim in life was to avoid trouble.

"I had to pull him up for telling me my job," Gotto was saying. "That's all. The foremen and shift bosses aren't supposed to tell *us* how to run the place, are they?"

Twigg looked up momentarily. "Well, no," he agreed. "That's quite right. Watch that." He seemed suddenly anxious to drop the matter.

"After all," Gotto went on dogmatically. "It's just something you can't have. You do trust me, of course? If you don't, you'd better have me back at Ma-Imi."

Twigg looked panic-stricken as he replied. "Oh, no, old boy. I trust you all right. That's why I sent you up here. Thought you were just the man for the job. Keep you busy till you go home. You've not long now, have you?"

Jimmy watched them with a sick feeling that he was doomed to spend the rest of his stay in Africa in Amama with only Gotto for a companion. With the amiable, too-easy-going Twigg as the one person who could alter the arrangement, he could see no likelihood of either himself or Gotto being removed.

144

After lunch, Twigg—who seemed glad to escape—disappeared in his car to see Romney and Swannack and made no further reference to the mine until he was ready to leave for Ma-Imi.

"Just keep that old ironstone coming down and you'll be all right," he said, pressing the starter. "And get along to see Indian Joe and tell him I'll put the District Commissioner on his trail if he doesn't keep off the rice."

"You could do so much more than we can, sir," Jimmy shouted as Twigg revved the engine. It was beginning to dawn on him that Twigg was throwing all the awful onus for curbing Gotto entirely on to himself.

Twigg waved again. "Oh, I don't know, old boy," he bawled as he let in the clutch. "Leave it to you two. Don't like to make trouble. Wait and see's my policy."

Two hours later, Jimmy accompanied Gotto to see Indian Joe. It required an argument that left him tired, an argument far too long for the heat of the late afternoon. Gotto obviously had no desire to worry about rice and he brought to bear every excuse he could think of : he was inclined to leave it until he got an official complaint. If Twigg wanted it doing, he should do his own dirty work. And so long as the Africans worked, he couldn't see any necessity to worry about it anyway.

"Listen, Gotty," Jimmy said patiently. "Making a success of this job here in Amama is important to you, isn't it?"

Gotto stared at him. "Yes," he said grudgingly. "I suppose it is."

"Well, if you get the shovel boys and the lorry drivers and the mechanics packing in because they're hungry, that won't be very successful, will it? After all, Alf Momo's worried about it and he ought to know."

"I'm not used to being told what to do by a wog, even when he's your pet." Gotto began to stoop, his head sunk

145

low on his shoulders as though he were in a fight. "I'm in charge, not him."

"Oh, Lord, man——" Jimmy suddenly lost patience, "let's stop talking about the Africans as though they were a species of monkey or something. And as for being in charge, it's probably because Twiggy couldn't spare anyone else— or because you didn't play for his blasted cricket team or something. Now let's go and see Indian Joe."

Joe Soloman's home was an overcrowded set of rooms at the back of his store, a makeshift bungalow attached to the main flyblown façade that belonged to the shop. On the iron roof, a couple of vultures hopped about, their scaly claws scraping and clattering on the corrugations.

Jimmy and Gotto were shown to the residential quarter of the building by Samuel Assissay who approached them from behind his counter at the back of the dark stuffy store. His glasses shone with his fervour and the rags Jimmy had seen him wearing on the journey from Ma-Imi had been replaced by neat khaki. Indian Joe was obviously looking after him.

"Oh, my people that dwellest in Zion," he proclaimed in a cranky chant that was made into music by the resonance of his voice. "Be not afraid of the Assyrian, though he smite thee with the rod——"

"We're *not* afraid of the Assyrian," Jimmy said, still in a bad temper. "We never were."

"You're getting the hang of things quickly," Gotto said from behind him. "Preparing to take over when you've edged me out?"

"You're not edged out yet, Gotty. So bear in mind it's your pigeon when we see Indian Joe. You're supposed to be in charge. You said so yourself. Remember?"

Zaidee Soloman met them at the end of a long passage that was crammed with sacks of what looked suspiciously like rice. The ceilings and walls were festooned with cheap kerosene lamps, alarm clocks, and buckets, and alongside were stacked rolls of gaudy cotton and silk. On the corrugated iron of the roof, they could still hear the feet of the vultures.

Zaidee came forward, a dramatic figure in a tight-fitting cotton T-shirt and the bright green trousers she had worn in church. It was quite clear she wore very little else besides and Jimmy began to understand Earnshaw's attachment to her.

"Good afternoon, gentlemen," she said, turning on them hot black eyes touched with kohl. "Please. This way."

The residential part of the house was furnished with bamboo and cane with an incongruous admixture of heavy Edwardian furniture that added to the gloom and stuffiness. Its smell was one of dust and sun-dried wood. On the walls were a gaudy print of the battle of Magersfontein and several enormous sepia pictures of children in the hats and lace pinafores of before the First World War. Over the door with a plan of the Allied battle fleets of 1941, cut from the *Illustrated London News* was a newspaper picture of the Queen pushed into a frame, and opposite were two or three pictures of Zaidee in what appeared to be a Freetown photographer's idea of a Hollywood starlet's pose.

Indian Joe was sprawled on a horsehair settee, his heavy body flowing over the edges. He was eating peaches with a spoon from the can. "Gentlemen," he said. "Peace be with you. This is an honour. Sit down. Coffee for the gentlemen from the mine, Zaidee, my daughter."

"Not for me," Gotto said quickly and, in an attitude of defiance, Jimmy accepted a cup of the thick, sickly coffee, conscious of Zaidee's bold appraising eyes on him as she handed it to him, and the disturbing shape of her high breasts beneath the T-shirt.

Indian Joe put down his can of peaches and spoon with a clatter and pushed a small table containing a whisky bottle and soda syphon into the centre of the room.

"Now, gentlemen," he said. "What brings you here to honour my household?"

147

Jimmy looked pointedly at Gotto who flashed him a desperate, baited glance. Deliberately, Jimmy buried his nose in his coffee cup and made no effort to help.

"Well, look here——" Gotto began to mumble.

"First a drink, Mr. Gotto!"

Gotto swallowed quickly. "Not for me," he said again. "Mr. Agnew?"

Indian Joe poured a drink and sat back, picking up the peach tin and starting to eat again, the thick syrup running down his flabby chin.

"You are new to Amama, Mr. Agnew," he said. "You like it?"

Jimmy glanced at Gotto who was sitting nervously on the edge of his chair, his expression one of distaste for his surroundings.

"Yes, I like it," he said shortly.

"That's wonderful." Indian Joe beamed, showing a mouthful of gold teeth. "Isn't it, Zaidee? Mr. Agnew likes our Amama."

Gotto caught Jimmy's eyes again and he began to speak.

"We came here——" he said when Indian Joe held up his fat hand.

"A moment, Mr. Gotto. Don't let us hurry too much. It's too hot to hurry in Sierra Leone."

Gotto subsided, flushing, his eyes glowing with anger.

"I like someone who comes to Sierra Leone and enjoys it," the Syrian went on. "I like to dwell on it. Too long it has had a bad reputation. Many years ago, your English Mary Kingsley wrote that anyone who makes up his mind to come to West Africa should promptly unmake it and go to Scotland instead." He laughed softly and Gotto leaned forward again.

"Have you read Mary Kingsley, Mr. Agnew?" Indian Joe said quickly, ignoring him, so that he remained leaning forward, rubbing his nose and trying to pretend he hadn't been about to speak.

148

The conversation continued with difficulty, with Indian Joe doing most of the talking, while the frustrated Gotto made several false starts to put in his complaint. Zaidee stood in the shadows behind her father's chair, saying nothing, her coffee face bland and blank-eyed as an animal's.

Eventually, Indian Joe looked up at her. "Surely we ought to provide these gentlemen with food, my daughter," he said. "We Syrians are noted for our hospitality."

"Not for me," Gotto said again between his teeth.

"Mr. Agnew?"

"Well—" Jimmy was almost enjoying himself as he watched Gotto's growing restlessness—"I think we ought to get on with what we came to see you about."

"Ah, yes! Of course. The thing you came to see me about. Well, now, Mr. Gotto—" Indian Joe turned round—"you have come to complain about the rice shortage, I suppose. Every time rice is short, Indian Joe is blamed. Always Indian Joe has some underhand reason for withholding food."

"That is the complaint against all Syrians, father," Zaidee said in her low voice. "Always we are guilty until we are proved innocent. Always we are the enemy. We have not the standing of the professional Englishman nor even of the hired black labourer."

"Oh, I wouldn't say that," Jimmy protested, while inside him some instinct shouted a warning of treachery too subtle to avoid. "That's not quite what we came to say!"

Vaguely, he could see Gotto fidgeting on the chair alongside him and as he finished speaking, he stood bolt upright, his face red.

"I can tell you this straight," he said loudly. "Any funny business and I go straight to the District Commissioner."

Indian Joe's smile was blank and indifferent. Zaidee's opaque eyes narrowed but her aquiline Syrian features remained unmoved.

149

Gotto glared, more embarrassed than angry at their calmness.

"Listen," he shouted. "I didn't want to come and argue with you over a sack or two of rice. But I was told to and so I have. I'm warning you. We're having no funny business."

"Mr. Gotto isn't threatening us, is he?" Zaidee asked.

"Oh, God!" His face crimson, Gotto moved to the door, stumbling noisily over the clumsy furniture. "What the hell's the use of arguing with them? They don't understand King's English."

Again Jimmy saw Zaidee's furious glance and he blushed for shame. He started to apologize, stammered to silence, then began to back out after Gotto, fell over the doorstep and found himself—dazzled by the flare of the sunshine after the gloom—in a dirt yard at the back of the house, in a puther of flying chickens. Gotto was standing near by, his face dark with anger and embarrassment, glaring round him for the gateway to the road.

Indian Joe's face was still unchanged as he stared through the doorway at them, the perspiration shining in small beads on his upper lip.

A chicken feather ludicrous on his hair, Jimmy made a last attempt at an apology, dried up, offered a sickly smile instead, then turned, trying to make out where he was.

They were surrounded by the three whitewashed walls of Indian Joe's home, shop and bar. The scrawny chickens were clustered now by the wall farthest away from them, clucking noisily round a pile of tin cans, most of which Jimmy noticed were labelled 'Peaches'. In the middle of the yard a bare white tree, like a bleached skeleton, threw the only fraction of shadow there was and the low sun beating into the yard rebounded from the walls like the open door of an oven.

"How the hell do you get out of here?" Jimmy said.

"God knows!"

"Well, you got us into this mess. You get us out."

150

"I didn't suggest coming here," Gotto retaliated furiously.

"Oh, hell, come on," Jimmy snarled. "We'll be standing here all day."

He turned and, followed by Gotto, ploughed his way through the group of hens which splintered immediately into a whirl of noise and flying feathers. A vulture, staring suspiciously from near the pile of peach tins, lolloped away, the dust spattering from its large feet as it flapped awkwardly to the bare skeletal tree.

They thrust their way through the banana plants and scrub that edged the only part of the yard which was not bounded by a wall and found themselves in the roadway again.

"That was a damned silly thing to do," Jimmy exploded in disgust as he slammed the car door after himself.

Gotto was slumped in the front passenger seat, deflated, his anger dispersed. "Let's get away from here," he said.

"Blowing up like that," Jimmy fumed as he pushed in the gear.

"If I hadn't blown up," Gotto shouted, sitting up straight, "they'd have had you eating out of their hands. I'm damned if I'm going to kow-tow to a wog."

"For God's sake," Jimmy snapped, "stop saying that!" He started the car with a jerk that clicked their heads back, bitterly conscious that what Gotto had said was true and that he had been hypnotized by Zaidee's handsome eyes.

He swung the car savagely round a bend in the road towards the mine. "Fat lot we got out of it," he said. "Now I suppose he'll be all the more determined to withhold the rice, the way you spoke to him. All that tripe about King's English. If you'd left it to me, at least we shouldn't have had a barney like that. I was just getting on all right with them."

"You'd have been inviting that damned woman down to the mine for dinner or something."

Jimmy flushed guiltily. "Don't talk rot," he snapped. "You've got to feel your way. You can't go insulting people.

151

We might have jollied the old boy into being more decent."

"I'm damned if I'm going to bow and scrape to a wog."

"Wog, wog, wog," Jimmy snarled bitterly. "Is that the only bloody word you know?"

Gotto gave him a long angry glare, then, as the car shrieked to a stop outside the bungalow in a cloud of drifting red dust, he climbed out and stalked away in silence. Jimmy sat staring at the steering wheel for a while, made all the more savage by the knowledge that he had not been particularly helpful and, indeed, that their humiliation could really be laid at his door for forcing Gotto to do the talking. It occurred to him suddenly that the quarrel had probably been deliberately provoked by the Syrian to enable him to evade the tricky subject of rice, and his frown grew deeper. Bitterly, realizing he was a tyro in the art of crafty diplomacy, he climbed out of the car and slammed the door with a crash that set it rocking on its springs.

Three

GOTTO would never have been an easy person for Jimmy to live with—there was too vast a difference between their temperaments—but after the visit to Indian Joe, the relations between them went from bad to worse.

It would have required a genius to have extracted much enjoyment out of Gotto's company, but Jimmy had managed to put up with him, neither liking nor disliking him particularly, until now, when he found himself dodging him at meal times, hanging about in the shower to avoid eating with him, or remaining at the office until he was certain he was out of the way.

He even began to take a delight in indulging in pinpricks, taking a perverse pleasure in making a great show of setting off for his evenings with Stella; going out of his way to be as friendly as possible to Alf Momo and the black foremen when Gotto was around; organizing his football team of small boys outside the bungalow at lunch time when he liked to doze and encouraging them to make as much noise as possible when the orange ball burst; deliberately describing Earnshaw as an African pioneer; trailing his coat all the time with every possible device, enjoying all the little things guaranteed to provoke Gotto to anger, knowing he was not mentally equipped to argue for long, so that he eventually retired hurt and unhappy into his shell. In his dislike, Jimmy began to enjoy even that.

It wasn't hard to cause Gotto misery. He was desperate for company and conversation but he seemed to have quarrelled with everyone who might help him. Even Amadu was by now conducting a feud of his own so that Gotto could never get his washing done properly or on time. Every other day he was involved in some noisy argument with the house-boy that brought him almost to tears with rage and frustration.

"My washing"—the contest took place with monotonous regularity—"why haven't I got any clean khaki?"

"Boss"—Amadu's black face was all innocence—"you no' lay 'um out."

"It was on my bed when I left the bungalow this morning."

"Boss, no." Amadu was placidly insistent, his light voice flat and unworried, his face smooth in its contempt. "No see 'um, Boss."

"Well, do it now then."

"Boss"—Amadu was still infuriatingly untroubled about it all—"no can do. Amadu no got charcoal for hiron. All charcoal used this afternoon to hiron Boss Jimmy's clothes. I no see yours. I catch charcoal tonight when I go to village."

Gotto glared, certain he was listening to lies, then he waved Amadu away. As he disappeared, his bare feet slapping on the concrete floor, Gotto sank into a chair, mopping his face.

"Why don't these black devils like me, Agnew?" he said wearily, his eyes anguished with defeat. "God, I try hard. They like that bastard Earnshaw, and look at the way he treats 'em. I can't even get my washing done properly. Yet Earnshaw kicks them and swears at them and calls them niggers and they'd do anything for him. Why?"

His scowl grew deeper as he looked at Jimmy. "How is it," he demanded angrily. "*you* can always get *your* washing done?"

"Try giving him a cigarette or two from time to time," Jimmy suggested. "Cigarettes seem to be good for the eye-sight. He never misses mine. It's a sort of blackmail, in case you haven't noticed."

154

"It's not just the cigarettes," Gotto snapped. "It wouldn't make any difference if I gave him hundreds."

Jimmy paused before he replied. "O.K.," he said slowly. "How about trying a little sweetness and light? That might help a bit."

As Gotto stalked to his room, still clutching a towel round his loins, to put on the crumpled khaki of the night before, Jimmy stared after him, aware that the argument would have its repercussions in the working of the mine. Like Earnshaw, he had now learned enough about Gotto to realize that no argument finished when the last word was spoken.

He was quite right. Immediately, there was a rash of incidents provoked by nothing more than Gotto's spitefulness as he worked off his feelings against Amadu on the boys at the mine. The only fisherman who dared to show his nose at the jetty was immediately seized by Sergeant Asimani on Gotto's orders and hustled down to the calaboose in Amama Town, and a dispute in the workings led to a deputation of union officials, which ended in a blazing row. Within two days, Alf Momo had appeared at Jimmy's side at the jetty with a complaint.

"Boss Jimmy," he said, his voice trembling with emotion, "I work for Boss Twigg since I was a piccaninny. The war come, I work for the Air Force building runways. I work with good man, bad man, clever man, fool man, but I never see Africans treated like this. That Boss Gotto, he is no good."

Jimmy wearily wiped the perspiration off his face with his hands. "You're probably right at that, Alf," he said.

"Boss, he is no good for Amama. He cause trouble. Boys no like him. He tell me 'You lazy.' He say 'You spoil the mine!' Boss, I am not lazy. I work hard for all the white bosses. Even Boss Gotto. I do not like him but I work hard. I wait for a long time before I complain. Now the time comes."

"I know, I know, Alf." Jimmy leaned heavily on the door of the station wagon, and offered a cigarette.

155

"Boss, I am not a clever man. I have not been to college and I could not get big job in big mine like Ma-Imi or Marampa. But I have taught myself to read and other things. What I know here I have learned over many years. I am not always wrong."

"Alf, I know that. You know I know it, don't you?"

"Yes, Boss Jimmy. I do."

"What do the union people think about it all?"

Momo frowned unhappily. "Boss Jimmy, union officials think they go to Freetown. They very displeased."

"I see. Alf, can you call 'em off for a while?"

"Boss, I am not union official."

"No, I know. But you're Alfred Momo."

Momo grinned, pleased at the implied compliment.

"Just for a bit, Alf."

"O.K., Boss Jimmy. I tell 'em." Momo grinned again. "Boss Jimmy, other black boys blame you. They think you like *him*"—he used the word as an insult. "But *I* know. I do not blame you, Boss Jimmy."

"Thanks, Alf. That's nice to know."

Jimmy felt a little overwhelmed. He had arrived in Sierra Leone to be a mining engineer and he was coping as psychiatrist, diplomatist and squire of Twigg's responsibilities. "Listen, Alf," he said. "I'll talk to Boss Twigg. As soon as I get the chance. Just hold on a bit. He's taking a long time to settle down. That's all."

"Plenty bad man, Boss," Momo insisted.

"Not really, Alf. He's sick, Alf. I'll get rid of him, somehow though. I'll tell Twigg. Honest I will."

But as Momo disappeared, Jimmy remembered the plea for mercy he saw in Gotto's eyes every time he was hurt or offended and he knew he never would.

Inevitably it was Earnshaw who first heard the rumours that the fishermen from King Tim were planning retaliation.

156

Earnshaw had sources of information that were denied even to Romney. In his hole-in-the-corner, catch-as-catch-can methods of business, it paid him to have his spies up and down the river at the various points where his boats put in with supplies, and it was through Suri, his coxswain, that he first heard the stories of revenge. There was a lot about Earnshaw that probably wouldn't have stood up to investigation. Everyone knew of the affair between him and Zaidee Soloman and why Suri waited late into the night on the verandah of her house. Everyone knew why the black Cadillac she drove for Indian Joe was parked under the cotton trees near Earnshaw's bungalow after the sun had disappeared and that it was not Indian Joe who kept her in the expensive clothes she fancied. Doubtless Earnshaw cheated at cards and was a congenital liar. Doubtless in his years of circling the earth he had forged cheques and seduced other men's wives, but there was something about him which daily confirmed Jimmy's first impression of him—that he knew where he was going and what he was talking about. No white man who lived and dressed as he did could have made a success of his life in Sierra Leone unless he did.

As he said to Jimmy: "I've poached pheasants in my time. I've poached salmon. I've poached blokes—agents outa Dakar and Casablanca up the coast during the war—and when I say the fishermen is after you, me old china, you can take it from me as the solid bar gold that they are. There's no flies on me."

"What'll they do?"

"Rifle the bungalow and mizzle with your dough. That's what Suri says, so keep your things locked up so the connivering bastards get the bare nixey."

Jimmy duly locked up his treasures in one of the warped drawers and, in his growing dislike of Gotto, kept the information to himself until his conscience got the better of him and

157

he passed it on. Gotto's response to the news was immediate and typical.

"No blasted black man can get anything out of my bedroom when I'm sleeping there," he said. "And they know it. They won't come."

But long after Jimmy had ceased worrying about them, they came silently in their canoes after dark and broke open the mine stores. Shadowy black figures, greased with palm oil, removed shovels, electric cable and spare parts for the lorries, most of them useless as loot, and carried them down to the canoes drawn up on the mud near the jetty. Then they crept to the bungalow through the bush, their bodies glinting under the oil in the faint light of the stars that peeped past the palm fronds, and removed food from the kitchen and all of Amadu's chickens from their hut at the back of the bungalow without a squawk. And finally they entered the bedrooms and made away with all the spare cash from the pockets of the trousers they found alongside the beds.

Gotto's reaction was one of fury at the theft and despair that the hated black men could get into his room and disappear again without being seen. Immediately, thoughts of being murdered in his bed rushed through his mind as he dragged Jimmy along to Earnshaw to demand the loan of a gun.

Not unnaturally, Earnshaw refused.

"Think I am?" he demanded. "Who you going to shoot, anyway?"

"Those damned wogs the next time they get into the bungalow."

"Don't talk wet, old lad," Earnshaw said calmly. "You'll never see 'em long enough to get a shot at 'em—even if you see 'em at all."

"You're on their side!" Gotto's anger burst out in a shout. "You have been all the time. You're another blasted nigger-lover like Romney. I'm going straight down to Sergeant Asimani. I'll get a guard."

158

"Whyn't you challenge 'em to a duel instead? Pistols for two and corffee for one. Or find the ringleader and beat each other to death with old banana skins?"

"That's stopped his little gallop," Earnshaw said to Jimmy as they watched Gotto drive away. "Catch me lending *him* a gun. He go and plug some bloke and then he be in real trouble. He might even knock you off one night, old lad, after you come back in the dark from your sprazzing at the Swannacks."

Jimmy was glaring along the straight sunlit road after the car. "What the hell am I going to do with the clot?" he asked angrily. "The next thing we know the District Commissioner'll hear about it and complain to Twigg. Then out goes Gotto. Even Twigg couldn't turn a deaf ear to *him*. It's all so stupid. They were doing no harm with their boats and Asimani's bound to be on their side. He won't stir himself much."

"No, he won't and when Master-mind cottons on to it, he's going to waltz hisself down to the District Commissioner and then the fat'll be in the fire anyway. He's a bright 'erb, that D.C., and he'd want to know what caused it all in the first place and then—napoo, out goes Gotto, and his ma's in the workhouse or something and me and you is calling usselves names for doing it across her."

When Jimmy and Earnshaw returned from the jetty at lunch time, they found all the labourers, digger-handlers and drivers outside the office in a ragged line that ballooned here and there and broke into groups of gesticulating men. There was quite a lot of noise and as they drew near they could hear an angry shouting that made Jimmy's heart sink.

"Archie," he said, as they made their way past the older men who squatted like frogs, under the trees, waiting with untroubled patience, accepting the uproar with the African's

159

bland indifference to time. "Something tells me he's cracking that whip again."

"He's a right boy, ain't he?" Earnshaw said wearily. "Every day he comes down here, brisk as a kipper, itching to spit in some bloke's eye for his morning exercise."

The crowd round the door opened to let them through and flooded after them, shouting indignantly. The noise inside the office was worse than it was outside. Protesting men were passing through in a line, Clerk Smith, his face contorted into a look of importance, searching them by patting their ragged shorts, in most cases the only garment they wore, while Gotto sat on the desk with a pad of paper, surrounded by cigarette butts.

"What the hell's all this?" Jimmy asked.

"One of these black bastards pinched my money,"Gotto said. "So I'm giving 'em the once-over. That's all. Simple enough."

"And are the fools letting you?"

Gotto grinned, a hard, humourless grin. "They've got to. I'm giving them a note when they've finished. Without it they won't draw their wages."

Jimmy's mouth dropped open. He spluttered for a while as his anger choked him, then he managed to burst out again. "Do you honestly think they'd be potty enough to bring your blasted money to work if they *had* pinched it? And, anyway, how will you identify it as yours?"

"There were some notes in my pocket," Gotto said cheerfully. "If we find any notes on these bastards, I'll want to know where he got 'em. I'll whip him straight down to Asimani. They don't get paid enough to carry notes around."

"Have you found any yet?"

"No."

"Nor will you. God, man, where would they hide it? Most of 'em only wear a pair of shorts."

"I've read stories of black men in the diamond mines hiding diamonds up their backsides."

160

Earnshaw, who was leaning on the window frame, bored, contemptuous and indifferent, gave a sudden dry laugh.

"Oh, Jesus," he said loudly. "You got a smashing job there. You looking at every one?"

"No, Boss"—Clerk Smith looked up with an important frown—"black boys no like."

Earnshaw nodded understandingly. "Perhaps they reckon their behinds is private," he said.

Gotto was walking up and down now, softly beating one fist against the palm of the other. "They might think they've got the upper hand," he said. "But they've not. An Englishman always wins the last battle."

Earnshaw looked up once more. "We at war again?" he asked.

Gotto spared him an angry contemptuous glance and looked round at Jimmy. "You've got to lick 'em in a thing like this," he announced. "Or you'll never get 'em to do as they're told."

Jimmy sighed. "Is it all that important?" he asked. "God, man, there are always stoppages over some damn' thing or other these days. It might interest you to know that Twigg's noticed the output's falling. Doesn't that mean anything to you?"

"Who told you he's noticed?"

"He asked me about it when he came up."

"Why didn't he ask me? Nobody asks me anything. And how did he find out?"

"He's got eyes, mate," Earnshaw said. "One each side of his nose."

Gotto pointedly ignored him. "I wish you'd stop worrying about the output," he said peevishly to Jimmy. "I've got everything under control. Nobody's getting agitated but you lot."

"Nobody but us lot and the nigs," Earnshaw growled.

Gotto sneered. "I'll soon sort *them* out. Never fear."

"You ain't been very successful up to press, old lad."

"Don't call me old lad," Gotto snapped, the sweat standing out on his face at his anger.

"O.K., old lad."

Gotto glared. "Perhaps you can do better. How about having a go?"

"No, thanks, old lad. I'll leave it to you. Besides, tomorrer, I'm off for a day or two to Freetown for me annual constitutional before the rains come. My advice is play ball with the nigs and your troubles are over. These chaps in Sierra Leone are a matey lot if you don't muck 'em about. Why not try and be pally with 'em?"

"Pally? With a lot of Africans? *You* can be if you like."

Earnshaw looked up at Gotto under a dusty grey eyebrow. "I am, mate. And *I* don't get no trouble. And them fishermen are a decent lot, if you treat 'em right."

"You think it was the fishermen?"

"Course it was."

"Right," Gotto turned to Clerk Smith. "You can let the rest go. I'll get Asimani in on this, I'll go through that bloody village at King Tim again—with a tooth comb."

Jimmy watched him walk away from the office and start his car. Earnshaw had sat down at the desk.

"Lemme out, lemme out," he was croaking in a dry dusty voice that sounded as though it had been dug out of a coffin. "It gets more like a mad-house every day. I wish somebody back home in London would decide he needs him in England." He lifted his head. "It can't be long, old lad, can it, before he goes?"

Jimmy was still staring through the door. "Archie," he said. "He's heading for Amama Town. He's gone for Sargy Asimani."

Earnshaw clasped his hands to his dusty hair in mock horror. "Oh, Jesus," he said. "And I sent him. What I gone and done now?"

162

Four

EARNSHAW turned up from his holiday a week later, with a hangover and eyes that looked like knot-holes in wood. His hand was unsteady and he was heavily disinterested in anything.

"How's it go, old lad?" he asked Jimmy as they met by the jetty. "Pardon my high spirits, but I got ever such a jolly mood on just now. I spent the last few days getting meself a beautiful crop of ulcers dodging in and out of bars. My inside's fizzing like a bottle of pale ale. How's the Daring Young Man on the Flying Trapeze? He take my advice?"

"No," Jimmy said glumly. "In fact, he's showing his contempt for it by working it off on the boys."

Earnshaw looked quickly at him, with a bleary eye full of the sad, stale wisdom of the Coast. "What's the matter, cock? You got saddle sores?"

"He's down with Sargy Asimani at the moment," Jimmy said. "He had his room raided again last night. They stole his clothes this time. And they've lifted more stuff from the mine stores. I've got Asimani to keep quiet for the time being but it can't go on." He paused, drew a deep breath and continued. "We had a bloke killed by blasting yesterday. It shouldn't have happened. It needn't have happened. But they were thinking too much about Gotto and not enough about their job."

Earnshaw took off his hat and mopped his face with a dirty handkerchief. "How's the rice situation?" he asked soberly.

"Lousy. Indian Joe got raided too, last night. They know he's got rice hidden away somewhere."

163

"You know something, son?" Earnshaw said. "Summat's going to blow up one of these days. I can feel it in me bones. He's dangerous. I know. I'm dead 'ot on danger."

"Thank God he's due to go home soon," Jimmy said fervently.

Earnshaw squinted up the winding road to the mine and nudged him. "Kid," he said. "Put on your dancing pumps and report to the ballroom for a waltz. Here comes His Master's Voice."

Clerk Smith emerged out of the approaching cloud of dust on his noisy old bicycle and almost fell into Jimmy's arms.

"What the hell is it this time?" Jimmy demanded angrily.

"Boss. Labourer done get hurt."

"Another?"

"Yassah. Bryma Komorra. De digger bucket done hit him. Boss Momo send for Ole Doc. He hurt plenty bad."

They found Romney kneeling on the ground alongside the still dusty form of one of the labourers whose black face was flecked with specks of blood.

"How bad is it, Doc?" Jimmy asked.

"Bad as it can be without being fatal. Fractured skull." Romney looked up, his heavy face serious. "How did it happen, Jimmy?"

Jimmy shrugged. "You know as much as I do, Doc. Arguing about Gotto, I suppose, like the last one, and not watching what he was doing."

He stared at the dusty ground and his eyes found their way to the silent figure of the injured man.

"What is he, Doc? Temne?"

"Yes, so I'm told."

Jimmy sighed. "I suppose that means a row in the town," he said.

That night the noise of mourning could be heard continually from the moment the sun set in its thunderous glory.

164

The drums began beating solidly and the mourning party spread a little under the influence of palm wine and native beer and the bottles of gin which Indian Joe had generously provided to assist the wailing, until it began to include people who were in no way related to the injured man—people who merely wanted to get drunk, noisy people and people who wanted to celebrate, and before long they could hear the shrieks of laughter, and the tinkling of the native xylophones chanting their monotonous tune. There were several big fires blazing round Amama Town and, inevitably, Samuel Assissay was doing the round of the parties, breathing fire and slaughter and making the most of the occasion to preach insurrection.

The drumming had reached a breathless pitch that set the whole town throbbing when Jimmy arrived at the Swannacks', and as he and Stella sat behind the mosquito mesh on the verandah, they could see a steady procession of people moving through the streets. The whole place seemed to be on the move, and the glow of passing lanterns and torches lit up the great leaves of the banana plants by Swannack's front gate.

Swannack seemed worried and the tufts of hair on his face which seemed to move about like a weather-vane according to his mood seemed limp and dispirited.

"Bad thing, this accident today, son," he said to Jimmy as he stood by the door, outlined by the fires that were burning down the road. He waved his cigar to shift the flies from round his head. "That's two in two days. The people are upset. There's a lot of noise down there."

Mrs. Swannack put her head round the door from the other room where she was conducting in hygiene and mothercraft a class of village women whose high-pitched chatter came through to them in bursts.

"There's too much laughter in the village, Father," she said aggressively. "Too much drinking. That poor man's soul's only an excuse for licence."

"They always make this noise," Swannack said patiently. "They're always looking for an excuse to make a noise. They sure are fast off the mark for a mourning or a celebration."

Mrs. Swannack glared suspiciously at the crowds. "I don't trust 'em," she said loudly. "They're too quick to celebrate these days but they don't come to church with the same speed."

"This is only high spirits, Mother," Swannack said gently. "The Lord will always prevail. If I went out and preached the Word now to them, they'd come, excited as they are."

"And probably burn the place down, the liquor they've been taking."

As Mrs. Swannack went back to her class, muttering rough-handed Old Testament texts, Swannack gave Jimmy his evening tot of gin—what Earnshaw was in the habit of calling "enough to drown a flea"—and settled himself down for a talk.

"Gin warms the soul as much as a good rousing hymn," he said, "but don't say *I* said so or Old Doc would tell me it's easier to make a convert with it than with prayer." He looked up at Jimmy. "Son," he went on seriously, "this afternoon I was approached in the town to denounce your friend Gotto in the pulpit——"

"Mr. Swannack," Jimmy pointed out, "he's not my friend."

Swannack waved a hand. "No, I guess not. But this boy who was injured today, he belonged to my flock and I was told I must denounce Gotto as an oppressor of the black races."

"Sounds a familiar line. Who by?"

"I don't know, Jimmy. Guy I never saw before. Looked like he came from Freetown. Smart suit. Glasses. Samuel Assissay was with him."

"I thought he might be." Jimmy's brow was wrinkled. "Looks as if the vultures are gathering. What did you say to him?"

166

Swannack rubbed his nose uneasily. "I figured it wasn't any of my business, son. I told him so."

Jimmy lit a cigarette. No, it's no one's business, he thought gloomily. Nobody wants Gotto. Not Twigg. Not Romney. Not Earnshaw. Not you. Nobody. That leaves me. Only me. He felt suddenly weary with the weight of his responsibility.

"What did he say?"

"Oh, he made oblique references to other means of getting rid of him."

"Father," Mrs. Swannack bawled from the other side of the house. "Aren't you tired of playing gooseberry?"

"Yes, Mother. Coming now." Swannack turned again to Jimmy. "I figured I'd better pass it on to you, son. Thought you'd like to know."

"Thanks," Jimmy said heavily.

"What are you going to do?"

"What do you advise?"

"Well——" Swannack rubbed his nose again—"I guess it's none of my concern. Gotto belongs to the mine. He isn't a member of my flock and the chances of me enfolding him into this church are small, I guess, now."

Jimmy sighed. "Anyway, thanks, Mr. Swannack."

"Sure. Nothing at all. Nothing at all."

"Father!"

Swannack scowled like a sulky schoolboy and the hairs on his face seemed to revive a little under his annoyance.

"Stella," he commented as he shuffled out, "your mother has more power in her command than the word of the Lord Himself."

Stella watched him disappear, flapping his hands in argument as he joined Mrs. Swannack round the door, then she began to stare towards Amama Town and the crowds again.

"They look too excited for comfort to me," she said. "That's quite a time they're having down there."

167

"I've a feeling it's not the last either," Jimmy said heavily. "I've a nasty suspicion that there's worse to come."

"Is it tough, Jimmy?" Stella asked quietly.

Jimmy nodded. "What did I pick myself in on?" he asked. "Who'd have thought when I signed up for this job that I'd find Gotto waiting for me. Hell, I think he hates the very earth of Africa. He hates the trees, the grass, the mountains, the sun, the swamps, and especially the mosquitoes."

"Hard to please, isn't he?"

"We haven't seen him for days. He spends all his time over at King Tim with Sargy Asimani trying to mount a full-scale investigation. Asimani's bored to tears with him but he's trying hard to satisfy him without actually picking him a winner."

"Have they found any loot?"

"No. Nothing. He's only managed to make a lot more enemies and hear a lot of noisy threats that keep him indoors as soon as the sun goes down. Since Earnshaw wouldn't lend him a gun, he's taken to sleeping with the light on. It only serves to make him more tired and irritable. He locks everything up now—everything—and gives himself the heeby-jeebies because he has to unfasten half a dozen locks every time he wants a handkerchief to blow his nose," Jimmy grinned. "Hell, he's only to shove his stuff in one of those warped drawers and give it a damn' good slam. It'd take six strong men to get it out then."

He looked at Stella, his smile dying again. "Stella, these people aren't hard to please. They're a good-natured crowd and there's nothing they like better than to laugh. If only he'd pull their legs a bit. They'd love it."

"You can't do that, Jimmy dear, with a temperament like he's got. Even supposing he tried it, it wouldn't go down the same way as when you and Earnshaw do it. And, anyway, I suppose he's not to blame for his temperament. The poor man's been starved of affection."

168

"He's been starved of something. Brains, I suspect."

"He's probably never had much love, Jimmy, from what you say. His mother doesn't seem to do much except complain. His girl friend doesn't come across."

"Neither does mine."

Stella ignored him. "In fact," she said. "Nobody seems to like the man."

"What do you expect? You get nothing out of this life unless you put something into it."

"He tries hard, Jimmy. Or he did at first."

Jimmy nodded. "I suppose you're right," he said heavily. "You usually are. But there's nothing I can do. God knows, I've tried hard enough. I even persuaded Earnshaw to try, too. You know what happened."

He looked at Stella. "Stella, what are we going to do with him? You're wise as well as beautiful. What would *you* do?"

"Under the circumstances, I know what I'd do. It's tough on him, but he's not the only one concerned. I'd let someone know."

"Oh, Lord, I can't go telling tales about him. He *is* supposed to be in charge. He *is* supposed to be my boss. I've got a certain loyalty."

"Women don't clutter themselves up with loyalties," Stella said firmly. "If someone hurts or annoys them, they don't worry about things like that. It's amazing how well it works out."

"It's an easy thing to say."

"Jimmy," Stella said urgently, worried by the nagged look on his face. "Are you sure you're not making more trouble for yourself by *not* telling someone?"

"Perhaps I am, but really, Stella, he's such a pathetic idiot. He's never cottoned on to the fact that these people are human beings. He regards them rather as a cross between animals and curiosities."

"Can't we set Mother on to him? She might be able to tell

him a thing or two. She's been here long enough to know and, when she's worked up, can she smite the Amalekites? She's just the person to show him how they tick."

"Nobody could show him anything about them," Jimmy said. "All his ideas were preconceived before he left England and he sees no reason to change them now."

"Mother's pretty hot all the same, Jimmy, and honest, you do look sore about it all. I don't like my Jimmy looking as though he ate something that disagreed with him."

Jimmy looked up. "*Your* Jimmy," he snorted. "I like that."

Stella laughed and, putting her arms round his neck, kissed him quickly and dodged away before he could grab her. "Now, don't get all worked up. You haven't got the kind of face that goes with a bad temper."

She took his hand. "Poor Jimmy," she said, the teasing note dying out of her voice. "Listen, don't let's quarrel with each other. Let's save our energies for dealing with friend Gotto."

"Damn Gotto," Jimmy snorted. "I'm sick of Gotto."

"Jimmy darling," Stella said patiently. "That's no way to deal with him. That'll get us nowhere. That's just accepting him and putting up with everything. We'd be much wiser to think up some way of getting rid of him."

"I've thought and thought," Jimmy said, a driven look in his eyes. "And, short of going to Twigg about him, I can't get rid of him. All I can do is put up with the fool."

Jimmy drove home in a depressed mood, along the dark road where the palms were lit by the flickering gold of flames. He could hear the steady beat of the drums and see dark figures swaying and singing round the fires.

Gotto's eyes had a tormented look in them when he arrived.

"This damned drumming," he said immediately. "They're all full of palm wine."

170

Jimmy laughed. "They're all right," he said. "I didn't notice any blood lust. Only the ordinary kind. I expect there'll be a few hangovers in the morning, that's all."

When he got to bed, he found he was unable to fall asleep for some time and the noise of the drums and the singing from the town didn't help. The following morning he woke late and when he went out to the station wagon, he saw Indian Joe waiting in the dusty Cadillac behind the bungalow. Zaidee sat at the wheel. While Jimmy was still hesitating, the Syrian heaved himself out of the car and came towards him.

He was smooth and silky and blandly friendly but also obviously angry.

"Mr. Agnew," he said. "This quarrelling with the fishermen does not become you. Haggling of this kind should be left to poor Syrians like me. We are the arguers on this coast. We are not able to become soldiers. We are too timid. We cannot become administrators. We are not clever enough. We have to be the shopkeepers. So we know how to quarrel. It is not fitting that the engineer of a mine should go in for haggling with the natives."

"Mr. Soloman," Jimmy said wearily. "How about coming to the point? Is all this because the fishermen have been raiding you?"

The Syrian raised his eyebrows. "How did you guess, Mr. Agnew? You have a Syrian's intuition."

No, I haven't, you old devil, Jimmy thought angrily. It's written all over your face. You're frightened they'll come again.

"Mr. Soloman," he said. "I'm busy. If you don't like it, hadn't you better go to the District Commissioner?"

Indian Joe threw up his hands in despair. "Mr. Agnew, if I go to the District Commissioner, I shall only make trouble —perhaps for Mr. Gotto."

"That's all right, Mr. Soloman. We don't mind."

Indian Joe's face lengthened with surprise then he turned

171

on his beaming smile again. "Ah, no, Mr. Agnew. I'll not worry the District Commissioner. He is a busy man."

"Are you sure it isn't because you don't want him up here finding that rice is short?"

"Mr. Agnew, I know nothing of the rice shortage."

"What was it they were looking for in your store the other night then?"

The Syrian mopped his moist face and stared at Jimmy without blinking. "Mr. Agnew, I have no rice. May Allah in his mercy strike me down if I lie. Mr. Agnew, I like you. My daughter, Zaidee, like you." Jimmy glanced at Zaidee's angry face in the Cadillac and wasn't so sure. "Very much she like you. We like you to come visiting. To have coffee with us. I would like to be your good friend. My daughter Zaidee would like to be your good friend, your very good friend——"

It was Jimmy's turn to raise his eyebrows.

"—but, Mr. Agnew, we cannot be good friends when we quarrel over rice."

"I'm afraid we'll have to dispense with the friendship for the time being, Mr. Soloman," Jimmy said seriously. "I've no control over the fishermen. I've no control over Mr. Gotto. If you want to do anything about it, the remedy's in your own hands. Take it to the District Commissioner."

He turned abruptly on his heel, leaving them staring after him, and drove to the mine with an uneasy mind.

When he got to the office, he found the lorry drivers and the shovel boys standing in a group shouting and arguing and immediately he felt that weight of foreboding like a rock round his neck again.

Momo came towards him, his face serious. "Boss Jimmy," he said. "Boss Gotto sack twenty-three Temne boys for coming late."

"Oh, my God!" Jimmy felt a wave of disgusted fury sweep over him. "What's the trouble *this* time, Alf?"

"Drinking last night, Boss. Temne boy hurt by digger.

172

You remember? Plenty boys come late. Boss Gotto give 'em all the sack. All Temne."

Jimmy was conscious of a frustrated, thwarted anger.

"Boss," Momo continued. "Boys always slow when they drink. Stop their money. But not sack them." He stared hard and accusingly at Jimmy. "You tell Boss Twigg soon, Boss Jimmy?"

At lunch time, Romney and Earnshaw arrived at the bungalow. Romney's face was dark with anger. Earnshaw wore his usual bored look—as though he were contemplating poaching someone's pheasants. They found the atmosphere already explosive. The tempestuous argument between Jimmy and Gotto had died down to an incommunicative silence but the air seemed to crackle with fury.

Romney wasted no time with explanations but came immediately to the point.

"What the devil's this mischief, Gotto?" he asked. "Twenty-three Temne shovel boys. Have you gone off your head?"

Gotto stared back defiantly. "Last time you complained because they were Mende. Now it's because they're Temne. Make up your mind."

"But twenty-three of them, man. Every Mende man in Amama Town's jeering."

"They were late," Gotto retorted. "I set on Mende—I found out they were Mende to please you—I try to oblige. They were there and willing to work. They hadn't been drinking."

"No, but they will one of these 'ere nights," Earnshaw put in heavily. "Then I suppose you'll sack all the Mende and set on a bunch of Temne again."

"Good heavens, man," Romney said. "If you've got to sack a few, mix 'em up a bit, can't you?"

"No, I'm damned if I can." Gotto was backing away into a corner of the room, the trapped, baited look he wore when

173

confronted with his actions on his face again. "When I cele- brate, I still have to be here at the proper time the next day."

"Celebrate?" Earnshaw gave a sudden harsh cackle of mirthless laughter. "You've never celebrated nothing in your life."

"The whole twenty-three of them are up outside Indian Joe's store now, listening to Samuel Assissay," Romney pointed out. "He's letting them have it good and strong about the rice shortage."

"We didn't cause it."

"I know you didn't. I suppose they do, too, if the truth's known, but at the moment while they're angry they put the two together and that fool's helping them. There's quite a crowd round and it's not all Temne. For God's sake, let's sort this thing out before there's any trouble."

"Trouble?"

"There could be."

"I'll warn Sergeant Asimani."

Earnshaw laughed again, harshly and mirthlessly as before. "If Asimani see any trouble, he'll lay low, mark my word, old lad. This place's grown too big for its police force." He flicked his fag-end out on to the dusty earth with his thumb and blinked at Gotto. "He got too much sense to try and argue with a mob with his few blokes."

"Mob?" Gotto seemed a little dazed.

"Ain't you 'eard?" Earnshaw started to scratch himself. "Out here, it's a mob job or nothing at all. I seen rice riots, mate. Proper caper, they was."

"Why not take these men on again?" Romney asked. "Before it's too late. Better still, why not leave the labourers to Alf Momo?"

"I'm having no African running this place. Besides, the law's on my side."

Romney drew a deep breath. He was very concerned and had been for some time with Gotto's activities. But, as he well

174

knew, his concern was largely a selfish one. He was anxious to see the last of Gotto and the villagers contented again, but he knew his wish sprang chiefly from his own desire for peace and comfort.

At the same time, although Gotto was a vain, tiresome, self-dramatizing fathead too much alert to suspicion, a man unable to exist alone and dangerous in a place like Amama, Romney knew that no one was more unhappy in Amama than he was and his loyalties were divided between his creature comfort and his humanity.

He gained control of his temper slowly and went on more calmly.

"Look," he said patiently. "It's not simply a matter of the law or taking sides. It's not even a matter of having principles. It's understanding that's required. Why not try to understand?" It seemed as though he were trying to force his own understanding and compassion into Gotto.

"You can't give and take on a matter of the law," Gotto pointed out with a stiff-necked hostility. "It has to be upheld. I suppose it *can* be upheld."

"Sure it can," Earnshaw said drily. "Only by the time they got the law out here to Amama to uphold itself, it might be too late, mate."

"There'll be no trouble," Gotto insisted. "You can't let these black devils get away with it or they'll be running the place before you know where you are."

He put on his topee with a gesture that ended the argument and stalked out of the door.

Earnshaw pushed his hat back and stared after him.

"Gawd," he said in wonderment. "Ain't he a beaut.? Ain't he the solid bar gold? Talk about tell me the old old story. He won't take a blind bit o' notice. Like water on a duck's back, it is, and him looking at us like we come to mend the lavatory."

175

Jimmy turned to Romney. "Doc," he said, a note of pleading in his voice. "Why does he do it?"

"Because he's a misfit, Jimmy."

"Well, why didn't someone realize he was a misfit? Why couldn't he stay at home and leave us alone?"

"He'd be a misfit there, too, I suspect. He'd be a misfit anywhere."

"Well, look here," Jimmy said angrily. "I'm getting a bit browned off with him. I don't care how long he has to go before the end of his tour. I'm all for telling Twigg. He's had his chance. How about it?"

Romney looked at Earnshaw, who drew a deep breath before he spoke.

"I've told him, old lad," he said.

"You've told him? What did he say?"

Earnshaw grinned sheepishly. "He said, 'Oh, that'll be all right, old boy'." He mimicked Twigg's high-pitched voice as he spoke.

"Is that all?"

"That's all. I telled him I thunk Gotto was going to be a proper old nuisance, as nice as I could—I let him have it all done up like rabbit stew—on me way up from Freetown yest'y—and that's what he say."

"But he must be mad."

"He ain't so mad, kid."

"He's reacted as you'd expect him to react," Romney said. "He's taking the easy way out. He knows he hasn't long to wait before Gotto goes home. He's hoping all the time he'll be able to avoid doing anything."

Jimmy turned desperately towards him. "Doc," he said anxiously. "What are the chances of him getting malaria?—a really good dose that would put him out of action for a bit."

Romney laughed. "Fifty-fifty, Jimmy. But then, it's also a fifty-fifty chance it might be you instead."

176

Five

In spite of their fears, however, there was no further serious trouble at the mine for a while. Always there were murmurings in the town, though, and the fishermen from King Tim, with the noisy pyrotechnics so beloved of the indignant African, indulged in a prolonged protest movement among the flies which hovered everlastingly in the shade of the palm-thatch market stand in Amama where they sold their fish. There was always an audience for them, for there are always idlers in an African village. And, in the evenings, Samuel Assissay, his fanatical eyes burning, could be seen on the raised stone causeway near Indian Joe's store, his back to the gasless gas lamp, haranguing the crowd, as likely as not with Indian Joe himself looking on from a chair in the doorway of his bar, fat, smooth, blinking like a cat in the late sunshine.

"De Lawd tell de humble black man to rise," was Assissay's battle-cry now. "He say dis mine which tear de black man's earth is de bringer of his troubles. Always dere is trouble. It is like de ten plagues of Egypt. We have no rice. We have no happiness. Always dere is de white boss with whip and spur to drive us on——"

Like the fishermen, he also was never without an audience. There had always been plenty of talk in Amama and there had always been heckling and interruptions when anyone got up to speak, for an African crowd loves an argument and, in a place like Amama, there was little else to occupy them. But now the mood of the listening crowd had become more silent and, in the silence, uglier.

177

He let it be known that Gotto was behind a movement to acquire farms in order to expand the mine and they accepted his words without demanding proof. From then on, it wasn't hard to convince them that wages were too low, and that the house tax should be removed. Fortunately, it came to nothing more frightening than noise with the exception of a few fights between the men who had been sacked and the men they accused of stealing their jobs; between the skilled and the unskilled; between the lowly labourers and the higher-paid drivers and mechanics between whom Assissay was driving his subtle wedge.

The Mende labourers, normally living in peace with the Temne men in the town, were now at loggerheads to a degree that was fantastic in a colony not noted for its passion. Small quarrels had always regularly broken out between them and heads had been occasionally cracked, fingers bitten or ears torn. But these were part and parcel of normal village life and no one had ever taken much notice of them. Now, however, at the first suggestion of a dispute, all the annoyances that Gotto had caused flared up and relatives were dispatched for reinforcements while the quarrel was still in its shouting stage.

As it happened, nothing much ever came of these quarrels either, because Sergeant Asimani was intelligent enough to know where the blame really lay and both Temne and Mende disliked Gotto more than they disliked each other.

But Gotto had sewn thickly the seeds of unrest and several shady people began to arrive in the town from the more sophisticated coast, prepared to use his stupidity for their own unscrupulous ends. Every one of the imaginary affronts and offences by African workers that Gotto so diligently nosed out at the jetty or in the workings were passed round for inspection over the rice bowls and round the fires and where men sat in their dim little huts at night.

Christmas came and went, a hot sun-sodden Christmas

without a great deal of cheer. Jimmy, in an excess of noisy Christmas spirit, draped the bungalow with pieces of foliage from the bush and lengths of red paper bought in Indian Joe's store. In this he was helped by a wildly excited Amadu, who sheltered behind his enthusiasm from Gotto's disapproval.

The celebrations in Amama Town started several days before Christmas with fires and dancing and drums, and Clerk Smith came daily to the mine with sad bloodshot eyes and a piece of string round his head to indicate a headache.

On Christmas Eve, the crowds moved about the town in procession carrying lanterns and torches, and the sound of dances and drumming became as natural to everyone as breathing. On Christmas Day, the Swannacks threw a party for all the white people in the neighbourhood and a few of the black ones. Earnshaw sang a ribald song and gallons of Mrs. Swannack's home-made wine were offered and refused— Earnshaw had a crate of beer and a couple of bottles of gin hidden in the withered grass at the bottom of the mission garden. They played games which made them far too hot and the party was notable chiefly for the noise and the speed with which the hymns were sung—Earnshaw's gin and beer had started to take effect by that time; for Jimmy kissing Stella in the garden in the dark; and for Gotto, who stumbled on them, losing his temper and going home in a jealous huff.

As a result, over New Year, with the dry Harmattan winds slamming the doors and filling the eyes and ears and mouth with dust from the Sahara, the mine bungalow was a cold, unfriendly place and as the New Year advanced into January Jimmy found himself leaving the mine at the first possible hour whenever he was free.

Sitting on the hot sand at Mansumana, Stella found herself playing the role of confidante, adviser and balm to his angry spirit all at the same time as she listened to the accounts of the councils of war over the iced beer in Romney's surgery. Every sun that rose and every moon that faded among the palms seemed to have brought some new foolishness, some fresh insult to Alf Momo or the workmen, some new outrage to Jimmy's sense of justice.

"Hell," he said plaintively, "why aren't we nearer to Freetown so that someone could find out about him without *me* having to carry tales and do the dirty on the poor misbegotten clot—without Twigg having anything to do with it?"

"Jimmy, the man's becoming a monster."

"You're telling me. And the future, with no prospect of relief from him, looks pretty bleak, believe me. Why doesn't his ticket home come through? It can't be far away."

"It must be rugged living with him."

"I don't live with him. I share the bungalow. That's all. I never speak to him if I can avoid it and he does the same for me. Meal times are marvellous."

"The conversation must be sparkling."

"It's easier not to bother. In the evenings I fiddle with the garden or sit on the verandah watching the sun. He stays inside."

"What does he do?"

"Get on his own nerves. Chiefly he rattles old newspapers, thrashes about in his chair like a wounded whale and reads and re-reads his letters from Doris, hoping against hope he'll find some affectionate bit he's missed."

Jimmy turned to Stella. "Honest, Stella, he's got everybody on edge. Sargy Asimani came to see me yesterday. He's worried. 'Boss,' he said. 'Soon I get every black man in Amama Town in calaboose.' He'd like to report Gotto but as it's Gotto who's doing all the complaining he's a bit stuck for something to report. He thought perhaps I could fix it."

Stella took his hand silently.

"Everybody expects *me* to fix things," Jimmy said indignantly. "I told him to go ahead and report him to the District Commissioner or whoever it is he reports people to. I don't care any more. But he won't. He's got nothing to

180

report. Gotto manages to be on the right side of the law."

"So what did you do in the end?"

"Told him to push him under a lorry."

"That's not very helpful, Jimmy darling."

"I know. But I couldn't think of anything else and he's got to wear his saddle like the rest of us. You're lucky. You'll be leaving soon."

"I'm not going," Stella reassured him.

Jimmy sat bolt upright. "The dry season's nearly over," he said. "I've been spending all of it getting used to the idea of you disappearing out of my life. You've no right to let me down like this. Why aren't you going?"

Stella turned and stared at him, smiling. "I'm staying because I've found a niche for myself in the school here. I've quite a talent for teaching little black boys."

"I don't believe you."

"Have it your own way. When I first came here, it was always part of the plan that I might stay and help my folks."

"You said you hated the idea."

"I did. But I don't any more."

"I think you're staying because you enjoy being with me."

Stella blushed. "You've got a big opinion of yourself, Jimmy dear," she said.

"No, I haven't." Jimmy was becoming aggressive and dominant. "But I'm a bit older than you and I know more about people. I haven't spent practically every evening with you since I came here without knowing something about you. I've watched you—I've never taken my eyes off you—I've listened to you. I've talked to you. And I know you enjoy being with me."

"Of course I do, Jimmy."

"Then that's why you're staying and the other reason's merely an excuse."

Stella laughed. "Dear Jimmy. My Jimmy. You look so cute when you're laying down the law. Anyway, you can rest

181

assured that I'm going to be right behind you against Gotto.
I'll be like a big sister."

"I don't want a big sister. That's the last thing I want
just now."

Stella's laughter died away quickly. "I know, Jimmy. I'm
only teasing you. I couldn't ever be just a big sister to you."

Jimmy looked up quickly. "Do I detect a faint breath
of hope for me?" he asked.

"Jimmy, there's always hope. But I'm being careful. I'm
still young and being married's like being dead. It lasts an
awful long time. And if you make a mistake it's worse than
being dead."

Jimmy returned her hand to her lap. "This is yours, I
think," he said heavily. "I don't know what I'm holding it
for. It doesn't seem to be any good to me."

"Jimmy dear," Stella said patiently. "Neither of us is
very old and responsible and this isn't the best place to judge
emotions. After all, it is rather unusual with no other men
about——"

"I suppose you want to be queen of the campus"—Jimmy
took refuge from his disappointment in sarcasm—"with a lot
of little college boys in Yale jerseys and crew cuts round
you."

"Thanks for all the understanding," Stella said more
coolly. "You've been seeing too many films. You need to
grow up, sonny boy. I'm only trying to be sensible."

"You don't 'be sensible' when you're in love. Listen, I'll
take you down to Freetown for the day and propose to you
in the lounge of the only hotel. Or in a club. Or on a railway
train. I'll propose on the steps of Fourah Bay College if you'll
feel at home. Anywhere you like, so long as it seems civilized.
I'm serious, Stella."

Stella sighed. But her anger had gone again before his
desperation. "Jimmy, we know so little of each other."

"I like the way you wrinkle your nose. We could get along
182

on that till we do." Jimmy looked at her for a while and sighed. "O.K. You win. So long as you're not far away I'll keep on hoping. Why are you staying, really."

Stella blushed again. "I sort of thought you needed a woman's intuition. Men are a bit hopeless when they have to deal with something a bit different. It was you, really. You looked so lost, you persuaded me that while my folks would have me I might as well stay. So, O.K., since I'd got to support myself, I'd got to get a job. So I teach little black boys in the Mission school. Satisfied?"

It so happened, however, that it was Jimmy, not Stella, who eventually disappeared from Amama. He was told to report down to Ma-Imi for a month for a short course on new methods and it was very obvious that Twigg was overlooking Gotto in sending for him.

He was met at the landing-stage as before by Twigg with the jeep.

"Thought I'd send for you instead of Gotto, old boy," Twigg said. "I'm not having that miserable clot down here, dripping round the place. How's the beautiful Stella?"

"She's all right," Jimmy said gloomily. He looked at Twigg for confirmation of what had always been Earnshaw's opinion and was now becoming his own.

"Sir, is that the reason you sent Gotto up to Amama?—because he didn't fit in down here."

Twigg, staring along the dusty road as he drove towards the Ma-Imi workings, gave him a sidelong glance. "Of course it is. You only just realized that? That's one of my privileges and your misfortunes. I'm sorry for you, old boy, y'know, but it was either that or everyone down here being upset. Honest, the way he drooped around the place, rubbing everybody the wrong way! He upset the foremen and got the other chaps' backs up. He didn't play cricket. He didn't play hockey. He didn't even play cards. He was no good at anything except

183

mining and not much good at that. All he did was complain. What's he doing at Amama?"

"The same," Jimmy said dispiritedly.

Twigg grinned. "I thought it couldn't go on much longer with you living in peace and joy with him. It hasn't been done yet. Thank God you've got him, not me."

Jimmy waved his hat to drive away the red dust that was blowing in. "Sir, he's becoming a damn' nuisance."

"I thought he would," Twigg said cheerfully. "There wasn't any *real* need for two of you up there, y'know. Any youngster fresh from mining school could handle that place easily. Jarvis did and spent most of every day shooting. *You* could run it, couldn't you?"

"Yes, I suppose I could."

"Well, we were one over establishment here so I took the opportunity of getting rid of Gotto. Sorry you've got to put up with him, Agnew, old boy, but he was becoming a damn' trouble-maker down here."

"He's becoming a damn' trouble-maker up at Amama, sir." Jimmy was irritated by Twigg's cheerful assumption that Gotto was safely out of the way.

"Trouble? Trouble?" Twigg cocked an eyebrow. "Oh, he can't cause trouble up there, old man. You're too far from the port. No fuss from unions and things up there. Besides, he's harmless, really."

"There's plenty of trouble, sir," Jimmy insisted. "Samuel Assissay's still around the place."

"Is he, by Jove? You want to keep your eye on *him*."

Jimmy felt depressed by Twigg's indifference. "And what about Gotto, sir?"

"Oh, hell, man, he'll be going home on leave before long. He's only about three months to go now and you can bet your boots I'll put nothing in his way. I don't want to sack the man. I'd rather wait until his tour's up and then get the London office not to renew his contract. Besides, there's always the chance he'll knock himself up. I've seen his type before—they work themselves to death or go home suffering from the sun. Just look out for the first outburst of temper."

"We're long past the first, sir."

Twigg seemed surprised. "Oh! Are you? Oh, well, London will look after him. They set him on. They can knock him off. I don't want to be held responsible. He's likely to cut his throat if I sack him. He's just the sort of damned idiot to do something foolish if I get rid of him."

"He's the sort to do something foolish if you don't, sir."

Twigg laughed. "He's getting you down, old boy, isn't he? Stick it a bit longer and I'll have you down here and send someone else up to handle him for a bit till he leaves." He flashed his brilliant smile at Jimmy. "I've a new chap coming out in a little while. We'll let *him* have a go. Introduce him to Africa."

"Sir, he's going to cause trouble up there," Jimmy persisted miserably.

"You're keen on that idea, aren't you? Well, we'll soon have him out if he does."

"It might be too late then, sir."

Twigg laughed again. "Don't worry, man. Now, how about the cricket team? How's it going?"

"We haven't got one," Jimmy said, too annoyed to lie about it any more.

"Haven't got one? But I thought you were organizing it."

A phrase of Twigg's occurred to Jimmy. "The bastards prefer football," he said shortly.

Jimmy's fortnight at Ma-Imi was shared between the face of the hill where the mechanical diggers ripped out the iron-stone, the offices where he learned something of the wider methods that made the amateurish efforts of Clerk Smith at Amama look silly, the laboratory, the loader down at the wharf, and finally the cricket field.

Twigg seemed to have arranged half a dozen matches especially for him, though the thought of cricket in the evenings appalled him. He had intended using all his spare time writing passionate letters to Stella in the hope of working some change in her mind.

"Don't let the fact that you haven't played for some time worry you," Twigg said. "We're all a bit rusty really. But I like to see a youngster have a chance at the wicket when he comes down here. I can usually fit him in."

Not half you can't, Jimmy thought to himself. He had noticed that all the older hands were expert at dodging the cricket fatigues.

"Fancy that clot Gotto down here," Twigg went on cheerfully. "He'd have complained to some blasted authority that I was making him play cricket—*making* him."

And he'd have been right, Jimmy thought sourly.

When his stay at Ma-Imi came to an end, Twigg threw his usual party to see him off.

"Got to see the boys safely back to the outposts of Empire," he said. "We river folk can't sit in plush-lined offices down in Freetown. We've got to make our own amusements."

The party began soon after the evening meal and went on late into the night. The same people as before were there and they all talked fifty to the dozen, all of them seeking some common denominator with each other, some town they knew, some book they'd read, some film they'd seen. Twigg got rather drunk and sentimental about the British Empire and its outposts, and a little envious and bitter about the people in Freetown, and their lot compared with that of the bush and river folk. The evening grew more stifling and Jimmy, desperate to get back to Amama and Stella, found his only interest was in manœuvring for a place under the fan revolving slowly in the centre of the ceiling.

He went to bed, conscious of the silence of his room and the jettiness of the dark after the noise and the smoky glare

186

of Twigg's house. Outside, the African moon, filling the whole sky and flooding the room with its light, seemed to balance on the mountain tops and Jimmy climbed under his net sobered by a sudden unexpected thought that came from nowhere of the wretched Gotto alone at Amama, afraid of the fishermen and the dark, conscious of failure and friendless, anxious to make good and desperate for the affection that his personality denied him. As he lay back on the pillow he determined for the umpteenth time to be kinder.

By the time he had been back in Amama an hour, however, he had forgotten all about it.

It was evening when he climbed on to the catamaran from the boat and up the ladder of the rickety jetty. Earnshaw was there, waiting for him, a scorched cigarette end between his lips, his leathery face expressionless.

"Good time?" he asked flatly.

"All right." Jimmy glanced at him quickly. "What's wrong, Archie?"

"Seen my jetty?" Earnshaw nodded in the direction of the pile-driver. Not a single pile had been driven into the mud since Jimmy had left for Ma-Imi. The place was deserted.

"Gotto?"

"I'll give him a smash in the chops one of these days. Straight up and no half larks I will. He's got everybody in the blasted place on edge. It wasn't for Alf Momo, nothing would be done 'ere at all."

"What about Gotto? What's he been doing?"

"Reporting some poor little nig to Sargy Asimani for pinching. He's got me chokker. He's got me two blocks. He has really. He found one of the shovel boys had swiped a bit of electric cable to hang a curtain on at home and he nearly had kittens. He had Asimani down on him like a ton of bricks. It's been like that ever since you went—the biggest old tear-up you ever see in all your puff."

187

Jimmy wiped the perspiration from his face. "What happened?" he asked.

"Case comes up tomorrow. I'm going down this time to stick up for the nig. I'll be in there, boy, I will, large as life and twice as nasty. I'll fix him. It'll be something nice to take 'ome with him when he goes on leave."

"Is he one of your boys?"

"Nah. I'm just sick of Master-Mind chucking his weight about. He's enough to put half-inch hairs on me."

"Oh, God!" Jimmy sighed. "I've not been back five minutes."

"You know who's running this place?"

"What do you mean?—running it? Who?"

"His bloody personal clurk, Smith. That's who. And a fine old caper it is, too. Master-Mind spends most of his time working himself skinny to nobble some poor little nig. He signs everything Smith puts in front of him. Alf Momo's going hairless."

"Oh, God," Jimmy said for the second time.

"Talking about Smith"—Earnshaw seemed to be wallowing in his gloom—"you 'andle much petty cash up 'ere?"

"At the mine? No. Why?"

Earnshaw shrugged. "Just wondered if our little playmate's been putting his fingers into it. That's all. That black-faced bastard, Clurk Smith, arrived at my place a few days ago, giving hisself a rare old treat with a fistful of notes. He offered me ten quid for that there gramophone of mine. He's a right boy, he is. I thought perhaps Gotto had been lending it to him and wondered where it came from."

"If Gotto's been lending that fool money he's sunk. I wonder where the hell he got it."

"Well, he had it, any road up," Earnshaw said. "So I 'ad to let him have the gramophone. I always said I would, if he could scrape up the dough. It wasn't worth a quid, anyway. I'd a *given* it to anybody but '*im*."

188

He paused and spat his cigarette end into the water. "It might interest you, by the way, to learn rice is short again—as if you didn't know. I 'ad to go up-river and fetch some for my boys. Indian Joe's sitting on it and the nigs is creating. There was a fight outside the store last night. Samuel Assissay, was there, o' course, blaming it all on the mine. You've got your 'ands full, son. You have, honest. The canoes is in the creek every night and Master-Mind gets raided regular. He's got Asimani out at night now. The poor old bloke don't know whether he's coming or going. Somebody's going to get his throat cut one of these nights. It's a proper game, played slow."

"Oh, God," Jimmy said for the third time. "You don't have to be away long, do you? Is it as bad as that?"

"It's worse. Don't you ever go and change rooms with him, son, in case they nobble you by mistake. Like to borrow a gun?"

"I wouldn't know how to hit anything."

"That doesn't matter much. Just pull the trigger and you're on the ball. It scares 'em if nothing else."

"Has Gotto got one?"

"Not likely. He been up after one again, but I'm not giving him one of mine. What'll scare in your 'ands'll rouse 'em to bloody murder in his, and then we won't half cop it. They hate him enough already. They thought he'd got a gun, he'd be a goner. I wish the flamin' rains'd come. Then he might die of malaria.

Gotto was out when Jimmy reached the bungalow. There were cigarette ends everywhere, the symbols of Gotto's loneliness, and in his room every drawer and cupboard has been fitted with a lock and hasp. By the bed with its rolled-up mosquito net was a heavy stick and torch.

The room made Jimmy feel depressed and just then he
189

felt he couldn't stand Gotto's bitterness. He hurriedly changed into clean clothes and drove up to Amama Town.

Stella's greeting was passionate and reassuring but, for Jimmy, tinged with a little unhappiness at the certain knowledge that she had by no means changed her mind. Swannack's face was grave as he came out on to the verandah to meet him.

"What are you going to do about your Mr. Gotto?" were his first words after their greeting.

"Mr. Swannack," Jimmy said, "everybody asks me that. But he's not *my* affair. If he was I'd have him out. I'm sorry for him, but he's trouble, bad trouble. As it happens though, *he's* supposed to be *my* boss."

"He's dangerous, Jimmy." Swannack stroked at the tufts of black hair on his cheeks. "Samuel Assissay's thoroughly enjoying all this and your Mr. Gotto's entirely responsible. There'll be trouble."

Stella's eyes were frightened as she glanced at Jimmy.

"Amama's no longer the happy place it used to be," Swannack went on. "I've spent years making this a happy church. Now I'm losing my congregation again and I can't stop the rush. What are we going to do?"

"Honestly, Mr. Swannack," Jimmy said, "I don't know. What would *you* do?"

Faced with a direct question, Swannack hummed and hawed. "I guess I'd wait a bit," he said unhappily, "and see what happens."

"That's what everyone says in the end," Jimmy pointed out. "Including me."

Six

THE weather had been growing hotter for some time and Amama became more stifling as the first clouds of the coming rains marched over the mountains that evening and hung on the tops of the cotton trees. Towards midnight came the first of the electrical storms of the season, violent forks of purple lightning that slashed across the sky, and sudden squalls of wind that heralded the rain as they set the palm tops thrashing.

Jimmy was saying good night to Stella when the first heavy drops fell, spattering the dusty road, then the rain came in a heavy downpour that drowned their whispers.

It was only a short shower but it turned the roadway into a river and filled the drainage ditches with a boiling torrent. Although the sun had long been set, steam rose from the sun-soaked earth in a sticky breath-catching heat, and the dust, lashed into mud, drank in the water greedily.

An hour later, as Jimmy drove towards the mine in the thin light of a moon hidden by encroaching clouds, he saw the lamps were still burning in Romney's surgery and he stopped the station wagon and went inside. Romney, his face glistening with perspiration, was dabbing iodine on a cut in the woolly head of Amadu, the house-boy.

The black man's eyes rolled round in Jimmy's direction, and Romney looked up, his expression angry.

"What happened to you, Amadu?" Jimmy asked uneasily.

"Boss"—the house-boy was almost in tears of rage and indignation—"black men wait for me. Dey say I no work for

191

Boss Gotto. I say I work for Boss Jimmy. Dey say again I no work for Boss Gotto. Boss——"

"Don't tell me," Jimmy said wearily. "They took it out of you."

"Yassah, Boss."

"Go on, Doc," Jimmy said. "Ask me what I'm going to do."

"No, Jimmy." Romney fastened a strip of sticking plaster across the wound in Amadu's head. "I know."

"Well, what?"

Romney patted Amadu's shoulder. "Wait outside, Amadu. Boss Jimmy take you home in wagon."

Amadu nodded gratefully and disappeared.

"Well," Jimmy repeated doggedly. "What?"

"Nothing, Jimmy." Romney mopped his face and began to stuff his old-fashioned curved pipe with tobacco. "You'll go on doing nothing. You'll go on hoping he'll solve the problem himself somehow——"

"How?"

Romney shrugged and poured drinks for them both. "His ticket home," he said over his shoulder. "It's due any day now. Malaria. Overwork. I don't know. But you won't do anything. You'll wait and let *him* do it. You'll hang on till he goes."

"I'm damned if I will," Jimmy burst out. "Ever since I came here we've been singing that song, 'He's going home soon. We've only to wait. Everything will be all right.' Well, I'm sick of it. We can wait until the crack of doom until that fool goes. How do we know that something isn't holding his ticket up? He'll never go."

"He will, Jimmy. And you won't do anything because of that."

"Won't I, by God? I've told Twigg already."

"And what did he say?"

Jimmy was deflated. "The same as he said to Archie: 'It'll

192

be all right.' That's all. Then he asked me if I wanted a game of cricket."

Romney smiled faintly, but his eyes remained troubled. "I'm sorry all this has happened, Jimmy," he said. "Purely selfish, I suppose, but I like Amama. We're very close to God here."

Jimmy stared at him, impressed by the old man's sincerity, and Romney went on. "Perhaps it's because I'm a big fish in a little pond," he said. "Perhaps it's because I'm an old man and I don't like change. You think I'm getting a little senile?"

"No, Doc. You just like the place. You like black men, don't you?"

Romney nodded. "Yes—but then, I like white men as well. Perhaps that's the root of Gotto's trouble."

He stood by the window staring out at the damp night air and the wreaths of mist that rose from the warm earth.

"These people who got Amadu," he said. "They're not Amama men. They're some imported gentry from down by the port. Sabby boys. Wide boys, if you like. Ruffians. There's more than just Samuel Assissay and Indian Joe in this now, Jimmy. A few of the political gentry are beginning to take advantage of it. There's at least one ardent pleader for a republic in the town to my certain knowledge."

"A republic?"

"Oh, there's always a crackpot bunch in Sierra Leone, as there is everywhere, who think the place could exist without the rest of the world. Probably a part of the National Council —the anti-British, anti-everything crowd. And that chap Gotto slung out, Melikuri Tom—remember him?"

"What's wrong with *him*?"

"He's an ex-soldier. He fought in Burma during the war with Wingate's lot. He got a medal for something. Now, of course, the ex-soldiers—and there's still a small drifting population of them—now they're yelling that they're not being treated fairly, that they're being denied their rights."

"God, he does pick 'em, doesn't he?"

"Yes, Jimmy, he does. But, unless you want him out, there's not much you can do."

"Not much more than I have," Jimmy said ruefully. "But Twigg just laughed. Can't you certify him or something? If not insane, at least queer?"

Romney shrugged.

"Well, where do we go from here?" Jimmy asked desperately. "Hell, everybody's blaming me for not slinging him out. It's not my fault. Come to think of it," he ended in bewilderment, "I suppose I ought to be thankful he hasn't slung *me* out. He's slung out damn' near everyone else."

He was silent for a while before he spoke again. "Doc," he said eventually, his smooth round face strained, "I've a feeling —something I can't explain—it happened when I saw Amadu just now—just a feeling—that something's going to happen. There's been a horrible inevitability about it all up to now. If only it hadn't been Twiggy who was in charge with his blasted trouble-dodging."

Romney took off his glasses and began to polish them hurriedly. "Or us with our wait-and-see," he concluded.

As the station wagon pulled to a stop in front of the mine bungalow, Jimmy saw someone slip down the front steps and disappear into the darkness.

Gotto was sprawled in one of the basket chairs and his glance at Jimmy was lustreless, unenthusiastic and bitter.

"Hallo," Jimmy said flatly.

"Thank God you're back," Gotto said fervently, and there was such a wealth of thankfulness in his words that Jimmy felt a twinge of sympathy beneath his anger. "They kept you long enough. Or didn't you want to come back to this hole and Snotty Gotty?"

"It was nothing to do with me."

"Might have thought about me all the same—stuck up

194

here on my own. Every damned night. Nothing to do. Those blasted drums. Dark as a cat's inside out there." Gotto's voice rose nervously.

"Well, I'm back now," Jimmy said wearily, trying to force a little reassurance into his voice.

"Not before time. I notice you didn't bother looking for me when you arrived. Went straight up to see your girl, I suppose."

Jimmy nodded, ignoring the sarcasm in Gotto's tones. "Who was it I saw leaving as I arrived?" he asked.

Gotto looked away quickly. "Smith," he said. "Clerk Smith. That's all."

"What's he want?" The question came sharply, abruptly, and, as he spoke, Jimmy's eyes fell on a couple of empty glasses on the table. "Have you been drinking with him?" he went on angrily.

"Why shouldn't I?" Gotto said defiantly. "At least, he doesn't go hunting imaginary butterflies."

They glared at each other for a while, then Jimmy sighed, sick of Gotto, sick of Amama, sick of everything about him.

"I brought some mail up from Ma-Imi for you," he said. "Did you get it?"

Gotto sneered. "Yes, the usual. Two letters. Both one-sheet jobs. One from Mother, complaining this time about the rent man being rude to her. God, I don't remember a time in her life when she wasn't yap-yapping at me about something. Nothing was ever right for her. The other was from Doris. She's found out about that old fool, Romney."

"Has she?" Jimmy was beyond caring, beyond interest in Gotto's trivial meannesses.

"Run out of town for some business," Gotto said gleefully. "Illegal operation or something."

"Well, that's his affair."

"I reckon it's mine as well. I've got to live here with him. Just let him say anything to me again. I'll give him a mouth-

195

ful." He paused before continuing, the eagerness going out of his eyes. "Doris got engaged to that swine back in England," he ended flatly.

"Did she?" Jimmy couldn't find it in him to be sympathetic.

"Dirty swine! Waits till a chap goes abroad and then pinches his girl."

"Oh, hell, man," Jimmy snorted, suddenly goaded beyond endurance by Gotto's self-dramatization. "You know damn' well she was never *your* girl. Why don't you stop behaving like an overgrown schoolboy about her? She'd never any intention of marrying you. You've been deluding yourself ever since you came here. Can't you find someone else?"

"As a matter of fact—" Gotto had calmed down quickly and he spoke casually, almost indifferently, "Smith's offering to introduce me to Zaidee Soloman. That's why he was here. She's been asking about me."

"Asking about *you*?"

Gotto looked indignant. "Why shouldn't she ask about me? By God, it'd make Mr. Bloody Earnshaw sit up if I pinched *his* girl."

Jimmy laughed. "Changed your tune a bit, haven't you? Come to that, she's changed *hers*."

Gotto stared at him angrily, then he rose and disappeared into his bedroom, slamming the door after him.

While Jimmy contemplated the closed door, it re-opened and Gotto's head appeared, nervously.

"Better put a club or something near your bed," he said. "We get regular raids now. That fool Asimani doesn't seem to be able to do anything about them."

196

Seven

THEY were troubled by nothing more that night, however, than the rain which came down in straight glassy splinters that shattered as they struck. It came in a devastating downpour that rattled on the tin roof with an unholy din that prevented sleep, and gurgled noisily in the ditches outside as it flooded away. The sound of it on the undergrowth was a steady roar threaded through by a hollow plop-plop-plop as it forced its way through the ceiling and fell to the floor in a monotonous drip. Although the place was panting in the torpid heat, Jimmy shivered as he climbed under his mosquito net.

There was another downpour the following morning but it didn't last long and even as the roar changed to the hurried patter of drips, the sun came out and the steam rose in twisting wraiths as the greedy heat sucked the moisture out of the earth. Already the dried grass seemed to be taking on new life and the withered plants began to throw out young shoots. A wild cucumber beneath the window of Jimmy's room seemed to have grown fatter already and a small plantain tree had pushed itself up a couple of notches.

In the living-room, Amadu had moved the table a little for breakfast. Where it had stood was a zinc pan into which a regular drop of water fell—zip plunk, zip plunk—all through the meal.

Gotto showed no hurry to leave for work and Jimmy, still too angry with him to argue about it, set off for the mine ahead of him. The zigzag road to the shelfings of the diggings was slippery with mud after the rain and already the boles

197

of the palm trees alongside it had had their coating of dust replaced—like raw wounds across the wood—by slashes of red mud flung up by the wheels of the Euclids.

Nobody appeared to be working and the trucks and the diggers stood silent. Jimmy was puzzled until, at the rock face on the lowest level, he found the drivers and labourers all standing in a group. The station wagon skidded to a stop in the mud and he jumped out.

"What's all this?" he demanded of the foremen. "Come on, get the boys on the job."

The foremen looked sheepish as they began half-heartedly to push the men back to their work. There were a few mutterings and someone shouted "White man, t'ief man," then Jimmy saw that in the centre of the group there was a black man in a white city suit, pith helmet and mackintosh. Beyond him was Samuel Assissay, his presence with his cranky doctrines symbolic of the bad feeling that had been growing. Although he was always making speeches, it was significant that until this point he had never made them on land belonging to the mine.

"What are you doing down here, Assissay," Jimmy demanded.

Assissay stopped speaking and turned slowly, and the man in the mackintosh slipped behind him.

"The loftiness of man shall be thrown down," Assissay chanted. "Proud white man shall be brought low. De Bible says so. Poor humble black man who loves de Lawd shall come to his proper place."

"Cut out that nonsense. What are you telling these people?"

"I tell 'em dat de white lawd perish when de revolution come. Black men rise up——"

"White boss go pinch black man's rice," someone shouted explosively from the crowd, the words flung out of the hubbub like a missile. "White boss stop black boys' fish."

"You'd better clear out, Assissay," Jimmy said quickly.

198

"Before I fetch Sargy Asimani and get you shoved in the calaboose. That kind of talk's dangerous."

"Black man no fear danger, Boss Jimmy," Assissay said calmly. "White boss Gotto make poor black man suffer. De Lawd watch over poor black man. White man Gotto ride black man with whip and spur——"

Jimmy's jaw set. "Hop it, Assissay. Now. One-time. Before I throw you out."

"No white man can lay hands on a black man," said the man in the mackintosh with a readiness that indicated he was well briefed for trouble.

"Who're you?" Jimmy demanded. "What are you doing here?"

"The men have elected me their representative."

"Their representative? They've got their representatives. They've got their union. You a union official?"

"I represent the New Africa Political Movement."

"Never heard of it. And I don't suppose they have either. You'd better get moving. You don't work here."

"I demand the right to speak to the men."

"You can speak all you want after they've finished work or when they knock off for chop. Not now. Get moving. Both of you."

The crowd began to edge round Jimmy again and he was very conscious of black faces all round him and the smell of sweat and earth and charcoal, that smell of Africa he would remember all his life.

"Black man suffer from white dictatorship——" the man in the mackintosh looked sideways at Assissay and started to speak, his attitude that of an orator.

Jimmy stopped him. "You're not an Amama man," he said.

"No." The other drew himself up. "I'm from Freetown. I'm investigating reports of oppression——"

"Leave that to the union officials and the government.
199

Now, off these workings before I throw you off. Both of you. I'll give you until I count five."

"No white man can lay hands on a black man."

"One."

"I demand the rights of the black slaves here in Amama——"

"White boss plenty proud," Assissay commented.

"Two," Jimmy chanted, at the same time uneasily measuring himself against the other two.

"We in Freetown are backed by powerful forces." The voice of the man in the mackintosh cracked a little nervously as he tried to continue.

"I'll bet you are," Jimmy said, his heart pumping wildly. "That makes three. You've got two more seconds."

"I will inform the District Commissioner."

"Four. Inform away. I'm going to sling you out first and he can ask questions afterwards."

The agitator stared for a second longer at Jimmy then he gathered his mackintosh round him like a cloak and turned in an undignified fashion up the sloping road, his feet slithering in the mud.

There were a few hostile murmurs from the crowd but no one moved and Jimmy began to advance on Assissay, who stared at him for a moment, glanced sideways at the dwindling figure of the man in the mackintosh, then turned abruptly, and began to stride away after him.

When Jimmy, in a passionate rage, arrived back at the bungalow, Gotto was still there as he expected, but to his surprise Clerk Smith was there, too.

The black man jumped up hurriedly as he appeared and bobbed his head in a half bow.

"Good morning, Boss Agnew," he beamed.

Jimmy glared at him, conscious of the stuffy heat that made his anger all the more unbearable and of a goading certainty

200

that of all Gotto's associates, this stupid, vain black man was the only one with the sense to realize he could be handled with flattery. "Clear out," he snapped.

"Boss, I just talking over t'ings with Boss Gotto——"

"Clear out!"

"I say to him dis ole world sad ole world wid all these bad t'ings happenings in Amama——"

"If you don't clear out I'll sling you out."

Smith's expression changed abruptly to one of panic and, reaching for his umbrella and hat, he edged past Jimmy towards the door.

"White man no fit talk black man all same dat," he said indignantly.

He finished the sentence sliding down the steps of the verandah on the heels of his white shoes as Jimmy gave him a violent shove, and he spun round in the wet red roadway and waved his umbrella, his glasses askew.

"You no strike black man," he yelled in his high-pitched voice. "I go tell Sargy Asimani. You go calaboose——"

As Jimmy snatched up a book from the bamboo table near the door and hurled it as hard as he could, he took to his heels and ran.

Gotto had risen from his chair. "You can't do that to a friend of mine," he snapped, his face taut and nervous.

"Friend of yours? You going native or something? That clown's one of the reasons why we're not getting any work done."

"He's a friendly little wog."

"Too bloody friendly! Listen, Gotto," Jimmy shouted, in a towering rage. "I'm sick of finding that clot in here. This is our bungalow. Mine and yours. And I'm saying he's not to come inside. The man's a menace. If you want to be matey with him, go up to the village and do it there. Not here. That fathead's one of the reasons why Amadu got a clout on the head last night. That's why I've just found some wide boy

201

from Freetown preaching fire and slaughter with Samuel Assissay in the workings."

Gotto laughed nervously. "Oh, God, man," he said fretfully. "You don't want to let that worry you. They're always arguing."

"They weren't arguing this time. They were listening. Only one of them was talking."

"Same thing."

"It wasn't the same thing. And if you were only half a clown you'd know it wasn't the same thing. That damn' man was trying to cause trouble."

"Well, we know what trouble is," Gotto said with a nervous snigger. "We've got plenty."

"Don't you damn' well care at all about the Africans?"

"They get their money. They get their rice. They get their jig-jig. That's all they're interested in."

"If that's what you think, then I was wrong and you're less than half a clown. You're probably a raving lunatic."

Jimmy glared, aware that Gotto would never see sense in any argument on behalf of the black workers.

"Listen," he went on. "There were never any troubles in Amama till you came up here. It's only through the grace of God and the fact that we're so far from anywhere that some official from Freetown hasn't heard of all this—that and because everyone up here's kept his mouth shut."

"Don't tell me that. All the trouble I've got on my plate is because of tale-bearing. It's not my fault Amadu got a crack on the head. I expect he'd been pawing some mammy and her husband caught him. They're all the same—bloody immoral."

"They went for Amadu last night because they hate your guts. That's why the canoe boys come."

Gotto was flushing angrily now. "I'll go straight down to Asimani and report them."

"Asimani my behind. Asimani's sick of the sight of you."

"I still say Asimani——"

"You make me sick," Jimmy raved, and as he went out he slammed the mesh door behind him with such force that it broke.

On the way to the jetty, he picked up Earnshaw who was walking down to his boats.

"Happy, son?" Earnshaw said.

"No," Jimmy snapped.

"I thunk not. Gotto?"

"Yes. The man's balmy." Jimmy turned to look at him. "Did you go down to the court as you said you would? You were going to stick up for that African against him?"

Earnshaw looked suddenly sheepish. "Christ," he said. "You can't go and stick up for an African against a white man in his position, daft as he is. Let him see his tour out."

"My God," Jimmy said angrily. "I don't think you've got the guts."

"No, I ain't got the guts," Earnshaw exploded. "And neither 'ave you. Neither has Romney. If you're so keen on the District Commissioner knowing what's going on, you go and tell him yourself. Go on, you've tried with Twiggy and failed, like I did. O.K., turn the car round and let's go down to the D.C. He's not far away. He'll see us. We'll warn him. He'll soon have Gotto out. They can't afford to have people like Gotto in Africa these days causing trouble. Come on, turn the car round."

Jimmy sat silently under the tirade until Earnshaw had finished.

"Hell," he mumbled in excuse. "It's hardly worth it. He's only a few weeks to go now."

"Right," Earnshaw said, satisfied. "I don't want to ruin the bastard. You don't think it's worth it. O.K. Now shut up and we'll do as we done before—let it slide."

As Gotto, on his way to see Sergeant Asimani, approached the outskirts of Amama Town, the rain began to fall again.

203

The heavy-bellied clouds that held the heat in suddenly split and down came the rain in a heavy downpour that punched holes in the muddy surface of the road and turned it into a quagmire again almost at once. There was no wind and the rain fell in solid sheets that brought down the dried palm fronds with it.

Sweeping round a corner, the red mud slashing from the wheels in waves, the water sluicing off the windscreen wipers, he almost crashed into the big American Cadillac which pulled out of a side road. Desperately, he swung on the wheel and the car slithered to a stop against a palm tree with the crunch of a collapsing front wing.

Gotto leapt out in a fury, the incident a personal affront to him, and splashed across to the other car, indifferent to the rain which soaked him in an instant. Dragging on the handle of the door, he heaved it open.

"What's the big idea?" he stormed. Then he stopped dead, his mouth open, as he stared at Zaidee Soloman, the anger in his eyes giving way immediately to a plea that she would treat him more mercifully this time than she had on the occasion of their first meeting.

"I'm so sorry," she said gently, unexpectedly humble. "Always I am so stupid. The water on the windscreen prevented the sight."

Gotto's voice stopped in his throat as he stared at her, mute with that hideous awkwardness that had always gagged him at times like this throughout his life.

"That's all right," he stammered, his anger drained away completely. "Nothing at all. Doesn't matter really."

He was hot with the thought of her contemptuous stare on the last occasion they had met, that disastrous afternoon when his request to Indian Joe to release rice had ended in a rout. But she was smiling now, in a way that made him indifferent to the rain which beat the brim of his bush hat to a dripping switchback and plastered his clothes in dark wet folds on his body.

Suddenly her eyes widened. "Quickly," she said. "You must get in. You get wet."

"Listen——" Gotto's gaping mouth shut with a click as, reaching over, she pulled him into the car alongside her.

"How much is the damage?" she asked.

"Nothing much," he muttered, wiping rainwater from his face. "Bust mudguard. Probably locked the wheel. I don't know."

"Where were you going?"

"Police," he mumbled, his hand hovering round his nose. "Make a report."

"You cannot go like that," she said, cool and aloof in a jumper that made him blush. "Never must white people appear before these black trash in rumpled clothes. Come to my house. My servant will iron it for you. It will dry it."

She started the big car with a jerk and headed it towards Amama Town, the rain roaring on the roof.

Gotto was struck dumb for a moment by the embarrassed panic which took the place of the mute gratitude that she had been kind to him. "No," he choked as he came to life. "I've got to get to Asimani. . . ."

The rain came down steadily all morning in a shining curtain that made the trees grey metallic shapes, until at noon the clouds parted once more and the sun began to drink the moisture from the pools.

Zaidee would not let Gotto move during the storm, her smiles dazzling him as they had Jimmy and before him Earnshaw and probably others. As he waited in the bungalow with its colourful European fabrics which were somehow African in their gaudiness—as though the blood that Zaidee tried to hide had still managed to peep through—he found himself to his

205

surprise unloading his troubles about the mine to her, glad to have a listener, grateful for sympathy.

"For one man it is too much without the support of his friends," Zaidee said firmly when he had finished. "A man in a lonely place needs friends he can trust, people he can talk to. I also am lonely."

"You are?" Gotto stared.

"Of course. Why not? I am not like all these others. I am not black. With whom can I be friendly?"

Gotto blushed and apologized. "Don't know why you stay here," he mumbled in bewilderment. "*I* wouldn't if I could help it."

"It is because here I am important," Zaidee said simply. "And our little wealth seems great. In Freetown or Takoradi I should be unimportant—just another Syrian—and my wealth would be small. I do not like that. I like to be important.

"Besides," she concluded. "Too much I am believed to be African. I am not. I am Syrian. You know my father. In Freetown, though, this story would do me no good. The women there would not accept me."

She spoke in a soft voice and from time to time she laid her finger tips against his arm to stress a point. As she reached across him for a cigarette, her shoulder touched his and left him red-faced and confused and devoid of speech.

She had the ability to give him confidence, though, and, because she appeared to enjoy listening to him, he opened out and talked, happy for the first time since arriving in Amama, probably for the first time since arriving in Africa. When he left, she drove him along the road towards the mine, passing the police station without his even noticing.

"I will drop you here," she said as she stopped the Cadillac alongside his own car, which was still jammed up against the splintered tree. "Then I must hurry away. I cannot be seen with you. My father is not trusted and it would do you much harm."

206

She laid a hand on his and she was very close to him as she spoke again. "We must be careful," she said. "You must not ruin your career."

"I don't care," Gotto said loudly. "I'm not scared."

Zaidee touched his hand again. "It is not so simple as that," she smiled. "To people who are surrounded by enemies, always caution is best. For both of us. We are alike. We are both unpopular. We are both lonely. Come this evening. I will meet you here. We will drink coffee again. It is good to have a friend."

"You're telling me."

"I have only my father. All he does is eat peaches from the tin. Otherwise nobody. Only black rubbish. I am not black."

Gotto blushed. "You're beautiful," he muttered.

"You also," Zaidee replied disconcertingly and Gotto gaped.

"With a nose like this?"

"With Syrians, large noses are a sign of great distinction," Zaidee lied without blinking, and Gotto would have fallen at her feet.

"They are a sign of distinction," she went on unblushingly, "because they are a sign of strength. You are obviously a strong personality." She held up her hand as he protested. "Because you have not been strong yet does not mean you are not strong. You can start now. That is all the black trash around us understand."

"Think so?"

"I am sure. I have known them all my life. Be firm. Be hard. Weakness encourages them to be lazy. I know this. That is why they do not like me. That is why I am alone."

She smiled again and leaning across, warm and soft against him, opened the door of the car. "It will be good to know I have a friend at last," she said, squeezing his hand. "Come tonight. It is good to talk. I shall be waiting here. You will come?"

207

Gotto nodded and mumbled his assent, confused, bewildered and utterly dazzled.

He watched the Cadillac draw away up the road towards Amama Town, in a sudden agony of doubt because she didn't turn her head to look back at him, then he swung on his heel towards his own car. As he did so, he almost bumped into Alf Momo and a gang of labourers.

He flushed crimson as he saw Momo's eyes flicker towards the disappearing Cadillac, then, fortified by the belief that his loneliness was over, he lifted his head and walked past the shift boss with a sudden new feeling of courage.

Eight

AMAMA was sodden and panting in the humid heat of the evening. The thermometer had started climbing again until the foetid air gagged in the throat. The clearing outside the mine bungalow was a sea of mud criss-crossed by the wheel marks of the station wagon and the car. Inside the living-room, the table had been moved once more. Bowls and zinc basins had been placed at various points about the floor and there was a puddle on the seat of one of the armchairs.

The wild cucumber under Jimmy's window was fatter and the plantain tree had grown another couple of notches. Behind the bungalow, the greenhouse shade of the bush had burst into life and the delicate new green was studded with trumpets and bells and lanterns. There was no wind and it was like being in a Turkish bath with the mirror blurred with moisture. Yet Amadu, like all the Africans, looked pinched and miserable.

Dr. Romney's gang of boys were moving in the neighbourhood, clearing the gullies and ditches of the sticks that choked them, so that the water could flow freely; spraying the stagnant pools with paraffin to prevent mosquitoes breeding. The river was a muddy-looking flood that brought small trees and fallen boughs and brushwood with it from the upper reaches where the falls gushed in full spate over the filling river beds.

Gotto hung about the bungalow until it was dark, hardly able to sit still in his nervous excitement. To be wanted, to have someone, and a woman, an attractive woman, anxious to see him a second and a third time, was a new experience

209

for the ugly frustrated man, and it was heady in its impact. Beneath the joy that kept bubbling up in him, however, doubt added a sobering caution. For too many years he had been the subject of rebuffs and laughter, and he was quite prepared for this sudden friendliness of Zaidee's to turn out to be a huge, humourless jest. His mind went daily through the mechanics of suspicion and self-assurance but the unmanageable tumult that Zaidee's interest had stirred up in him was too strong to be held in check merely by misgiving and he found it difficult to read, to work, to concentrate on anything beyond the exhilarating thought of Zaidee.

Jimmy watched him pottering about the bungalow, smoking cigarette after cigarette, expecting half the time for a safety valve to blow off in a cataclysmic burst of temper.

"What's got you?" he demanded. "You're like a cat on hot bricks lately?"

It was on the tip of Gotto's tongue to tell him the truth, to brag about Zaidee, the Zaidee who had always attracted wolf whistles in Freetown from the sailors off the ships, the Zaidee who was coveted by half the white men who came to Amama, and hated by all the white women. He wanted to boast, to feel he was a conqueror and to let everyone know he was a conqueror. It was with difficulty that he hung on to his secret.

"Nothing's the matter," he said, his voice quivering with excitement.

Jimmy watched him putting matches and cigarettes and money into his pocket, obviously in an elated mood. "Thought you'd got a girl or something," he joked. "Thought it might be Zaidee, in fact," he ended with a quick glance over his shoulder.

Gotto whirled round, obvious happiness bubbling in him and his words burst out in his excitement louder than he had expected. "That'd make 'em all sit up, wouldn't it, if it were true?"

210

"It would if it were but let's hope it's not," Jimmy said pointedly.

"What do you mean?" Gotto's brows came down and his jigging movement stopped abruptly.

Jimmy picked up a newspaper with a yawn and started to read. "Where Zaidee is, Indian Joe's just behind." There was a pontifical finality to the statement. "The only thing I like about her is the way she walks—especially in trousers."

Gotto stared at him from the middle of the room, his mouth working with rage, then he whirled on his heel and disappeared through the mesh door. A moment later, Jimmy heard the car start up and the sound of the engine dying away.

For the next few weeks, Gotto never went near the mine. He claimed sickness as his excuse, yet he looked better than he had ever done, and he was strangely dominant and boastful. He refused naturally to take his so-called sickness to Romney for a diagnosis and went off every day in the car.

"Must get some air," he claimed. "Must get to the hills a bit."

As he drove away on the third day, Jimmy stared after him through the sheeting rain which made every leaf of every palm stream like a waterfall and set the drips clunking like an arpeggio into Amadu's tin dishes about the floor. Then he grabbed his hat and oilskin and searched out Earnshaw.

"He's gone off again," he said, avoiding Earnshaw's eyes, "but, as it happens, it suits me fine. If he wants to play the fool somewhere, now's my chance to make the mine hum. And I'm taking it."

Alf Momo was called to the office immediately and Earnshaw, dropping in later on his way to the jetty, found Jimmy already installed behind Gotto's desk, holding court with a sulky-looking Clerk Smith.

"There are the loading returns, the fuel tally and the accounts," he was saying. "See that Suri gets 'em to take down

211

to Ma-Imi. He's responsible enough. He'll see they get to the right department."

"Boss—" Smith's high, whining voice had an aggrieved note in it—"already I am too busy."

"Not for this, Smith, old son," Jimmy said briskly, brushing aside his objections. "Get 'em typed out. Savvy?"

"O.K., Boss," Smith mumbled. "Tomorrow I do it."

"No. Not tomorrow. Nor the week after. Today. Now. They're overdue."

"Boss—" Smith sounded indignant as he hugged the papers to his breast—"today I muss tell labourer boys where to go."

"Never mind the labourer boys. Your job's to type. *I'll* tell the labourer boys what to do."

"Boss Gotto say *I* tell labourer boys——"

"Well, *I* say you don't."

Smith's face became desperate and crafty as he sought an excuse—any excuse—to avoid the menial tasks of the office. "Boss. De telephone. Boss Gotto tell me to git it repaired. I go now."

"Oh, no, you don't! You stay here."

"Boss Gotto tell me."

"I know he did. *And* the clock. And half a dozen other things as well. And they're still not repaired. Well, never mind, we've managed up to now. We can manage a bit longer."

"Boss—" Smith twisted his face into a forced smile as he tried another avenue of escape—"you clever boss——"

"That's right, Smith," Jimmy said with a grin that made the black man's heart sink. "I am. Too clever for you. Now hop it."

Earnshaw grinned, took up his usual position against the doorpost and lit a cigarette.

As Smith went out, grumbling to himself, Jimmy turned to Alf Momo by his side. "Right, Alf," he said. "There are three lorries unserviceable at the moment. Get 'em going again. If you have any argument with the mechanics, shoot 'em in here. I'll sort 'em out."

"Yes, *sah!*" Momo grinned happily. "This good, sah, to see you in that chair, Boss Jimmy. You belong."

"Thanks, Alf." Jimmy didn't even look up as he pawed through the papers on the desk. "And when you've got 'em serviceable, take one of 'em and go and get some of that rice you know of. We'll see the boys get one good meal at least. I'll be responsible. I'll square Twigg if there's any fuss. We'll get it first and he can ask questions afterwards. O.K.?"

"Yes, *sah!*" Momo's face seemed to be one big smile.

"And when you've got the lorries sorted out, come back here and you can help me go through some of this damned rubbish. I shall need a hand. I don't think it's been done since Jarvis left."

As Momo turned away, Jimmy halted him again. "Oh, and Alf, before we do that, we'll scout round the workings in the station wagon with one of the foremen. I think we can divert some of this damn' water that's flooding them. To-morrow, we'll go and see the headman at King Tim and sort out *that* little problem. Think we can do it?"

"You and me together, Boss Jimmy, perhaps we can." Momo gave him a gay little mock salute and disappeared.

"Blimey," Earnshaw said from the door. "Ain't you the boy for work? What's 'appened to all that bumph what was on the desk?"

"Dumped," Jimmy said. "Most of it was Gotto's tripe. A long list of wrongdoers for Asimani. All neatly tabulated. He must have spent hours over it. What a mind he must have. I've had Asimani up already and told him to forget everything that's happened. We'll start afresh."

"What 'e say?"

"I think he was relieved. Saves him a lot of work."

"Not 'arf. And what about all them rules and regulations
213

Master-Mind was writing out? I seen a great pile of 'em 'ere the other day. You dumped *them*?"

Jimmy laughed. "Yes. That's all dumped, too. The next thing that's going to be dumped will be Clerk Smith if I can manage it. I'll get a boy from Swannack's school. He'll soon learn to type."

"You going to tackle the rest of the troubles?"

"Yes. I'm going over to King Tim to see the headman. I'm taking Alf Momo."

"Taking an escort?"

"No. I'm not afraid. I'll get nothing out of 'em with a gang of Asimani's boys."

"Think you'll get anything without 'em?"

"Yes, I will." Jimmy's young face was hard with determination and Earnshaw nodded.

"You might at that, old lad," he said.

"I'll call off this damned quarrel or bust."

"How about the mechanics and labourers? They've had a beano lately."

"You're telling me. I'll see them tomorrow."

The following day, the African employees found a whirlwind descending on them. The mechanics in charge of the lorries, used to laziness under Gotto's indifferent rule, had already been driven back to work by Alf Momo and were occupied in straightening out the bent mudguards which had been the meagre excuse for useless vehicles for weeks. Electricians were set to work on ignition troubles and a tireless Jimmy, spattered with red mud, drove the labourers to fight against the clock to repair banks broken down by rain, to clear gullies jammed with rubbish that was diverting water through the workings, to remove earth washed from the hillside across the roadways.

"Alf," he said, pointing through the rain, "if we fell those few trees along that bank, we can make a quicker route to the jetty. Save time on every trip. Get the boys on it, will

214

you? They can use the logs to shore up the sleepers on the railway. If it sags any more, there's going to be an accident and the whole outfit's going to finish up on top of someone."

"Jeeze," Earnshaw commented. "Them boys of yourn don't know what's 'it 'em."

"I haven't started yet," Jimmy said.

"Gawd help 'em when you do."

Jimmy grinned. "I don't know," he said. "I honestly think they're pleased. After all, work means money for 'em."

"You fixed the fishermen yet?"

"Yes."

"How you do it? That boyish smile o' yourn?"

Jimmy grinned again. "Alf helped. I drank a lot of palm wine, I know that. It took all morning and I'd got a hell of a head afterwards. Alf drove the station wagon home. But we're all pals together again now."

"They coming back to the jetty?"

"No. I'm clearing 'em a strip of mud just outside the mine area. The boys are on it now. That way, Gotto won't be able to sling 'em off again when he comes back."

"Cute, aintcha? Perhaps he won't come back. He ain't got long now."

"Suits me fine if he doesn't."

"Seen any more of Assissay and his pals?"

"No. I think they've heard what's happened. I don't think they'll come."

Earnshaw grinned. "I don't think they will, kid. Keep it up. You're doing all right."

The chatter and roar of the diggers began to echo again through the trees as new targets for output were set—and reached—and in a remarkably short time, shelters that had slowly wilted through three or more rainy seasons were straightened and men laboured more willingly beneath them at the ends of the conveyors.

"Boss—" Clerk Smith in his office was bewildered and
215

complaining at the amount of work that was suddenly thrust on him—"dis no good for black man. Too much busy."

As they entered the third week, Jimmy became aware of a new tidy appearance about the mine that existed in spite of the weather, and what was better, a new spirit. All the sullen resentment that had existed seemed to have vanished and the labourers were singing their rhythmic songs again as they swung their shovels in the rain.

"Nearly three weeks he's been away," Jimmy told Stella gleefully. "Three more weeks off his tour. Three weeks nearer to him going home. If only he'll stay away a bit longer, we'll make this mine begin to look like a paying proposition."

"Jimmy"—Stella looked worried—"do you know where he goes?"

"Maybe," Jimmy said. "But I'm not very bothered. So long as he keeps out of the way."

"Jimmy dear, the Mission boys are talking about him. They're saying he goes to see Zaidee Soloman."

"I should say they weren't far out."

"There's more to him than we suspected, Jimmy. I mean —being able to get Zaidee."

"Wonder how it happened," Jimmy mused. "I wonder what she used as bait. He'd run a mile if she winked at him. I wonder what's she after, too. Probably trying to make us keep quiet about the rice or something."

"Isn't it dangerous?—Zaidee and Gotto, I mean, Jimmy."

Jimmy frowned. "Could be," he agreed. "But personally, I'm inclined to let him have his bit of fun. It might sweeten him. And, anyway, it keeps him out of the way and let's me get on with the washing. If she can only keep him amused and away from the mine a little longer, we'll make a job of it yet."

The steady and sickening descent of the rain went on, the brown water boiling in the ditches and bubbling under the eaves of the bungalow, while every banana leaf and every blade of grass dripped its weight of water to the sodden earth in differing notes. The roads became red sheets of mud and the undergrowth, glittering with dripping diamonds, was bright green again as the dust of months was washed away. The wild cucumber under Jimmy's window was swollen and almost grown now and the plantain tree had reached the sill itself. The river was a seething dark brown torrent which roared round Earnshaw's trembling jetty in swirls of creamy foam, and the mangroves held wraiths of mist which never seemed completely to disappear. Mildew spread on books, clothes and any unused objects faster than the house-boys could track it down and brush it off, and there was an atmosphere of gloom which came not so much from darkness as from absence of sunshine.

But, in spite of the weather and the discomfort, the work at the mine went on and Jimmy couldn't contain his pleasure.

"We're doing it," he said, as he swung Stella into his arms and danced an indecorous fandango on the verandah of the Mission bungalow. "We're doing it. We're beating him, Stella."

Gotto had other ideas, however, and when he finally re-turned to work he was angry and domineering. And there was a subtle difference now. His anger came not from lack of confidence so much as from imperious over-confidence. Those little tricks which betrayed his temper as worry were gone, though there was still nervousness in his gestures, as though he were being driven by some outside force he wasn't sure of and at a pace that was barely within his control.

Tempers suddenly grew more frayed again and nerves were on edge once more, and Samuel Assissay was seen at night with the men in Freetown suits and glasses, which stood out among the tattered shorts and dirty shirts of the crowds who listened to them. The half-forgotten grumblings started again with their assistance and fights broke out so that Romney's surgery was busier than it had been for years. That very

217

isolation which left Amama untouched by the worst of civilization also permitted the murmurings to grow without reaching the District Commissioner.

Within three days of his return, Gotto had sent the dhobi boys and latrine boys on strike and had driven down to Sergeant Asimani's twice to report some imagined offence. Tempers rose still more rapidly so that a shoving match between one of the foremen and the driver of a ditched scraper became a fight and the foreman was stretched on the ground with a blow on the head from a lump of rock.

Clad from head to foot in an oilskin, and bitterly disappointed at the turn of events, Jimmy managed with a considerable amount of tact to sort out the grievance and get the boys back to work.

"Listen, Gotty," he said, confronting him. "All I've done since you came back is sort out arguments. What's come over you? The output's going down like stink again and we'd managed to pull it up a bit."

Gotto stared coldly at him. "O.K.," he said. "If you know what's wrong, you look after the workings and I'll look after the jetty. If you're so clever, let's see what *you* can do."

He seemed anxious to be rid of the responsibility and glad to take over the simpler supervision of the pile-driver. But the outburst of temper he immediately displayed by the leaking steam engine was monumental enough to result in a noisy demonstration of those gymnastics of anger so beloved of an African crowd with a grievance, and black hands, having failed to make an impression by gesticulation, began to reach for brickbats.

As Gotto strode away, he was startled to see a large piece of rock land in a spattering of mud by his feet. He turned round to see where it had come from and was just in time to dodge another as he bolted for the car.

He found Jimmy in the workings talking to Alf Momo.

"Mutiny," he shouted as he tumbled out. "Get Asimani
218

and his men! Send someone down to the District Commissioner! They've been stoning me!"

"My God," Jimmy said. "It doesn't take you long, does it? Stay here. I'll sort 'em out."

"They'll murder you."

"I'll chance it."

"They're throwing rocks."

"I'm good at rock-throwing myself."

Gotto turned towards the car. "I'll go down to the District Commissioner's," he said.

Jimmy pushed him aside and climbed into the car himself. "If you don't want a quick ticket home, I should stay where you are."

He drove towards the jetty, his heart thumping painfully near his throat, depressed by the certainty of calamity. He found the pile-driver labourers in a large group shouting and quarrelling, and as soon as they saw Gotto's car the stones started flying again.

"White man de oppressor!"

"White man go home!"

The windscreen starred as a rock struck it, and Jimmy stopped and opened the door. A piece of wood hit him on the shoulder as he climbed out and stones began to splash round his feet and bounce off the car as he slammed the door behind him.

"Git for go! White man git for go!"

"Samuel Assissay say white man no good!"

Jimmy straightened himself up abruptly and advanced on the labourers. Gradually the shower of stones dwindled, then as the ringleader bent to pick up another missile Jimmy shoved out a foot and he went down on his face in the mud from what was nothing more than a neat schoolboy trip.

Immediately, the expressions of the volatile Sierra Leoneans changed to broad grins as the unfortunate man picked himself up and began to brush the mud from himself.

219

"You damned great fool, Malaki," Jimmy said angrily. "What the hell do you think you're doing, throwing rocks at me?"

"White man no good," the black man spluttered, spitting out mud.

"Don't be a damn' fool or I'll tell your wife about you. She'll handle you. She doesn't want you to go calaboose, you fathead."

The grins of the crowd grew wider as the black man began to look sheepish, and Jimmy laughed, a strained laugh that sounded unnatural to him. "You great clown," he went on. "What have I ever done to you for you to heave rocks at me?"

The black man's head began to hang and Jimmy turned to the rest of them. "O.K., the rest of you get back to what you were doing and let's have no more of this damn' nonsense."

"Boss Jimmy, dat ole Gotto——"

"Never mind Gotto," Jimmy interrupted quickly before the complaints could become a torrent. "I'll see to Gotto. Now get back to your work. And if I see any more of this bloodiness, there'll be real trouble. Savvy?"

When Jimmy arrived at the Mission bungalow that evening, he found that Swannack's state of mind matched his own.

"Son," he said. "The atmosphere around here is something I've never known before."

"It's that fiend Gotto," Mrs. Swannack shouted—inevitably from another room where she was sorting out schoolbooks. "Father, why don't you go down to Asimani and complain?"

"Asimani's got enough people complaining," Swannack said, immediately starting to flap his hands in agitated defence of his theory.

220

"Well, why doesn't he pass the information on to where it will do some good?" As she appeared in the doorway, Mrs. Swannack looked like Samuel itching to get at the Amalekites. "Jimmy, they catcalled me today in the town. Me and Stella. In Amama. Me! 'White Missis go home,' they said. One guy threw a stone. It hit the car. Scratched the paint. I got out and told him what I thought of him. If I could have laid my hands on him, I'd have had him down to Asimani's double-quick. I've been brought up on the Old Testament. He quit when he saw me coming. He sure did. There's too much bad feeling in this town. You know what they're saying, Jimmy?—that Zaidee Soloman's behind all this. Everybody's talking. Gotto's been seen at her house at night. Now, what would he be wanting there? There's only one thing I can think of for she's a sinful, deceitful woman."

She turned to Swannack again. "There's mischief afoot," she said dramatically. "It needs stopping. Everybody in the town knows about it. Why don't you let me report that Gotto to Asimani, Father?"

Swannack looked baffled and the hair on his face seemed to droop with his bewilderment. "I guess it's on account of the poor guy being busy enough already," he said. "It seems real silly for me to report Gotto to him when it's Gotto who's doing all the complaining."

"Then report him yourself to the Commissioner, Father." Mrs. Swannack's sharp eyes gleamed with the prospect of battle. "Or let me. I'll go. I sure will. I'll be glad to."

"Our duty is to the Lord," Swannack said, beginning to grow flustered. "Not to the law. It's our duty to pray for the poor misguided man that he'll be set on the right road, not to engineer his downfall. They tell me he's the sole support of an aged mother."

"Oh, Lord, that mother of his," Jimmy whispered to Stella.

When they were alone, Stella turned to him.

"Jimmy," she said, "when I arrived here, everyone seemed to enjoy life. Everybody was God's children. Now they're all griping and ready to quarrel. I was with Mother in that car today. Jimmy, it terrified me. Mother must have been ashamed of me. I'm not made to do battle with Philistines as she is. She wanted to get out and set about them. She didn't turn a hair."

"I'll bet she didn't," Jimmy grinned.

"Jimmy, they just stood around and hissed and yelled. A great mob of them round the car. Samuel Assissay was there. I heard him shouting. 'White man go home,' they were saying 'White missis t'ief missis.' Jimmy, what's happening to us all? My folks are missionaries. They're not here to harm anyone."

Jimmy scowled at the floor.

"Stella, this business is getting too damned organized for my liking. They stoned Gotto today. They tried to stone me——"

"Jimmy, no!"

"Oh, it didn't last. But these two incidents—Gotto and me—they couldn't have been connected with your little circus here in Amama. Obviously there's someone in the background encouraging it on. And it isn't Samuel Assissay. I don't think he's got the brains. And it's not Indian Joe. He loves it, of course, but all he does is let it take its course now. That's what worries me—these people who are organizing it. The big cheeses are joining in. I've caught one of 'em at it already, a nasty-looking piece of work with a smart suit and all the answers. I don't like those boys. They're too clever."

He looked out at the rain which was falling again, sparkling as it crossed the beam of yellow light from the windows, gurgling in the gutters and hissing in the pools.

"Stella," he said. "When I got back from sorting out that little lot at the jetty for him, you know what he had the nerve to say to me? 'You've got to insist on what you know is right.

You've got to force your will on them. That's all these black trash understand.' Even after he'd been stoned. What do you do with someone like that?"

"Sounds dangerous talk to me," Stella said. "Sounds the sort of stuff you get out of a political pamphlet. Clerk Smith's talk."

"That's what I thought. But nobody in their senses believes that rubbish."

"Friend Gotto obviously does."

"I suppose he does. He can convince himself of anything. He can transform facts simply by brooding on them. I expect he repeats his own version over and over to himself until the rights and wrongs of it are as sharp to him as the blacks and whites of a crossword puzzle."

Stella smiled. "Mother sees things a bit like that with religion, bless her."

"When I told him I'd already reported him to Twigg, all he said was, 'I thought I could rely on you to stab me in the back.' He's so certain he's right and that everyone else's wrong. Stella, how much longer dare we let him continue? How much farther can we let him go? Every stupidity we've evaded responsibility for has been followed by a worse one. We've got to do something eventually." He shrugged. "But all we do is think he's getting near his leave and put it off till the next day in the hope that Twigg will do something instead. We've been doing that ever since he started."

He looked at the rain again. "Blast Gotto," he said angrily.

"Jimmy," Stella said, "ought we to let this affair with Zaidee continue?"

"We can't stop it. It's not illegal. They frown on these affairs with coloured women but they still go on."

"But shouldn't Twigg know? Or the District Commissioner?"

"They couldn't do a thing, Stella darling."

223

"Well, Earnshaw then. *He* could."

"God, no!" Jimmy turned quickly. "*He* mustn't know. Or there'd be murder done and then Archie would be in trouble. We don't want that."

"He's bound to find out sooner or later."

"So long as it's later. Gotto might have gone home by that time and then it'll be too late."

"Jimmy dear, are you sure you're being wise?"

"No, I'm not sure," he admitted. "But I've got to chance it. Damn him, he's caused me more trouble than all the black labourers put together. And he's worse than ever now. He was bad enough before when he was just miserable. Now he's getting vicious and he's dangerous."

He looked hard at Stella. "Listen, Stella darling," he said seriously, taking her hand. "Do me a favour, will you? Don't wander far from the Mission—at least not till Gotto goes home and this thing sorts itself out a bit, not till it settles down."

"Is it bad, Jimmy?"

"Bad enough."

"All right, Jimmy. I'll stay home."

"It's just that I don't want you to get into any trouble, that's all." Jimmy glanced at her and scowled. "Oh, hell, you know what it's all about. I love you and I'm worried."

"Jimmy darling, please don't talk about that. You know what it'll lead to: Just an argument and then we'll quarrel. And I don't want to quarrel. There are already too many people quarrelling."

Jimmy kissed her gently. "Stella, I won't. We're not going to quarrel. There's nothing so important as us being happy. Neither Gotto nor Amama nor the mine nor anything. We haven't so much longer together. You'll go home eventually, I suppose. I only want you to believe in all the things I've said about us. I want you to trust me——"

"Jimmy, I do——"

"—and more than that, I want you to need me. One day

you probably will. I hope it won't be too late when you do."

Their anger against Gotto had dispersed when Jimmy had finished speaking, and they sat in silence for a while, not looking at each other, then Stella glanced up under her eyebrows.

"Jimmy."

"Yes?"

"Jimmy, you'll be careful, won't you? I mean, with Gotto. And the people in Amama."

"Don't tell me you're worried about me."

"Of course I am. Be careful, Jimmy."

Jimmy gave her a grim smile. "Stella," he said slowly, "where I come from, they resisted the Romans, the Norsemen and the Normans. They resisted Napoleon and finally Hitler. And the Agnews were always there in the front shouting the odds and making a damn' nuisance of themselves—to both sides. Let 'em all come. The bigger they are the harder they fall. It would take more than Gotto to scare me—more than Gotto or any damn' trouble he cares to stir up."

"Jimmy, will it get worse?"

Jimmy kissed her and did his best to reassure her, then spoiled it all by trying to impress on her that if trouble did arise, she would be his first concern.

Stella looked at him, her eyes shining with trust. "Would you really come and look for me, Jimmy, if this trouble comes you say isn't going to come—in spite of everything? In spite of me saying no all the time, Jimmy?"

"You know I would, Stella. You know damn' well I would."

"Oh, Jimmy!" Stella moved closer to him and held his hand as he put his arm round her. Suddenly she felt very close to tears.

Nine

JIMMY was awakened early next morning by Amadu, whose face was grey under his black skin. His hand was trembling so that the cup of tea he held out spilled into the saucer.

"What's the matter with you, Amadu?" Jimmy asked, as he pushed the mosquito net back.

"Plenty trouble, Boss. Plenty plenty trouble."

"Black boys been after you again?"

"No, Boss." Amadu beckoned. "Come, Boss. Come with Amadu."

Puzzled, Jimmy followed the agitated man, still in his pyjamas, still holding the cup of tea. Amadu led him through the bungalow and on to the verandah where he stopped and pointed to a bunch of chicken feathers and cowrie shells which had been tied to the unpainted wooden upright which supported the roof. The previous night's rain still dripped into the puddles below and the feathers were wet and bedraggled.

"What's that?"

"Boss—" Amadu was quaking—"that ju-ju. Bad ju-ju."

"Ju-ju? What, that?" Amadu nodded furiously. "What's it mean, Amadu?"

"Bad ju-ju on house. Mean all die. Boss, I go. I leave."

Jimmy studied the black man's trembling form. "I take ju-ju down, Amadu. What then? You no leave?"

"Yassah, Boss, I leave," Amadu gabbled, his voice rising. "Ju-ju bad. All people die. Medicine man fix 'um."

"That's nonsense, Amadu," Jimmy said gently.

226

Amadu shook his head feverishly. "No nonsense. All men die for ju-ju."

"Well, look, Amadu, I give you good dash—plenty money —if you fix breakfast first. Savvy?"

Amadu stared at the chicken feathers on the upright then his greed overcame his fear, and he nodded. "Boss," he said. "I fix breakfast. Den I go."

Jimmy stared at the bunch of feathers and shells, his face thoughtful, remembering all the stories he had ever read about witchcraft and black magic, suddenly aware of the dark forces that existed in Africa, and continued to exist in spite of the white man's wisdom.

Amadu was watching him carefully, then he turned and picked up a bunch of bananas from the table on the verandah "Boss Jimmy," he said. "I bring you dese. I bring dem befo' I see dat ole ju-ju."

"Thanks, Amadu. What are they for?"

"You good, Boss Jimmy. Not like other white boss. You dash me plenty cigarettes. You bring me home when black boys in Amama Town go sock my head. You no get angry wit' me. My piccaninny called Jimmy."

"Thanks, Amadu. That's nice of you." Jimmy felt oddly touched.

Amadu's eyes flickered once more to the chicken feathers. "Boss, I go git de breakfast," he said quickly. "Den I git for go. I no come back."

As he hurried into the back of the house, Gotto appeared in his dressing-gown.

"What's got that stupid idiot?" he asked.

"How do you feel, Gotty?" Jimmy turned slowly towards him, sipping his tea. "You all right?"

"Yes. Why?"

"No pains? No headaches?"

"No."

"No stomach cramps? No touches of colic? No bowel disorders?"

Gotto frowned. "No, you fool. Why?"

"Just wondered, because you've got a ju-ju on you."

Jimmy indicated the bunch of chicken feathers. "They've put a spell on us."

Gotto stared at the feathers for a while then he laughed. "That boloney doesn't take you in, does it? They're just a lot of savages."

"Maybe," Jimmy said thoughtfully. "Perhaps it *is* all boloney if you don't believe in it. But at least it's a symbol of what they think of us."

"What do you mean?"

Jimmy drew a deep breath. "Even if it can't do us any harm," he said, "at least it means they'd *like* it to do us some harm."

Gotto sounded less convinced as he replied. "You don't believe all that nonsense, though, do you?"

Jimmy turned to him. "Do you?"

Gotto laughed again. "Me? Not damn' likely." He stopped and looked again at the chicken feathers, frowning suddenly. "There isn't anything in it, is there?"

"Well, I remember reading a story by Somerset Maugham who'd lived in the East long enough to know a bit about these things. It was about a chap who'd had a ju-ju put on him—a white man. He didn't believe in it either, but on the boat going home—long after he was away from the place—he got hiccups."

"What happened?"

"He couldn't stop and gradually he lost weight and——"

"And died?"

"Yes."

Gotto laughed again, but more nervously. "Author's licence," he said. "That's all. Author's licence. It couldn't happen. I mean, could it?"

"Ask me another."

Gotto stared hard at the chicken feathers, his face sharp and suspicious now.

"What do they do?"

"Romney tells me they do all the usual mumbo-jumbo. Kill a goat or something and dip the feathers in the blood. Something of that sort. Then the old witch doctor recites his rubbish over it. And that's that."

"I've heard of witches making little clay models of people and sticking pins in them." Obviously Gotto was not so sure of himself and his opinion now. "It all depends on how much you believe in it, doesn't it? That's all. It's as simple as that."

But he went on staring at the bunch of feathers, his eyes narrow and glittering and suspicious, his long bony nose out-thrust, his forehead puckered by a frown. And Jimmy noticed he lit a cigarette quickly as he walked away.

"I'm going to Asimani with this lot," he said as he re-appeared shaved and dressed. "I'll have that witch doctor shoved away."

"Then the fat *will* be in the fire."

"I'll risk it."

Jimmy studied Gotto with a feeling of baffled frustration. Nothing seemed to exhaust his capacity for punishment. "I should wait until after breakfast," he said. "Amadu's offered to make us some before he leaves."

"Is he leaving?"

Jimmy nodded at the ju-ju. "That was enough to convince him he didn't like the smell around this place."

"I'll soon fix that." Gotto threw away the cigarette in his fingers and bawled into the kitchen quarters at the back of the bungalow. "Amadu! Come here! One-time! Double-quick!"

Amadu appeared, rolling his eyes and keeping his distance.

"What's all this damn' nonsense about leaving us?"

"No nonsense, Boss. I go."

229

"Because of this thing here?" Gotto flung an arm in the direction of the ju-ju.

"Yassah, Boss. Plenty bad ju-ju. I go."

"Don't talk rubbish. Who's going to look after us?"

"No savvy, Boss. Amadu go."

"I'll raise your wages."

"No, Boss. I go."

Gotto had started in what for him was a reasonable manner, but seeing he was getting nowhere and that Amadu was proving stubborn, he exploded.

"You're a fool! That thing can't do you any harm!"

"Plenty fool, Boss. But I go, Boss."

"Oh, get the hell out of it, then," Gotto shouted. "But send us another boy up. Get us someone else."

"No get, Boss. No boy come. Ju-ju frighten 'um away. All boys know."

"Why? Have you told 'em?"

"No, Boss. But all boys know. All people in Amama know."

"Jungle telegraph, eh? Listen"—baffled and infuriated, Gotto made a sudden dive for Amadu but the black man dodged round the table and watched him warily from the other side.

"Come here," Gotto raved.

"No, Boss. I no come."

"I'll bloody well shake some sense into you!"

"No, Boss. You no catch Amadu!"

"Gotty!" Jimmy put down his cup and stepped between them. "Don't be a blasted fool. Can't you see this is important to him? Perhaps we can get Swannack to find us a Christian boy who won't worry about it."

Gotto turned away towards the verandah. "I'll find out who put it there. I'll get Asimani on the job."

"Oh, for God's sake—" Jimmy's temper flared up— "leave the poor devil alone for a bit. God, man, haven't

230

you noticed yet? He's bored with your complaints. He couldn't care less."

Gotto stared. "Oh, couldn't he? Right, I'll go somewhere else then."

"Gotty!" Jimmy tried to introduce the subject of Zaidee in the hope of offering a warning or clearing the air a little. "Where are you going? I know there's something going on in the village. What are you up to?"

Gotto's expression was sly. "Wouldn't you like to know," he said.

"Gotty—" Jimmy became silent as he turned away unheedingly. He watched him start his car and rocket on to the main road with a groan of springs, then, as he turned back into the bungalow, he almost trod on Amadu who was waiting just behind him.

"Hello, Amadu. My breakfast ready?"

Amadu gave the bunch of chicken feathers a sidelong glance. "Yassah, Boss," he said. "Chop ready now, sah!" He paused as he turned away. "Boss."

Jimmy stopped on his way to the bathroom.

"Boss Gotto no come back?"

"I dunno, Amadu. Why?"

"Boss, I stay cook your chop dinner-time. I 'gree for you, Boss Jimmy. I no 'gree for Boss Gotto. He come back den I go."

The rains came more heavily during the morning and the river was full of logs, driftwood, torn-up bushes, and even, occasionally, a great tree. The palm-trunk supports of the ancient jetty trembled under the feet as the weight of the water struck them. The conveyor belt, that rickety system they used for loading the boats, looked if anything less safe than it had ever done.

The pile-driver stood untended and the native labourers crouched, pinched and cold, in the shelter of the trees with

231

wide banana leaves over their heads. The concrete piles were sinking into the sea of mud that was forming on the low ground where they lay.

The mine office, its dust gone, its walls wet with the fine moisture that seemed always in the air now, was a cheerless place when Earnshaw stormed in to Jimmy. It was typical of him that he had no umbrella and that the banana leaf he held over him as he ran through the rain looked as though he'd slept in it.

"My jetty," he said savagely. "My flaming jetty! You seen it?"

"I know, I know," Jimmy said wearily, drained of energy and sweating in his oilskin. "It's falling down. But so's the conveyor. So's the explosive store. There hasn't been a pile driven in for days. His Lordship spends all his time in the foreman's hut yarning with Clerk Smith or off in the car somewhere up-town."

"We'll be losing them boats," Earnshaw said. "And then I'll sue you—or at least I'll sue Twiggy. No offence to you, old lad."

He stamped the length of the office and back, then he jabbed a dirty finger at Jimmy. "Down there at that jetty that bloody Clurk Smith's doing as he likes these days. 'Im and Gotto get on like they was running a three-legged race. Proper matey, they are. Just like two of cheese."

"Except when he goes off in the car."

Earnshaw stared at Jimmy through the grey rain-filtered light, his eyes narrow and suspicious. " 'E got a girl?—a bit o' black stuff?" he asked.

"I doubt it." Jimmy laughed nervously, trying to cover up his incautious remark, and pretended not to hear Earnshaw's next comment:

"He behaves like a bloke who's feeling his oats."

While they were talking, Alf Momo appeared in the doorway, holding an umbrella. He smiled wryly and entered the office.

232

"Boss—" he began and his very manner made Jimmy groan.

"Don't tell me," he said. "I know. Gotto."

Momo laughed, a deep, rich laugh, then his face became serious immediately. "Boss, bad man. It is good you know what he does."

Jimmy glanced at Earnshaw and went on quickly. "I know only too well what he does, Alf. Gives everybody the pip. That's what."

Momo grinned again, but once more his face became serious quickly.

"Boss, this old mine no good any more. Jetty does not get built. People all unhappy. Boss, union officials have decided to make complaint to Freetown."

"They have, have they?" Jimmy felt a vague sense of relief. "That's that then, Alf."

"Boss, he does not pay attention. Mine no longer matter. He go other place. Bad place. I see him."

"You do?" Earnshaw leaned forward eagerly. "You hear that, Jimmy? Alf knows where he goes."

"Oh, it's nothing, I suppose," Jimmy interrupted quickly.

" 'Course it is. Out with it, Alf. Where?"

Momo fiddled with his umbrella for a while and glanced at Jimmy and they listened in silence to the tricklings and gurglings of the rainwater outside until he spoke.

"Boss Earnshaw, you don't know where he goes?"

" 'Course not. Why you think I'm asting you?"

Momo turned to Jimmy. "Boss Jimmy, you don't know?"

Jimmy turned away and nodded slowly. "I think so, Alf," he said quietly. "I think I know."

"Well, come on," Earnshaw said impatiently. "What we waiting for? Why don't someone tell *me*?"

"Boss, every day he go," Momo said earnestly. "Every night he go. Plenty bad."

"Spit it out, old lad. Where?"

"Boss Jimmy," Momo said. "It is good he knows."

" 'Ere—" Earnshaw was becoming suspicious—"what's going on? Where *does* he go?"

"Zaidee Soloman, Boss."

"Zaidee Soloman?" Earnshaw gave a howl of rage, quite out of character with his dry, dusty manner. "What's he doing there?"

"Boss, I don' know. Sometimes, he stay plenty late. I see him go. My house down the road."

Earnshaw swung round on Jimmy, his face dark with anger. "Did you know this, old lad?" he asked dangerously.

Jimmy nodded.

"Well, why the hell didn't you tell me?"

"I thought it best not to, Archie."

"Best not to! Same old story, eh? The old husband's the last to know about his wife. Jesus, the laugh's on me. I reckon he thinks he's got me by the short and curlies. That's what I reckons he thinks. But he's not, you know."

Earnshaw seemed on the point of bursting with fury. He began to stamp from one side of the office to the other, swiping papers to the floor and shouting. "If he thinks he's getting anything there, he's got another think coming. I'll give him a smash in the chops. It's me as pays for that bloody bungalow —not Indian Joe. If he thinks he's going to push *me* out, he's proper in the dripping he is. He'll get a smack on the earhole. I'm a right boy to handle that randipoling streak of whitewash. He'll feel like a sick cat when I've finished fixing him."

Jimmy watched him storming about the room for a while, like a cyclone in a bottle, before he interrupted.

"Dry up, Archie," he said soberly, his face serious. "Gotto never pinched anybody. He isn't capable. If Gotto's paying regular visits to Zaidee, she made the suggestion."

"She never!" Earnshaw howled. "She wouldn't. Not after the way I help to keep her." He stopped dead, his expression
234

of furious anger giving way to one of crafty suspicion, and went on in a low furious voice. "She would though, you know. The bitch, she would. I've 'ad it afore. I'm always warning 'er."

"Oh, come off it, Archie," Jimmy said. "It isn't love Zaidee's after. Don't kid yourself. You're probably twice the man Gotto is. I'll bet Indian Joe's behind all this. They had a go at me but I didn't bite."

Earnshaw stared, calming down, then he slapped his leg. "By God, you're right, old lad! She's more Syrian than African any time." He turned and pointed. "That's where Clurk Smith got his money to buy the gramophone. Zaidee and Indian Joe gev it 'im to 'elp 'em."

"That's where he was for those three weeks," Jimmy said bitterly. "Love and indoctrination. Brain-washing par excellence. He'd fall for it hook, line and sinker. It must have stood out a mile to them the time we went to complain about the rice that he was wide open to that kind of treatment."

They were still talking when they heard Gotto's boots on the concrete step outside and, instinctively, they drew apart as he stopped in the entrance. His face was working with rage and he was saturated to the skin.

"The swine slashed my tyres," he spluttered. "While I was with Asimani. I had to come home on the rims. Christ, that finishes it! I'm going to the District Commissioner. Where's Smith? Get him to get 'em changed. There's a spare set in the store."

He suddenly became aware of them all staring silently at him across the room.

"Ha," he said sharply. "A conference, eh? To find a way to sink a knife in my back. Ganging up on me, the whole damn' lot of you."

"We're falling over backwards to *avoid* ganging up on you," Jimmy said angrily.

"Never mind ganging up on anybody," Earnshaw snarled. "What's all this we 'ear about you and Zaidee?"

235

"She's not your property!" Gotto backed away to the door immediately, his face drained of colour as he realized his secret was known. "And why not, anyway? She's the only person in this blasted place who's been decent to me."

"Decent! I bet she's been decent. I know 'er."

Gotto's eyes were bright and his face was devoid of colour. But he was defiant, and in his defiance there was confidence, something they had never seen before, something that came from the belief that someone wanted him.

"You can howl," he shouted. "But none of you lot ever helped. Whenever I appeared, you all shoved off. It was Ma-Imi all over again. Snotty Gotty. I know what you called me, all dashing off to each other's houses to talk about me and laugh at me. At least, Zaidee never did that." His voice choked in his throat. "She was the only person who wanted me around."

"Wanted you?" Jimmy hated himself as he pricked the bubble of Gotto's happiness. "God, man, it's not *you* she's after. It's the mine."

Gotto sneered. "Who's been telling tales out of school? You, Momo?"

Momo looked wretchedly unhappy. "Boss, Zaidee no good. Bad woman. All black people say so."

"Shut your great mouth, you swine," Gotto shouted, tears of fury springing to his eyes.

Momo's face twisted. "Boss, she agree too much for Indian Joe. They like that." He held up two fingers. "What she says, he tell her. She plenty wicked woman."

"You dirty rat!" Gotto made a wild swing at Momo, who received a glancing blow on the jaw that sent him staggering back, and Jimmy and Earnshaw immediately leapt on him and held his arms.

"You bloody fool," Jimmy shouted.

"That swine's not going to slander a lady—he's not going to spread his filth about a friend of mine!"

236

Between them, Jimmy and Earnshaw got him on to the verandah still storming at Momo and struggling in their arms.

"Gotto, you thrice-damned fool," Jimmy yelled above his raving. "You can be pinched for that!"

"Not after what he said about Zaidee!"

"You sawny bastard," Earnshaw roared, his fury at his punctured pride forgotten. "What he say is right enough! Christ, I don't care about the bitch! Take her if you want her. There are plenty more."

Gotto struggled in their grip, his eyes wild and not quite sane. Flecks of foam appeared on his lips as he glared at Earnshaw.

"You bloody immoral, dirty-minded drunken swine," he shrieked. "I've a good mind to do the same to you."

"Listen, Gotto," Jimmy shouted, "if you don't stop this blasted nonsense, I'll clout you myself."

With a strength that came from fury, he shook Gotto until his hysterical rage died down. Then they released him and they all stood staring foolishly at each other on the verandah, not knowing what to say, with the rain gurgling behind them from the low roof into the gutter below.

Finally, Gotto turned abruptly and stalked away past his car towards the station wagon, heedless of his umbrella which lay trampled on the floor.

"He's gone towards Amama," Jimmy said.

"And good riddance. Come on, let's have a shufti at Alf."

They turned slowly and went back into the office where Momo was still rubbing his bruised jaw.

"Alf," Jimmy said. "If you want a witness, I'll willingly speak for you."

"No, Boss." Momo drew himself up with dignity. "I no tell police. Boss, *you* muss tell."

"Alf, I will," Jimmy said earnestly. "I promise I will."

237

"Boss—" Momo's voice was full of reproach—"that what you said last time."

Jimmy flushed. "Alf, I will this time," he said. "I'll tell Twiggy straight away."

"You muss tell District Commissioner this time, Boss Jimmy," Momo went on seriously. "Bad trouble coming. I know, Boss. I African. I smell death, Boss."

Jimmy stared at him. The chickens were coming home to roost. All his own certainty of approaching disaster seemed to have culminated and crystallized in Momo's warning. He glanced quickly at Earnshaw whose face was unexpectedly grim.

"Death, Alf?" Jimmy said. "Whose death?"

"I do not know, Boss. Only death. I smell the fine-driven rain. I hear the noise of the trees, Boss, and feel the cold Harmattan wind. I know ju-ju. I know these things about Africa."

He picked up his umbrella and went out into the rain.

"Come on, Archie," Jimmy said to Earnshaw. "Let's go up to Old Doc's."

Romney dismissed the black man he had been treating in the surgery and listened to them with grave eyes that stared unseeingly through the dusty mesh of the windows. He stood with his back to them as they told him their story in excited, panting bursts, each one treading on the heels of the other's words in their hurry to get it out. All the time, his mind was dwelling more on Amama than on Gotto and on the problem that assailed him every year at this season.

'This damned rain,' he was thinking. 'Nothing thrives because of it. Nothing ever comes out right. If I could only find out how to beat it before I die.'

With a start, he turned as he realized they had finished and were watching him.

"Well?" Jimmy asked. He was seething with anger and

238

itching to destroy Gotto without mercy. "Which one of us goes down to see the District Commissioner? I'm damned if I'm going to cover up for the clot any longer. I'm sick of picking up the bricks he drops."

Romney held out a hand. "Just a minute, Jimmy. Going to the District Commissioner wouldn't perhaps be the best thing. We must think of Amama itself, and the mine after he's gone. We can't afford to let the trouble-makers think they've scored a political victory by getting him removed or they might be tempted to try again. After all, Amama must go on, the mine must go on."

Jimmy rose abruptly as he finished and started to stalk about the room, then he halted by the window where the moisture from the heavy rain drifted in through the mesh.

"Are you suggesting we leave it to Twigg?" he demanded and Romney nodded.

"Fat lot of notice *he'll* take," Jimmy commented.

"I think you'll find he'll *have* to take notice this time," Romney pointed out. "And if Twigg removes him, it will be done quietly—for Twigg's own sake. He doesn't want a scandal."

"No! To hell with Twigg!" Jimmy's answer was sharp and decisive. His eyes fixed on Romney's and held them until the older man's fell. "Alf Momo said not Twigg. It's got to be the District Commissioner this time."

"Jimmy——"

"It's no good, Doc. I'm not having Twigg. He'll put us us off again as he did last time."

They became silent again and Romney knew they were waiting for him—as they had always waited, as Amama had always waited—to set the seal of approval on their decision by his word, to accept the onus of what they were doing, and he felt the weight of responsibility on his plump bowed shoulders. Suddenly he felt he had grown too old for decisions of this kind.

He sighed as he was driven by their silence to take the initiative. "All right," he said heavily. "Let it be the District Commissioner. Someone must tell him." He took his glasses off and began to polish away the moisture, his mind working like a tired machine. "But *you* can't leave Amama, Jimmy. You must stay here to keep an eye on him in case there's further trouble."

Earnshaw looked up at him, shrewd as an old fox. "And you're too old," he said. "That leaves me. You said it nigh on as good as I could have done meself, give the time and place. O.K., I'll be spot ball. I'll go down tomorrow—early."

Romney turned to Jimmy who, it was clear, would have preferred to be the instrument of Gotto's downfall, and occupied his uneasy mind with trying to placate him.

"This way, Jimmy, you can't be accused of engineering it so you can take over his job," he pointed out. "People talk too quickly about these things out here." He was speaking rapidly, nervously, still unconvinced of the rightness of what they were doing.

"Don't worry about him, Doc. Just leave it to me," Earnshaw said in his rasping crusty voice and Romney saw with a feeling of guilt that he was relishing the task. "He won't know whether to laugh or sing hisself to sleep the time I've finish with 'im. I'll play it big and use both 'ands. He'll be up here with half the Protectorate Police Force. It's all over bar the shouting."

They stared at Romney again, the surgery tense in the silence. Outside, the steady roar of the rain was interspersed with the drip drip drip from the eaves into the puddles.

Romney sighed and turned back to the window. It was done now. The decision was made. It was out of his hands. Probably it was better, he thought, but he still could not divorce himself from a feeling of ruthlessness. He felt like a judge who has just pronounced sentence.

240

Part III

Part VII

One

AMAMA was quiet as evening approached. Romney, busy in his surgery, failed to notice the arrival of darkness. Earnshaw, as was his occasional habit when he was drunk—and he was drunk now because his sour thoughts on Zaidee had encouraged him to be so—occupied himself with teaching Suri and two or three other members of his crews the intricacies of housey-housey, something they never managed to master. Gotto was shaving himself to see Zaidee and, at the other side of the bungalow, unspeaking, hugging his secret to himself like the guilt of murder, Jimmy was preparing for his usual visit to Stella Swannack.

In the early evening before dark a storm of particular intensity broke over the town. For an hour or more, there were violent electrical disturbances, with purple flashes and great squalls of wind that set the palm tops tossing. Then the thunderstorm stopped abruptly and the rain died away, leaving only the weeping leaves. The atmosphere was heavy, humid and depressing.

With the thunderstorm, however, everyone felt a little happier for thunderstorms usually meant the approach of the end of the wet season, a relief from the inexorable descent of the rain, and everyone took it to be the first sign of the long-awaited break in the weather.

It was this feeling of relief after the cheerlessness of the heavy downpours that first started the celebrations. Someone, happier than the rest, decided to get drunk and from his solitary beginning, the excitement spread. The first drum started shortly after dark. Pay day, coinciding with one or two other local celebrations and a wedding caused people to bring out their palm wine and home-brewed beer. Fires were lit, kerosene lanterns and torches appeared, and as the rain gave way to a bright sky with stars pricking their way through the palm fronds in the first clear evening for several weeks, one or two more people joined the few drinkers in premature parties. The biscuit-tin zithers began their flat plink-plonking. A juggler started his act and a snake-charmer brought out his ugly performers. Another drum, the shape of a long cylinder, joined the one at the central fire, then another like an hour-glass, and another, until eventually there were more than half a dozen, and black hands were fluttering over them and the bom-bom-be-bom-bom could he heard as far away as King Tim where the fishermen, scenting excitement and dances, got out their own instruments and set off to join in.

Then some lean-flanked labourer from the mine started a dance. He was joined by a big man with an umbilical hernia and in no time there were thirty or forty of them shuffling and stamping and clapping and chanting in front of the fire, a swaying mass of black figures silhouetted against the flames, their flat feet stamping down the wet earth into a hard-packed, concrete-like platform.

Women began to join the crowd and palm wine and beer were passed round more often while forgotten children dropped asleep in the nearest doorways. Before long, the whole of Amama Town had joined in among the native huts.

Clerk Smith, unable to join the tribal celebrations by virtue of the starched suit, spectacles and sun hat which put him in a race apart, bought beer, palm wine and a bottle or two of gin from Indian Joe with the money Zaidee had given him and, with it, enticed a drummer away from the main dance to start a party of his own with his family and relations. Since he was doing most of the talking and not keeping an eye on the drink, several hangers-on joined in and started a

244

smaller party of their own outside the hut and eventually, as Smith became a little more noisy, the two parties merged into one, a xylophone of split bamboo was produced, and a song started.

> "On de banks of Moa River,
> On de banks of Moa River,
> On de banks of Moa River,
> Dat whar I make ma home."

Suddenly, Smith remembered his newly acquired gramophone and held up his hands in the doorway for silence, a skinny figure in the firelight, his spectacles glistening importantly, his face shining with perspiration.

"All come," he shouted joyfully, enjoying his new role of a man of wealth. "All muss come to my party. Personal Assistant Smith famed along de whole Coast for de size of his parties. Personal Assistant Smith de mos' famous man on de Coast. He read. He write. He type better dan de Queen England. He dance better. He make better music."

The small boy he dispatched for the gramophone returned with it on his head, followed by another carrying the solitary badly scratched record of Carmen Miranda with a reverence which would have been fitting for the Crown Jewels. Smith placed the record on the turntable with due ceremony and started it for the enthusiastic members of his party.

"—yi yi I like you vairy much," came the sudden thin screech of a female voice in the middle of a sentence, competing none too successfully with the various scrapes, scratches and roars which made it sound more like two bush-cats mating in the hills. "I yi yi yi yi I theenk you're grand——"

"White mammy," Smith pointed out gaily. "Finest singer in de whole worl'."

He signed to the drummers to take up the tune and the

245

two different rhythms competed in a cacophony which was not allowed to stop, for as soon as the record had ground its way to its end Smith started it again.

"Come," he said, when the party was well enough under way for him to be able to direct its destinies as he pleased. "We go see my friend, Boss Gotto. Boss Gotto welcome us. Boss Gotto my good friend. He go sleep my udder friend, Zaidee Soloman, who buy me de gramophone."

The noise of the party passing penetrated to Romney's surgery but he had heard it hundreds of times before, at Christmas, public holidays, births, deaths and marriages, and the celebrations of the various secret societies which existed round Amama. His mind still occupied with his conscience, he hardly lifted his head, for he knew the Sierra Leonean as a happy soul by nature who was always seeking something to celebrate in his noisy fashion. In his own untidy bungalow, Earnshaw—Zaidee completely forgotten by this time—never even heard it. As with the doctor, the noise had been his background for so long it was as familiar to him as the sound of his own breathing, and, for the same reason, just as unnoticeable. And, besides, having instructed his boys in the use of the housey-housey counters, he was now beginning to play the game for money.

"O.K.," he was saying. "Eyes down for the count. Clickety-click. Sixty-six. You'll soon learn. That's two sixes together like this 'ere. Legs eleven." He paused to glare at Suri. "Two ones, you soft clot. Don't you know yet? You're a proper sawny, you are. Bed and breakfast. That's a two and a six. No, you great soft donkey, you can't 'ave won yet. I've only called three numbers. Use your swede a bit, can't you?"

Half a dozen black brows were contorted in an endeavour to understand.

At the Swannacks, Jimmy and Stella listened to the noise with something like awe.

246

"It's like this for weddings," Jimmy pointed out, glancing hopefully at Stella.

"Don't let's talk about that, Jimmy," she said. "Let's just enjoy the moment."

"No two normal people," Jimmy said very deliberately, "in full possession of their faculties and the normal amount of hot red blood in their veins, can go on like this. After a while, you get to thinking more of what you ought to be thinking about—marriage and the things that go with it— and less about what the other's saying. It's the most natural thing in the world. It's like the hen following the egg."

Stella looked stubborn, though there were tears in her eyes, and ten minutes later they were clinging to each other in a kiss which only served to make Jimmy more doggedly sure of himself.

Gotto, leaving a sleepy-eyed Zaidee Soloman to hurry back to where he had left his car with its new tyres in the shadow of a group of cotton trees on the road to the mine, listened to the drumming and the shouts and was not reassured by her claim that it was all noise and palm wine and no danger.

He had heard drumming and noise before but nothing quite so intense as this, and he looked uneasily at Zaidee's black maid who was to show him the way, wondering if he could trust her. The slashed tyres and the stoning of the previous day had unnerved him, but he hadn't had it in him to withstand Zaidee's command and he had arrived at her bungalow as usual after dark.

As he set off for home, the series of events which were to become known in the official records as the Amama Incident were set in motion.

Earnshaw was deep in a noisy argument over the housey-housey. He had been drinking gin all evening and Suri had had more than one with him, a treat Earnshaw allowed him

247

from time to time when he was feeling mellow. The others had all been drinking native beer.

"Listen, you stupid black clown," Earnshaw was bawling at the top of his voice as he pounded his fist on a housey-housey card. "I keep telling you you don't shout 'House' until you've filled your bloody card up!"

"Boss, I filled 'um," Suri was shouting back, equally indignant.

"Yes, you silly old fool, and with all the wrong numbers. You're the balmiest old duck I ever see in all me puff. There's one 'ere, for instance, what you've filled in and it ain't been shouted yet."

"Shouted?" Suri and the others stared, baffled by the white man's bewildering games. "I muss shout it, Boss?"

"Oh, Christ!" Earnshaw took a flying kick at the housey-housey card and counters and sent them across the room where they rolled clattering under the table to join those left from the last violent argument. "Let's 'ave another drink. Pass the bottle, Suri, you ugly bastard, and 'ave one yerself. It's enough to make a man go mental."

He rose with his glass of neat gin and walked towards the verandah to get some of the hot still air of the evening, and as he opened the door, he almost fell over the flying figure of the small black boy he employed to sweep the decks of his boats and make tea.

"Boss! Boss!" The boy's thin voice shrieked a warning. "De jetty done go bust!"

"What?" Earnshaw slammed his glass down with such force that it shattered. He swore and crammed a cut hand into his mouth. "What's that?" he mumbled through his fingers. "Let's have it again."

"Boss, big tree come. Jetty go bust."

"Jetty's bust? Oh, Christ, just like I say! That bloody Gotto! Suri! Bryma! You, there, Sam! Off you go! Sharp

248

now!" Earnshaw flung out a hand and pointed, dripping blood. "Get down there and rescue them boats. Go on, Shorty," he said to the boy as the others tumbled out of the room, sending chairs and bottles flying. "What else?"

"Boats go get plenty mix with piles, Boss. Boats go get on mud."

"O.K., Shorty. That'll do. That's enough for any man." Earnshaw was already moving purposefully about the room, pushing a knife into his belt, reaching for his battered bush hat. "You stay 'ere. You savvy Boss Jimmy?"

"Yassah, Boss." The boy's face split in a grin.

"Well—" Earnshaw paused to suck his cut hand again— "you nip around between 'ere and the mine bungalow and Missis Swannack's and Old Doc's. When you find Boss Jimmy, tell 'im the jetty's gorn and we want more help— more black boys. O.K.?"

"O.K. Boss."

"Right. Off you go."

As the boy slipped away in the darkness, Earnshaw set off at a heavy trot after Suri and the others, stumbling and falling more than once in the deep ruts made by the Euclids. The sky was still clear and the air less stifling now that the grey clouds had rolled away, but as he staggered towards the jetty, his shirt was sticking to his back with the heat, his face running with perspiration. He was already stone cold sober.

At the jetty he saw the glimmer of hurricane lamps and the flash of Suri's torch. Where the loader had stood was a wreckage of twisted iron and palm-tree logs, some of them splintered and broken, with the conveyor belt half submerged in the brown water that swept about it. Occasionally, a piece of drift-wood broke surface, heaving round in the creamy foam, then submerged again and disappeared.

Of the jetty there was nothing left beyond one or two uprights and the huge tree which had wrought the damage, grey-green and slimy, its branches shattered, its roots worn to stumps. The rest of the jetty had brought up farther downstream against the few piles that had been driven into the mud as the foundation for the new concrete loading station. The whole trot of boats appeared to have been wrecked. Two were jammed inextricably between the concrete piles and a third stood half on its end between them, grinding and groaning in the pressure of the swollen river. About them were the remains of the hut where passengers waited on the jetty in the rainy season, the grey-brown planks and the poles, and the bent corrugated-iron sheeting.

"Christ Almighty," Earnshaw breathed. "O.K., you boys," he shouted. "Lay 'old of some crow-bars and ropes. Bryma, get aboard there and see what you can do. Suri, get a 'andy billy from the store. We might be able to 'aul it off between us."

As he finished speaking, he waded down the slipway and stood waist-deep in the swirling water, his shoulder against the outermost of the three boats, trying to assist the scrambling black man above him. Suri came running back with the handy billy and Earnshaw made one end fast to the bow of the outer boat and the other end fast round one of the inshore piles.

"Now, you black sinners, pull! 'Eave!"

While Earnshaw and his boys were sweating by the ruined jetty, Gotto was approaching the spot where he had parked his car.

As always when he had left Zaidee, he was anxious to be home and in the familiar surroundings of the mine bungalow. He had never fitted into Zaidee's background of gaudy shawls and bead curtains and the antimacassar atmosphere of Amamã, of pictures on the walls cut from the *Illustrated London News* and the *Tatler*; and now, as always when he had put her behind him, he was eager to be back among the things he knew, the dusty area of the mine and the scarred trees, the rutted roads, the foliage broken by turning Euclids. The fires behind him were synonymous of evil and in the thump of the drums were all the mysteries of Africa.

He crept along the dark paths between the tall grass and the banana plants, and round the backs of the houses, following the black girl who trotted along just ahead of him. Once he had to back deep into the undergrowth as he heard a group of men approaching, noisy, laughing and clearly in a high good humour. His pulse throbbing in his throat, he realized that a month or so before he would never have dared to walk along this path in the dark either with a guide or alone, but Zaidee's passion and, even more, his loneliness, had driven him to do things he would never normally have contemplated.

Stumbling against a couple of figures in the dark, he stifled a yelp of fear and hurried past as he realized it was a young man and his girl darting away from the firelight and the noise, as anxious to avoid being seen as he was, and he burst thankfully out of the wet head-high grass on to the road alongside the cotton trees where his car was hidden. Zaidee's maid halted alongside it and smiled with a flash of white teeth. A mosquito whined near her and she smeared it down her arm without even looking at it—instinctively, as though she had been doing it all her life.

Gotto dropped a few washer coins into her hand and started the engine of the car. Then, thankfully, he rolled and bumped along the last few hundred yards of the uneven road towards the mine, splashing in and out of the unseen potholes in the dark. Several times, he saw fires burning at the roadside and heard laughter and even had to avoid groups of white-clad figures standing in his path. But the mood of the crowd seemed to be good and one or two of them even waved to him.

His fear had dropped away from him as he turned the car into the clearing in front of the mine bungalow, and he frowned as he saw the lights were on. He had expected to be first back and had hoped to avoid the chilly silence with which Jimmy

251

would be bound to greet him. Their furious argument that morning over Momo had not yet gone from his memory and the temper that had risen in him still left a sour taste in his mouth.

As he climbed out of the car, he heard the sound of laughter and singing and even drumming from inside the bungalow and he stopped dead.

"My God, a party," he said aloud. "At this time of night."

The thought of facing Jimmy and a hilarious Earnshaw, both of them ready to torment him with private jokes and quicker wits than he could muster, made him seethe with anger. For a moment, he debated whether to walk boldly through or go to his room via the house-boy's quarters, then he recognized in the voices the peculiar high-pitched note of excited Africans.

Red rage surged over him as he stormed towards the bungalow steps. Inside, the living-room was a wreck. There were twenty or thirty black men and women in there. Bottles littered the floor and at least two unconscious people were lying in corners. Chairs and tables had been pushed back and in the centre of the room Gotto recognized Earnshaw's ancient portable gramophone, screeching out its tune at tremendous speed.

"IyiyiyiyiIlikeyouvairymuch,
IyiyiyiyiIltheenkyou'regrand."

The words, with the speed regulator advanced to its limit, came out only as a gabble and the group of drummers in the corner sweated and rolled their eyes in their efforts to keep up with it as the tinny tune scraped across the room with the sharpness of a chalk dragged across a slate.

Clerk Smith, his spectacles, white suit, umbrella and topee discarded, danced a frenzied shuffling dance round the gramophone, clad only in a pair of tattered underpants.

252

"What the hell's all this?" Gotto roared and the drums stopped immediately. Several of the black men scrambled to their feet and moved back and, in the sea of silence that flowed after Gotto's shout, the gramophone still screeched its gabbling tune, a reedy pipe punctuated by the roars where scratches marred the record.

For a second or two, Smith continued to dance, then the absence of the drums edged in on his senses and he stopped, panting and sweating, his eyes wild. Recognizing Gotto, he approached him, obviously very drunk, his hand extended, a wide, white grin on his black face.

"Boss Gotto," he said gaily. "My friend Boss Gotto. All my friends here now. Boss Gotto go sleep my good friend Zaidee."

"Shut your mouth, you clown," Gotto shouted, shoving him away violently.

Smith's eyes clouded then he grinned again and advanced once more.

"Boss Gotto make joke," he said. "We no laugh. Ha ha! Clerk Smith, you de stupidest damn' ole fool in de whole worl'. Boss Gotto make joke. You no' laugh."

"I'm not making any joke," Gotto raved, suddenly scared of Jimmy arriving unexpectedly and finding the party in possession of the bungalow. "Get this mob out of here, you clown. Get out!"

"But, Boss, we come join you. We come make laugh and dance and sing. Plenty palaver."

Gotto could hardly speak for the rage that engulfed him. "Out," he stormed and, seizing Smith by his skinny black arm, swung him almost off his feet in a great scything movement, that sent him skidding along the concrete floor on the seat of his grubby pants. One foot jarred against the gramophone, ending the song in a violent shriek that added one more scratch to the record, then he crashed into a basket chair, and, with its shattered remains round his neck, ended upside down against the wall.

253

At once, as though at a signal, the room emptied. There was a rustle and in silence all the other black men and women disappeared through doors and windows until the room was clear. Even the two unconscious figures were whipped away, the drums, everything. Only two or three empty gin bottles lay on the floor, one still rolling—and a few dirtier bottles which had contained palm wine.

Smith climbed shakily to his feet.

"Boss Gotto, you my friend," he said hesitantly, game to the last, but Gotto gave him another violent shove that sent him flying down the steps on to the muddy moonlit earth outside. Almost before he had landed, his clothes came flying out of the door after him, then bottles, then the record of Carmen Miranda which shattered at his feet, and finally the gramophone. It landed by his side with a crash and the twang of a broken spring, and became silent, the turn-table still spinning idly of its own volition.

Smith stared at the gramophone for a while then, still only in his torn underpants, he flopped on his knees beside it in the mud with a wail.

Frantically, he wound it up and waited for the turn-table to spin. When it didn't, he moved it with his finger and watched it run down again to a stop.

"Dis ole t'ing go break," he howled in an outburst of misery, tears coming to his eyes.

He wound up the machine again and tried once more to spin the turn-table, then still on his knees, he searched round for the broken parts of the record.

"Ole Carmen Mirandy no sing no mo'," he mourned noisily. "Dat ole Gotto go break 'um."

He turned towards the silent bungalow as his rage burst out of him. "You bloody damn' ole white bastard," he shrieked at the closed door. "You go break my Carmen Mirandy! You break my gramophone! You damn' bloody fool white man, why you no' open de door? I t'ink you my friend. I tell Sargy Asimani. He come take you for calaboose."

For some time, his spectacles awry, he stormed at the unresponsive bungalow, then, still shouting and muttering to himself and with tears of rage and unhappiness streaming down his black face, he scooped up the gramophone, cradling it to his skinny bosom like a mother with an injured child. He picked up the pieces of record and what he could find of his clothes and began to stagger out of the clearing towards Amama.

On the main road, his friends met him, first one or two, emerging from the shadows where they had hidden to watch the fun, then in groups.

"Dat old Gotto," Smith shrieked at them in English. "He go break Carmen Mirandy. De music no play. No parties. Clerk Smith go tell Sargy Asimani."

They commiserated with him noisily and offered him a drink. Eventually, he permitted someone to carry the gramophone for him while he retained his clothes and the pieces of broken record, then the whole lot, drums, bottles of palm wine, broken gramophone and all, set off towards Amama Town, bewailing the villainy of Gotto for spoiling their party, Smith's arms going like a set of station signals all the time, his crumpled white suit flapping in his hands as though in distress.

As they moved slowly along the road in the faint light of the stars, passing in and out of the shadows that striped the silver, others joined them, most of them not very interested in Smith's sorrows but all of them enjoying the noise and the shouting.

Driving towards the jetty with the half-dozen labourers he had rounded up on receiving Earnshaw's S O S, Jimmy passed them as they entered the outskirts of Amama Town. They were straggling across the highway, still drinking from bottles, pushing each other and quarrelling among themselves, the major issue lost in the presence of a dozen smaller

255

ones. Their black faces were almost invisible but their clothes stood out, disembodied and wavering about like ghosts in the starlight.

As he edged past them, they shouted at the station wagon and one or two of them even shook their fists, but they all moved back and offered no sign of violence.

He had hardly halted the vehicle at the jetty when Earnshaw appeared out of the darkness, smeared with black mangrove slime, his face drawn with exhaustion.

"How many you got, old lad?" he asked.

"Six," Jimmy said. "I crammed 'em in. I can easily fetch you some more if you want 'em."

"Don't bother. Any more'll only get in the way. Come on, old lad, help me get 'em on the job. A couple of the boats is 'oled and there's some more on the mud down-stream."

He pushed a crow-bar into Jimmy's hand and they set off towards the dim outline of the pile-driver and the ghostly shapes of the piles that stuck out of the mud like gravestones.

"What's all that shouting going on up there?" he asked.

"Party, I think," Jimmy said. "They've all been celebrating. I passed a bunch on the road arguing about something."

Earnshaw grunted and indicated the boats jammed against the concrete piles. "This is a fine old lark, ain't it? Your pal, Gotto."

"He's no pal of mine."

"If he'd got on with the job, that jetty would have been finished."

"It would have been finished if he'd only let the men get on with the job."

"Have it your own way. Anyway, my bleedin' boats has gone. *And* my jetty. *And* if it interests you, your conveyor. Christ, he won't half catch a cold when I see him. I'll let him have the length of me tongue, I will proper."

256

"Much more sense to let the D.C. have it tomorrow," Jimmy said soberly.

Clerk Smith's party duly arrived back in Amama and the drumming and the dancing and the drinking there stopped long enough for his followers to swell to a hundred or more. They swept up the centre of the town towards the police station, with Clerk Smith lost in the middle of them, hugging the gramophone to his breast again while someone else carried his clothes. He was still shouting and weeping alternately.

"Dat damn' bloody ole Gotto," he was wailing. "He go smash de music. Now no dance. No drumming. No parties."

Those round him who could not hear properly assumed that Gotto had forbidden dancing and music, and the noise grew louder. Outside the police station, Sergeant Asimani, uneasily comparing his few court messengers with the number of Smith's supporters, tried unavailingly to break up the milling crowd, but it was still there when Samuel Assissay and the city-suited gentlemen from Freetown arrived out of the shadows and started to harangue the fringes. Indian Joe, sitting in his chair at the entrance to his bar, smiled his mouthful of gold teeth and leaned forward delightedly to see better.

"De Lord say de white man go pinch all Africa from de black man," Assissay was yelling. "De Bible, dat good book, say all men equal. Black man rise up, go punish de brutal white man."

The spectacled, suited gentlemen from Freetown took up the chant. "Go punish the white man," they shouted. "Down with the white man who steals the African's land."

The crowd had been good-natured up to this point but, like all African crowds, it was easily stirred to excitement and anger, and the words of Samuel Assissay and his friends fell on ground sewn with discord by Gotto. Before long, they were surging up through the centre of Amama Town again and

Swannack and his wife and Stella watched them pass with worried eyes.

"That's a big crowd, Mother," Swannack said quietly. "Biggest I've seen yet, I guess."

"Sure is, Father," Mrs. Swannack shouted. "I don't like the look of it. It looks ugly."

"Is anything going to happen?" Stella asked.

"I don't know, child. I hope not."

"I wish Jimmy were around," Stella said half to herself. "He'd know what to do."

"I figure there's a lot of our flock there, Father," Mrs. Swannack observed, eager for battle, her eyes bright as she peered into the darkness. "We should go and talk to them."

"They look as though they want more than talking," Stella said uneasily.

By this time the crowd filled the whole of the open space in the centre of Amama Town, a mass of moving figures and wavering torches that etched reddish highlights on black faces. Occasionally, someone was trampled on or knocked on to a fire and suffered minor burns. A woman was crushed against the wall of a house, and a mud hut was pushed over. When Clerk Smith, fortified and encouraged by the enormous number of what he took to be sympathizers, set off back towards the mine bungalow, the crowd accompanied him, sweeping round him and in front of him and behind him where Samuel Assissay's friends were whipping in the laggards. There were dozens of dogs on the move with the mob, and more dozens of small boys, running and leaping in and out of tne huts, shouting, yelling, taking the opportunity to create mischief. One of them set fire with a torch to the grass roof of a hut out of sheer devilment and the owner, a Mende, having rescued his family, set off, protesting noisily, to search out the nearest Temne on whom he could wreak his vengeance.

Assissay was marching next to Clerk Smith now, urging on the mob.

"De children of the Lord God," he was yelling, "go fight de good fight. Onward, de soldiers of de Lord."

Someone, not knowing what the uproar was about, started to sing 'Onward, Christian Soldiers', as he had been taught by Swannack, and it was taken up like a revolutionary hymn by a section of the crowd, which immediately became involved with a group of pagans and a secondary brawl started.

Smith was in his element. "I go punch dat ole Gotto in de nose," he was shouting to those around him who were really no longer concerned with his troubles in the general excitement.

"I go tell him, Boss Gotto, you no do dat to Personal Officer Smith. I tell Sargy Asimani. He come pinch you for calaboose. I come punch you on de nose. I no' agree for you no mo'."

He squared up, his thin arms in the stance of a pugilist, and shadow-boxed with himself for the next hundred yards until one of his flying elbows hit his neighbour in the eye and started another scuffle. His clothes had long since been stolen and all that he now possessed were his topee, his spectacles, and his muddy cotton pants. Even the gramophone had disappeared, knocked out of the hands of its bearer, trodden on and kicked into a water-filled gulley out of the way of bare toes. Carmen Mirandy had been ground to dust in the confusion.

"I punch him," Smith was shrieking. "Like dis. One—two—t'ree."

"Down with the white oppressors," roared Assissay.

"Down with the white men," shouted the agitators from the fringes and back of the crowd well away from the front where they might get hurt.

"Down with the whites," roared the crowd delightedly, neither honestly meaning it nor sincerely understanding why they shouted it, but enjoying the noise, the mass movement. It was all far better than the dancing.

Two

GOTTO heard the crowd approaching the mine bungalow while it was still more than a mile away. As he went to the door to see what was happening, he was knocked aside by the frantic figure of Amadu, their former house-boy.

As he shot past, Gotto grabbed him by the collar of his shirt which promptly split down the back, and the two of them staggered apart. Amadu turned and stared at him, his eyes rolling so that only the whites showed.

"Where Boss Jimmy?" he panted.

"God knows," Gotto snapped. "What's going on? What's got you?"

"Dat ole Clerk Smith. Big crowd. Dey come for fight. Shout 'Down with white man.' Where Boss Jimmy?"

"What do you want him for?"

"I tell him go hide."

Even in a moment of panicking fear, Gotto was bitterly aware that Amadu was not including him in his warning.

"What do they want?" he shouted, leaping across the room and grabbing the house-boy's wrist.

"Boss, it dat ole ju-ju. Black men come. Big numbers. Plenty plenty men."

Gotto twisted the black wrist until Amadu yelped with pain.

"Are they coming for me?"

"Yassah, Boss. Boss, where Boss Jimmy?"

"To hell with Boss Jimmy." Gotto flung Amadu away. "I'm getting out. Which way are they?"

260

"De Amama Road. Boss, where——?"

"How far away?"

"All de way. Dey just leave Amama Town. I come plenty quick. I run."

"All the way, eh?"

Gotto thought quickly. Not far along the road was Earnshaw's house and, beyond that, Romney's. He knew he could reach them before the crowd from Amama did, and he knew the respect with which both were held. He pushed Amadu aside and ran for the car. Starting the engine and letting in the clutch, he shot off with spinning wheels and rocked out of the clearing into the road.

The vehicle slewed half round in a skid as he stopped at Earnshaw's sprawling bungalow with its overgrown garden and empty bottles and the petrol tins of geraniums on the verandah. In the distance, as he leapt from the car, he could hear the shouts of the crowd, could even see the pinpricks of red light where the flames of the torches danced against the dark back-cloth of the trees. Then, in a couple of bounds, he was inside the bungalow.

The lights were still burning, and chairs were overturned, and there was a half-empty gin bottle on the table where Earnshaw had left it when he had been called hurriedly to the jetty.

"Earnshaw," Gotto shouted, his voice cracked with strain. The echo came back to him hollowly from the back of the house. "Earnshaw! Where the hell are you?"

Obsessed by the darkness, the silence of the bungalow and the noise of the approaching crowd, he was caught by a shudder of fear.

"My God," he muttered. "They must have got him."

As he turned towards the door again, his eyes fell on Earnshaw's rifle lying, as usual, on the old-fashioned horsehair couch he used. Gotto's long legs took him across to it in a couple of strides and he snatched it up. The breech was

261

empty and he looked round wildly, wondering where he might find some ammunition. He began to plunge about the bungalow, panting, the sweat streaming down his face as he opened drawers and cupboards in frantic haste, tumbling tins and dishes to the floor.

Finally, in a drawer of the old-fashioned treadle sewing machine warped to sticking point by the damp, he found a solitary bullet, typical of Earnshaw, thrown there at some time when he was emptying his pockets.

Gotto thrust it into the breech and slammed the bolt home. Then he ran for the car and drove madly towards Romney's.

The doctor was standing on the verandah, smoking and listening to the noise of the crowd. As he saw the car come to a stop, he turned abruptly and went inside, followed by Gotto.

"The mob's coming," Gotto panted, flourishing the rifle. "We've got to hold 'em off."

"Don't be so dramatic, my dear lad," Romney said mildly in an effort to calm him. "This isn't cowboys and Indians we're playing."

Romney's calmness made Gotto feel stupid and in his embarrassment he shouted louder.

"They're coming, I tell you. They're up the road. They've already got Earnshaw."

"Not they. He's the last person they'd ever get, even supposing they wanted him, which I doubt. There's been a lot of drinking, I suppose, and they're excited about something, but they'll do no harm if you don't do anything stupid."

His eyes fell on the rifle in Gotto's hand. "What are you going to do with that?"

Gotto looked down at the weapon, suddenly foolish in front of the unperturbed old man. "Hold 'em off, I suppose," he mumbled.

"Is it loaded?" Gotto nodded. "Then don't be stupid.

And for God's sake don't let that crowd down the road see you with it. It's just the thing to cause trouble."

"I'm not letting go of this," Gotto said viciously. "Not likely."

"Don't be a damn' fool. Give it to me."

"No. They're not going to catch me."

Romney half turned and seemed to be studying the reply, when he suddenly swung his arm. His podgy fist caught Gotto on the end of his bony nose as he dodged back, and made tears come into his eyes. By the time he had recovered his wits, Romney had snatched the rifle from his hand and thrown it on the table.

"Now don't be such a damn' fool," he said sharply. "You don't use guns against black people."

"I expect you've got a gun hidden away somewhere for yourself," Gotto yelped, furious with pain and the humiliation of being disarmed. "You want those black devils to get me."

"Better have a drink," Romney said calmly, offering him a glass.

Without a word of thanks, Gotto swallowed the drink, spluttering and coughing as it burned his throat.

"It's all right for you," he shouted as he got his breath back. "You've nothing to live for. You're a damned old criminal. That's what. Dodged out here to avoid the police. An abortion case in Birmingham."

Romney's expression didn't alter and his very indifference made Gotto feel foolish.

"So you managed to find out," Romney said. "How?"

"My girl wrote and told me. You can't hide things like that, you old crook." The new imperious Gotto, bolstered up by Zaidee's encouragement, was eaten away by panic and was crumbling back into the old querulous mean man.

"And what do you intend to do about it?" Romney asked.

"I'll see that everyone knows. I can soon tell Swan-nack."

"My dear boy, Swannack knows. It's true enough. I've never denied it. It was a poor devil of a woman with seven brats already and a lout of a husband who knocked her about. I'd do the same again given the same circumstances. As it happened, I wasn't responsible but I told her what to do and where to go. But they bungled it and I was implicated. But this is Amama, son, not Birmingham. They don't care two hoots here why I came."

Gotto stared, infuriated and thwarted, aware that Romney was right, and that his news, the well-stored piece of scandal he had intended using as a threat, was worthless.

Romney glanced through the open door before turning back to Gotto. They could hear the crowd, still in the distance but clearly drawing nearer.

"And what are you going to do now?" Romney asked.

"What can we do?"

"Well, what you *ought* to do is to go down to the mine office and stay there."

"On my own?" Gotto's words came in a thin shriek.

"If *you're* there, they won't touch anything."

"Don't be a fool. That's asking for trouble."

"Listen, son," Romney said in his gentlest voice. "These people are excited and probably will be all night, but they won't touch you. The penalty's too high. Just have a bit of courage and stay down there with the lights on. They'll make a lot of noise but they'll eventually go away if you don't do anything foolish."

"I'm not going. I'm staying here with you." Gotto's words were almost a plea.

"You're responsible for that mine." As he spoke Romney remembered they were even then hoping to remove him from that responsibility but he realized that if they could tell Twigg he had stayed at the mine throughout the uproar it would at least stand in his favour. "It's your job to look after it," he ended.

264

"Not damn' likely. Think I care about the mine? Where's Agnew? Let *him* go. He should be here."

"I'll find him and send him down at once. I'll send Earnshaw, too. They won't attempt anything with Earnshaw there. I'll get the boy to find them immediately."

Romney took a step closer to Gotto.

"Think, man, what will Twigg say if he hears you just left the place? This is your life. This is your career." As a sop to his conscience, he was trying to persuade Gotto to redeem all his stupidity with one small fragment of courage and commonsense that might be held to his credit when they were weighing up his record. "And after all," he ended. "They might not even get as far as that."

It was this final point that convinced Gotto.

"All right," he said unwillingly. "Are you coming?"

"I've got a maternity case here. Looks like being complications. I can't leave it."

"That's a good excuse."

Romney ignored the comment. "You'd better go. Jimmy and Earnshaw will be along in no time."

Gotto was left alone as Romney turned to the back of the house, shouting for his house-boy. He was trembling violently, aware of things out of his control, things he didn't understand, of the violence of Africa, its darkness, its size, and all the shadowy things that went on that white men didn't know about. He lit a cigarette jerkily, then his eyes fell on the rifle on the table by his side and he reached out quickly and put it outside the door.

Romney returned. "I've sent my boy to find them. I'll send them straight along. You'll be all right. Don't forget to put all the lights on. Conspirators don't like the light."

As he turned again towards the back of the house, Gotto ran towards the car, picking up the rifle as he passed. He was determined not to be separated from that rifle and its single bullet if he could help it. Its shiny stock with its brass plate

265

gave him a feeling of greater confidence as he felt it in his hand.

Although there was still a lot of laughter, the mob that moved along the muddy road was getting somewhat unruly round the fringes. One or two people were taking advantage of the confusion to pay off old scores. One or two more grass thatch roofs had gone up in flames en route and there had been several cracked heads.

As they drew closer to the mine, Clerk Smith found himself in the lead, thrust forward by all those who had no wish to be in front if Sergeant Asimani and his men should appear before them with staves and fists and feet. He was glistening with perspiration and he had now lost his topee and his spectacles, those symbols of his education and respectability. He was quite drunk, not only on his own verbosity and the noise, but on the palm wine that was constantly being thrust on him by laughing well-wishers who were looking forward to the fight with Gotto.

"Bim bam bom," he was shouting as he swung his fists in the air. "I fight Joe Louis, dat ole champion man. Bim bam bom. Down go Joe Louis. Clerk Smith de champion of de worl'."

At the back of the mob, the city-suited gentlemen were encouraging the passing round of palm wine, shoving forward with cries of encouragement any who looked like growing bored and slipping away into the darkness. Samuel Assissay was lost in a fanatic circle of his own noise, singing hymns, reciting psalms and quoting thunderous prophesies from the Book of Isaiah which was the only part of the Bible he had ever absorbed.

"Behold, de Lord's hand is not shortined, dat it cannot save; neither his ear heavy dat it cannot hear. Advance, de slaves and hear de word of de Lord to arise."

Sitting in the silent mine office, gnawing his nails, with the rifle across his lap, while the bugaboos of being made to sleep alone in the dark as a child came rioting back to him, Gotto licked his dry lips as he heard the shouts in the distance.

Following Romney's advice, he had switched on all the lights about the place, even the arc lights outside, where moths immediately crowded round in fluttering multitudes, but he had felt naked and too visible to his enemies and one by one he had switched them off again, first the ones outside, then the office lights, and finally those in the room in which he sat. He could hear the generator putt-putting in the distance like the ticking of a time bomb, in its chatter a suggestion of power, but nothing would have induced him to switch the lights on again.

He had no idea what he ought to do and he was praying aloud that Jimmy and Earnshaw, the scruffy, immoral Earnshaw he had always detested, the capable, uncrushable Earnshaw who was never upset by any crisis, would arrive and take the unbearable responsibility off his shoulders. He sat in the shadows of the unlit office, his feet rustling the gritty mud beneath his boots, petrified by fear of the darkness, yet unable to bring himself to move.

He had parked his car among the trees at the back of the building where it would not be seen and he was still hoping the mob would sweep past him and leave him alone.

The prospect of being in the middle of two or three hundred black men—drunken, noisy, argumentative, probably awkward black men—terrified him and he found himself wondering if anyone would miss him if anything happened to him, and whether Doris would ever even think of him again. His mind still held clearly the emptiness of her last letter.

His thoughts fixed on the blurred image which was all he found he still carried of her in his mind, he listened again to the sound of the crowd as it approached the opening in the banana plants where the road ran into the mine yard.

267

Outside, he could see the night watchmen slinking away, anxious to avoid being caught up in any trouble. Then, in the faint light of the stars, he saw the first of the mob come sweeping into view, tumbling and rolling between the trees, crushing down the foliage like some vast flood, boiling over the ground, breaking into smaller rivulets as they eddied round obstructions, to end in a seething mass in front of the mine office.

Trembling from head to foot, Gotto remained seated with the rifle across his knees, wondering what he ought to do, trying desperately with all the courage he possessed to resist the craven desire to dodge silently through the back door of the office and into the bush.

He knew perfectly well that what Romney had said was right, that while there was a white man at the mine the mob would do no damage, and he knew that what he ought to do was switch on all the lights and stand in the doorway and tell them to go away. But Gotto simply could not bring his will to force his legs to function. They seemed separate entities from his body and the message from his brain was not carried by his numbed nerves to his muscles.

The mob was still milling up and down the mine yard, shouting and calling, occasionally throwing things, but to his surprise doing no actual damage beyond trampling down the few flower beds Jimmy had planted and smashing the small trees and shrubs. Finally, they halted in front of the office, and he realized that the skinny black figure in front of them, wearing nothing but a pair of linen shorts, was Clerk Smith. It was only the high-pitched voice that gave the figure identification.

"Dat ole Gotto," he was shrieking. "He go break de music! Stop de party! I fix 'um! Bim bam bom!"

His bony arms were flailing but he was incapable of any other action beyond talk. He was too drunk to stand up straight and his monkey-like chattering was an incoherent babble

268

from which Gotto could pick out only the recognizable words like his own name.

For some time the crowd swarmed round the yard while Samuel Assissay urged them in his strident voice to "Rise against de white man," and the agitators on the outskirts tried to whip up greater enthusiasm. But the crowd, many of them mine-workers, were too well brought up to the knowledge of law and order and respect for the property which was also their livelihood to do more than make a noise.

Gotto was not aware of this, however, and as they seethed nearer to the door of the office, he clutched the rifle more tightly, still incapable of standing on his feet.

Then someone at the back, more drunk than vicious, threw a stone, which crashed through the window of the next office and the sound of broken glass tinkling to the floor in the darkness brought Gotto to his feet at last.

Smith was standing in front of the crowd, carrying out a violent soliloquy above the catcalls of the others, threatening, demanding, complaining all at once, the only thing in his mind the broken gramophone and the humiliation it had caused. Assissay was driving that magnificent voice of his through the din like a battering ram punching through wood—"Rise de workers of de Lord, and take over de white man's t'ings"— but he was careful enough to do no more than shout. Gotto, in the dim interior of the office, unheard and unseen by the crowd, clutched the rifle in his sweating palms, holding it out in front of him like a lance as though he were afraid of it, conscious only of hundreds of black faces and hundreds more shouting mouths and wild eyes and waving arms, and the depth and thickness of the darkness.

At last, Clerk Smith, like the rest of them unable to pluck up courage to do anything more than shout, backed again into the crowd, only to be thrust out once more by two or three laughing men who were enjoying the spectacle he was providing, and he staggered forward, drunk, stupid and half-doped. As he swayed he was given another shove and, still wailing and shrieking and beating his breast, he stumbled towards the office steps.

Gotto watched him coming, his throat dry with fear.

"Dat ole Gotto," Smith was yelling. "I kill him dead. I cut his throat from dis ear to dat ear. I tear him to pieces, de damn' bloody bad man!"

While he was still cavorting on the top step, Gotto fired.

He was not conscious of pressing the trigger. One moment, he was holding the old rifle in front of him vaguely in the direction of Clerk Smith a couple of yards away, outlined in the doorway, and the next the crash and the flash of the flame that leapt from the muzzle burst through his numbed senses. He caught a whiff of the cordite that blew back towards him and he saw Clerk Smith leap into the air as the bullet hit him in the throat, his arms outspread, his fingers clawing like talons at the empty air. He heard the thud as the body clattered on the wooden steps and rolled over, head over heels, heels over head, appearing to spin on its skull, legs kicking wildly in the air, then crash flat on the trampled earth and quiver to a stop, sightless eyes staring at the stars.

The yelling died at once and a vast sigh rippled through the crowd, then the shouting broke out again as they began to back away and eventually fled howling through the undergrowth and down the road towards Amama Town.

Gotto stood in the dark office, still holding the now useless rifle, staring at the empty space in front of him where the crowd had been and at the sprawled corpse of Clerk Smith, still quivering in the mud, one foot twitching slightly.

For a moment he was horrified by what he had done. Then the fact that the crowd had dispersed began to make him feel bold and brave and resourceful. What Zaidee had said came back to him—"Be strong. It's the only thing they understand" —and he began to feel he ought to have acted more boldly

270

before. Then he stared at Smith again and it dawned on him he had killed a man, had committed a murder.

He had never seen a dead man before, not even a decently dead one, let alone one who had met his end as violently as Clerk Smith had. It seemed impossible to Gotto that anyone who had been as noisily alive as Smith had been a few seconds before could now be so silently dead.

"Don't do anything stupid," Romney had said, and he had done the most stupid thing of all.

Even as he caught his breath at the enormity of it, he realized that the mob hadn't disappeared for good, but had only gone for reinforcements and weapons, and that it would be back in a far uglier mood than the light-hearted spirit with which it had originally invaded the mine.

He dropped the rifle with a clatter to the floor and ran through the rear door of the office, his only idea to get away before the crowd returned. Vaguely, there was a feeling in him that Zaidee would know what to do.

He started the car, crashed into gear, and shot out of the mine yard.

Three

LABOURING by the shattered remains of the jetty, Earnshaw and Jimmy heard the shot which killed Clerk Smith but, preoccupied as they were with the job of getting the boats free before the falling tide left them high and dry, they barely noticed it and put it down at once to Swannack out shooting somewhere nearby.

It was the glow in the sky which first really caught their attention and halted them in their task.

Straightening his aching back to mop his face, Jimmy caught sight of the red glimmer over the trees from the direction of Amama Town.

"Archie," he said. "What's that?"

Earnshaw stopped working long enough to glance over his shoulder. "Nigs celebrating," he said. "There was fires all over the shop when I first come down here."

Jimmy continued to stare over the silhouetted trees. "It's damn' big, you know," he said. "There's more than a palaver fire or two burning there."

Earnshaw looked again. "Come to think of it, old lad," he said. "Perhaps you're right."

"Did you hear a shot a while back?"

"Swannack."

"That's what I thought," Jimmy said. "But Swannack was busy when I left. And surely he wouldn't go shooting as late as this."

Earnshaw, too preoccupied with ropes and tackles to be interested in a solitary shot, looked up with an irritated scowl.

272

"Romney then. Shooting a rat."

Jimmy's face, picked out in flickering yellow by the glow of the hurricane lamp, was worried. "Archie," he said. "I don't like it. When I came down here, I passed quite a crowd charging about the road——"

"Oh, Christ," Earnshaw said angrily. "Leave that lark to Gotto—worrying, that's *his* job."

Jimmy turned back to his work, his mind heavy with the certainty of disaster which had been on him all day. "All the same, I don't like it. That crowd on the road. The shot. Those flames over there." He squinted towards the trees again. "Archie, they're bigger than they were."

"Well, what do you want me to do about 'em? Spit on 'em and douse 'em? I got enough on 'ere, ain't I?"

"How much longer are you going to be?"

"Not long. We'll get one free and have done. If you wanting to be off, scarper. I can manage now and you're all bloody thumbs, anyway."

Jimmy grinned briefly. "O.K., Archie," he said. "I just want to be certain that fool Gotto hasn't started something."

"Started something? What could he start?"

"He could start lots of things."

Earnshaw glanced shrewdly at the glow in the sky. "O.K., kid," he said. "Off you go. I'll see you back at my place for a drink."

His brow puckered, he stared after the tail light of the station wagon as it disappeared. He glanced towards the trees again and the glow in the sky, then he shrugged and turned back to his work.

He had almost finished when he heard the slap of bare feet on the muddy road and turned round to see Amadu totter down the hill and out of the shadow of the cotton trees.

"Boss Earnshaw! Where dat ole Boss Jimmy?"

"What's up? What's happened?" Earnshaw tossed aside

273

the crow-bar he was using and grabbed hold of Amadu, who almost collapsed into his arms, panting.

"Boss Jimmy——"

"He's gone. Up there somewhere. What's up? Come on, spit it out!"

"Boss, plenty trouble. Clerk Smith done get shot."

"Well, button my belly button! I expect it serve him right though. He hurt?"

"Yassah. He plenty hurt. He dead."

"Jesus!"

"Black men go look for Boss Gotto. Dey set houses on fire."

Having lived at peace in Amama longer than he cared to recall, Earnshaw couldn't believe his ears now that the trouble he had been expecting had arrived. "Gawd," he murmured "A riot."

"Yassah," Amadu panted. "Boss, you come quick."

When Jimmy reached the mine yard, the place was deserted. There was no sign of the watchmen but there were obvious indications that a large number of people had recently been there. The foliage at the entrance was crushed and the flower beds he had so laboriously planted had been trampled flat. There were also odd things lying about in the mud—a hat, a few bottles, a stick or two, stones by the dozen—and Jimmy stood by the station wagon in front of the office with the feeling of being in the presence of ghosts.

The windows of one or two huts were broken and as he entered the office the glass crunched under his feet on the verandah.

Clerk Smith's body had long since been dragged away and was at that moment being paraded on a litter through Amama Town, while slogans stamping him a martyr were being shouted by Assissay's friends.

Back at the office, however, there was no sign of what

274

had happened beyond the few silent objects lying about the yard. Jimmy switched on the lights and immediately saw the rifle Gotto had dropped lying half under the table.

He recognized it at once as Earnshaw's and he found the hair on the back of his neck tingling with the certain knowledge that something evil had happened there. He threw the rifle into the station wagon, closed the office doors, and set off in search of the night watchmen. His headlights throwing a dancing beam before him on the wet zigzag road, he explored the workings and toured round the silent diggers and the deserted Euclids.

As he reached the mine yard again, he noticed that the glow from Amama was greater than before and that he could actually see sparks flying into the air in the hot up-draught of a big blaze, and he decided to go back towards the river and collect Earnshaw.

He met him on the muddy slope, toiling up with Amadu and they jumped into the station wagon thankfully.

"Better get along to your place," Earnshaw said immediately. "Summat's up. Amadu says the mob's out in Amama. It sounds like the mother and father of all riots. Somebody shot Clurk Smith. Amadu says he's dead. He thinks it must have been Gotto."

"Gotto? Oh, God!"

"That's what I said," Earnshaw said laconically. "Or more or less. It's come at last, old lad, and we're too late to stop it after all. I only 'ope they tear 'im limb from bloody limb."

They halted for a while at the mine bungalow where the litter from Clerk Smith's party still remained.

Earnshaw's bungalow was also empty, but Romney's seemed to be full of black people, most of them bandaged and frightened.

Romney came forward to meet them with a worried expression. There was blood on his shirt and his thin grey hair

275

was awry on his head so that he looked frail and elderly as he told them what he knew.

"They tell me Clerk Smith's been shot dead by someone— I suspect Gotto——"

"I found a gun at the mine office," Jimmy said.

"*My* gun," Earnshaw pointed out.

Romney stared with narrow eyes at the weapon. "That's the one. He had it when he came here. I took it off him but he must have got it again."

Jimmy looked towards the flames in the sky. "What about the Swannacks?" he asked.

"I wouldn't like to say, Jimmy," Romney went on cautiously, oppressed by the thought of his own bad advice. "Amadu tells me the mob have burned down the police station."

"Oh, Jesus," Earnshaw said. "Poor old Sargy."

"He's safe," Romney pointed out. "They took to the bush. Asimani will have sent a runner for help by now if I'm not mistaken."

"Is it bad, Doc?"

"Looks like it, I'm afraid, Jimmy. Amadu says they're after Indian Joe now. It'll be Gotto next."

Earnshaw looked hard at Romney as he fished for a cigarette in the pocket of his bush jacket.

"Doc," he said, unearthing one at last. "You want me to go and get him? I will if you want me to."

"I think we'd all be safer here," Romney said, worried that further deaths might be on his conscience. "If he's not at the mine, God knows where he is—probably up in Amama Town with Zaidee Soloman."

"I'm going up there," Jimmy said suddenly.

Earnshaw popped the cigarette into his mouth abruptly. "Don't be a fool, old lad," he said. "They class you with Gotto. They might nab you, too, and you can't tell what might happen if they do. They're not responsible when they're like this 'ere. I seen 'em afore."

276

"All the same, I'm going. I'm going to try and find Stella. Doc, can I bring them back here?"

"Of course you can. I don't think they'll touch us here."

"Right." Jimmy set off for the door, but Earnshaw's hand on his arm swung him round.

"Hold it, kid," he said gently. "Don't take the station wagon. It ain't all that far. They'd spot you immediate. Use Shanks's pony."

Jimmy grinned nervously. "O.K., Archie."

"And kid"—Earnshaw's hand still held his arm as he turned away again—"black your face. That'd make it harder still."

"O.K. What with?"

"Plenty of slosh outside."

"Right." Jimmy darted outside and, on his knees in the road, scooped up handfuls of mud and rubbed it on his face and hair and legs and arms. Earnshaw nodded approval.

"Lovely, kid," he said. "Now, how about changing clothes with old Amadu 'ere? Them things of yours is a bit too smart!"

He watched Jimmy soberly as he stripped off his shirt, his body smooth and boyish-looking. "Reckon I'd better come with you," he commented.

"You'd be better employed going to Ma-Imi for help."

"Perhaps you right at that." Earnshaw grinned and slapped his shoulder. "So long, kid, and good luck."

Dressed in the charcoal-smelling clothes of the house-boy, his face plastered with drying mud, Jimmy set off at a jog trot for Amama Town. The road seemed full of people, mostly in large groups, shouting, gesticulating, arguing, straggling across the highway, clotted in the doorways of huts. They were still noisy and angry but suddenly they were drunk only with excitement. The gaiety had gone.

Jimmy kept to the shadows and wherever possible used the bush paths off the road. Once he crashed into a staggering man who caught hold of his arm and seemed loath to let

277

go, and Jimmy set him reeling back with the only native oath he knew, a word of considerable obscenity Amadu had spent hours explaining to him.

'Fools rush in,' he thought as he set off again. The angels seemed to be scurrying like mad past him in the opposite direction.

His heart was beating wretchedly in his chest and he was covered in perspiration which carved white marks in the mud on his face, but he was indifferent to his own discomfort in the agony of fear he felt for Stella. His mind was filled with all sorts of horrors and he found himself muttering out loud as he ran.

'Stella—I'm coming— Look, my darling—I'm going to get you out of this—lark— You're going to marry me, see?'

Once, as he drew near to the town, he ran into a crowd which had spilled out of a house. They were armed with bottles and sticks and stones and were in an ugly mood. In the light from the doorway, he saw a man in torn clothes and bleeding from the mouth being dragged hither and thither and beaten by staves and fists. A woman screamed and he saw the thatched roof go up in flames.

He stopped dead in his stride, panting, suddenly conscious of the night scents about him struggling through the smell of burning foliage. For some reason, they calmed the panic in his heart and his breathing slowed.

'Steady, The Buffs,' he said out aloud.

He had a feeling he ought to confront the mob and clear a path for himself simply by the coldness of his eye and the immaculateness of his bearing. Then he realized that his bearing, in Amadu's stained clothes, was anything but immaculate, and that the mob was a large one and in a nasty mood.

'Better submerge!' He dived into a clump of banana plants at the side of the road and immediately found his arms round a woman, who squealed and crashed off into the bush.

278

Terrified, he sprawled in the tough grass for a moment, then he realized the woman was probably hiding from the crowd as he was, and he crashed off after her in the darkness.

Amama Town was teeming with people, its rutted roads solid with black figures.

"Death to the whites," Jimmy heard again and again as he slunk between the houses. Several times in the shadows, he crashed into someone, and once had to use his fists, shoes, everything he possessed, to drive off a man who tried to grab him.

The banana plants which marked the entrance to the Mission bungalow were broken down, and littered about were the scraps of clothing and dropped weapons which marked the passage of the crowd. His heart in his mouth, Jimmy stumbled up the lane towards the bungalow and he stopped dead as he saw the schoolroom had been razed to the ground, the charred timbers still glowing in the darkness. The doorway of the bungalow swung open, symbolic of loneliness, of disaster.

'God, oh, God, no,' he said to himself.

He moved through the silent building, holding in his hand a stave he had uprooted for a weapon. Cupboards and drawers were flung open and clothing was scattered about the floor. Under the table, he found one of Stella's cameras and the bush hat her mother sometimes wore.

As he searched the place, his eyes smarting with tears, odd things, broken and shattered as they were, brought back to him vividly the happy times he had spent there with Stella—a wireless they had tried to dance to, a trampled alarm clock, two or three tattered notebooks, a shoe with its heel torn off.

There was no sign of a living soul about the place and he laboriously searched all the rooms with a torch he found in a cupboard, holding it shaded with his hand. Then he examined the garden with the seat where he had sat often with Stella drinking coffee, now overturned and broken. Among the still smouldering ruins of the schoolhouse, he found slates with charred edges and crumpled books, and a blackboard, smashed into two pieces down the centre.

He was in an agony of apprehension as he searched under the bushes, his mind heavy with shock as he found nothing —nothing but a ragged old black man lying by the entrance, smelling strongly of gin. Whether he was alive or dead, Jimmy could not tell.

He sat down wearily on the steps of the verandah and tried to make his mind function. It seemed reasonable that the Swannacks would have had sufficient warning from the noise to get out and he decided to make for Alf Momo's house for help.

Picking up the torch and the stave again, he trotted heavily down the lane towards the main road, his feet like lead now, his clothes sticking to his sweating body.

Once some hothead had set fire to the police station and Sergeant Asimani and his men, unable to do a thing against the numbers that had now collected, had disappeared into the darkness for their own safety, the crowd seemed to lose all control.

It had returned to Amama Town from the mine, stirred to rage by the shot which had killed Clerk Smith, to gather reinforcements and fortify itself with more drink. Arriving there, it collided with a large number of fishermen who were on their way from King Tim to join the celebrations which had started the riot and, thinking in the dark they were police reinforcements, had promptly begun to stone them. Fights with fists and staves broke out and spread through Amama, and the Mende in the general confusion began to take it out of the Temne and vice versa. Christians were beaten up by pagans, and the artisans at the mine, mostly decent men sheltering in their homes, were dragged out by groups of labourers incensed by all the false rumours that Gotto's activities had

280

started, and kicked and punched and threatened. When all the private scores had been settled there were several houses blazing and more than one bleeding figure left for dead, sprawled in the gullies and under the banana plants.

The flames seemed to incite the crowd even more and, suddenly remembering Indian Joe and the rice shortage, they swept up towards his premises.

They smashed down the barricaded doors of his bar and helped themselves to liquor, then pushed in the front of the store and, inevitably, found the rice that had been stored there. For a while they milled round outside, sharing it out, carting it away in sackfuls, bucketfuls, pocketfuls, hatfuls, carrying it in anything they could get to hold it, fighting among themselves as they snatched it from one another. Then they started to help themselves to whatever goods they found in the wreckage, and by the light of the torches they carried away buckets, kerosene lamps, toilet powder, alarm clocks, a bicycle, the old-fashioned shoes Indian Joe bought by the crate, the ancient frocks and shirts and hats, wearing them over their normal clothing. The deafening noise was increased by the sound of splintering wood and the clanging of stones raining on the corrugated iron of the roof.

Indian Joe, horrified by the turn of events, had clung to his house to the last in the hope of saving his store, and there was no chance for him. He could not drive the big Cadillac parked behind the building and he knew Zaidee would not come near the place from her own bungalow on the outskirts of the town. He was discovered under the sofa surrounded by tins of peaches which he had obviously gathered to him in case of seige, and was dragged out, pushed and punched and flung through the crowd, beaten to his knees, his face bleeding, his clothes torn to shreds. His greed had recoiled on his own head and his desperate hope of saving the store was his death sentence.

He was kicked and hammered with sticks and stones until

281

there was no life left in his fat body, which was then flung into the wreckage of his store. Some madman, egged on by drink, flung kerosene about and tossed a torch on to it and the store went up in smoke. Within a few minutes, the ancient wood-work, tinder-dry in spite of the rainy season, was caught by the flames which the up-draught dragged through the building, so that huge sparks were flung through the air, filtering like fireflies through the palm trees, to drop on the thatched roofs of other huts in the vicinity. Within half an hour, there were a dozen buildings burning round the vaster conflagration of the store.

Jimmy, edging round the backs of the houses, his face plastered with fresh mud, his clothes grimy and torn, his skin seared by the heat of the flames, was staggered by the violence. The savage mood of the mob, he realized, would not allow much sympathy even for the Swannacks. The hotheads were in control and the more sober spirits were carefully keeping out of the way or preparing to defend their own property. What few had protested had already been beaten up them-selves.

He knew his own safety was precarious. The mob was quite beyond reason now. No one knew how the riot had started, but from being an argument over a broken gramo-phone, it had developed into a frenzied desire to smash and loot and maim.

Alf Momo stood in the doorway of his home with a machete in his hands, prepared to defend it if necessary but hoping against hope the mob would sweep past without noticing him. He had seen Indian Joe's store go up in flames and had stood by helpless while others were beaten up.

His house was full of people, all huddling there behind the respect that most of the township held for him. And away at the back, farthest from the doorway and the light of the torches, the Swannacks huddled, Swannack himself bewildered by the events, hurt by the actions of the crowd, with his arms round his wife and daughter.

Mrs. Swannack had been all for staying to fight it out with the crowd. She would doubtless have given a good account of herself and might even have saved their home, but Swannack had wisely advised caution, and they had hidden in the bush behind the bungalow when the mob arrived, wide-eyed and horrified as they saw the schoolroom burned down and the mob storming through their home, flinging their possessions through the windows. They had decided to try and get to Romney's but, half-way there, had been cut off and had had to make a detour through the ditches and the bush paths to Alf Momo's. They were all three of them grimy, sticky with perspiration, tired and hungry.

"Pop," Stella said in a shaky voice. "Jimmy's out there somewhere. How long will it last?"

"I don't know, child," Swannack replied in a grieving voice, wounded beyond measure that he had had to shelter for his life, shattered to realize that the word of the Lord, in which he had always had faith, would have been useless against the temper of the mob. "I guess it will die out when daylight comes. Oh, Lord," he murmured, thinking of Gotto, "we pray that Thou will take the soul of this unhappy man to Thy bosom and forgive him this night."

"Do you often have these fun and games?" Peering past Momo's lean frame in the doorway, Stella interrupted with another nervous question. "It looks as though the Marines have landed out there."

"Should have let me talk to them, Father," Mrs. Swannack said loudly. "Now the Mission's gone."

"It was wiser to hide," Swannack insisted.

"They'd only have got in over my dead body."

"That's just what I mean," Swannack said more sharply.

Momo turned and signed for silence. "Please, Missis. No noise. They must not hear you."

283

Mrs. Swannack closed her mouth until it looked like a seam sewn in her face and glared through the open doorway of the dark house at the torches and the lights moving along outside.

The mob had passed now and only the stragglers were left, jumping in and out of ditches in their excitement, turning somersaults, fighting, scuffling as they went.

One of the last of them, his face grimy, his clothes filthy and torn, a stave in his fist, approached the house and Momo gripped his machete tighter.

"Oh, my God," Stella said, hiding her face in her father's shirt, and her mother, upright as a grenadier, glared at her as she spoke.

The man approaching the house stopped as he saw Momo, then he grinned.

"Hold it, Alf. It's me."

"Boss Jimmy!"

Momo lowered the machete and dragged Jimmy inside quickly and pushed him to the back of the hut.

"Alf," Jimmy demanded immediately. "The Swannacks? I've been looking for them everywhere."

He had got no farther when Stella, bursting through the black people between them, flung herself into his arms, sobbing.

"Oh, Jimmy, Jimmy, Jimmy! You came to look for me. I knew you would."

His cheek close to hers, Jimmy was speechless with relief for a time. His arms holding her tight, he took in everything around him, the dark native house with its solitary lamp, the black faces and white eyes, the mammy consoling a whimpering infant at the breast, and in the background Swannack, grimy, older suddenly and tired-looking, and Mrs. Swannack, hard as nails, straight-backed and fierce of eye.

For a minute, he held Stella silently, his mind flooded with relief.

"Jimmy," she whispered. "What's happening?"

284

"Oh, nothing," he reassured her lightly. "The boys are having a bit of a tea-party."

"Jimmy, I knew you'd come. I knew you were out there somewhere. I was worried stiff about you."

"Honest, Stella?" Jimmy's grimy face lit up. "Honest, darling?"

"Jimmy, I thought you were one of the mob at first. I thought it was the end. I thought I was going to die without ever seeing you again. That was the horrible part."

"Stella"—there was a lump in Jimmy's throat. He had to stop speaking and Stella looked up quickly at him.

"I feel like having a good old cry," he said quickly. "Silly, isn't it?"

Stella's fingers were tenderly feeling his muddy face and he managed to smile. "It's all there," he said.

There were tears in Stella's eyes. "Oh, Jimmy, you've grown up suddenly."

"Well, that's what you always wanted, wasn't it?"

"Yes, but I mean, I—I guess—oh, Jimmy, your funny old face's gone——"

Jimmy allowed himself only another moment of pleasure, then he turned to Momo.

"Alf," he said. "Can we all get to Old Doc's? I think we'll be safe there."

"Safe here, Boss Jimmy."

"Not Mr. and Mrs. Swannack. I think I'd better take them."

Momo nodded. "O.K., Boss. I come also. I know quick way through bush. My sons guard this home." He indicated three strapping young men in shorts.

"Fair enough, Alf. As soon as possible then. I suggest we black our faces."

Jimmy turned to Stella. "Stella, we're going to Old Doc's. You'll be safer there. Alf will show us the way. He can find you something to wrap round you and something for a head-

285

cloth. Make you look like a mammy. Think you can make it?"

Stella nodded speechlessly but she was suddenly cheerful again, her mud-streaked face and untidy hair the banners of her courage.

Jimmy patted her shoulder and went to the doorway to scoop up a handful of wet earth. "O.K.," he said. "Hold up your face, darling. You're going to have a mud-pack."

They reached Romney's house almost without incident, to find it more crowded than ever with black people. Romney looked tired and Jimmy noticed there were more stains of blood on his trousers. There was hardly any room in the house now. Every available chair was taken and there were people sitting on the floor.

Someone rose to let the newcomers sit down, and Swannack flopped into a space but Mrs. Swannack remained standing as though it were an act of defiance.

"Where's the crowd now, Jimmy?" Romney asked.

"Coming this way. I think they're on the way to the mine again. Think I ought to go there?"

Stella's frightened eyes swung in his direction, and Romney shook his head. "I think not," he said. "There's plenty to do here. Perhaps Mrs. Swannack and Stella will give me a hand in the surgery?"

Mrs. Swannack headed for the door immediately, rolling up her sleeves, looking as though she were going to give battle instead of succour to the injured.

"And perhaps you, Swannack, will get this lot singing or something. Get a prayer going. Anything to take their minds off what's going on."

Swannack rose quickly to his feet, and Romney turned again to Jimmy.

"I've got a fractured skull and one or two broken bones. And one man with his wrist slashed with a knife. Nasty job. Cut the tendons. I've had to stitch it up. That's the worst

286

though, thank God. See if you can find anyone among the crowd with any knowledge of first aid. We may need them."

He was directing operations like a general and as he and Jimmy moved towards the surgery they heard Swannack reciting a psalm in the other room.

"Yea, though I walk through the valley of the shadow of death——"

Below his tired voice they could hear the murmuring of the others, then the psalm became a prayer and eventually a hymn, sung hesitantly, wavering for once without Mrs. Swannack's brassy confidence to give it strength.

"Doc," Jimmy said. "Where's Archie?"

"He's trying to get downstream to Ma-Imi."

"Good enough." Jimmy paused for a second before continuing. "Doc, I'm going to look for Gotto."

"Jimmy, no!" Stella's words burst out of her involuntarily and Jimmy took her hands gently, his eyes still on Romney.

"You don't have to, son," Romney said soberly. "It's Tom Tiddler's ground up there."

"I know. I saw it. But the idiot will only get himself into worse trouble."

"It's his fault, Jimmy," Stella begged. "It was always his fault."

"I know, Stella, my darling, but that's no excuse for not going. I shan't be long. I'll have a scout round. I might find him."

"But, Jimmy, the mob——"

"Don't worry, Stella"—Jimmy's voice had taken on a possessive note now as he spoke to her, a confident note that indicated he was sure of her at last—"I've got the hang of this game now. They won't get me."

He kissed her cheek. "Give the doc a hand," he said. "It'll take your mind off things a bit."

Before she could say any more he had slipped out of the door.

By the time Jimmy came up with the mob again, it was sweeping back towards the mine. They were still carrying Clerk Smith's body on its litter, jolting it about in the pushing and shoving, sometimes almost upsetting it in the excitement. The skinny Smith had never commanded such attention in his life as he did in death.

The crowd was moving much faster this time than before. Though there were more of them, they were more drunk, more angry, after their success against Indian Joe's store, and Melikuri Tom and a gang of ex-soldiers had joined in now, bolder than the rest with their wartime experiences. Samuel Assissay was almost forgotten in the noise he had stirred up, and his city friends, sensing that things had gone too far, had slipped away silently.

The mob swept round Romney's house and hospital, singing ribald songs and shouting catcalls.

Romney appeared on the verandah, while everyone inside held their breath, and found himself face to face with Assissay, whose fanatic eyes were blazing with excitement.

"Hallo, Samuel," he said. "So you managed to get it going then?"

Assissay stared back with an earnest conviction that was impressive. "I de leader for de Lord. I lead de black men, de mammies and de piccaninnies, back to de new Jerusalem. De Lord say so. De Lord protect de black men from evil."

"The Lord's not a police force," Romney said slowly.

"De Lord punish de wicked. De Lord say all men equal."

"You seem to have rather a monopoly on the Lord."

"Black man rise at last against white man."

Romney lifted his eyebrows. "Well, tell 'em not to do any damage round here, Samuel, or there'll be trouble. Headman and chiefs put ju-ju on this place. Just you clear 'em out. Savvy?"

Assissay glared at him for a moment, baffled by his matter-of-factness, then he turned to the crowd, holding up his hands. "Any you niggers go catch anything belong Ole Doc, I fix 'um. Savvy?"

The crowd parted for him to make his way to the road, and started to disperse in silence until they reached the highway when the shouting commenced again.

As Romney watched them go, he heard Swannack behind him.

"Say, how do you do that?" the missionary asked bitterly.

Romney turned to look at him without speaking, his heart sick inside him.

The mob swept once more into the mine yard. The grudge they felt had become a personal one. Their rage had been worked off on Indian Joe and now they were looking for Gotto. Most of them had suffered in some small way, directly or indirectly, from his stupidity, yet none of them had previously dared to do anything on his own against authority. Now, however, now that hundreds of them were moving in unison, they found their courage. They all wanted to see the destruction of Gotto—yet none of them really expected to be the instrument of destruction. Every man there believed it would be the man next to him in the jostling crowd and not himself.

They approached the mine offices warily at the spot where Clerk Smith had been shot then, realizing they were empty, surged forward, shouting, and proceeded to tear the place apart. Chairs, tables, filing cabinets, plans, maps, were all flung through the doors and piled on the fire that had been started, then someone flung a torch into the office and the whole building began to burn.

Eddies of the crowd ran to the mine workings and to the lorry park. A whole row of vehicles went up in flames as petrol was poured over them and ignited. There was a crash as the boom of one of the diggers collapsed and buckled, and a yell went up as someone set fire to the explosives store.

Meanwhile, leaving the offices burning behind them, the main bulk of the mob began to move again, on to the mine bungalow, still in the hope of finding Gotto. They poured through the building, shouting and slashing at everything within reach of their machetes, putting torches to the curtains and furniture.

Jimmy followed them, hanging about in the darkness on the fringe of the mob, not knowing quite what to do, hoping against hope that if Gotto made a dash for it, he would see him first.

Four

EARNSHAW'S arrival at Ma-Imi caused an uproar. Twigg was having one of his periodical parties and Earnshaw's appearance in the middle of it, weary, muddy and in a mountainous temper, provided quite an eruption.

He arrived just when the party was at its height, red-eyed with the smoke, his shirt scorched by flames, his hands bruised and his body aching with his efforts to launch an overweight Susu canoe.

He had struggled with Suri and two other boys in the swiftly ebbing tide to float the only boat he had salvaged from the wreckage of the jetty and had managed to pole it down-stream in the darkness to King Tim. There he had begged a native dug-out, a cigar-slim affair half full of dirty water and fish guts, and he and Suri had pushed themselves off again.

Twigg's amiable drunkenness disappeared as Earnshaw told his story, downing great gulps of whisky and soda while he talked.

"There they are," he was saying, surrounded by wide-eyed men and women holding glasses, "burning and smashing everything they can lay their hands on. You've lost your mine office by this time, Henry Twigg, or my name's not Archibald Earnshaw. You've lost your bungalow, too, I'll bet. But that's nothing. Indian Joe's lost his life and so have one or two others. It's a proper barney, believe me."

"The swine," someone said from the back of the crowd. "The treacherous swine."

"Treacherous, my backside," Earnshaw said hotly. "It was just the way it happened."

"But, I mean, setting about everybody like that."

"Listen, old lad," Earnshaw said aggressively, "it ain't the wogs what's to blame, so don't you make no mistake about it. If anybody's to blame, it's that flaming Gotto."

"Gotto," Twigg said in amazement. "What's he done?"

"What hasn't he done? I reckon he's upset everybody in the whole of Amama."

"How long has he been doing this?"

"Ever since he went up there."

"Well, why didn't someone tell me?" Twigg's voice rose in a welter of indignation.

"Listen,"—Earnshaw half rose, his eyes angry—"somebody did tell you. I did. Young Jimmy did. If you'd taken some notice it wouldn't have happened."

"But I thought you were only acting the fool."

"You know bloody well we wasn't acting the fool. You didn't want him down here. That's the trouble."

"I hope you realize what you're accusing me of," Twigg said with an intoxicated dignity.

"Not half I don't. And if you don't stop arguing about it and get on with something a bit sharpish, *everybody* up there'll cop it. Young Jimmy. Swannack. Romney. The whole lot."

As Earnshaw finished, Twigg was galvanized into life, hiding his confusion at knowing he was in the wrong by violent action.

He ran out of the room shouting for the house-boy and sent him in search of the native drivers. One of these he sent in a lorry for the police, others to load vehicles with supplies of all kinds, food, bandages, and tents.

Then, with his jeep full of people and the lorries behind crowded with more people, black and white alike, and followed by an odd procession of cars, they set off towards Amama, in a nightmare drive up and down the house-side hills and round the hairpin bends of the bush road.

The mob had split up a little now, beating at the under-growth in the shadows round the mine bungalow. They were howling with rage, cheated of what they were seeking. All the hatreds and enmities that had been worked out during the night had crystallized now into the greater one—the mad desire to get their hands on Gotto. Everything was being laid at his door, even Indian Joe's treachery and greed, even the Mende dislike of the Temne and the Temne hatred of the Mende, even the resentment of the ex-soldiers. Every little quarrel was being blamed on Gotto. Houses had been burned, people had been beaten up, and everyone seeking vengeance seemed to be seeking Gotto.

Their quarry, hiding in a drainage gully beneath the black base of a banana palm, watched them shouting and screaming through the burning bungalow with eyes that were shocked with fear, his own peculiar brand of obsessed fear of the dark-ness and black African faces. Most of the mob had clubs or staves or bottles, but he could also see the flash of machetes and even an occasional spear.

His face was stiff with horror and his muscles were frozen into immobility again. For the life of him just then he couldn't have moved. He could hear his own name shouted over and over again with the lusty hatred of the half-crazed mob, washed backwards and forwards like driftwood on the tides of sound.

He had fled from the mine office after Smith's death and had tried to get up to Romney's but there were still sufficient stragglers from the mob in the roadway to prevent him pass-ing. In a state of panic he had hidden in the bush and eventually had returned to the mine bungalow, hoping Jimmy and Earn-shaw would find him there, but again he had waited too long in an agony of indecision, and when he had finally tried to creep away again he had been stopped once more by growing groups of whooping black men, the vanguard of the returning crowd. Several times since he had been almost trodden on as they dashed past him and now they seemed to be everywhere, all round him as he lay beneath the banana plant, naked and vulnerable without the car and petrified by their violence.

Beyond the fear the noise engendered in his mind was only one emotion—resentment. There was no feeling of guilt, just the firm belief that this horror had been wished on him by the treachery of others—Jimmy, Earnshaw, Romney, Twigg, Alf Momo, even the people back in London who had tricked him into coming to Sierra Leone.

From the first day of setting his foot ashore in Freetown from the ship which had brought him from England, he had been fighting this mounting sense of indignation. The romantic Africa he had read about had not emerged—only a raw, ugly land of poverty-stricken dwellings and dirty villages, with the inevitable congregations of vultures and starving thin dogs that sickened him, and the hundreds of millions of insects, grossly huge or infinitesimally small, that had scraped at his nerves until they were paper-thin.

He had been unsettled from the start by the heat and the savage splendour which had given him too many impressions to cope with at once and, try as he might to see Amama as Jimmy saw it, the palm trees had remained just palm trees and the mountains had remained just mountains.

He lifted his head as the noise seemed to die down and for a moment he thought the crowd had dispersed. Then he realized they were systematically beating the bush around the bungalow for him, their silence an indication of their determination. They were moving slowly round the building, beating at the foliage and the grass with their machetes and staves, and he suddenly knew the feelings of a rabbit trapped in a dwindling field of corn as the reaper draws near.

Inside his brain was still the nagging feeling that he must reach Zaidee Soloman, that she would know what to do. That her advice up to now had been wrong never occurred to him. She had not criticized him. She had let him make his clumsy love to her, and that was sufficient. The bludgeoning of fright on his mind seemed to hammer that point further home as he thought of the crowds he must negotiate to get to her—all the black faces, more sinister with the darkness.

The line of men moving through the bush was only thirty yards from him when his limbs suddenly found their life again and he leapt up and began to crash through the foliage towards the road. Fortunately, there was so much noise of trampled undergrowth no one noticed him until he left the darkness of the bush and ran for the hidden car.

A yell went up as the engine started and he was recognized immediately, and the crowd streamed after him. Frantically, he took off the brake and let in the clutch. The rear wheels spun in the mud as he accelerated violently and for a moment he thought the car would never move away, then it jerked forward, almost throwing his hands from the wheel.

Jimmy was watching from the fringes of the hullabaloo, always keeping in the shadows, armed with a stave as much for disguise as for his own safety, making as much noise as the others and taking refuge in anonymity in the hope of finding Gotto before the rest of them did. He saw the angular form leap from the darkness, and, with his heart in his mouth, watched the car jerk away out of the shadows and roll violently on to the road. He was in the tail of the crowd as they set off, yelling and shrieking abuse with the best of them as they streamed after it.

A hundred yards along the road, they began to turn off through the bush, and he realized they were taking a short cut to Amama Town. Panting and exhausted, having to stop every now and then to apply more of the mud that his own perspiration threatened to remove, he struggled along with

295

them, weary, horrified, sickened by the noise, the violence and the destruction. He had watched his own bungalow go up in flames together with all the lorries and all the equipment. He had watched the destruction of the explosives store and the wreckage of all the other hutments and shelters they had built so painstakingly, but the thing that moved him most was the trampling of the flower beds he had built and the plantain tree growing outside his window, and the knowledge that, fried in the burning bungalow, were the dozen bananas that Amadu had brought him as a gift.

Fortunately for Gotto in his headlong, panic-stricken flight which was without conscious direction of reasoning, the mob was mostly behind him when he set off. Only isolated groups of angry men and women were along the road and none of these, momentarily petrified by the headlights, attempted to stop the car as it thundered down on them, and he was able to make the town with safety.

Amama was silent by this time, the mob, its violence there expended, having moved to the mine. A few flames still licked at the ruins, and in the light of blazing torches, a few scantily clad figures were trying to salvage their belongings from the wreckage of their homes. Once he saw a woman crouched by the sprawling figure of a man, beating her breast and tearing her hair as she wailed her misery, and that panicking drumming of fright that threatened to take away the power of movement came round again.

He fought it down, however, as the need to find Zaidee in this hell of burning buildings and mad shouts became a thunder in his mind.

Even through his panic, he was shocked by the sight of the Swannack's ruined home, and the burned-out shell of the schoolroom. There were still a few looters picking through the remains of Indian Joe's store and bar but most of what was valuable there had been removed in the first assault.

296

Gotto drove past desperately, not quite seeing where he was going, knowing only that he must find Zaidee and escape with her along the bush road away from Amama until the riot subsided. He knew that what he was doing was dangerous but the importance of finding Zaidee had suddenly become an obsession.

As he reached her house on the outskirts of Amama Town, he stopped the car violently, skidding on the muddy road, convinced in his stubborn, unthinking way that she who had advised him once could save him now.

There was no sign of life but the house's distance from the centre of the town had saved it and the mob had not been near it. He ran through the rooms, flashing his torch, shouting Zaidee's name, sobbing and bewildered and lost as a small boy when he was not answered.

It had started raining again in heavy hot drops when he eventually found her in a hut in the garden, where she was crouching with her maid. They were in total darkness huddled together, Zaidee wearing only a native lappa in the hope of being mistaken for a village woman.

Suddenly, she looked more African than Syrian with the naked fear showing in her face, as though she had renounced all her white blood and was just a scared black woman with rolling eyes.

"Zaidee," he croaked. "I've come. They're after me."

Zaidee glared at him, her eyes baleful through her terror. She had not seen Indian Joe's store wrecked and fired but she had been well informed and she knew quite well what would happen to her if the mob found her.

She hadn't been able to escape herself, for Indian Joe's car had been burned with the store and it had never occurred to the languid Zaidee, who had never used her feet in her life to walk, that she might make her way safely up the bush road on foot. Conscious that the plot she had worked out with her

297

father for the destruction of the mine had recoiled on their own heads, she stared angrily at Gotto for a moment from her hiding place, feeling that he was to blame that it had gone awry, then she became aware of the white glare of headlights on the foliage round the house.

"The car?" she said. "Have you got the car?"

"Yes, it's in the road." Gotto never noticed that the concern in her voice was not for him.

"Outside, then! Quick! Quick!" Zaidee clutched the lappa high round her waist and scrambled to her feet, pushing him in front of her while the little black maid brought up the rear snivelling with fear. "Drive as fast as you can! Up-bush! Anywhere!"

Thankful to have found her, thankful to be told what to do and blind to the sharp opportunism in her voice, Gotto led the way back to the car. They ran through the silent house, clattering and crashing into the furniture in the darkened rooms, and out into the road. The doors slammed as they crammed inside and Gotto started the engine. The drops of rain were beginning to tap more quickly on the roof and Zaidee's hair was limp and dank with it already.

Gotto's mind was numbed with the impact of the evening's events but suddenly through the beating fists of fear, came a feeling of courage, of strength. He had found Zaidee and was rescuing her. He was suddenly carried away by a feeling of pride in himself.

He jammed his foot on the accelerator and swung the car confidently on to the road again, the rain like brass knives now as it slashed across the beam of the headlights. Even as he heaved on the wheel, however, the first of the crowd, broken and distorted by the water on the windscreen, burst out of the trees a hundred yards away, between them and the bush road.

"My God!" Gotto yelped. "They've cut us off!"

"Turn round," Zaidee shrieked, pounding his shoulder with her fist. "The other way! Towards the coast!"

The mob had seen the car now and were streaming towards it. Even at that distance they could hear the yelling.

Backwards and forwards, Gotto reversed the car in the narrow road until he was facing the other way.

"Quickly! Quickly!" Zaidee shrieked. "They're here!"

Gotto put his foot on the accelerator again and the wheels flung up mud as the car lurched forward. But the first of the crowd had caught up with him and a wet black hand came through the side window and wrenched at the wheel.

Fighting with his free hand against the African who was being dragged along with them at increasing speed, Gotto struggled to keep the car from being swung to the right side of the road. Almost before he knew what had happened, Zaidee leaned across him and, in a savage gesture that appalled him even then in his panic, she sank her teeth into the black hand that held the wheel. The African yelled with pain and, releasing his hold, went rolling into the ditch. Immediately, the steering wheel, freed of the tug towards the right, swung back in Gotto's grasp to the left and the car leapt towards the opposite side of the road. There was a violent clang as the near-side tyres dropped into the drainage ditch and for a yard or two the car scraped along on one wheel, with the water slashing up in a brown wave, until the nose slewed round and it rolled on its side, scoring a great wound on the muddy earth, and they were all flung to the left-hand side of the vehicle.

Zaidee and the maid were both kicking and screaming in terror at the bottom of the pile as Gotto pushed himself clear. His booted feet sank into soft flesh as he fought his way free, and as he fell on his hands and knees beside the car, the heavy rain chill on his face and arms, he saw the crowd still approaching. He yanked Zaidee half out of the car, lost his grip on her and fell into the shadows at the side of the road, wrenching his ankle. As the shouting swelled up, his fear caught him again, and instead of turning back to her he plunged into the wet foliage. He heard her shriek of terror as the mob surrounded

299

the car and black hands started to grab at her. He halted for a moment and swung about, his hands against the bole of a palm tree, and in the instant, by the flames of the torches, he saw her half in and half out of the car fighting them off as they clutched at her. As he watched, one of the grabbing hands seized her clothes to pull her over, and like the peel from a banana the lappa came away and left her body shining in the glow of the torches. Then her feet slipped and she disappeared inside the car again and he heard the 'woof' as the petrol went up, and the bush in front of him was suddenly lit with the glare from the burning vehicle which flared up with orange flames touched with sooty black. As the crowd shrieked its delight, he flopped into the grass, weeping and muttering with anguish, beating his fists on the ground, horrified and sickened that Zaidee had not escaped and he was again bereft of help.

It was some time before he could drag himself to his feet. Sobbing with horror, he eventually found himself at the backs of the houses near the centre of Amama. Most of them were barricaded and barred, and occasionally between them there were the charred remains of a burned-out dwelling.

He stumbled along, numb to everything—to weariness and hunger and the pain in his ankle—to everything except the idiot knowledge that Zaidee, the one person he had felt he could trust, the one person who had been kind to him, was gone and he was friendless again. Then, through the haze of rain that filled his eyes, he recognized Alf Momo's house and he crept whimpering to the door. His clothes drenched and torn, his eyes wild, his mouth hanging open, he stumbled forward, prepared to throw himself on the shift boss's mercy.

Alf Momo had returned and was standing guard again in the entrance with a machete when Gotto appeared.

"Momo! Alf Momo," Gotto begged in his cracked voice.

Momo's head swung round but Gotto saw no sign of

300

recognition in his face, and the machete came up in front of him at the ready.

"Momo! Let me in! You've got to save me!"

Momo still kept the machete in position, his eyes narrow and cold.

"It's me! Gotto! I'm a white man! You've got to help me!"

He could hear the yells of the crowd in the distance once more. The burning of the car had held them up for a while but they had discovered he had escaped and they were still hot on his heels.

"Momo! For Christ's sake, Momo," he begged, his voice breaking.

"You cannot come in here," Momo said at last. "Nobody can come in here tonight."

The yells of the crowd sounded in Gotto's ears like the baying of bloodhounds.

"Momo! Momo!" Gotto's voice rose to a thin shriek but the shift boss suddenly turned his back on him.

Whether his action was caused by the desire to protect his own house, or because he deliberately refused to give him shelter, Gotto never found out. He could hear the mob not far away now and he swung round, desperate, frantic, blinded by the rain, and set off stumbling down the road again, his feet splashing in the puddles.

The mob saw him as he fled and the yells grew louder. Dodging, zigzagging, he staggered on, slipping in the mud, his breath scalding in his lungs as he struggled for air. Then he saw the path obstructed by half a dozen older men who had obviously not been able to keep up with the crowd in the short cut through the bush and had entered Amama from the other end.

Gotto halted. "No," he shouted despairingly and swung off towards the black bush again. But, as he tried to turn, his weary ankle collapsed under him and he skidded on the wet road and fell into the ditch.

301

He had not even time to raise himself to his knees before the first of the mob was on him.

Huddled and drenched in the shadows at the other side of the road as the shrieking crowd swept round, his body trembling with exhaustion, Jimmy hid his face in the thick leaves of a banana tree and, overcome by weariness and revulsion, broke into a fit of sobbing.

"Oh, God," he said out loud in an agony of pity. "Gotty. Poor Gotty."

Five

THE sun rose on a silent, deserted Amama. The rain, which had pounded down during the night, washing the charred embers of the burned-out houses into sooty puddles, had smothered the violence of the mob. It was as though the soaking they had received had brought them to their senses and they had quickly dispersed, suddenly aware of what they had done. The flames from burning cars and houses gradually died down in a sickening smell of charcoal and burnt foliage, and the smoke that had filled the town was sluiced away.

The following morning the climbing sun drew steam from the earth to mingle with the thin wisps of blue smoke that still curled lazily from the charred ruins. There was a strong smell of crushed grass and a spicy aroma of burned vegetation, and Africa looked all of its age in the fine antique air of the new day.

A few shame-faced Africans were moving about but mostly they were keeping out of sight. The ringleaders of the rioting had disappeared into the bush and were doubtless already miles away. The fancy-suited gentlemen had vanished in the direction of Freetown, innocent of any outrage. The most that could be said of them was that they had jollied along the the uproar when it had looked like stopping and most of them had been sufficiently adept at that to have done it unnoticed.

Only Samuel Assissay, dignified and unashamed, had been taken by the police who had arrived in two lorries and swooped among the native huts just as the sun climbed over the ridge of hills to cast the first brassy glare on the destruction. Sergeant

Asimani, having sent one of his men off on a battered bicycle for help, had emerged as soon as the riot had quietened down and had successfully got Assissay into custody. By the time the first of the police had arrived, the riot was over. Only the charred poles which had supported the wrecked houses and the scorched palm trees gave any indication of the fury of the night before.

When noses were counted and the losses totted up, it was discovered that the noise had been greater than the violence. There were many injured but only six dead—Clerk Smith, Indian Joe, Zaidee Soloman and her maid, one unidentified African, probably a fisherman from King Tim, and Gotto. His body was found still huddled in the ditch where he had fallen near to Alf Momo's, half-submerged by the water which it held back as a dam in the narrow gully.

Covered with a blanket, anonymous like the other blanketed figures, he now lay in the ruined police station guarded by a couple of court messengers. Only Jimmy had seen what had happened to him and, when it was all over, he had crawled wearily back to Romney's, soaked and covered with mud, with eyes for only one person in the crowd of blacks and whites who waited there. He had collapsed beside Stella where she sat, still grimy and tired, on the floor of Romney's living-room and, before they had even got any story out of him beyond that Gotto was dead, he had gone to sleep, dirty, exhausted, his clothes scorched, his muddy urchin face covered with great soot marks, and flattened against the boards. Stella had waited in silence alongside him until daylight, his hand in hers, and had fiercely kept away the police officers who had come to question him.

Amama was full of policemen now, and they had been questioning the crowd at Romney's for the whole morning.

"I tell you it wasn't a racial riot," Romney had said a dozen times. "It was nothing like that."

"Well, who started it?" The white police officer who was

doing the questioning was very persistent and a little impatient.

"Nobody started it. It just happened." Romney was obsessed with an oppressive sense of his own guilt that he had not prevented what he had known—what they had all known—was inevitable, that none of them had had the courage to destroy Gotto and had therefore destroyed far more—and Gotto as well. He had drifted into it as he had drifted into everything else, to please people—medicine to please his mother, disaster to help a distraught woman, and now this mess to avoid hurting Gotto.

"Riots don't just happen," the policeman was saying coldly, convinced Romney was lying.

"No, I suppose they don't." Romney took his glasses off and began to polish them. "But it wasn't racial. It wasn't political. It started when someone got shot—accidentally, I believe."

"Riots don't start because someone is shot accidentally."

"No, I don't suppose they do."

"Whose fault was it? Samuel Assissay's?"

"Not really."

"Gotto's?"

"No." Romney almost barked the word, wretchedly aware of how they had failed to help, of how they had vacillated and waited and relied on everything coming out all right—and it hadn't—of how much it was their fault and especially his own because the advice they had acted on had been his and it had been wrong. "No, it wasn't Gotto's fault."

"Well, whose fault was it?"

"I don't know."

"You must know. Somebody must know."

The policeman's face was suspicious and distrusting.

Twigg and his officials were wandering round the mine premises, followed by one or two newspapermen who had arrived—the enthusiastic Creoles from the Colony press, and the hard-faced international man who had driven up an hour before. Twigg was trying to assess damage. One or two natives had been arrested for being in possession of such things as inkwells and rulers, possessions of the mine, or blankets from the bungalow, but everything else lay in sorry charred heaps in front of the ruined buildings, trampled into the mud.

Twigg seemed dazed and took no part in the efforts of his assistants to organize some sort of relief, to salvage what they could. Instead, he wandered about the mine, a lost expression on his face, as though someone had cheated and he had been the victim.

"God, they'd only got to tell me," he kept saying to his surveyor. "I could have shifted him. They'd only got to say."

Earnshaw had stoutly refused transportation. It was his intention to stay in Amama, an intention that was fortified by the knowledge that he had been right all the time. His smirk as the police interviewed him was smug and self-righteous and there was no trace of sympathy in him when he heard of Gotto's death. "That's stopped his laughing in church," was his only comment.

His bungalow had been wrecked but not burned and he and his boat crews were collecting everything into untidy piles, and he had already organized a building party to erect him a new house. Zaidee's fate seemed to have left him unmoved and he had already been seen with a bright-eyed fuzzy-headed child whose lappa he had replaced with a hideous jumper and skirt.

Jimmy reappeared at midday when the heat of the sun made sleep restless. He was gaunt with the smoke that had scarred his eyes, and haggard still with weariness. Everywhere he went, whether it was answering the persistent police or the odd few officials who had appeared with a sudden new interest in the place—the worried District Commissioner, the Church workers, the men from the Government departments on the coast—or trying to help Twigg at the mine, he was accompanied by Stella. Indifferent to the heat, she followed him everywhere, still in her scorched and torn clothes, indignant as his tormentors nagged him with inquiries.

Twigg's questions to him were fretful and irritated, sour with a sense of injustice.

"Why didn't someone tell me?" he kept saying. "I'll be held responsible for this lot. I mean to say, all the Euclids gone, the diggers smashed, the buildings burned. It's going to cost thousands and London will want to know what's been happening. Why didn't the District Commissioner find out what was going on?"

Because, Jimmy thought, like a lot of damned fools we were all doing our best to stop him.

"It's a damn' poor show," Twigg went on. "And I don't think anyone could blame me if I told the truth about it. I'll have to make out a report, y'know."

You do, Jimmy thought bitterly. And stress your own part in it.

He stared at Twigg, feeling a great deal older than his superior. He was weary with a weariness that dragged at his limbs, but he was also uplifted by the knowledge that he no longer need feel uncertainty about Stella. He had no job— at least, his job had disappeared—and he would without doubt have to leave Amama because there was no longer any reason for him to be there. It was most unlikely after this affair that the directors safely back in England would permit Twigg to continue with his experiment. At least, however, Jimmy thought with mixed feelings, there was no longer Indian Joe to take over and carry on where they had left off.

Finally, he grew tired of listening to Twigg's complaints and, taking Stella's hand, he drifted back to Romney's house where the indefatigable Mrs. Swannack had started something akin to a soup kitchen for the homeless and a créche for lost babies.

"There's one thing, Stella," he said to her as they approached

307

the hospital. "We can start making plans for the future. I suppose I shall be going home. I have a suspicion that, things being as they are in Africa and as I was mixed up in this blasted affair last night, they'll be only too glad to get rid of me."

Stella said nothing, waiting for him to continue, and he shook his head, a little bewildered. "I'm sorry you're going to marry a man without prospects," he said.

She smiled and held his hand tighter. "Not for long, Jimmy dear."

"It's a pity I've got to leave," he went on sadly. "I quite liked Amama. I got so I was attached to the place. I liked the people and old Amadu, the house-boy. Apart from Gotto, I don't think I was ever happier. Still"—he shrugged—"it wouldn't be the same again. Perhaps it's as well."

He was feeling, like Romney, an uncomfortable sense of guilt.

"They'll never let me stay here now. I was in charge with him. I'm associated with failure, with Gotto, with murder even."

"Oh, Jimmy!" There were tears in Stella's eyes as she sensed his unhappiness. "It wasn't your responsibility. You're not to blame."

"That's just it. I am. I should have stopped it. It was every-body's responsibility. Not just Gotto's. We hadn't the guts to do anything about it. Earnshaw was right all the time. Dead right. We should have had him out." He paused, wondering at the alchemy that had made the uneducated Earnshaw so right when he and Romney, with their superior advantages of intellect and learning, had been so wrong. He put it down to the fact that Earnshaw hadn't been blinded by sympathy and his reactions had been instinctive. It was a triumph for instinct over intellect, he decided bitterly.

"Poor old Gotto," he said aloud. "I reckon we didn't help him much, poor devil."

The police remained, but Twigg's lorries left late in the

afternoon. They were packed with the few things the Swannacks had been able to salvage and what little of Jimmy's gear had escaped the burning of the bungalow. The Swannacks left in the first lorry, Mrs. Swannack tight-lipped and dictatorial and firmly convinced that the riot was caused by inefficiency in high places, Swannack arguing and flapping ineffectually as usual. It was their intention to reach the coast and get in touch with the Evangelist Missionary Society to replace their belongings before returning to Amama—an event to which Mrs. Swannack at least was looking forward with a burning zeal.

Jimmy and Stella left in the second lorry. With the Swannacks' consent they were going to Ma-Imi for the time being. From there, Stella was going to rejoin her parents until Jimmy discovered where his future lay. After that, wherever he went, she was intending to follow him.

They said good-bye shyly to Earnshaw and Romney and Alf Momo. Suri and Amadu, in the background, were weeping openly, either with misery that Jimmy was going, or with the flooding sentimentality of the African at the thought that he and Stella were going to be married.

"You'll not be stuck fast for long, old lad," Earnshaw said, and he had obviously dismissed Gotto from his mind already as good riddance to bad rubbish. " 'Ave a nice wedding. My brother was a fireman and he had an archway of fire 'ydrants. It look ever so nice. I shouldn't rely on Twiggy for a job. I think you've had it there. He wouldn't touch you with a barge pole now. Riots ain't popular in Africa these days and Twigg's scared to death of being dragged in. You mark my words, he'll dodge any blame what's coming."

"It won't be Twigg who'll get the blame if there's an inquiry," Jimmy said, thinking of Gotto.

"I think you'll be right, Jimmy," Romney said heavily. He sighed, thinking of the conscience he had to live with for the rest of his life. "But they'll all be wrong."

The sun was already low, and the vultures high in the sky

309

were picking up glints of it on their dusty undersides when Jimmy helped Stella into the back of the lorry and climbed in after her.

The engine roared noisily and the driver let in the clutch with a crash of gears. The noise seemed to Jimmy typical of everything in Africa—not quite correct but workable; raw but promising.

The familiar smell of charcoal, that smell Jimmy would remember to the end of his days, was more than ever strong as they moved away. After the rain which had washed away the soot, the foliage seemed greener than ever and it seemed to Jimmy that Romney had got his wish—Amama hadn't really been damaged, and the mine, its only flaw, had disappeared and would go back to the lizard and the mosquito and the prowling bush cat.

The place seemed more lush than ever, and the red earth richer with its false promise. The trampled grass would grow again, thick and lush and beautiful. Even the broken plantain tree outside what had been his window would recover and grow over the ruins. The advancing green of the bush would tramp over the burned houses and Amama would be the same as before, everlastingly Africa.

The sun was shining on Romney and Earnshaw and the little group of black people who clustered near the hospital as the lorry drew away. Jimmy sighed. What was left in Amama was now solely Twigg's worry—as it always should have been. Only Gotto and Clerk Smith and the others who had died were lost and none of them mattered or would be missed. Amama itself would be there when he himself was an old man, whether more mines came or not; still Amama, still with the never-ending hills and its cathedral groves of trees.

He turned to Stella who was watching him silently. On either side of them the palms raised their crests into the air above them, always moving, always graceful. The deep red road ran on endlessly, towards the coast, striped with shadows and dotted here and there with a solitary walking figure, the symbol of Africa.

They raised their arms in a final wave towards Earnshaw and Romney and the others as the road curved and they re-appeared briefly in an opening in the bush, then they were lost to sight, and Amama was gone.

As they turned away from the tail of the lorry, the sun disappeared behind the hills and the first of the bull frogs began its croak, the first of the crickets, and the red and gold of the day became blue and the brilliant sky became a jade green flecked with salmon-pink clouds in a fan of light.

Before they had gone another mile the sudden dusk had descended and the palms, the bush, the everlasting hills faded into a misty greyness that was anonymous and the interior of the lorry was dark.

THE END